The Beginning

Adventures in Valdore
Book 1

W. M. Stahl

For: My cousin Kayla Clemenhagen and my friend Greg Tabor both of whom have characters named for them that they may live forever within these pages.

The Beginning
Adventures in Valdore Book 1
Second Edition
Copyright © 2015 by W. M. Stahl
Cover design by W. M. Stahl

Published March 2015 by W. M. Stahl and Strange Mind Publications

About the Author:

W. M. Stahl was born and raised in a small village in central New York. Has traveled extensively throughout the U.S. and is now residing somewhere could be anywhere, but wherever he is, he isn't there. And he can prove it.

"Having been from here to there and back again I can safely say that I all I really need is a library full of books, an endless supply pens, paper, and cocktails." W. M. Stahl

Legends:

Before history was written, it was spoken, handed down in stories from generation to generation. When words or deeds began to fade from memory, they would be replaced or exaggerated. Each generation of storytellers would do whatever they could to pass the story onto the next generation, as best as they could. By the time it was able to be written they were written as they were remembered. With history lending itself as it does to the history of those that came before, the stories may not have been exact. What was truth and what was not is all mixed together until no one can or could remember what was real and what was not. Everyone knows that legends are not legends until they have been handed down over several generations. Until they become legend they are only stories that have been passed on from family to family. Yet each time they pass from one generation to another they begin to take on a life of their own. Still, there is one more thing that needs to happen before they can be considered legends. The last step, of course is when no one alive can remember when the story took place, or be sure if or how it all happened. Legends are born of truth mixed with half-truth and no truth at all to become as they are. So, if you can follow that, then you should not have any trouble following along later on.

It was some time ago while working for a friend renovating an old house that I came across a medium sized wooden box. Believe me when I tell you that the house has no importance in the story than what you are now reading. The box was heavy and made no noise when I shook it. I showed it to my friend who looked at it once and told me that I could toss it out if I wanted. But the box was well crafted and I thought that maybe one day I would find a way to open it without breaking it. Hoping it would

1

make a nice piece for a desk, I decided to keep it. I put the box in the toolbox on my truck and thought nothing more of it for more than a year. I know you're thinking; how could I have forgotten all about a box I found in an old house. What can I tell you, it happens; get over it. I can't remember the exact reason I was digging around the bottom of my toolbox when I came across it again. I took the box to a locksmith who, after a few attempts, was able to open it without any damage other than breaking part of the lock.

Inside we found one light green crystal the size of a boy's fist, one small blue stone mounted in silver, one silver dagger, one pendant with a tiny green stone, a gold ring with a tiny green stone, and four books written by hand wrapped in oiled parchment paper. The books appeared to be intact and in quite good shape; unfortunately they in a language that neither I nor anyone I knew could read. I figured that if someone had taken the time and energy to save these books, there just might be something interesting in them. So, I made several copies of one of the pages and sent them to every linguist I could find the address for.

Months passed and I was beginning to think that it was going to be a useless search. I decided that I might as well give up on ever learning about the books. I packed them away one day while thinking that what I had was some nice conversation pieces. I could bring them out at parties for people to wonder and talk about. I had given up until a young woman in California contacted me. She thought her grandfather might be able to help me with the language. She told me that she was not positive, but she was sure she had seen the writing in a few books that her grandfather had shown her some years ago. She said that he had always tried to teach her the language but she was afraid that she could not remember any of the words. Either way she said she was sure that he would be able to help me. She also told me that I should not delay in visiting him as he was up in years and was ill at the time. I packed up the contents of the box and headed to the forests of Oregon where he was living at the time.

I immediately showed him the box when I arrived not wanting to waste much time. His eyes grew wide with amazement as I handed it to him and I knew immediately that I had finally found the one person that could help me. He pulled a watch from his pocket and fumbled with its chain. On the end of the chain was a key and it seemed to disappoint him when it would not work the lock. I did explain to him that we had broken it when we opened it

2

but he was still disappointed. As he sorted through the contents his disappointment changed to a large smile, and his eyes lit up as he unwrapped the books from the oil soaked parchment. He began reading them stopping now and again to tell me a story about the box and its contents. He spent little time that day with the other articles but he held those books in his hand and would flip through their pages as he told me about them. He told me that they were thought lost and long ago destroyed by those that knew the story the best. More than once he would forget that he was telling the story and just sit and read. It was some hours later when he finally finished and told me that he wanted to show them to me. He said that he could not teach me everything about them in just one day. He invited me to stay so that he could teach me the letters and words of the language so that I could carry on in the event that he could no longer. He only spoke of it as the language of the ancestors and those that came before. It was a few months after my arrival that he shared more books written in the same language all telling a part or version of the story. I spent just less than a year in that home in the woods with the old man reading his books, learning what I had come to call his language. Each book held a part of the story. Together they told the history of a long ago Kingdom, long lost to the world. While he taught me how to read the language he told me no more of the story than he had on that first day. Instead he allowed it to unfold to me as I will let it unfold to you.

My time spent learning from him and reading the books was outshined by the turn in his health. He went from a frail man to a vibrant being full of life. His family believed that he had even begun to look years younger. I am not suggesting that by reading this book you will become younger or that your health will improve. No, that I believe can only be the work of an immortal or an ancestor. Is the old man such a being? I cannot say for sure, I can only tell you what I know and what I saw happen to him over that year.

The culmination of that trip and the time I spent with him has become this book that you are now holding in your hands. I give it to you to read translated as best that I could. While not in the language or even in some cases the exact framing of words, the story does not lose itself on any level. It is as it was, the same in any language. He has asked that I not use his name in connection of this writing, for what reason I cannot say for certain. I wish only to honor him by sharing with you this story of a Kingdom long ago forgotten.

Fact, fiction or folklore you decide. I know what I read and I know what I wrote, and I saw with my own eyes the transformation of an old man ....

The Beginning:

The story of the Kingdom of Valdore begins some time before history was written in books. A legend in the making still mixed with truths and stories yet to happen. A Kingdom, that once was but is no longer. To every history there must be at least two sides; it is true even in life. There can be no good without evil, no birth without death. This is true also of the Kingdom of Valdore. It rose from the death of other greedy selfish Kingdoms, from those that saw their people and land only as a way to wealth and power. King Valdore was a kind and honest leader, known for his fairness and just laws, and for many years the Kingdom flourished and grew. It is written among the legends that the ancestors formed Valdore to settle the disputes that were tearing the world apart. It was once the largest Kingdom ever known and said to have had castle villages numbering over sixty-five, with many small villages and farms scattered throughout the lands. Most of those sixty-five castles were believed built in the same place of those before them.

Some believed that the Kingdom rose and fell with the hand of magic. That one man was given the power to first defeat those that would destroy the world and then unite the scattered castles and Kingdoms under one flag and one rule. All to bring peace to the land and to those that lived in it. The length of the rule of Valdore has been, like many other things, lost to time. However long ago it was, legends now tell of the Kingdom and its rise and fall. They also tell of the time that the Kingdom would rise again. That one would come and they alone would have the strength and power to reunite Valdore.

After its fall, the villages that had spread throughout the Kingdom in the peaceful time of Valdore began to disappear. Of the villages that remained, most were midpoint between the old castles of Valdore. Moreover, those were the only ones that still showed on any maps that were made during that time. Those villages that still existed that were no longer on any map were lost to any of those that may have remembered them. One of those lost or forgotten was Penif, and at one time an important village of the lost Kingdom of Valdore. Although it is just one of the small villages that survived and grew after the Kingdom of Valdore disappeared from the world. It was once a proud and thriving place visited by kings and other royalty, its glory days were now long in its past. While few in the village ever did know the reason for their visits, none if any still knew.

The village of Penif sits next to a small lake surrounded to by rolling hills covered in tall grass. In the distance to the west and south are tall snowcapped mountains that seem to rise from the ground for no reason. While beyond the rolling hills to the north and east lay dense forests that appear to have no end. Yet, if one were to look close enough, they would find the remnants of roads scattered about that were used long ago and now forgotten. Few villagers were known to ever have ventured out on those roads. None that did were ever known to have come back. North of the village, about a day's walk away, lay the remains of a stone wall. There were many stories about the wall and the reason it was there, but no one alive could tell which were true and which were not. The stories of castles and palaces were many and in the end, no one could say for sure what the truth was. The one thing for sure was that the wall was there and that it was part of something quite large.

It was then, in his fifteenth year, that he left his home of Penif. The snow had left the valley but the wind was still cold. Pulling his light blue cloak tighter around his neck, he stood on the crest of a small hill that overlooked the village. Standing in the wind he watched as the village came to life. The sun was just rising over the forest lighting the valley and catching the light brown hair that covered his head. He could see his father's home near the center of the village. It stood out among the others, as it was one of the largest homes. His father, the most famous man in Penif, was an elder, which meant little towards his fame. It was his skill with stone that had allowed him to afford such a home. His stone cutting and carving skills were known in Kingdoms all over. When his father was younger, he traveled to many Kingdoms carving and cutting stone, helping to build or rebuild many palaces, statues, and other works. Even when he stopped traveling it was not unusual for him to receive orders for specific carvings from Kingdoms far away. It was from here that he decided to go out into the unknown. To experience the life that he felt was passing him by in the out of the way village of his birth. He took his time looking around at the surrounding areas committing it all to memory. He was not sure if he would ever come home again, he was not even sure if he would want to come home again. It was as if he were trying to convince himself that leaving was still what he wanted to do.

Reaching down he pulled up a handful of grass and tossed it into the air. Turning in the direction the wind had blown the grass; he pulled the hood of his cloak up over his head. Throwing his small pack over his shoulder the traveler walked away from his home for the first time in his life. As the blades of grass led the way, he headed north toward the wall that stood near the middle of the long valley. The new meadow grass was filled with blossoming wild flowers that filled the air with their sweet smell as he walked past. With any luck, the villagers would not have to go too far up the valley to get the winter supply of hay. He remembered many times when they would have to go out to the old wall to get enough hay for their animals. Smiling he thought of some of those summers when they would come out with the other villagers to cut and collect the grass for winter. It was hard work, but his father would always try to make it fun for him, telling stories of his travels and of the kings and queens he had met. The boy did not always believe him, but they were entertaining just the same, and everyone looked forward to them. It seemed that everyone from the village would show up to bring in the grass for the village's animals. They would eat a midday meal among the cut grass before loading carts with all they could carry and return to the village. But he had been much younger then. Now the village was smaller and there was little if any need for them to go far from the village unless there had been little rain.

As the sun warmed the day, the traveler shed his cloak, rolled it up and tied it to his small pack. His light brown hair, which just covered his ears, caught in the wind while his light gray eyes looked out across the landscape. His face was that of a boy his age. It lacked the chiseled look that he was sure to get as he grew older, but that did not stop many of the girls in Penif from following him around. He stood just less than average height for a boy his age, yet stronger than most, if not all the boys and some of the men. He never once showed himself as a fighter or as anything like it. He was considered by all that knew him as a quiet unassuming young man. In the fall and throughout the winter months the markets were full of those from the village and sometimes a few outsiders. Contests of all types would spring up between those that had been drinking too much ale or wine. Then there were contests that were sponsored by some of the passing merchants. Each one hoping to bring out the villagers to buy their goods or whatever it was that they happened to be selling. The contests that would bring out the most crowds were those of strength. They were held every month by one of the many traveling merchants that passed through. Some of them were easy contests; they were given baskets with dirt or stones to lift. While others were different types of wrestling contests depending on their age. The boys that would win were given small trinkets or maybe a few small coins. The men could win a gold coin or two depending on whether there was any betting to be had. The winner, of course, would most often be someone with the merchants. There were times when someone from the village would win the gold coin, but not always. Many would turn out and show off their strength every month at the marketplace. He almost always found himself standing nearby watching them. His father would always tell him, 'A wise man does not show their strength, as more often they are also showing their weaknesses'. Still there was one time that he had decided to enter one of the challenges. He was about to win before thinking about what his father had told him of the contests. With that thought in his mind, he lost and never again entered any of the challenges.

About midday, he began to catch sight of the old wall as he would crest one small hill after another. Stopping on the crest of one of those small hills, the traveler sat and stared out over the fields in front and behind him. In the distance he caught a glimpse of the corn and wheat fields that dotted the lower meadows of Penif. Beyond that even though he could not see them, in the foothills of the mountains were the village vineyards.

'It is too bad that the wind had not been blowing to that direction earlier,' he thought. 'I could be enjoying some wine with my meal right now.'

The truth of it was that it had not mattered which way the wind was blowing. He had always known that he would be leaving the valley in the direction he was now headed. Shaking his head he put away his bread, slung his pack over his shoulder and started off again.

It seemed to him that he had remembered the wall all wrong. Somewhere in his mind he always saw it standing tall and long in the field, that it was thick and sturdy. He always remembered it as a whole wall with two finished ends but that was not what he saw as he reached it. Lying about the ground were broken pieces of the crumbling wall that were now being covered over by weeds and ivy. What was left standing of it was not that tall but it was thick. It was made up of three layers with an outer layer of smooth faced stones on either side, with dirt and smaller stones between them. Each of the layers were about equal in width. He guessed that he could lie down over each layer with his hands over his head and not reach the edges of them. It stood just a few inches higher than he could reach but nowhere near as high as he had remembered. Vines of ivy clung to parts of the wall making their way up and over the top. He noticed that in places it seemed to be standing more from sheer will than by design. A short distance from the wall he found what looked to be a rabbit run. After placing a couple of traps on it he went back to his small campsite and built a small fire pit.

He stood once again at the base of the old wall and thought of the stories he had heard about it over the years. He was beginning to wonder more than just a little which story, if any of them, were true. A small stream about a foot or so wide ran along the wall and off through the field. Cupping some of the water in his hands he took a drink of the cool sweet water bringing back even more memories. He laughed to himself as he remembered them. Whenever they would come out to the wall for hay he would always try to wander off and follow the stream. The first time he had tried to follow it he was about five years old. He did not get far before his father and some of the other villagers had stopped him saying that it was too far away for him to go at his age. He had, as he got older, on many occasions been able to follow it back to the village as it cut through the hills on its way to the lake. It followed a near straight line past the wall to a point where it met up with another stream. Then together the two found their way into the lake. Sitting, he spent an hour staring out at the distant mountains, the forest and rolling hills that surrounded the wall. He was amazed at how beautiful the area was. He did not think he had ever thought of the area as beautiful before. It was almost as if he had begun to have second thoughts about leaving. Those thoughts were not unusual, and there had not been a day that went by that he had not second guessed himself. In the end it always came back to one thing, his desire to leave.

Perhaps somewhere there was a deeper need that he needed to fill; one could argue that it was his destiny, if he believed in such things. He had heard all the stories when he was younger of destinies and things that may have happened and even stories of magic. He knew them only as that, stories and nothing more. Never once could he begin to believe any of the stories that included magic. There was no such thing as magic in his eyes. To him everything had an explanation, in nature and in man. That explanation never included magic or anything, at least in his mind that did not exist.

As the sun began to drop behind the mountains the traveler cut some vines from the wall and built his first fire. Once the fire was burning he checked his trap and found a rabbit for his dinner. When it was done he sat down and looked at the crumbling wall as the sunlight faded and the fire's light struck against it. Later he stoked the fire one last time, curled up on his grass bed and looked to the stars in the night sky as he drifted off to sleep. It would become his habit, to stare at the stars and think of home, whenever he was able and there were no clouds.

Later, when his fire was just about out. With the darkness closing in on him, he began dreaming of his father's stories and of the places he hoped he would soon see. Many were only real to him because of stories told by his father and the odd traveler that would come to his home with work for his father to do. It seemed to him that the older he became the less work his father received from other places. Once when he was about ten his father went away with one of the travelers and was gone for almost two years. He had wanted to go along but both his mother and father agreed that the trip would be too much for him at his age. When his father finally returned he spoke little of his trip, and had become ill shortly after returning. To the day of his departure the illness still affected him from time to time. It was a hard decision for him to make but he did not let it change his plan to leave.

As the traveler dreamed of what might lie ahead of him a mist rolled in covering him and his campsite. The fire flared up lighting the area driving back the mist, clearing the air around and above the sleeping boy. At the edge of the firelight the tall figure stood looking down at him. Dressed in a long blue coat the figure moved closer to the fire, the mist separating ahead of it, and sat across from him. The figure reached into their coat and pulled out a small box, placing it on the ground. Leaning over the fire the figure rubbed its hands together as if trying to get warm. It was several minutes before the figure moved again, almost as if they were stuck hunched over the fire and unable to straighten up. When they finally moved it was only to pick up the box before hunching back over the fire and lifting its cover. Reaching inside the small box with three fingers they grabbed at some of its contents. They brought the three fingers up to their face; as if to study the amount it held in its fingers. A second later the hand flew toward the fire, releasing the powder that it held into the fire. The fire flared once then died down before turning from orange-red to pure white. The brilliant white light of the flames began to grow higher, lighting up the entire campsite as if it were day. The face of the figure finally caught the light enough to show a short beard and wrinkled face. The face had seen better years; what was once a handsome face was now hidden beneath old age and wrinkles left by time and struggles. Opening his coat the man stood and went over to the sleeping boy. Bending down he touched his face with the fingers that had held the powder from box, leaving remnants of it on the boy's face as he did so. Running his well calloused and crooked fingers over the contour of the young face, the old man knelt down and took the boy's hand.

Opening his eyes the boy sat up and looked into those of the old man that knelt next to his grass bed.

"Father," the boy whispered, "what are you doing here?"

"You were dreaming of me," he began.

"Dreams are for children," the traveler smiled back.

"Dreams are for everyone, even those that leave home."

"Are you mad that I have left home?" the boy asked. "Is this why you come all the way out here?"

"I knew that you would leave home from the day you were born."

"You are not angry then?"

"No," his father chuckled, shaking his head as he spoke. "I could no more be angry with you for leaving than I could be at your mother for having given birth to you."

"Then you do not come to get me to return home?"

"No, I come because you are dreaming of me."

"So you have told me," the boy said as he stared into the fire. "Why was I dreaming of you if I am meant to leave home? Why is it that I think you are angry with me? Why, if it is all not true? Why is it that I am meant to leave home and for what purpose?"

"So many questions," his father began. "There are things that I cannot tell you, much of which you must learn for yourself, even more still that will be told to you. What has been kept from you has been done so for your own safety and those around you as well as my own. Everything will be reveled in its own time my son. Now that you are out of the house you can begin to learn of these things. You will be shown what lies ahead of you. They will come to you and tell you all that has been hidden from you. All that I have kept hidden to protect you."

"I should be the one that is angry then I suppose."

"If you think that it will serve you."

The boy lowered his head and stared at the fire as if he could no longer look at his father.

"You will see many strange and new things on this journey of yours," his father began. "You will meet many people in the days ahead of you. Some will know who you are before you tell them, and others will know of you, or have heard your name spoken in whispers. There are those that have been awaiting your arrival for more years than can be remembered by just one person in a single lifetime. I have had to allow you to grow up without the knowledge of your ancestors and destiny to protect you and myself as well. You now go out and among a world that is in the best of times harsh and unforgiving and at its worst deadly. A friend has been sent to meet you, to help you prepare and train for what lies ahead. This friend is but the first of many that you can and will trust with your life. There is no need to test them; you will know each that you can trust when you meet them, their loyalty is a given. One that will be closest to you will never let you close enough to know everything about them. Their secrets are theirs to keep, just as your secrets are yours. This journey will take you many places and far from your home but there is one thing that you must always remember."

His father jerked his head around to look over his shoulder as if he had heard a noise. Holding his hand up to his son he turned in the direction of where the sound came from. Assuring himself that it was safe, he turned back to his son.

"If there is only one thing you remember from our talk this night, remember this always," the father said leaning close into his son. "When there comes a time when you believe all is lost. When you feel you have no strength to carry on and are faced with what can only be certain death, all you will need to do is think of me and through me you will gain the strength needed, for I am with you always. I wish you good journey my son. I wait with your mother for your return."

His father rose and walked away from his son. The mist closed back in on the campsite again engulfing it and his father. Soon all that could be seen was the mist.

"Make sure you leave nothing out," he told the two as he passed them. He did nothing more to acknowledge their presence as he passed them, but somehow he knew they were there.

"We will do what we need to do, you can count on us as always," said the taller of the two.

"We will tell him everything," the second added, "if there is time."

The boy's father reached out into the mist and grabbed the second by the front of their cloak. Lifting them off their feet and he pulled them towards him.

"The two of you will do as you have been told, you have but one thing left in this life to do. I would suggest that you not waste any more time. You were to have been here many nights ago. He was to know of his heritage and ancestry before he left."

"You seem to forget that you have not been honest with him either. You could have told him everything as well."

"What I have done is what I was supposed to do," he said trying to control his anger. "I was to protect him, and to allow him to grow into what he is and to what he will become, nothing more. Yours was to teach him the rest."

"He has been too sheltered. He is far from ready for what he is about to go through."

"Then the two of you will have to be with him and show him what is needed until the end of his training."

"Dear brother we have too many things to do that are far more important than to watch over your son once he has been told."

"Then I suggest that you both do your job now," he added lowering the figure as he spoke. Then you can attend to your other things. Do not cross me sister," he said, finally lowering the second figure. "You seem to forget who I am."

"We can never forget," said the other. "You always find a way to remind us."

"There is nothing to worry about brother I will make sure that she does what is needed."

"If either of you mess this up," he added as he walked away from them, "I will make sure that you both pay for the mistake."

They watched their brother as he disappeared into the

darkness before turning toward the sleeping boy.

"I am not so sure that he is ready for this."

"Ready or not our brother would not hesitate to see out any threat that he has made toward us."

"At least he is our other brother and we know what he can do." The two shook their heads as if to keep themselves from thinking about what could happen to them.

The two slender figures, dressed in long hooded cloaks, seemed to float towards the fire. They moved closer to the sleeping traveler before stopping just outside the ring of light that his fire created.

"I told you, we have no time to do this."

"We have to make the time."

"Look at that, he just moved, he's waking up."

The two figures moved back into the mist and darkness of the night. The first pulled on the other's arm to move them even further from the sleeping boy.

"Well we cannot approach him when he is awake."

"If I leave it up to you we just may have to."

"Besides, it will not be long before he begins to learn on his own."

"He will not learn what we have to teach him on his own, that is why we are to tell him before he begins his training."

"Us telling him is not going to help him learn to fight and survive."

The first figure made a low huffing noise and disappeared into the heavy mist, the second smiled and followed. As they walked away the travelers fire returned to the state it was in before their visit.

He woke as the morning light was reaching his camp and began to warm the ground around him. The dream of his father was forgotten as if it had never happened. Coals were all that remained of his fire from the night before. After tossing on a small dry vine he brought it back to a point where he could warm what was left of his evening meal. He sat hunched over the fire warming his hands as his rabbit warmed trying to remember something that would not come. After he ate his morning meal, he gathered his belongings and stood among the dew covered grass and studied the wall one more time. When he finished he turned in each of the directions that offered themselves to him. It was almost as if he were trying to decide which to follow. He turned several times in each direction. Even though he had said he would go whichever the wind took him each day, he had already chosen his direction when he was just five. That was the first time he had tried to follow the stream north. Tossing his pack over his shoulder he followed the stream as it led away from the wall. A childlike smile crossed his lips as went remembering the times he had wanted nothing more than to follow it upstream. As the sun passed its highest point that day he came to a point where the stream split. Stopping just for a minute, he was torn between his desire to find out where the stream came from and where the other part of the stream went. Smiling again he knelt down and refilled his water pouch one more time before continuing on.

That night as he began to look for a nice place to make his next camp he came across the beginning of the stream. At least it was the point where it bubbled up into a pool from under rock ledge, forcing itself a few feet up from the ground around it. The pool was not quite large enough for him to lie in, but it did seem like it was deep. Not that he stuck anything more than his hand into it, but still he did not reach the bottom. Finding what looked to be a comfortable place to camp he sat in the grass and set his pack down next to him. It was a warm night and he found no game in the area, so he did not start a fire. Once the sun set he laid down and used his pack for a pillow as he had the night before and would again no doubt every night that he would be gone. He again stared at the stars while falling asleep, a pattern that would follow him as often as he could. Off in the distance the two stood watch and argued with each other. Yet in his dreamless sleep the traveler noticed none it.

It would be three days after he set out from the wall before he would put the grass covered rolling hills behind him. It was as if he had stepped through a door into a new world; the ground before him laid broken by rocks and a few scattered trees. Blackberry bushes found their way up from the rough terrain and became thicker the farther he walked. Thorns seemed to jump out at him if he got too close to them; scratching at his clothing and fingers, when he would push them out of his way. It was the first time that he began to regret not accepting one of his father's horses.

After what seemed like several hours, he reached the top of a small hill and found himself standing at a roads end leading away from him. It was as if the road sprang up from nowhere as there had been no sign of a road up to that point. Was it where the road ended or was it the beginning? He wondered if the road might have been built to connect with another that was never built.

Perhaps it had even run through the rolling hills that he called home. Then again, maybe the Kingdom that had started it had run out of money, or just no longer wished it built. Perhaps the stretch of broken ground proved too much work for the worth of the road. Whatever the reason for it, the road existed there in the middle of nowhere. Whether it was the beginning, the end, or the middle, it made little difference to him. He welcomed its hard grassy surface under his feet. Ruts from wagon wheels formed its edges. How many wheels had to have rolled over the road to have formed them?

In truth the road had been built many years before he had ever stepped foot on it. Its purpose was long ago forgotten. The road had been built when the crumbling wall had a purpose, it extended over the rolling hills and through its lush grass. It cut through the wide valley on its way south skirting the east side of the lake where Penif now stood. It was intersected by still other roads that came from the mountains and forests that surrounded the valley. It was built by a long ago forgotten Kingdom; to serve a castle that no longer existed. Stories had once been told of the vast armies that used to pass through the valley and tales of adventure and death that came with them. Like the roads they were long ago forgotten, no longer told to the children so that they would remember and pass them on.

Walking the road proved much easier going than the previous few hours over the broken rocks and through the brush had been. Trees lined the road on either side and he would have made much better time had it not been for the nuts that he found scattered about them. Being late spring most were leftover from the previous fall and many of them were no good. Still he took his time picking his way through them to find the best ones. As he walked over the road he ate his fill of the nuts, leaving the road here and there so that he could pick up more for later. On one of his excursions off the road he found himself stepping into the shadow of a tree, and pressing himself against the trunk. Standing still against the tree he held his breath and listened. He did not understand what it was that he was listening for or why he was hiding from it. Pressing himself tighter against the tree, he seemed to disappear into the shadow of it. It was not long before two men armed with bows and carrying swords walked past him on the road. They too picked at the nuts and talked of the deer that had escaped their grasp earlier that morning. The two took their time and even joked about having nothing to take with them except the nuts. Trying not to make a sound he stayed in the shadows long after they had passed.

As it was getting late in the day he decided to make his camp there among the trees on the side of the road. Gathering some fire wood, he set a trap on what looked to be a rabbit run, lit a small fire and looked around taking in the scenic view of the area. A snowcapped mountain range loomed far north off in the distance. There were two mountains though that stood out in front of the range. It seemed as if they had been cast out by the others and forced to stand alone against the wind, and rain. Clouds covered the tops of the two mountains in the almost cloudless sky. The late afternoon sun reflected off of them coloring them in a light orange hue. A light hazy cover lay over the rest of the land that he could see between him and the two mountains. After a while he checked his trap, finding a small rabbit and with some of the nuts he made himself an evening meal. With his fire still burning he sat eating and watching the last of the sun as it disappeared and the sky changed from day to night.

Having been raised in a peaceful village he never had to worry about trouble. He never once thought that anyone would harm him; even after having seen the two well-armed men on the road. The only protection he had brought with him was a small knife from his mother's kitchen and a dagger that his father had given him on his birthday. So to him the thought of putting out his fire so as not to be seen was unheard of. He was relaxing on the small patch of grass, and did not hear the old man as he approached. He was sitting down at the fire before he even knew he was there.

"Thank you for building this fire," the old man said. "I almost passed you by."

The traveler jumped at the sound of the voice and began looking for his knife.

"I mean you no harm son," the old man said. "I just saw your fire and thought it would be a good place to warm my bones."

"You are welcome to the warmth of my fire," he replied regaining himself. "I am sorry to say that I have no food to offer you. I have been living off of nature and I ate all that I had earlier."

"I am in no need of your food," the old man replied pulling his own rabbit from beneath his cloak. "Perhaps you will allow me to cook mine over your fire."

The traveler stood up and tossed a couple of small branches on the fire and looked for more wood nearby. The old man placed his rabbit on a stick and readied it for cooking.

"This road is a dangerous place for one as young as you," the old man said to him. He kept talking to him each time he would return with more wood for the fire. "Things have a way of killing boys like you out here. I have been out here many years. Each one of them had their own dreams of fame and fortune. Many just like you that know nothing of the world. Except the only thing they find is the blade of a sword or an arrow stuck in their chest."

He tried to ignore the old man as went back and forth among the trees. Only it was not as easy as he hoped as the words began to sink in.

"Where are you off to son?" the old man asked when the boy seemed to finally have all the wood he wanted.

"I go wherever the wind may take me."

"Ah, do you seek fame and fortune, or just life and adventure?"

"Adventure."

"Adventure," the old man scoffed. "Why would you be in search of adventure? Have you not had adventures in your life by now? You have had adventures, have you not?"

"I have had no adventures yet. I want to go out into the world and see things that cannot be seen in my village."

"Well, then perhaps you are not the one," the old man said softy enough that the boy was unable to hear him. He looked closer at the young traveler, his light gray eyes giving little away under the light brown hair of his head. With more features of a boy than a man, the old man had a feeling that the traveler was much stronger than he appeared. He noticed that he was a good looking child but showed nothing of the strength that he knew that the traveler possessed. "What is the name of your father?"

"Tarsus," he returned, "he is an elder in my village. Do you know of him?"

"Tarsus," the old man repeated nodding his head. "Of the village Penif; yes I have heard of him, a stone carver as I remember. Although I will admit it has been some years since his name has passed into my ears."

"You have heard of my father?" the traveler asked.

"I have lived a long time, traveled many Kingdoms, there are few anywhere that I have not met or at least heard of before now."

The traveler accepted the explanation, as he knew that his father was known to many kings and Kingdoms for his work as a stone carver.

"And you old man what brings you to this road?" he asked as if an afterthought.

The old man turned his rabbit over the fire. Reaching into his cloak he pulled out a small pouch no bigger than his fist and sprinkled some of its contents over his meat.

"I am on my last and final journey," he answered finally

"Where is it that this final journey takes you?"

"I travel to the twins," he said pointing in the direction of the two outcast mountains. "The twins of Valdore. Have you ever heard of the Kingdom of Valdore?"

He shook his head for indeed he had never heard of such a Kingdom and if he had, he could not remember.

"You have lived in a small world. Have you never gone anywhere outside of your village before now?"

"When I was younger my father would take me to see some of the kings that passed near and through our village. They would always tell stories of their Kingdoms and where they had been. Many of them were so far away that they had not been home in more than a year. I remember one such king who stayed in our village for several months while recovering from an illness. He was always telling me tales of small human like creatures as well as demons and monsters. Many of them I only ever heard of in childhood stories that were told to frighten children into behaving. I have heard many stories told in my short life and I can admit that I never once have heard any mention of the Kingdom of Valdore."

When he finished he turned away from the old man and the fire, not wanting to talk about his home any longer. It had only been a few days and he missed his home already. But he tried not to think of it so that he would not want to return before he had any adventures.

"Ah, sheltered from the stories by your father Tarsus no doubt." The old man turned his head as he spoke. "I would not put it past my brother. So tell me, Sarn of Penif, where do you think that this adventure will lead you?"

He did not hear the old man's words as he had fallen asleep, lost again in his dreams and the warmth of the fire. As he slept the old man sat by the fire and ate his rabbit and considered the boy that lie before him. He looked through the items that the boy had seen fit to bring with him on his first adventure. A change of clothes, a knife, some spices, and near the bottom of the pack he found a book. No doubt the book was placed in the pack by his father. He was sure that he had not found it yet. If he had, he would not have been able to say that he had never heard of Valdore. The old man remembered the book from his youth. It was a tale written about another brother, though he doubted that the boy's father had told him that. Holding the book away from him the old man passed it over the fire once, twice then four times. He reached into his cloak again and pulled out a different pouch. Opening it he sprinkled some of its contents onto and between several of the pages. When he finished, he passed it over the fire one more time. He smiled as he flipped through its now blank pages before returning it to the bottom of the boy's pack. There was no reason to allow his nephew to learn any more than he already knew.

"With any luck," mumbled the old man, "you will be dead long before you ever get a chance to learn anymore."

Turning back he stoked the fire with the remaining branches. The fire leapt higher until the flames began licking at the hanging leaves from a nearby tree. Still smiling he sat back and finished his rabbit. Afterword he knelt over the boy and placed his hand on his forehead.

"If, by any chance, you ever reach the end we will meet again. Although you will have forgotten me long before then, and will not remember anything about this night." Laughing the old man stood and walked away from the campsite.

It was just before dawn when Sarn woke to the smoldering fire and found himself alone. Shaking the sleep from his head he tried to remember if the old man had been in his campsite the night before or not. He tossed some twigs and small branches on the fire to get it going again. At least going enough to warm up, he thought, and perhaps a quick morning meal. That is if he could find something to eat. Near the spot where the old man had been the night before he found a pheasant, a couple of chicken eggs and a small jug. He thanked the absent old man as he sat back down and cleaned the bird.

When it was done he ate half of it along with one of the eggs, while sipping on some of the liquid in the jug. To his surprise it tasted like his father's breakfast wine. When he was convinced the old man was not coming back he ate the other egg and put the rest of the bird up so he could eat it later in the day. He got closer to the small fire warming himself and his clothes one last time before tossing dirt on it to extinguish it. Lifting his pack to his shoulder he looked around one last time for the old man before he moved on.

Over the next few weeks his days continued as they had, with him walking alone looking at the world around him and taking in the scenery. He had yet to come on any villages or farms, yet there were many meadows that broke up the forest along the old road. On the bright side he did find himself getting better at trapping and hunting game for his meals. While most of it was rabbit, there were a few squirrels and some birds mixed in as well. Still, there were some nights that all he had to eat were some nuts that he would find along the way. What remained of the memory of the old man's visit was lost to him shortly after it had happened. Even before it was lost to him, he had begun to wonder if the old man had been there, or if it was all just a dream.

It was the next full moon before he dreamed of his father again. A fog settled down around the campsite just as it had that first night when he dreamed of him. Tarsus walked through the parting mist up to the ring of light that the small fire threw. He raised his hand as if he were trying to stop the still sleeping boy from getting up from his bed of grass. The fire turned again to a brilliant white clearing the fog away from his son. The boy stirred before waking up. Rolling over he sat up and turned to face his father.

"You have gotten some distance from me in your time away."

Sarn said nothing, instead he just smiled up at his father as he heard him speak.

Tarsus came closer and sat next to the fire. He put his hands out as if to warm them on the dwindling flames as he spoke. A short time later he began stretching his feet toward the fire as well so that he could warm them. It was then that he noticed that his feet appeared to be covered only by a thin sock. He began rubbing his hands together over the fire, and as he did the flames grew higher.

"You have managed to travel alone so far," he began finally. "Soon though, another will join you and will teach you what you need to know to survive. You will learn many things from them if you only allow yourself to learn it. I had hoped that you would know more of your destiny and ancestors by now, but that does not seem to be the case."

He tried to talk several times but nothing came out. Tarsus sat with his son for what seemed to be hours asking him of his days and if he had met anyone, yet he did not give him a chance to answer. Not that he could answer him; it was as if his voice was taken from him as he listened to his father.

"Have you found …." he began, but stopped.

He jerked his head around and listened into the silence of the night. Standing, he smiled and turned his back on his son. He stood in silence listening to the night picking out the sounds that belonged and those that did not.

"I must go now," his father said finally turning back to his son. "Remember all you have to do is think of me."

The fire fell to a smoldering sizzle and returned again to its normal color of orange as Tarsus walked away into the night. As he left his son, so did the mist that had settled around the camp. Both disappeared into the night leaving no trace that either had ever been there. As his dream faded and with the mist gone again the full white moon slipped over the tree tops and through the night. Three figures that had started toward the campsite of the traveler now stood near the edge of the forest arguing. It would not be too long before they too turned and disappeared into the forest.

Sarn woke just before daylight and tossed the rest of the wood he had gathered the night before onto what remained of his fire. Smoke began to roll out of the pile as dead needles on some of the branches and the remaining coals connected. It was not long before the flames were rising up again and he was drying some of the dew out of his clothes and body. He smiled as he went about his morning routine. Not because he remembered everything or anything for that matter of what his father had had said in his dream. No, all he knew was that he had dreamed of his father and that made him smile, remembering that his father was not angry that he had left home. In his dream he was about four years old and sitting on his father's knee, like he would after his father had returned from a trip. There was a large fire burning in the kitchen hearth; his mother was baking breads and cakes for a festival. Their smell filled every room in the house. Looking out past the animals he could see snow falling in large fluffy flakes. No one spoke, but he was warm and snuggling closer to his father as if at any second he would be gone.

As he woke he lost all memory of what had happened the night before. All but the memory of being in his father's lap, the smell coming from their kitchen and the big snowflakes that fell in the distance. All the same he found himself pouring the contents of his pack on the ground in front of him. Everything that tumbled out was just what he remembered putting in it. That is until the book fell out from the bottom of his pack, making a hollow thud as it hit the ground. Picking it up he flipped through the blank pages, not quite knowing what to think. He wondered which of his parents had put the book in his pack and why had they chosen a book with nothing written inside. Placing everything back he made sure to put the book on the top. So that he could give it a closer look another day in the hopes that he had missed something. Only it would never trouble his mind again and somewhere along the way it would be lost.

He spent most of the morning in a grove of hazel nut trees. Taking his time he filled all the small canvas bags he had, on the chance that when he came to a farm or a village he might be able to use them to trade. He was hoping they would be enough for a few pieces of smoked meat or perhaps a home cooked meal with vegetables and a bed. He never gave much thought to the vegetables that his mother always seemed to have on the table for dinner until now. Especially since he had none and had not seen any since leaving home.

It would be three days after the dream of his father when he finally reached what had once been a small farm. The burnt out shell of the house steamed as the sun warmed the air and took away the dew that had gathered during the night. Sarn stood where the door had once been, looking into the burnt mess as if he were reconstructing the house. He wondered if anyone had been home when the fire had started, or even if the fire had been an accident. The meadow grass was high but the ground still looked hard and unable to be plowed.

Walking behind the house he found the well, lifted its cover and tossed the bucket in. It fell a long way but it finally landed with a splash. As he hauled it up he noticed a garden just a short distance away. It was overgrown but one could still make out the garden from the weeds. How long the farm had been in this condition made him begin to wonder. When the bucket reached the top of the well he got an answer to at least one of his questions, but it also raised more. In the bucket along with water, looked like part of an animal hide and some bones. With the rock walls of the well and its cover, it was not likely that the animal would have been able to fall in. Even if the winter snow had been high enough the cover would have stopped anything from falling in. Tossing the bucket back into the well, he cut the rope and placed the cover back over the opening. A few steps away in the garden he found himself amongst a variety of growing vegetables. Even though it was early spring he was still able to figure out what was growing there.

The plants were scattered as if they were a second or third year of wild growth. The thought of potatoes and cabbage had been on his mind for several days, but it was too early in the season for any of them. He did find a few spring vegetables coming up. As tempted as he was to try some of the potatoes he found from the year before he thought it best not to. He remembered that his father had told him that they would not set well. Sarn picked some of the vegetables and some of the greens that were growing. They were young and not ready but that did little to stop him. Beyond the garden and just before a small pen was a swift moving stream with good cool water. He set a trap on one of the rabbit runs that made its way across the barnyard and out into the meadow. He found some firewood and built a small fire and rummaged through the wreckage of the house looking for a pot to cook with. After several minutes of looking he found nothing that would help him. Abandoning his search he gave into the fact that he would have to roast them or eat them raw. He heard his trap spring as the rabbit cried out; he did not think he would ever get used to their cries. The rabbit in his trap was one of the largest he had caught on his trip. It looked as if it were well fed, no doubt because of the all the food in the area. With that thought in mind he figured the burnt out farm would be a good place to spend an extra day or two. He would use that time to smoke some meat to fill his sack and work on the furs he had begun to collect in the hopes of being able to sell or trade with them. He had spent some time on them already, but they would need more work if he was going to be able to sell them. Sitting by the fire he cleaned his rabbit, placed it on a stick and began to cook it. He set up a quick bed promising that he would make a better one the next day. As the sun neared the horizon he returned to his search for anything that he could use as a pot, again the search turning up empty. Perhaps tomorrow he would have better luck in finding something to use to make a stew in.

As the sun's final rays slipped under the horizon he turned back to sit near his fire. Just as he was about to step out of the burnt out house he noticed something different. Looking toward the fire he saw what appeared to be someone sitting next to it. He worked his way back to the fire, being careful where he stepped, trying to make his way with as little noise as possible. Coming up behind the uninvited guest he reached out to tap them on the shoulder. A second later he found himself lying on the ground on the other side of the fire.

"Do you think that you will ever get anywhere if you travel but a few paces a day?" his uninvited guest asked as he landed in a ball. "And if you call what you just did sneaking up on me, then you are going to need more training than I was told."

Pulling his knife Sarn was slow to get up off the ground. The intruder stood and took a step back away from the fire.

"There is no need of your knife," his uninvited guest said before stepping back into the light of the fire. "I mean you no harm."

"If that is true," he paused as he brushed himself off, "then perhaps you can tell me why I ended up over here on the ground completely on the opposite side of the fire than I started out on."

"It is not always wise to come up behind someone that is only waiting to talk to you." The intruder held back a chuckle as they tugged at the hood of their cloak.

"Then talk to me and be on your way," Sarn said becoming a bit irritated.

He thought for a minute about what the intruder had said and felt that it would not hurt to at least give them a chance to speak. Relaxing his stance and putting his knife down by his side he waited for them to tell him what they wanted. After all, had this person wanted to harm him he would have already been injured or dead. Either that or the two of them would be fighting instead of talking.

"Why is it that you have not gotten far from your home?"

"I am in no hurry; I take my time so that I can forage for nuts or roots or whatever I wish," Sarn spoke out as he gathered himself to sit on the rock that he had pulled earlier to the fires edge.

"I am sorry; I am not the old man you met several days ago."

"What old man?" he asked, not remembering having met anyone except for the intruder since leaving home.

His answer puzzled the intruder enough that they wanted to get a closer look him. Sitting down they missed the mound of dirt where they had been earlier. Landing instead on what had once might have been some type of plow that was now waiting to be added to the campfire. The stranger jumped up, straightened up, and shrugged their shoulders before sitting again. This time they found the spot they were looking for the first time. Sarn had all he could to do to keep from laughing. Thinking of the fact that the stranger had not laughed at him when they had tossed him over their shoulder helped.

Lowering their head they pushed the hood of their cloak back and off their head, before covering it again just as fast. It was hard for Sarn to see exactly what the intruder looked like in the darkening night air. The low light of the fire was not enough for him to get a good look at the figure. He did guess that they were both about the same age. The stranger had light reddish brown hair that was cut short and a bit shaggy, as if it had been cut with a knife. Their skin was light maybe even a bit pale and looked smooth from where he sat. While he could make out little else in the light, there was something about him that seemed to put the traveler at ease. He just was not sure what it was that made him feel that way. It was as if something inside him was telling him that this stranger was going to become important in his life and that he was able to trust him.

"I am Silver Dagger," the stranger said out of nowhere. "They call me Dagger. I hope you have something to eat. I have come a long way and I am hungry."

His words were more a statement than a question.

"I have this rabbit cooking over the fire here," Sarn said pointing to the fire. "And I have some nuts and baby vegetables I picked from the garden over there. There is a good rabbit run just behind the farm house if you wanted to set a trap."

Sarn tossed Dagger a bag of the nuts and reached across the fire with some of the vegetable greens. The bag landed in the newcomer's lap and seemed to startle him, as did the handful of greens. While Sarn seemed not to notice, the intruder was quick to recover from the surprise.

"I would, if you think I might do any good setting it out so late in the evening."

Dagger was trying to be funny but the only way one could tell was by the expression on his face. Being dark he was not able to see it well, and Sarn did not notice. He was too busy looking at Dagger's hands. They were smaller and looked more delicate than he thought they should be for someone his size.

"I think that it would be too late to set a trap for another rabbit and this will not be enough to eat. And these greens and vegetables are no good raw." Dagger shifted a bit on the mound and then sat still for a second before continuing.

"As I said, I have only the one rabbit and you are welcome to share it," Sarn began. "I am sorry to say that I had not expected anyone would be joining me this evening so I only set one trap. I have nothing to cook the vegetables in either."

"Well then Sarn of Penif," Dagger began, "perhaps you would be so kind and get that rabbit over there with the dagger sticking out of it."

As Dagger finished he pulled a long silver dagger from under his cloak and threw it into the ever-darkening night. Sarn did not notice where the knife landed, nor did he realize that Dagger had called him by name for the second time. What he did hear was the rabbit cry out as the dagger struck it. Sarn picked up a piece of wood from the fire to use as a torch and headed out towards the area where the cry had come from.

"You can grab the other one while you are out there as well."

Sarn felt the breeze of the next dagger going past his head, followed by another cry of a rabbit. A few steps later he found the rabbits with the daggers buried into their heads from behind in almost the exact same place. He was surprised that the rabbits had had a chance to cry out. They were as big if not a little bit bigger than the one he had trapped earlier. Sarn took a couple of minutes to dress out the rabbits before bringing them back to the fire. By the time he returned Dagger had started eating the first rabbit. And it surprised him to see a cooking pot setting next to him into which he was tossing the vegetables.

"Why don't you skin those rabbits and I will put these vegetables in the pot that I found and we can have a stew before too long."

Sarn shook his head in disbelief having no idea where the pot could have come from. He was sure he had searched the area earlier and there was no sign of a pot anywhere. Sitting down he began to skin the rabbits and tried not to think about it.

"Where is it that you think you are going?" Dagger asked as he worked.

"I have not given it much thought," he answered. "I only intend on going as the wind carries me."

"It appears to me that you must need that wind to move," Dagger added, "as each day you go no further than an early morning breeze."

"I am in no hurry. I go as fast or as slow as I feel, taking my time as I wish. I have nowhere to be. I left home for adventure, and I expect nothing more no matter how fast I travel."

"I see," Dagger was trying to be sarcastic but missing the mark as was his usual problem. "Then perhaps you would like to travel as my aide. In exchange I will train you. You will need to know more than how to forage for nuts and rabbits if you are to go... how did you say, as the wind carries you."

"What makes you think I need your help?"

"Because like most your age, you are young and foolish."

"I do not believe that you are much older than I."

"We are near the same age, Sarn of Penif, but unlike me you have just come to traveling as where I have been traveling all my life."

"And you believe that you could teach me things."

"There is another rabbit in the same area as the first two," Dagger said handing him one of his daggers, "kill it."

He was a bit confused, but started out from the fire with the same torch he had used earlier.

Dagger shook his head and grabbed his sleeve as he passed to stop him.

"From there," he said pulling him back then pushing him to where he was sitting. "If you can kill that rabbit from there, then I will be happy to leave you to your own means."

"I do not know how you were able to kill those others from there," he said returning the dagger. "There is no way that I can do it from here."

Dagger smiled before cocking his head to one side and then to the other, forcing himself to hear. He smiled again as he flipped the dagger from one hand to the other. A second later he let it fly through the night air.

Sarn had just sat down when he heard the cry of yet another rabbit coming from an area not too far away from where the last two rabbits had been. Going to where he heard the cry he found the third rabbit with a dagger again buried in the back of its head. He began to realize that perhaps Dagger was right and there was something he could learn from him. On the way back it finally dawned on him that Dagger had used his name when he had not told him his name yet.

"I think perhaps that maybe I could travel with you so that you can train and teach me things," he said when he got back to the fire with the rabbit. "But, as an equal, not as your aide."

"An equal," Dagger replied. "Perhaps, there is still a chance that we could do just that, but you will need many days of training before you can travel as an equal."

Dagger stared off into the night as he tossed the final rabbit into the stew pot. As the stew cooked he seemed to be talking to himself and yet he was not loud enough for Sarn to hear him.

"Tell me this," Dagger began after the stew was ready. "Why is it that you have left your home for adventure? Do you not have a father and mother that will miss you?"

"I am sure that they will miss me as any parent would miss their only child. But I have wanted to leave my village for as long as I can remember, and now was the time."

Dagger gave no response only nodded his head before lying down, back away from the fire.

After the meal he laid back on his makeshift bed just as he had each night over the past few weeks. Looking up he began to relax as he watched the moon and the stars before drifting off to sleep.

When he woke in the morning, Dagger was gone. Sarn ate a few nuts for breakfast, along with some of the stew that had been left over from the night before. He spent the rest of the morning building a small shelter and a better bed. After all there was no sense changing his plan just because the one who called himself Silver Dagger had left.

As he worked he thought that he heard a sharp clicking noise coming from the edge of a group of trees. He spent the next several minutes looking over his shoulder trying to see if he could figure out where the noise had come from. After not seeing or hearing anything he went back to his chore.

Just inside the small group of trees two figures were trying hard to blend in among them.

"I still think that this is a bad idea. We need to tell him."

"What can happen, if we tell him the end will be the same, things will be as they will be if we never had."

"So that is the reason that you are going to give our brother when he asks if we have given his son his inheritance."

"He will not need it; he has the thief to give him all the training that he will need. You agreed that if the thief was here we would wait. Besides we cannot go to him in daylight. We would be found out and would never be able to finish it."

"That is not what I said," one of the figures said shaking its head as it turned and walked away.

The two continued to argue as they disappeared deeper into the forest.

When Sarn was finished with his chore, he turned around to

find that Dagger had returned with his own nuts and a deer.

"Just how long do you think we will be here?" Sarn asked when he saw him, "a few rabbits, a pheasant or three sure, but a whole deer?"

He tried hard not to show any sign that he had just snuck up on him again. After all it would do no good to let him know that he had.

"We will be here as long as it takes," Dagger began. "And if your lack of being able to tell when I am coming and going is any hint, then we will need more than just this one deer. It no doubt will run out long before we are finished."

He was not sure how he had meant the statement, but he decided to take it as a joke and laughed.

"It would have been easy for me to have killed you last night in your sleep, then again this morning, and just now. That will never do." Dagger shook his head at the laughter and turned away, making himself busy again with the deer. "You must be able to tell who is where at all times and if they are the one that has been sent by the gods as your assassin. Do they have more or less to lose than you; is their magic more powerful than yours, can you escape if you have to? What about your weapons, are they better than theirs? There is so much that you need know in that first moment. If you are not able to know that in that first second, then it might be too late for you to survive it all."

Sarn lowered his head and stopped laughing almost as fast as he had started.

"Then again," Dagger added, "you did know to hide in the trees when those two soldiers came along the other day. Had they noticed you, you would not have made it this far."

"You were following me?"

"No," Dagger returned, "I was following them and we just happened on you."

"Why were you following them?"

"That is of no concern now Sarn of Penif. They are," he paused as if he were looking for the right word to use. His knife never once stopped its work on the deer carcass. "Well, they will bother no one any longer and I have made right their wrong."

He must have killed them, Sarn thought. That is the only way that they could 'never bother anyone any longer'. He tossed what remained of his building materials aside so that they could be used as firewood.

"That's another thing I have been meaning to ask you," he

began. "How is it that you know my name?"

"Are you just going to stand around all day or are you going to help me with this?" Dagger asked, ignoring his question. "At least make yourself useful and scrounge around to see if there is anything we can add to our meal."

"My name?" he asked. "How did you know my name?"

"You told me your name I am sure," Dagger replied. "It would have been impolite if you had not."

"I do not remember telling it to you."

"Hmmm," Dagger added and said nothing more.

Sarn shook his head as he walked away toward the garden. He was not sure why he was so accepting of Dagger, but somehow he knew that he and Dagger would become close friends. Somehow he even knew that he could not have done any better in finding someone to train him. Although he had no idea why he would need to be trained in anything more than he already was. After all he was an apprentice stone cutter, and that was all he ever felt that he would ever need.

"Just what do you plan on teaching me?" he asked from near the small garden.

"The one thing that you will need most."

"And what is that?"

"How to survive, to live, to not be killed," he returned. "If you know how to survive everything else is of no importance."

"You have little to no trust in me. I can tell."

"I have as much trust in you as you need me to have."

Dagger never once stopped his work as the two talked back and forth. Turning his head back to the deer he shut out anything more that Sarn could say.

"Then I guess I will need no training at all," Sarn laughed, knowing nothing was further from the truth.

Still laughing he foraged in the garden pulling what he figured would be enough for their meals that day. Knowing that each extra day the now wild vegetables had of growing, the better they would be.

Dagger was on his knees now still cutting away on his deer when Sarn return to their campsite. He was rocking back and forth while he worked and it seemed to Sarn that he was singing, although he could not be sure. There was a chance that his new companion was talking to himself as well.

"What do you sing?" he asked him.

"I was not singing." Dagger stopped moving, putting his knife down for the first time since he had returned with the animal.

"Then what were you saying as you rocked back and forth?"

"You must have been hearing something that was not here," Dagger smiled. "I do not sing, nor do I talk to myself."

"If that is what you want to tell me, then I have little choice than to not believe you," he chuckled.

Grabbing the small pot from the night before, he went to the stream to fill it. As he walked he began to get the same feeling he had earlier, when he had thought he heard something in the stand of trees next to the farm. He felt himself crouching as he continued to make his way to the stream.

There is nothing out there, he kept telling himself over and over. Still he found himself searching the edge of the trees and everywhere that he thought someone might hide.

When he returned Dagger had taken over his shelter.

"You should make yourself a shelter like this one that I found. It feels like it is going to rain in the next day or so," Dagger told him

"I will see what I can do about that but I am not so sure that I have the ability to make such a good shelter," he returned, holding back what he had wanted to tell him. It sure would have been easier than biting his tongue, although something told him it would be only part of the price he would have to pay for his training.

Dagger stood, turned around once then twice, whistled, and sat back down. He missed the rock that Sarn had put in the front of his shelter and fell backwards to the ground. He laughed as Dagger found his seat. Sitting up Dagger shrugged his shoulders.

"I meant to do that," he said as he made sure he was all the way on the rock.

"I can only guess why," he returned still laughing.

A few minutes later an orange and black striped animal came up beside Dagger.

Sarn was frozen in his spot having never seen such an animal before. He rose after a minute with his knife in his hand ready to confront the animal.

"Easy," he told him, holding up a hand as the animal sat beside him. "It is just Tig; he is my friend and protector."

Sarn sat across from the pair still wide eyed with fear and amazement. Dagger reached over and pulled off a pack that Tig was carrying, almost falling off the rock again as he did so. Reaching into it he pulled out another small pot and handed it to him.

"Go get more water."

"When do you plan on beginning my training?" he asked, not moving.

"It works much better if you take that to the stream to fill it with water," Dagger returned.

Sarn let out a sigh before getting up from his spot near the fire.

"Everything in its own time," Dagger said finally answering his question. "Did anyone ever teach you to have patience?"

He could not help but notice that Dagger had been telling him what to do and what needed to be done from the moment he showed up. The thing that was beginning to worry him the most was the fact that he was doing it without question. Shaking his head he began to laugh to himself again. One thing was sure, it looked as if Dagger was full of surprises.

When he returned from the stream, Dagger was feeding some of the deer and its bones to Tig. The two spent the rest of the day cutting and slow cooking thin strips of the meat over a smoky fire. Dagger took his time with each strip of meat. Rubbing each of them with some herbs he had found and some he had in pouches before placing them over the fire. By the time Dagger felt they had enough strips cut, the stew was well on its way to being done.

That evening Sarn had the best meal he had had since leaving home. They did not talk as they ate, both seemed happy just enjoying it. Dagger and Tig curled up under Sarn's shelter and drifted off to sleep shortly after the sunset. Sarn lay back and looked up to the stars and watched them as he always did before he too fell asleep thinking of home.

It was in the second half of the night when Sarn sat upright in his sleep. Turning to the fire he rubbed his eyes to find his father sitting on the rock where Dagger had been earlier that day.

"Your thoughts give you away my son," his father said. "You need not worry about Dagger, he will teach you most of what you need to know. Your friendship will keep you well. He will not tell you of his secrets yet he knows many of yours. Listen to him and learn well for the knowledge that you gain from him will keep you alive. Your paths are joined and you will save each other's lives more than once before you part company. Sleep now and rest easy knowing that Tig watches over you now as he has been watching over Dagger." His father reached out to pet the animal on its head, as Tig placed it in his lap.

"But, father how will I learn if he does not teach?"

"Your days here will be well spent," Tarsus said before leaning over and whispering into Tig's ear.

Tig sauntered up to Sarn, licked his hand, and then returned to Dagger's side.

Sarn lay back down and his dream ended as fast as it had begun. Unlike the other dreams of his father, this one he would remember. He would remember it differently than it happened, but it still stuck with him.

In the morning he began to build himself another shelter. He thought as he built it that he should thank Dagger for taking his first one, as the second was much stronger and a little bit bigger.

Let the rain come, he thought, as he placed the last of the pine boughs for his bed.

After a small meal of nuts and smoked venison Dagger leaned over and whispered to his ever present protector. The animal tilted his head before running off into the fields surrounding the burnt out farm.

"Tell me then," Dagger said after straightening up. "What do you know about protecting yourself?"

"I know enough to hide," Sarn laughed.

Shaking his head Dagger told him to get some water for their pouches and then to meet him in the field.

The two worked in the field on his training throughout the afternoon. Sarn kept getting frustrated when he did not do as well as he hoped. Dagger was quick to notice his frustration and was not about to let up. He kept pushing him until finally Sarn threw the stick they had been using as a sword off into the field.

"The problem is you have no patience," Dagger yelled at him. "Do you think that just because you are Sarn of Penif that everything you do will be ... will be ...?"

"Will be what?" Sarn asked losing his frustration.

Dagger turned away for a minute as if he had heard something that did not belong.

"Will be what?" Sarn asked again.

"That you will be able to do all," Dagger answered finally hoping that he had not said too much.

"Maybe you are right," Sarn began lowering his head, "maybe I am expecting too much, for the first day especially."

"Perhaps we should stop for today," Dagger added. "Go and get us some firewood now."

Sarn looked at Dagger for a second before heading off to find some more wood.

With his training begun he would spend his day in the fields with Dagger and Tig. In the evenings he was busy getting water, cooking, gathering firewood and anything else Dagger would think of for him to do. His nights were spent working on the rabbit pelts he had collected and now the deer pelt as well.

"Why do you spend so much time on these skins?" Dagger asked one night.

"I plan to sell or trade them for anything I can get," he told him. "Besides it is not good to waste what nature has given to us."

"I think you will find that you will not get as much gold as you hope. Then again, if you find yourself in some farm land and you need a female companion for the night I am sure you will fare much better."

It would not be the only night that Dagger would say something about the skins that Sarn was working on. Still he would spend each night working on the furs and would ignore whatever his comments were.

Over the next few days he learned fast, with his teacher pushing him harder each day. The frustration from the first few days was soon gone. It was replaced with a desire to learn, and was quick to go from him swinging sticks around to using Dagger's own sword. The weapon was not a great fit for him but Sarn improved each day. It was not long before the teacher had his student in full battle training, where the young traveler was also a quick study. Although, it was not without the pain of his teacher's stick thrust into his stomach or rapped up the side of the student's head. By the end of the week the young traveler was beginning to show signs of becoming a real swordsman. It would not only be battle training and defense that he would begin to learn. His second week of training began as it had every day, but it was after their midday meal and rest that Dagger began to teach him something new. While Sarn had no idea what he was being taught, it reminded him of the contests that he had watched in Penif. Dagger never told him what he called this type of fighting, without a weapon, using only his hands and strength. The boy found that this new training did not come as easy to him as his sword training but he still liked it. He was not sure if he could kill with it if he had to, but he did know that he would at least be able to use it with his strength to get away from trouble.

It would be another two weeks before the two finally left the burnt out farm. Dagger was happy that he could at least count on the boy to do as he told him and perhaps if he was lucky save his life if needed

As they headed out Tig stuck close to Dagger, the small pack on his back brushing against his master's legs. It was not until midday that he noticed that it looked as if Tig was guiding Dagger down the road. The animal would push against him here and there as if to help him to avoid hazards. Thinking back over the past few weeks he began to realize that he had never seen Dagger walking around by himself. Dagger was the first one in the field each morning, moved only when he did in small areas, and was the last to leave at the end of the day. When their training was finished for the day Dagger would always send him off for firewood or on some other task. By the time he would finish whatever his given task was for the day, Dagger would be back sitting just outside of his shelter. He pushed the thought out of his mind thinking that there was no way that he could be sightless. He did nothing to lead him to believe it, other than the way the animal acted and Dagger's reactions to him.

"I keep telling you, you have so much to learn," Dagger said with a slight laugh when he noticed that Sarn had stopped. "Why it is that you have taken so long to notice what you think you notice now is quite disturbing. I would have thought that you were much more observant Sarn of Penif."

Their conversations were short as they walked with Sarn doing most of the talking. With him telling stories that he had heard from his father and the merchants that had passed through. Dagger true to form, rarely ever talked, walked at a brisk pace with Tig always by his side. It kept Sarn guessing whether his new companion was blind or if Tig just liked being close to his master. Every time that he thought he had it figured out Dagger would do something that he was sure he would not or could not do if he were blind. Like the puddles of water that he would sometimes jump over, but then there were other times when he would walk through them. Then he would seem surprised that he had just done so. Yet there were also times that he seemed just as surprised that he was able to jump the puddles or streams. Whatever happened, he would always say that he had meant to do it or that he had known all along if he was ever asked about it.

It would be three days later that the two travelers came across their first village together. Sarn was nervous not knowing what to expect being in the first village he had ever been in other than his home of Penif. Tig disappeared long before they reached the first houses of the village. Dagger seemed unsteady at first but as

Sarn walked so did Dagger. They bumped into each other, but it was no more or less than any other time they had while they were walking. Dagger matched his companion's step and noticed as he would move around the obstacles that were in the pair's way. About half way up the ever-crowding street, Sarn turned away and stopped. Shaking his head Dagger too stopped in his tracks. It was as if his companion had disappeared from him. He chuckled a bit before reaching inside his cloak. A few seconds later he seemed to find what he was looking for. Laughing out loud now he held onto a fist sized crystal and moved on ahead of his companion.

"As I have said before, you have much to learn yet," Dagger said still laughing, but only to himself now.

Sarn stood on the side of the street looking at him as if he had just seen the most incredible act ever seen by man. He had stopped there deciding to find out once and for all if his feeling was true and that Dagger was blind. After the weeks spent in his presence and the days that he had just spent pondering the question he was beginning to think that he was right. Now he was unsure and not any closer to the truth than the day he had met him. He thought of asking Dagger about it but thought better of it on the off chance he would get angry. Then he decided that it did not matter anyway; and if it were an issue he was certain that his new companion would tell him. At least he felt that he should. So he decided that it was best to not ask or say anything more, for now anyway.

Dagger smiled to himself as he strode up the street. All while weaving around the obstacles and people that were beginning to wander up and down it with great ease. In truth, Dagger was stone blind, not that he would ever admit it to anyone and most that knew him were too frightened to ask. Those that were lucky enough to gaze into his eyes could not tell that he was blind, as his eyes looked like anyone else's in the seeing world.

The locals in the village seemed used to strangers as the pair did not get much of a first look let alone any second looks as they went. Dagger kept walking up the street toward the center of the village until he found what he was looking for. Sarn followed behind, not close but he followed him just the same.

Dagger walked into the tavern, ordered ale and sat at a long table close to the fire.

"Would you care for a bite?" asked the old semi-toothless cook squatting near the fire.

He was a small man, with a constant hunch. No doubt from spending a lifetime in front of the fire pit. His hands were scared from cuts and burns and it looked as if they could not open all the way. Making them look more like claws than hands and fingers. Dagger looked at him and said nothing before turning away. The old cook placed a bowl in front of him before pouring some type of stew into it from a ladle. It was a few minutes before Sarn finally came through the door. Standing just inside the tavern he looked around for Dagger in the darkened room. It took him a little longer to find his companion than he had expected. The tavern was not much to look at, a few tables here and there with a long bench along one wall. There was a couple of planks that served as the bar along another wall, behind which stood the innkeeper. He was a short stocky built man that looked as if he had seen more than his fair share of fights, but not always on the winning side. There were three or four tavern girls sitting in a corner eating a meal, trying not to look impatient. Along the other wall he noticed the old cook and a young raven-haired girl working next to a large fireplace. He finally noticed Dagger in the corner sitting at a long table by himself, his ever present hood over his head. He almost thought he saw a smile on his companion's face, but the room was dark and his cloak hood, as usual, covered most of his face. There was not a time in his training that he ever did see his trainer's entire face. He often wondered as a joke if his face was anything more than chin.

As he sat down next his companion the cook placed a bowl in front of him and filled it with the same stew. Sarn began to wonder if the coins his father had given him would be enough or even accepted as payment for his meal. Dagger told him not to worry about paying for his meal, as if noticing his slight concern about it. He was a bit shocked at the timing of his words, but not that he had said them. If there was one thing he was sure of, Dagger could not tell what he was thinking, no the timing was nothing but a coincidence. They each ate their bowl of the stew and drank the first of many ales they would have that night. It was not as if Sarn had not had ale before, his father brewed ales and made wines to sell and for the family to drink. The ale that the innkeeper served to him was not quite as strong as that of any his father brewed, but Sarn went easy on them just the same.

As the evening went on the tavern began to fill. Some of the patrons were quick to come and go. Still others would disappear upstairs or behind the curtain on the back wall with one or more of the tavern women. Several times during the evening the two travelers were approached by each of the women. Dagger would always brush them away declining their advances, and also declined to buy them wine or ale. The two listened to stories being told by other travelers around them, as each one tried to out tell the story before them.

"I am Willie," a man said out of nowhere as he tried to stand from one of the tables on the opposite side of the crowded room. "And I can beat any man here."

The room went quiet as if they were waiting for someone to take the drunken man up on his challenge. A second later the crowd erupted into laughter as the man fell backwards over the bench when he attempted to sit down.

The raven-haired girl that worked alongside the cook kept her eyes on Sarn from the moment he walked through the door of the tavern. She was never too far away that she could not see what he was doing or which of the women approached him and his companion. He could not help but notice her and the attention she was giving him. From the time she cleared his bowl when he had finished to wiping the table in front of him almost before it got dirty. What else could he do but notice her. Not sure what he could do about the attention she was showing toward him, he decided it would be best to act as if he had not noticed. It was not as if he did not think she was worthy of his attention, he just was not sure if he should be paying her any attention at all. The question was if he would have time to do anything about her attention. Chances were the two would be leaving again in the morning and that no doubt would not be long enough for him to get to know her. Each time she passed, or he would look her way, she would smile at him. Whenever she would wipe the table in front of him she would be sure to touch him. Anything to make him look up at her, so that she could look and smile at him. When she was able to, she made a point to tell the rest of the girls that he was not theirs to be had.

When Sarn thought that Dagger had enough ale, he tried to ask him about his sight, but his questions went ignored and unanswered. His new friend seemed intent on getting drunk and staying drunk throughout the night. He was quite sure he would have to help him out of the place. He was not new to taverns but he sipped his 'second ale', as the tavern owner called it. He claimed that the boy was too young to be drinking anything else, let alone the good stuff. After his fourth, or was it the fifth, he was beginning to agree with the tavern owner, but not quite.

Dagger seemed to be feeling the effects of his ale as well. After a couple of hours he began to stand up every once in a while and look around as if he were looking for someone or something. He would then have trouble finding the bench he was sitting on again, falling to the floor each time he tried to sit back down. Sarn had a hard time to keep from laughing at him. As he looked on Dagger would shrug his shoulders each time and give a little chuckle before claiming that he had meant to do it. Then he would again try to find his seat.

"What or who are you looking for?" Sarn asked after about the third time he stood up.

"I am not looking for anyone. They are looking for us."

The crowded tavern began to thin out again. The tavern girls were disappearing with their chosen companions for the night. The tavern owner was tossing out the drunks and cleaning up behind them.

"You two over there," the tavern owner called to the travelers. "Why are you still here? Pay up and leave. It is time to go. Either go upstairs with one of my girls or be out the door."

Dagger slipped the hood of his cloak back just a little, something that he had not done the entire evening, and glared at the innkeeper.

"It would not be in your best interest to push me out the door like your other patrons." Dagger rose as he spoke weaving a little as he tried to make himself seem taller than he was.

"You owe me for food and ales, of that I cannot forget," the innkeeper said starting toward them. "I wish to close my doors and sleep with my wife."

"We do not wish to leave yet," Dagger said, his words slurring together as he sat back down. "Now bring my friend and me another round of ales, and no more of this half ale stuff."

Dagger's speech was slurred but it still had the ring of authority.

"Give him what he wants Calid," called a voice from the darkened corner on the other side of the room.

Calid turned to face the voice as if he were going to say something. Instead he turned back and went behind the board as the man came out from the shadows.

He was a tall man dressed in a long coat with dark hair and beard; he seemed to dominate the now empty room.

"You must be Ryn Mar," the man said as he got closer to the

two. "And who might this little one be?"

"You know who I am Galdar," Dagger began. "The boy is of no concern at the moment; just know that he is my friend. You may speak around him, he knows what I know."

"If I am to pay for his food and ales as well as yours, I will know his name and where he comes from." Galdar towered over the two as they sat at the table.

"I am...," Sarn began, trying to keep the man from getting angry.

Dagger cut him off by placing his arm across his chest.

"His name is his to keep," Dagger shot back. "As I said before he is not your concern. We have a deal to discuss, let us be on with it before I change my mind about helping you."

"As you wish," Galdar grumbled. "Just tell me if this boy is to be your second in this affair?"

"If he wishes, then it will be so."

Galdar shrugged his shoulders, and sat down across from them at the table. His face was battle scarred. It was hard not to notice the long scar that ran from his temple to his chin on the right side of his face and the all but closed left eye. It left little doubt that Galdar had seen many battles in his lifetime.

"What I have for you is simple. There is a stone tablet that was stolen from me some months back. I have traced its path and I want it back. You will find it in the third Kingdom of Valdore. I am told it is in a room in the King's palace. Which room it is in depends on who you talk to, but I am sure you will be able to find it. Return it to me and I will pay your price, even though I am not happy with it."

"My price included horses," Dagger returned. "I saw no horses when I arrived."

"Your two horses will be waiting for you upon your return."

"Then we do not go," Dagger began, his words no longer slurring together. "The horses were to come first, and since you insist on breaking our deal I guess a new deal is in order. I will remind you of the old deal as I make you aware of the new one. The horses were to be here when I arrived. Now I will need four horses; two for me and two for my friend. There was also to be a payment of a hundred gold coins before I left. Now I must insist on three hundred gold coins before we even attempt to go after the tablet. And of course when I return it to you, you will pay us another four hundred. We will keep the animals if we wish, and you will bother me no more. I tire of your summoning me on a whim."

Sarn gulped when he heard the price for returning a tablet.

"I only summon you when I need you," Galdar grumbled back. "Besides I have never heard you complaining about how often or how I summon you when I count out your pay."

"Nor do you see me riding off to return your tablet on my horse."

"I was not able to get them here. They are a few miles outside of town. You can walk there in the morning."

"My feet are sore. I have had to walk for many days to get this far. If I have to walk a few more miles, you will have to compensate me another hundred coins for my feet. That being the case, I think that you will agree that our usual agreement for supplies and outfitting will also need to apply. I need new foot wear and some new clothes. I lost my supplies and horse when I took on your last easy job, which almost cost me my life. My friend here also needs to be equipped for the journey, you will see to it as well."

"That is not part of this agreement."

"Then I am afraid that we will no longer be in a position to help you. Now leave us."

Galdar stared angrily at Dagger, stood and took a few steps away from them before turning back to face them.

"You will have the accounts as usual to buy what you need," Galdar gave in. "Just know that it will come out of your final payment if you succeed."

"And four horses out front in the morning," Dagger replied. "Not too early, I wish to sleep in. The supplies will be attributed the way they always have been, as your loss when I return, as your gain if I do not."

"You are nothing but a common thief Ryn Mar," Galdar added as he came back to the table.

"If I were a common thief," Dagger began, "I would not be so expensive. I doubt a common thief would return the tablet to you once they found out its real worth. I imagine our old enemy Lord Crel would be pleased and quite generous if I were but a common thief and held it for the highest offer."

Galdar lowered his head realizing that Dagger was right.

"You will have all that you ask for. Your horses will be out front before you are ready to leave."

Galdar went to the board and paid for their food and ale. Turning he hefted a pouch in his hand then tossed it towards

Dagger. Dagger did not even reach for the pouch as it went past his head and it hit the hearth behind him, spilling out onto the floor.

"There are just over sixty gold coins in that pouch. You will find the rest with my men in the morning along with your horses," Galdar told them before storming out of the tavern.

All eyes were on the pouch as it hit the hearth and spilled out on the floor. The blonde that had been watching Dagger and the raven-haired girl were first to jump for the coins, but Sarn was also on top of the pouch. Before any around them knew what was happening Ryn Mar had one of his silver daggers out and thrust up to the throat of the blonde. She dropped the coins in terror as she felt the blade of the dagger pushing into her throat. The raven-haired girl continued to pick up the coins but was placing them into Sarn's hand as she did so.

"I am just picking them up for you my lord," stammered the blonde. She was certain that the blade had drawn blood, but after he let go of her she found that it had only been sweat.

With the help of the raven-haired girl the gold was collected in no time. Sarn counted the coins assuring Dagger of the number. With that Dagger thanked the raven-haired girl as he stood and headed toward the board and Calid.

"We will need rooms, one for me and one for my friend. If my friend wishes one of these women, make it happen. I wish a bath this night and then to be left alone until morning." Turning to Sarn, Dagger counted out half of the coins. "I suggest you get a bath as well and perhaps that pretty dark haired girl there in the corner. The one that has found it impossible to take her eyes off you all night."

Sarn nodded. He was not sure about the girl, but the bath sounded good to him. The stream at the burnt out farm was too cold to do a good job at bathing, but it had worked well enough at the time. Now in the middle of the night the thought of a warm bath was beginning to appeal to him.

"I would like a bath," Sarn stated before heading toward the stairs. He looked back over his shoulder, and caught the dark haired girl's eyes sparkle in the low light of the fire. "I want her to fix it for me. I will not trust any other."

He pointed a thumb in the direction of the raven-haired girl and turned to the stairwell. The girl hurried to be by his side, leaving the chore she was doing. Calid was not impressed by her action but thought better of saying anything. He had never seen anyone handle Galdar the way Dagger had. After that, he was no longer in any hurry to confront either of the travelers, whoever they might be.

Calid ordered the blonde to show Dagger his room and to prepare a bath for him. He grabbed the arm of the raven-haired girl as she passed.

"Hurry back and finish your chore," he told her before letting her past him. "Remember you are only a scullery maid, nothing more."

Sarn was ahead of her on the stairway and did not hear what Calid told her. She caught up with him before he reached the top of the stairway and showed him the rest of the way to his room. Dagger and the blonde were far ahead of them as the two made the top of the stairs. Opening the door for Sarn she took his hand and led him to the bed. Smiling; she let go and opened the window letting a nice cool breeze into the room. She said nothing to him as she set about preparing him a bath. The room was large considering the fact that they were meant to be used and reused throughout the evening. There were windows on either side of a large four post bed. Along another wall was a large bureau and a small table with some chairs. The girl worked in silence and as she pulled out a short round tub from a cabinet on the wall. Sarn sat on the bed and watched her as she worked. It was then that he realized that she was about the prettiest girl he had seen so far in his short life. Her eyes sparkled as she worked, and she would flash him a smile every time she looked up. If he didn't know any better he would think that he was having feelings for this girl. The kind his mother told him that he would have on more than one occasion, and soon. The girl had a smell about her that was more than the sweat from the heat of the fire or of the smoke. It was a much sweeter smell, and it reminded him of flowers. Each time the girl returned with a bucket of water she would smell more like flowers than of fire and sweat. His bath was ready before he knew it and he was just getting ready to get into it when Dagger poked his head into the door.

"I see you are taking my advice," Dagger said, his hand tucked inside his cloak.

Dagger looked at the half clothed boy and turned away. So many things he wanted to say but it was too early in their friendship for him to learn too many of his secrets let alone his biggest one. He found himself stammering as the girl returned with one more bucket of water and poured some of it into the tub.

"I am sure that I am no longer needed," Dagger chuckled, sounding a little nervous as he closed the door behind him.

"Your bath is ready," she called to him. "If you need anything else, just call for me. My name is Sala."

She walked away as Sarn came to the edge of the tub. He was standing with one foot in the tub when Sala came back towards him with his clothes in her hand. Sarn covered himself with his hands as fast as he could, turning red as he did so.

"You are very shy," she said smiling, as she continued looking him over and liking what she saw.

The candlelight reflected off his muscular body causing Sala to inhale deeply as she caught sight of him. Even with his hands covering what they could and the redness of his face, she wanted to always be with him.

"I have never been undressed in front of a girl, except my mother. That was a long time ago," he answered trying to cover himself further.

"Just how old are you?" she asked stepping toward him.

"I am nearing my sixteenth year."

"Just be sure that Calid does not discover your true age."

"Why should he care how old I am?"

"He owns this inn. He knows you are young, that is why you only got half ales all night. I think fifteen might just be younger than he wants here, let alone up in one of his finest rooms."

"You do not look any older than I," Sarn added looking closer at her.

"I am in my sixteenth year."

"How long have you been a tavern girl?"

"I am not a tavern girl," Sala said as a matter of fact. "I work as a cook's helper and I clean some rooms when I am not busy. I do what I want, when I want, and if I so desire it, who I want."

Sarn laughed to himself. It was difficult, but he managed not to show his amusement. After she turned away, he finished getting in the tub and began washing himself. He paid no more attention to her as she went about the room opening and closing windows, pulling down the covers of his bed. She was doing anything she could just to keep in his presence.

He found himself thinking of Dagger and wondering too of Tig, especially of Tig. Where could the animal find a place to sleep in the area without being noticed? What if Tig were to get hungry and kill an animal? He was sure the farmers in the area would hunt him down and kill him if he did. Still it was not long before he began to relax in the comfort of the tub.

Sala took his clothes down to the kitchen. She gave the girl there a couple of her own coins to get her to wash them with the other laundry first thing in the morning. She snuck back up to his room as soon as Calid had gone into his own room.

By the time Dagger reached his room after peering in on Sarn and assuring himself that the inn was secure enough, his bath was ready. He dismissed the blonde without as much as another look. She was hesitant to leave and he could not help but notice her hesitance. He removed his cloak and walked toward the tub. He tossed her a small coin for getting his bath ready and again told her to leave.

"I will not spend any gold on you," he told her sounding angry. "You need to leave now. If you return I will be more than happy to slit your throat."

Dagger plunged one of his silver daggers into the table next to the tub to emphasize his meaning. The blonde nodded her head before turning and going out through the door, but the smile she wore once in the hall told of other ideas. Dagger went to the window and opened it, a few seconds later Tig bounded into the room, and lay next to the tub. Closing the window behind him, he pulled the curtains before quickly undressing then getting into the tub.

"There is no moon tonight, is there my friend? It is a good night to be me."

Tig raised his head to look at his companion, and Dagger reached down to stroke the animal's head.

The two had seen many taverns and many moonless nights in their time together. Yet Tig was the only one, outside of his family, alive that knew exactly what he meant.

When Sala reached Sarn's room again, he was stretched back against the tub wall half asleep in the warm water. She slipped back into the room unheard and made her way to him. Sitting next to the tub she reached in and began to bathe him. He jumped at first but her hands were gentle and soft. She smiled over the top of the tub at him, her eyes catching the candlelight making them sparkle. They showed a side of her that he had not thought that she would have. He offered no resistance as she removed her clothes and joined him in his bath. What he did do, was turn a bright and deep shade of red.

"I thought you were a cook's helper and scullery maid, nothing more?"

"After chasing them away from you and your friend all night long," she whispered, "do you think I would let any of those others come sneaking into your room? They are still out back arguing over who is going to sneak into your room as well as your companions."

"And so you just beat them to it," he said chuckling, all while trying to keep from jumping out of the tub.

She said nothing more as she laid the wash rag aside and began to kiss his chest and neck.

Sarn woke in the morning with Sala sleeping next to him. His clothes were cleaned and folded at the foot of the bed. Looking down at her head on his chest he realized how comfortable he had become in just one evening. Stretching he turned toward the still sleeping girl, her head slipping off his chest he as cradled her in his arms. He thought how easy it could be to stay in the soft comfortable bed, in her arms, for a week or longer and not miss a thing. Waking she lifted her face to him kissing his lips. Yes, at least a week right there he thought, smiling to himself.

A minute later a scream from outside of the room brought him back to reality and the two lovers came up off their bed. Sala ran naked out of the room, with Sarn close behind, that is, after he took the time to put on his pants. Reaching the bottom of the stairs they found the blonde girl lying in a pool of blood close to the front door. Her throat was cut from ear to ear. She had been dead for some time; a few hours at least. She was pale and her limbs were already stiff. A couple of minutes later Dagger made his way down the stairs. Without saying a word he pushed past the growing crowd in the tavern.

"She robbed me," Dagger said emotionless when he reached the bottom of the stairs. "I only did what was right. Bury her and buy yourself another girl."

Dagger handed the tavern owner a small handful of coins and said nothing more of the incident. Calid may not have been happy about the dead blonde, but he agreed with Dagger. Besides it was not the first time she had been caught stealing. The blonde had stolen many times from his customers as well as from him. She already had cost him some customers. If word were to spread that he was running a bad house, his business and his reputation would be ruined.

"It would be best if you were to leave and not return again," Calid told them both, before turning to Sala. "As for you wench.

Since you seem to be working on your own anyway, you can take her place. That is unless of course you would rather be turned out into the streets as a common whore."

Sala's eyes widened as she listened to Calid before turning away in tears. Running back upstairs she made her way to the room she had shared with Sarn. She did not want to take the girl's place. She was happy working as a cook's helper. She had kept herself too useful as a scullery maid and a cook's helper for too long to let herself be turned into a common tavern girl like that. There was no way she was going to let Calid make her take the blonde's place. He may have paid for her, but she was a scullery maid and cook's helper and that was all. She had been in the tavern for just over three years and was only a few gold pieces away from being able to buy her own freedom. If Calid made her become a tavern girl, she no doubt would be at least two more years away from being free, more if the men liked her. According to the other girls once you were a tavern girl you could never pay off your 'debt' to him, especially if you were well liked.

"Say your farewell quick," Dagger told Sarn. "We have things to do before we leave and we have a long journey ahead of us and now we must leave today."

Back in his room Sarn finished dressing in silence, while Sala sat on the floor near the bed crying.

"Please, take me with you."

"I do not know what to do, or what I can do."

"Please my love," she began, "I can care for you and your companion. I can cook, I will treat you well. You know how loving I can be. Please, do not make me stay here and become one of…, of them."

Sarn was not sure what to say or do for that matter. What would Dagger say? Would he even let her come along? What could he say to this sweet girl that would help? If he brought her with them there was the chance that Dagger would leave her in the woods or somewhere alone on the road. When he was finally dressed he lifted Sala from the floor and held her close. Holding her still naked body, he took in her smell and the feel of her soft skin, not wanting to let go. She continued to plead with him whispering in his ear to help her.

"If I were to give you enough gold, would you be able to get yourself away from here?" Sarn asked, finally realizing what he could do that would not anger his companion.

Sala smiled over his shoulder and she had a plan as soon as

he asked. Hugging him tighter to her, she did not want him to forget the night they had shared, then again she was not about to give him time to. He let go of her long enough to reach for his pack. He reached inside for some of the coins that Dagger had given him the night before. He did not count them as he pulled them out of the pouch that they were in. He only knew that it was just about all he had, other than those that his father had given him. Sarn handed her the coins before taking her back into his arms. They kissed for what seemed forever, neither of them wanted to let go. When the two finally did let go of each other, Sala dressed and with her gold in hand she took off to her room. Closing the door behind her, she pulled her own coins from their hiding place, counting them over and over. As she worked through each step of her plan she placed the amount of coins aside that she would need. Calid could have three new girls by the evening meal hour with the money that she would give him. She figured she would have enough left over to buy a horse from the stables and enough food to get her away from the village.

"She did not try to rob you, did she?" Sarn asked Dagger as he entered his room.

He was not sure why he asked him the question and was not even sure he wanted to know the answer.

Dagger turned to face Sarn, staring at him with his sightless eyes from under the ever present hood of his cloak.

"You should not question what I do, or think that I do not tell the truth when I speak." Dagger shook as he spoke, pulling the hood of his cloak even lower over his face.

Sarn backed away from his companion as the stare sent an eerie feeling through him. It was a cold shiver that ran through him then pressed against his chest as if it were meant to crush him. He would never again ask of the blonde or question a word that Dagger would tell him.

The truth was, she came into his room just as he was getting into his bed, Dagger said to himself, as if to keep his conscious clear. He was not paying attention and did not hear her until it was too late. It was then that she tried to rob him, but by then she had learned his secret. At that point she could not be allowed to live long enough to tell anyone.

"We need to get you the proper clothing of a thief, some better boots, a sword or two and some better knives for protection." Dagger pulled at Sarn's arm as he spoke.

The cold pressure left him as fast as it arrived and he found himself being pulled out of the tavern. He counted his coins in his mind as they walked down the street. He hoped that he would have enough to get what he needed. Asking Dagger for more coins was not something he wanted to do.

"You gave the girl half of your gold," Dagger said sounding more disgusted than surprised. "These girls do not care for you; they only wish your money. You could have done just as well to have tossed the gold out the window."

"She is not a tavern girl like the others," Sarn began. "She works as a cook's helper, not as you think. She can save what I gave her to buy her freedom back from Calid."

"Ah an indentured," Dagger said catching on. "But, make no mistake; if Calid wants her to be a common tavern wench, then that is what she will be. No matter what he has to do or how long it takes to get the message across."

The two walked farther down the street toward the village shops in silence. They were watched along the way by more than one of the villagers. Children passed them as they chased each other playing some game or another. Some of the children were fighting each other with wooden swords or sticks, taking turns dying. Smells from the bakery and butcher shops combined to create one smell that carried throughout the village. Carts crowded the street as they worked their way up and down it. Each one caused the two to move out of their way as they passed them, their drivers nodding hello as they went past. Men with bows and pikes kept a close watch on the travelers, as did the young women. Giggles and whispers came from groups of girls and scowls from the men with bows and spikes. Sarn was stopped more than once by a dropped handkerchief or some other item or parcel. Dagger ignored the items as his companion continued to stop and pick the dropped items up. Even though there were just as many meant for him as for Sarn.

"You should not pick them up unless you think her beautiful or wish to know her," Dagger told him after he had stopped for the fifth time, twice from the same girl.

"But it is what is expected, is it not? What is wrong with that?" he said smiling. "I can see nothing wrong with it."

"Expected, yes, but only if you wish to get to know her or if you like her or wish to bed her."

"Again what is wrong with that?"

Dagger raised his eyebrows and shook his head in frustration. He said nothing more about it as the girls continued to follow them and he continued to pick up their 'dropped' items. He was certain he even heard one of the girls whisper words of love in his companion's ear. As much as he wanted to comment on what he heard, he let it all go and walked in silence while looking for the shops they would need.

"Besides," Dagger said, interrupting the silence, "we do not need to use any of our gold. Galdar will be paying for what we need. He will no doubt want to take the cost out of our final payment, but we can deal with that when we return to his summer palace with the tablet."

The streets were beginning to fill with farmers, fishermen and others trying to sell their goods. The two had no trouble finding the blacksmith where they found a short sword and a couple of daggers. The smith had made them for a boy about Sarn's size, but they had never returned. Afterwards they found their way to the cobbler and the tailor. In each case they were well received and able to find everything they needed. Within a couple of hours they had everything they needed to begin their journey and they returned to the inn. When they got back they found four horses tied up in the front, two saddled and two with packs.

"Good day to you boys," Galdar greeted them both. Then turning to Dagger, "I see that another mortal has died at the hands of the legendary Ryn Mar, and the legend continues to grow. No doubt she was another in the dying line that discovered your secret."

Dagger did not answer. Instead he shot him one of his cold, chilling stares from his sightless eyes. If it was the death of the young woman or the supposed legend it was unclear. But Galdar seemed to back down from any further questions that he may have wanted to ask Dagger.

"One day Ryn Mar I too will discover your secret and then I will know why it is that you kill for it."

"Not if you expect to see the light of another day."

A nervous laugh escaped Galdar's lips. He had seen ten of the thirty rumored to have been killed for 'robbing' Dagger. Most of those that he had seen had been decapitated, their heads were never found as far as he could say. Another had been found cut in half, yet another had been staked to the ground in the woods and left to be mauled to death by Tig. He had no intention of becoming number thirty-one or rather thirty-two if the blonde was to be counted among them.

Galdar took Dagger by the arm and led him away from the

tavern as they again discussed the tablet.

"Why is it that you want me to steal this tablet?" Dagger asked as they walked away from the others.

"It is an important piece of my ancestors' history. It was stolen from my family over a hundred years ago. I intend on bringing all my family's artifacts back together. I also intend on restoring my family name and honor. With your help I will do just that."

"I meant what I said," Dagger stared out from under his hood at Galdar. "This will be the last time I come to your call."

"Ryn, be reasonable, we need each other," Galdar half pleaded, half chuckled as he spoke.

"I am unhappy with the way you have treated me."

Galdar looked to see if he could make out any expression on his face, but his hood was too low to tell.

"There has to be a way that we can fix this, make things better. Tell me what it is that you want from me."

"You can start by telling me which tablet it is that we are going after."

Galdar was not sure what to say to him, whether to tell the truth or to continue the lie.

"You hesitate," Dagger began again. "You are either trying to find the right lie or you are trying how not to tell me the truth. Either way it will end the same."

"It is known as the Tablet of The Spirits," Galdar began, realizing that it was best if he were to tell Dagger the truth, or at least some truth. Finding out his secret was not the only reason he would kill for. "That is all I can tell you. I am not sure which of the four tablets that this one is, but it belongs to... I know it is the one. It is just wider than a tavern bench and no longer than the arm of a man. It should be easy to get, providing of course you get to it before Jares passes it off to Crel. You remember him; tall man wears black, not so good looking. Killed your last partner if I remember, right?"

Galdar's sarcasm did not go unnoticed. Although it was not taken well as Dagger stopped, turned toward him and shoved his ever present hood back from his face. His eyes locked on him in their cold sightless stare. Grabbing him by his shoulders Dagger shoved him against the wall of a home and held him there with one hand as he struggled to get free.

"He would not have been able to if you had told me that he was going to be there." Dagger scowled as he moved in close to Galdar and wrapped his free hand around his throat. "If I were you right now, I would tell me everything that I want to know and I would leave out my former partner. You are not worthy of thinking about him let alone speak of him."

Galdar gasped for air as the hand around his throat squeezed tighter. He felt a small pop in his neck just before Dagger let go.

"You could have killed me," Galdar coughed. "I swear to you I know nothing more that I can say for sure about the tablet. No one that I know that has seen it can read the inscriptions to be able tell me for sure which of the ancients' tablets it is. Although, I am sorry about Paytruk, I hear he was a good man."

Dagger said nothing more after letting go of his throat. Instead he turned, thrust his hands into his cloak and stormed off in the direction of the tavern. Close behind him, Galdar tried to regain his breath as he continued to apologize for speaking of Paytruk.

As the two walked away Sarn took his time and looked over the four horses. There was one thing that he had learned in his short life and that was horses. His father spent many hours with him showing him the best features in horses. It taught him how to tell the difference between one that would be good and one that would not. One of the horses in particular caught his eye. It was almost pure white with just a small spot of brown on its right cheek. The other three were near identical, gray with speckles of black. Each of the horses were well bred and seemed more than suitable for a long journey. For Galdar to be willing to give them these horses he had a good idea what the rest of his stable might be like.

When Dagger and Galdar returned, Dagger handed Sarn another handful of coins. He said nothing, but he knew why he had given them to him. Now all he had to do was find Sala. Galdar rubbed his throat as he instructed Calid to gather whatever food the travelers might need for their journey.

"I cannot have you stopping every couple of days to hunt and forage," Galdar began. "This journey is too important for any more delay."

Galdar shook his head and coughed several times as he mounted his horse. He glanced first at Sarn then to Dagger who turned his back to him as he left them.

"See that Calid does not cheat us," Dagger told Sarn as he again reached his hand into his cloak. "I will be back shortly. I have one more thing to take care of before we leave this place."

Dagger walked with great care up the same streets the two had walked earlier. Sarn watched him until he turned a corner and disappeared.

"Follow me, I have everything you will need," Calid chuckled as he led Sarn into the cellar of the inn. His son was already there making a pile of things on a table. Smoked meats, flour, and spices topped the list, along with brandy, wine and some ale.

"Perhaps you would also enjoy a jug or two from my personal stock as well," Calid added, reaching under a large barrel and pulling out two jugs.

Sarn nodded his head before asking him if he thought that they had enough. Calid told him that he was pretty sure they would have more than enough for the trip. He watched the two of them as they began putting the supplies on the packhorses. Making sure to write down every item that they had gathered to be sure the two forgot nothing. He was not sure how much they would need but he did see to it they would take all the packhorses could carry. He also kept looking around trying to find Sala, who was nowhere to be found. He had hoped that she would be around so that he could spend a little more time with her. Perhaps even explain why he didn't feel that she should come with them. At least he could try to explain anyway. Calid had even been calling for her to help them bring the supplies up from the cellar and help pack the horses. When she would not answer, he would mutter to himself under his breath, and then as if giving up he finally said what he was thinking.

"Whores," he spat. "Nothing but trouble in the tavern, I have to almost beat them to serve the tables. They are too lazy to do any work except on their backs."

Sarn grabbed him by his shirt and shoved him against the hitching post. He kept pushing until he had the man bending over backwards on the post. Pulling his new knife from under his shirt he pushed the point hard against Calid's chest.

"Yours will be the second death at your tavern this day if you speak of her that way again." His kind soft eyes began to change to a hardened glare of red.

"So I was right, she was in your room last night," Calid said starting an ear to ear grin, not noticing his attacker's eyes. "I should charge you for the pleasure."

"You can add it to our account, if you think that it will make you happy. I am sure that Galdar will pay your flesh money," Sarn added, pushing the knife harder into his chest and drawing blood before letting him go, but still not backing away from the tavern owner.

He could not believe the words that had just come out of his mouth. Never had he thought the way he did in that moment. He had never killed a human before and yet he felt nothing stopping him from doing so now. He hated Calid for speaking the way he had about her and began to wish he had told her that she could join them. After a few seconds of silence he backed away from him and returned the knife to its hiding place.

Sarn turned his back to Calid and went about checking the packhorses to make sure the supplies were secure. Calid had pulled his son close to him and began talking to him about how difficult it was to keep the women in line, as he said. They both had their backs to the traveler as he worked at his chore. He ignored the man and his son, trying hard to avoid any further conversation with them.

"Perhaps Galdar will wish to have the pleasure of her as well." Calid spoke to his son as if they had been far enough away from Sarn for him not to hear them. Yet he knew that he could hear every word of it. "Yes, I am sure she will be quite the prize for a while then she will become as the rest of the whores that pass through."

Sarn spun around pulling his knife as he did so, not quite sure if he should or could kill Calid for saying what he did, but he did want to hurt him. The knife flew from his fingers as he came about, its pointed blade driving into the back of Calid's raised right hand. Sarn surprised himself at his aim and the speed at which the knife flew from his hand. It was as if the knife knew where he was going to throw it before he even knew. The knife buried itself to the hilt, before driving his hand forward and pinning it to the outside wall next to a window of the tavern. He let out a scream of pain as the knife hit its mark bringing his wife running from the tavern thinking it had been her son that had been hurt. His son turned pale at the sight of his father's hand pinned to the wall and took off on a dead run into the tavern thinking he was next. Yet his wife seemed to take great pleasure in her husband's situation as she freed his hand. It seemed to all that could see her that she was trying not to laugh. But an uncontrolled chuckle escaped her as she looked at the blood streaming from her husband's hand.

"I am not surprised to find you in trouble. No doubt it is your mouth that has caused this knife to become lodged in your hand."

"You are being no help," Calid screamed as she removed the knife from his bleeding hand. "You are as useless at times as those whores."

She made no reply but did hold the bloody knife near his neck as she looked over the wound on his hand.

"I told you to never speak of her like that again, and I would tell you now that I have more than one knife."

Sarn's eyes seemed to turn a deeper shade of red as he spoke. Calid ignored him and his words looking instead to his wife who was more or less caring for him.

"He could have killed me," Calid said to his wife as she pulled the knife back away from his throat.

"Perhaps he should have killed you for saying what you did," his wife answered as she wrapped the hand in a cloth to cover the wound. "It sounds like you should take his advice and choose your words with great care."

"I am ruined. I will no doubt lose my hand."

"You will be fine in no time at all you old fool," his wife told him when she had finished with his hand. "I will send our son to retrieve the surgeon. Until then I am sure you will be fine."

She whipped the blade of Sarn's knife off and walked it back to him offering it to him handle first. Taking the knife back he lowered his head as if he were ashamed of what he had just done. In a way he was, but only because the tavern owner had not done anything to threaten him directly.

"I would not worry too much of him," Calid's wife said. She ran a hand through the boy's hair as a mother would to sooth a child that had just been scolded. "I am thankful that you did not kill him. He may deserve death more than you realize and much more than I am willing to admit, but I am thankful just the same. Besides, I think I would be offended if I did not have the pleasure of killing him myself one way or another."

She smiled as he lifted his head. As she looked into his eyes a shiver ran down her spine and out through her fingers as if she had just been struck by lightning.

"You... you are the one," she said as if she immediately knew everything that he did not. Placing both hands to his head she looked into his eyes again. "Yes, I know of you, but yet I think that you do not. Your adventures have just now begun. Good travels young Sarn of Penif, good travels indeed. May the ancients and the ancestors protect you both."

She kissed his forehead while running her fingers through his hair one last time before turning away. She did not look back as she left him, leaving the puzzle-faced Sarn standing alone next to the horses. He did not know what to say or do after she had left him except to return to checking the packhorses. Calid, left behind by his wife, was muttering to himself and holding his hand. He motioned to his son to follow him, leaving Sarn in the front of the tavern to finish his task.

After leaving Sarn to see to the rest of the needed supplies Dagger made his way down the main street. He knew that he was being watched as he turned up the alley behind the village butcher shop. Going to the furthest door he knocked twice and waited for a reply.

"Cousin," a voice from inside called out as the door opened and Dagger stepped inside. "It is a shame that another has robbed you."

"If you say so," Dagger replied with no emotion. "What took you so long to get here?"

"Well…"

"Never mind just tell me of the tablet."

"It is as Galdar has told you. It is the Tablet of The Spirits, yet it does not belong to him or his family. You do need to hurry a bit as Lord Crel is on his way to retrieve it. I do not have to tell you what will happen if in fact Crel gets to the tablet before you do."

Dagger said nothing in reply before turning toward the door.

"Will you need us cousin?"

"Not for now cousin but be ready." Dagger did not look again to his cousin before closing the door behind him.

"Good to see you again as well cousin, and as always we will follow you and be ready," his cousin yelled behind him. "Not that you would give to us any other thought."

While waiting for Dagger to return he again looked over the saddled horses. He knew that by all rights Dagger should have the first pick of the horses. Although there was something about the white horse that kept drawing him to him. He was by far the best of the four horses. This one he was sure would take care of him, and at that moment the two made a connection.

"Pel," Sarn whispered in the horse's ear, "I think I will call you Pel."

The white horse nodded his head as if to agree with him. Pel lowered his head allowing him to look the horse in the eye and he did not move until Sarn did. His father always told him that if you could look a horse in the eye, the horse would trust you. If the horse did not try to turn away from you, you could trust the horse to never let its rider down. At least that was what he had been told. It seemed a familiar thing for the horse to do and he wondered where his father had learned it. By the time Dagger had returned the two had become fast friends.

Saying nothing Dagger grabbed at Pel's reins as the horse pulled away and reared up at him.

"You may have this one," Dagger told Sarn as he turned and began to mount the saddled gray.

Sarn smiled to himself as he took Pel's reins and mounted the horse.

"I hope that nothing was left out of our supplies as we will have little time for hunting and I dislike going hungry. I am surprised that your woman is not here to see you off," Dagger shot over his shoulder, as if to get back at him for smiling.

He did not wait for him to reply as he pulled away from the hitching post with one of the packhorses in tow.

"Well, it is getting late," Sarn replied. "We should be on our way. We have no time to waste waiting for a girl."

He was also trying his best not to show his disappointment, or let Dagger know that what he had said bothered him.

With one hand in his cloak and the other on his horse's reins Dagger led the way out of the village. A minute later Sarn followed him with the other packhorse close behind. The small group was an hour from the village when Tig bounded out from hiding to greet them. Dagger's horse tried to throw him, and the two packhorses spooked as well almost spilling their packs, while Pel just stopped in his tracks and backed away, before Sarn reassured him that the animal would not hurt him.

Dagger cursed his horse and then Galdar for giving the animal to him.

"That man should know better than to give me horses that would spook so easy," Dagger cursed. "He knows of Tig."

"Perhaps he wanted to get back at you for costing him more gold than he wanted to pay," Sarn returned trying not to laugh.

Dismounting Pel he took a few minutes to check on the packhorse's ropes. His statement did not help Dagger's disposition as he continued to mutter to himself. With the horses checked and Sarn back on Pel the travelers began again. They continued riding in silence, each lost in their own thoughts.

It was well past sunset before the two would stop to make camp. The moon lit their way as they passed through fields and into the clump of trees were they found the spot where they would camp for the night. Sarn spent the first few minutes collecting wood while Dagger led the horses to a small stream that wandered through the trees. With their fire lit Sarn went about going through their packs finding what would become their night's meal. Sala rode up to the fire jumped off her horse and began making the two their evening meal. She did not speak to them, nor did they speak to her. It was as if she was expected and was just doing what she was supposed to be doing. Sarn was glad to see her but did not show it. Dagger, while not as happy to see her as his companion was, showed no emotion. Instead he decided to reserve his thoughts until after they had eaten.

"I think it is good if she comes along," Dagger began, after their meal, knowing that Sarn was glad she was there. "I have grown tired of your cooking."

It would be all that Dagger would say about the addition of the girl at least that day. There was no real reason that she should come along, except that perhaps it was expected of her. That night she snuggled up to Sarn and vowed to herself that she would not leave his side no matter where his travels would take them.

It might have been sympathy that made Dagger to allow the girl to come along with them, but she was proving to be a useful addition. With her along he could spend more time with his student and his student had a better chance of learning quicker than he was already. Yet there was more to it than that. It was easy for him to give in and let her come with them, easier still to send her away. Sarn's feelings for her had nothing to do with it as he would have sent her away as soon as they were within a day's ride of another village. That is if sympathy were the best reason he could come up with for letting her come along. He could think of many more reasons that she should not come with them, but none of them would make a difference.

Sala in turn took care of the two as best as she knew how. Each evening, she made sure there was enough wood for the night's fire, cook for them and see that they wanted for nothing. She even took on the task of seeing to it that Tig was well fed. She knew that if the animal never went hungry she would not have to worry that she would find herself as a juicy meal. Tig warmed quick to having the girl around, finding her a welcome addition. Much to Dagger's surprise Tig showed that he was more than happy to have the girl along. As far as he could tell Tig never seemed to have much use for most females. Yet would watch over and protect her as he did the two boys.

While Dagger had thought about it from the first day, it would be close to two weeks before including her in their training. She was not as quick to learn as Sarn, but she did show some signs that she might become a useful fighter someday. Most of her early training was spent teaching her more about defending herself and less on attacking. Later, he thought, he would teach her more about attacking, that is if she survived long enough. Each night as the three would train, Tig would take up his familiar place of watching over them and keeping an eye out for any signs of trouble.

Some nights he would not be alone in his watch.

"So tell me young Tig, where is it that they found the girl?" the figure had asked the first night they came after the group had left the tavern.

Tig had stretched his head up toward their hand as if he were trying to make them pet him. Reaching out and touching the animal's head the figure saw where and how the girl had come to join the group.

The figure would return many nights after that, either alone or with another dressed exactly like they were. Each time they would come around Tig would curl up at their feet and allow them to pet him. With that, they were able to see what the travelers had been going through and where they had been. Once they found out whatever it was that they wanted to know, Tig would curl up and sleep. Leaving the two to argue how best to help the travelers, if at all.

"I think it is enough that we have given the one this animal to use and to help him in any way."

"Some days I think you would make them a meal and say that is all the help that we ever need to give them. And besides we gave the one this animal when they both were young."

"Are you saying that just because we gave the thief the animal when they were both young that it should not count?"

"I am beginning to think that you are not serious about we do."

"Why is it that you think that? I do exactly what I am supposed to do, except those things that we have not done yet."

"How can you say such a thing and be serious? As long as I keep letting you talk me out of doing what we have to do, I will never think that you are serious."

"Then why do you never walk up and just tell him what he needs to know and get it over with?"

"You know that it is impossible to do it that way."

"Just because our brother wants us to tell him together what makes you think that we are supposed to?"

"You are impossible. Why do I get the feeling that this will be yet another huge mess that I will have to take care of because of you?"

The words may have been different some of the nights but they always had the same effect. One of the two would turn and leave mumbling as they went. Yet no matter how it all worked out Tig would always be asleep at the feet of one or the other of them. Leaving whichever one that did not walk away to watch over the travelers. No matter the ending by sunrise they were gone again and Tig would be walking through their campsite as if they had never been there at all.

It would be almost a month and a half after leaving Calid's Tavern before they would enter the valley of the fifth Kingdom of Valdore.

In the mountains high above the group the sentry watched as the three thread their way through the narrow mountain pass. The trail was not much wider than the packs on the horses. It was just one of five ways into the valley, but it was the least likely anyone would travel so early in the year. Luckily for them, it had been a mild winter and the mountain passes had cleared early. With his hand wrapped around the crystal, Dagger led them as they threaded their way through the narrow pass. The first sentry they passed was about to sound the alarm until he noticed that there were three of them. There were to have been only two of them, at least that is what they were told. Turning back to his small cooking fire he returned to cooking his breakfast, and failed to see Tig following the trio a short distance behind them.

They had spent the night near the top of the pass taking shelter just inside of an old mine. It had been a cold night and they had spent it without a fire. Tig seemed the only one that was not cold as he lay at the entrance of the mine. The travelers huddled together keeping warm by talking of hot summer days and winter nights around a fire. Telling of times of drinking hot wines and cider helped but only a little.

The trio began their descent a few hours before sunrise. By the time the travelers reached the valley floor they had been noticed by four such sentries. Each discounted the group as the one they were looking for when they noticed that there was three of them. None of them noticed Tig who was keeping himself away from the group and being ever watchful over them. It was not until much later that the travelers were recognized. By then the trap that had been laid was far behind them.

As the alarm when up, Dagger acknowledged for the first time that he had noticed the sentries.

"It would seem," Dagger said turning to the others, "that our job will be more difficult, than first hoped."

Dagger pointed to the black smoke trails behind them leading back through the pass.

"What do you think they will do now," Sarn asked.

"One can never be sure. There is little if anything they can do to us from there. Although as soon as news of our arrival reaches the castle I am sure they will come looking for us," Dagger told the pair. "And that my friends; will make it that much harder if not impossible to get through the gate."

He showed no sign of concern in his voice as he spoke. Instead, he kept up the pace that they had been traveling all day. It was still a few hours before midday and there was nothing but fields between them and the castle. But there was still close to half day to reach it.

The smoke from the closest sentry fire turned from white to dark gray as they spoke.

"There goes any chance of getting any closer to the castle before they notice us," Sarn added as he watched as the smoke from each of the sentry fires ahead of them began to turn from white smoke to gray and then to black.

"It is a good thing we had not just spent hours trying to sneak into the valley," Dagger laughed, with Sarn joining him.

In the distance they could see men coming from the main gate of the castle carrying the flag of King Jares, the unlawful King of Nefrendel. The valley had few places for them to hide. There were a few barns that dotted the fields that could offer them some chance to hide from the sentries, if only for a short time.

"I think I can get us to the castle," Sala chimed in. "Well, I think I might know of a place we can hide at least."

Dagger and Sarn both looked to her unsure of how or if she could do as she said. It was against Dagger's better judgment, but he also realized that they had little choice but to trust the girl.

Sala led them to a group of peasant huts that made up a ramshackle village about a mile from the castle at the edge of a group of plowed fields. It had been almost eight years since she had been in the valley. She could only hope that they were still there. They made their way down the makeshift main street as Sala, trying to remember where she was going, led the way. Each of the houses looked as run down and neglected as the next. Sarn was wondering how anyone could tell one from another. They would turn down more than one street that ended in a place she did not know or seem to remember. The boys were beginning to wonder if she even knew where she was. It was just before the sun set when Sala seemed to find the place she was looking for. Hoping that she was right she led them to a small stable next to one of the neglected homes. They stayed in the stable until long after it was dark. Each took a turn keeping an eye on the sentries as they roamed the area searching for them.

Watching the travelers from the darkest corner of the stable, praying they would not be found, were a small boy and an old man. The two hoped that the trespassers would leave soon. After several minutes, the boy moved, causing Dagger to turn sword at the ready. Tig pounced in the direction of the movement knocking the boy to the wall. His paws set steady on the boy's small shoulders. The old man moved forward with a wooden pitchfork in hand, rearing back to hit Tig. Sarn threw himself toward the old man tearing the pitchfork from his hands as he went past him. The boy began laughing as Sarn picked himself up from the floor. He thought that the boy was laughing at him until he caught sight of Tig who was licking his face. The old man let out a sigh of relief at the laughter, but still searched for anything he might be able to use against the trespassers.

"Grandfather?" Sala asked, staring into the dark stable.

The old man turned toward her, cocked his head to the side and squinted trying to see her face. He thought he recognized the voice, but it could not be who he thought it was.

"No, it cannot be," the old man said aloud after a minute. "No, Sala is dead. She has been dead for four years now."

"Grandfather," Sala continued, "it is me, I am Sala."

As soon as Tig released the boy he ran to Sala, looked up at her, threw his arms around her and squeezed. The boy immediately began to cry as did Sala.

"It is her grandfather," the boy said between tears that flowed now in a steady stream from his eyes.

The boy was about eight and was still quick to recognize his older sister even though they had not seen each other in four years. The old man rushed forward, tears streaming down his face as he took her into his arms.

Dagger put his sword away as he realized that no harm was coming to them, for the moment at least. Sarn joined the growing group in the middle of the stables.

"I did not know that you could move so fast," Dagger whispered to Sarn, as they watched the reunited family.

"That was no faster than any other time," he returned with a puzzled look on his face.

"You will have to move like that in your training. We can work on how to use that speed later," Dagger said ignoring the fact that Sarn did not believe how fast he had moved. "It will come in quite handy sometime. You will have a deadly combination once we have the time to get you a better sword to use."

When the three lost family members broke away, it was the old man that spoke first.

"Come; let me get you all into our home. It is not much but it keeps our heads dry, most of the time." He said leading them back through the stable into the home that was attached at the rear.

The old man and the boy led the travelers into a warm kitchen. An old woman was crouched in front of a low stone fire pit, stirring a pot. The boy ran to the woman and whispered in her ear. When the boy finished, the old woman rose from her position and turned to find Sala. With outstretched arms the two rushed together. Tears flowed between the family members as the grandfather led Sarn and Dagger to a small table. There was a window next to it, but they had little worries of being seen. On a clear day one would have been lucky to make out the shapes of those that were near it.

"We have little but you are welcome to what we have," he said turning back to his granddaughter.

They in turn thanked him before testing and then sitting in the well-worn chairs. Tig, as always, was quick to adjust to his new surroundings as he curled up by the warm stone of the fire pit.

The fake would be King Jares stood in an anteroom and waited for the news that the thieves had been killed. He ran his fingers over the face of the tablet. The tablet looked as if it had just finished being carved. Figures and forms stood from the stone with crisp and clear cuts that had been chipped away. It came nowhere near telling of its true age and that it was so old that none alive could say when it had been carved or read the words that were on it. It did not take long for Jares to get the bad news. The sun had set and the night had just settled in when the sentry begged his forgiveness for bursting in on him. Jares was quick to forgive him knowing that it would be the news that he was waiting to hear. Telling Jares what had happened was another thing as he stammered through how the thieves had gotten away from them.

"They are dead?" he asked as another one of his guards entered the room.

"We missed them," he said lowering his head knowing that Jares would not take the news well. "We have them trapped in the peasant's village outside of the castle. It will only be a matter of time before they are found."

"How could you have let them get that far? They were supposed to have been dead before they reached the bottom of the pass," Jares shouted, slamming his fist to the table that held the stone tablet. "You were told the route they would be using, how could you be so useless?"

Jares turned and approached the first guard with open arms, asking for forgiveness for his outbreak. Instead of putting his hands on his shoulders he pulled a dagger from the guard's belt and slit his throat from ear to ear. Wiping the knife on the dying man's shirt as he fell, he turned toward the remaining guard. Smiling he asked again if they were dead. The remaining guard gave no answer except to step back unsure of what his King would do next. Jares said nothing more and began to walk away, turning only once. He stopped, throwing the knife and hitting the guard between his eyes, burying it into his skull. Smiling, Jares turned and ran through the halls of his palace towards the throne room. He was laughing and yelling that he would give fifty gold pieces to anyone that would come forward with the location of the thieves. When he reached the next floor he ordered the tablet moved to another room. Saying that he had no intention of letting Dagger and his thieves just walk in and steal it. If by chance Dagger did get inside the palace, he knew that there would be little they could do to stop him from taking the tablet. He needed to stop them before they got in or make it so they would not make it out of the palace alive. Either way he vowed that he was not going to make it easy. He was too close to his reward for taking it away from its previous owner to have it slip through his fingers now. If it got away from him Lord Crel would be as forgiving with him as he had been with his guards. Crel had been quite excited when Jares told him that he had found the tablet and could get it for him. Of course he had no idea what having the tablet meant to Crel or for that matter if it meant anything at all to him. He only knew that it was important enough that he was to given 'great rewards'. It was just a few more days before Crel would arrive. Then he could take his reward and leave the godforsaken Kingdom once and for all. Then as far as he was concerned the tablet would no longer be his problem.

"Tell me what is so special about this tablet that we are after," Sarn asked as they huddled at the small table.

"I am not sure that I can tell you," Dagger replied.

"I think that we have waited long enough for you to tell us about what we have been led here to steal."

"You chose to be here when you began your training," Dagger began, smiling at him knowing that Sarn did not exactly ask to be where he was now. "We my friend are not stealing it, we are returning it to safer hands than Jares and his master. You can think of us as reclaiming it for its rightful owner."

"I still believe that I should know more about it all the same."

"I am going to give my family some of our food if that is all right with you," Sala interrupted. "I am sure that we are not going to need all that we have left."

Dagger waved her away nodding his approval.

"We will not be spending much time cooking after this. I trust that you will give them only what we cannot use," Dagger returned before leaning in closer to Sarn to continue. "It will also help to hide us. Jares is no doubt offering gold to anyone that knows where we are. Unfortunately for us, the temptation for gold to feed one's family often outweighs even that of blood."

Sarn looked around at the surroundings as if he was just now noticing how poor the family was. The dirt floor, the clothes they were wearing having been sewn and patched many times over and were no doubt the only ones they owned. The only furniture was the table, two chairs, three benches, and it was all in desperate need of repair. Smoke from the cracked stone fire pit wound its way up and through a hole in the roof of the house. He could only imagine what the three had to sleep on, a thin rug perhaps and some rags or hay to put under their heads.

"I guess you could be right," Sarn added finally. "That does not mean that you cannot tell me about the tablet now that we are here."

"I think that you may just wonder way too much for your own

good my friend," Dagger laughed at him. Shifting in his chair, he settled into tell the story. "If you are sure that it will make it easier for you to help return it to safer hands, then I will tell you, but I doubt that you will believe me."

Dagger stopped and cocked his head to the side listening to the night. In the stable he heard Sala and her brother taking care of the horses; her grandmother as she was going through their packs; villagers as they walked past on the street. There were no were horses in street and that meant no sentries. Finally he nodded his head agreeing to tell him about the tablet. "I do not know for sure of the origin of the tablet and I do not know if any one knows for sure. I can tell you that it is old, just how old no one seems to know," Dagger began. "It is as long as your arm and not much wider than that bench over there. Words and figures believed to be from a people long lost to this world decorate both sides, as well as the edges of it. There are those that have studied it that claim that the words are a spell. One that holds closed the door between good and evil, while the symbols tell of where to find the door. Some others that have studied it claim that it was carved by the spirits themselves and holds the secrets of all life on the face of it. While on the back is the spell that will undo life as we know it, so the world can be recreated in any image that whoever calls up the spell wants. Perhaps the symbols representing life, death and rebirth that are on it are just decorative, I cannot say for sure."

Dagger paused again to listen to the sounds of horses coming from the street. The horses of the King's army kept on their path and did not stop. Tig too raised his head, as if he were ready to pounce from the comfort of his spot by the fire pit. Dagger took a drink from the cup that had been placed in front of him, before continuing again.

"There are others that believe the tablet is not as powerful as that. They too believe that the ancients carved the tablet. Although they think that the words and symbols contain a spell that hides the fairy folk from the world. Invoking the words on the tablet will reveal their hiding places allowing them to be found. The ancients hid the fairy folk from the world after someone began killing them off. It is thought that Jares has stolen it so that it can be used to find and kill them once and for all. I know that this is too much for you to take in and believe in such a short time. I only ask that you give yourself time to see all that I have told you before you tell me that you do not believe." Dagger finished speaking and turned away from Sarn and faced the wall.

Sala had finished in the stable and was busy helping her grandmother at the fire pit. Stopping when Dagger did, she turned towards the two.

"There are no fairy folk any more, if there ever was," she said half laughing, wiping her hands on her grandmother's apron. "Everyone knows that they are only story characters, made up to scare or put children to sleep. No, if they ever were real they have been dead long ago."

"You may believe as you wish," Dagger returned. "I only know what I have been told as well as what I have learned and have seen on my own."

The thought of fairy folk being real was too much for Sarn as well, although he kept his laughter to himself. As for the tablet being some door between good and evil, or destroying life and starting over, no it was all too hard for him to believe.

"It being some magical thing I can believe," Sala began. "I have seen the use of magic and know that it is real, but fairy folk, no I cannot believe that they exist."

"No matter the use of it or what it hides," Simon, Sala's grandfather spoke up. "It sounds to me that it is an important object to a few select people."

"You could say that," Dagger replied.

"So, you will need to get it in safer hands than those of King Jares," Simon added.

"Have you heard of Lord Crel?" Dagger asked.

Simon had been facing the window until Dagger asked his question. His face turned stark white as he turned and went to the fire pit placing his hands on his wife's shoulders. He did not answer Dagger, as he stood staring into the fire. After a minute or two he began pacing the dirt floor. Finally grabbing his cloak he smiled at his wife, she nodded in return and he left without saying a word. Sarn noticed how scared he looked when Dagger mentioned Lord Crel. It was only the second time he had heard the name and the first time he had seen this reaction, but it would not be the last. He thought it best though not to question Dagger about the name then and there. Deciding instead he would find another, perhaps quieter time to bring up the question of the name.

Sala brought soup to the table for the boys while her grandmother came up behind them and thanked them for returning Sala, as she said, from the dead. She kissed them both on the forehead, while the two protested saying they had nothing to do with finding her.

"If she had not been so taken by the young boy here," Dagger said patting Sarn on his back. "She would not have gotten it in her head to follow along no matter the cost."

"Then perhaps I should be thanking you for her return," Tera said as she turned Sarn's face to her and looked deep into his eyes.

"I did nothing," Sarn returned, turning red. "She did it all herself."

"He gave me what I needed to buy my freedom and get a horse," Sala told her. "Falling in love with him was just a plus."

Sala and her grandmother both laughed as Sarn turned three shades of red.

"It was enough, whatever you did, to deserve the thanks." Tera held his face in both her hands and kept looking into his eyes. "What is your village?"

"I am from Penif," he began, "it is a small...."

"I have heard of this village," she interrupted. "There is a stone carver there named Tarsus that lives there with his wife Tara, is there not?"

"Yes," Sarn answered a bit surprised that she would know them. "They are my parents."

Tera was the one surprised now, but showed little sign of it as she continued to hold his face and look into his eyes. She smiled and kissed his cheeks and squeezed his face before whispering in his ear.

"You are welcome to my home and all that I have. May the gods keep you and bless you as you go about your life." Tears streamed down Tera's worn face as she let go of him and turned away.

Simon made his way towards the tavern near the center of the small village. He stopped several times on his way in an attempt to avoid being seen by the sentries as they continued to search for the thieves. Reaching the tavern he made his way through the crowded room to the far corner. Simon waited in the corner until he was sure that no one was interested in what he was doing. He was no stranger to the tavern but it was rare that he would be there after dark. It was not long before he saw who he was looking for. Getting up he crossed the floor and sat at his table.

"I need your help," Simon told him.

"I have told you many times, I can do nothing for you old man."

"You still work in the palace and I have a friend that needs to go inside without being seen," Simon continued, not caring what the other had said. "You used to tell everyone in here that you knew this castle better than any man alive."

"That is true, there is not a crack in any wall that I cannot tell you where it is and what caused it."

"Then you are just what they need," Simon knew that there was little chance that he would help Dagger, but he had to try. Anything that might keep Crel from ruling over the Kingdom was worth whatever lie he could make up. "I can promise you gold if you help them. "

"Gold, your friends must be desperate or stupid to have sent you Simon." He put his arm around the old man as he spoke trying to reassure him that everything would be fine. "But, since we have known each other for so long I will meet with your friends and see what it is that I might do for them."

Simon thanked him and told him that they were in immediate need of his help

"Meet me outside," he told him. "I will not be long."

He watched as Simon left the tavern. When he was sure that he was outside the man went to another corner where two sentries had been watching them. He leaned over to where they were sitting and whispered in their ears before leaving. The two soldiers nodded their heads and smiled at each other as the hunched over man left.

"We were poor," Sala began. "My parents brought little Simon here to be with my grandparents to help them. On the way back home they sold me to a man that had said he needed someone to take care of his children. They did not tell me what they had done. They just disappeared in the middle of the night. I learned that he had no children. When I would not bed him he sold me to a woman that went to poor villages and paid gold for children. She would sell the best looking girls or sometimes just the youngest girls to taverns or to old men as servants and pleasures. As for the boys, the handsome ones would be bought by widowed women and even some men for the same reasons as the girls. Any of the children she could not sell that way, she would sell to work in mines or quarries, wherever the need for labor was greatest and would bring her the most money. We went from village to village staying just long enough to sell some of us. I did everything I could to not be sold off to the mines. I would take care of the smaller children and keep them out of her way. Although I knew it was only a matter of time before it was my turn. When we came to Calid's tavern I knew I would not be leaving anytime soon. I think she knew that I would have nothing to do with selling myself when she sold me to Calid. I think that she did not like him. I have never figured out why but the cook stood up for me. I was placed in his care in the hopes that I would one day 'come around' as Calid had always said. Three and a half years later and I still had not come around, when you two walked into the tavern."

Sala stopped and turned back to the fire pit with her grandmother and began preparing the rest of the meal. Dagger had sensed that she had more to tell them but decided that he could wait for her to finish. Although he was not shocked by the tale, Sarn had nothing to say about it either. Sala's story did get them both thinking of their own parents. Dagger wondered if he was being sought out by his, while Sarn wondered how his parents were getting along without him. Not that Sarn's parents were old and frail. It was just that there was quite a lot that needed to be done each day, and many things that his father could no longer do alone.

"I knew that there was something special about the two of you that would make everything different for me. And that nothing in my life would be the same again," Sala began again, as she brought the two a plate of meat and flat bread. "In a way I knew the minute you came into the tavern that one of you was there to bring me out of that life. I had only survived so long because Borthen, the cook, protected me and kept me safe from Calid and those that would have no doubt raped me. I had tried to befriend Calid's son in the hopes that he would at least want me for himself, but that did not work. As the two of you sat by the fire I could not stop watching you and wondering what you were doing there. Neither of you seemed to have any interest at all in the other girls that were trying to force themselves on you. I waited still hoping that I was right and that one of you would pay some attention to me. It was not until I caught Sarn's hand while picking up the gold pieces that I realized that he was the one that had been sent to help me, to love me. I was sure then that I was destined to follow him whether I wanted to or not. I only hoped that he would want to take me from that tavern. In the morning when he gave me the gold I saw in his eyes that he wanted to take me with him. I also knew that without your say so Dagger, he could not offer. With what gold I had saved and the gold Sarn gave me I had enough to buy my freedom from Calid with enough left over to buy a horse. It would not be a good horse but Borthen gave me all the money he had been saving as well and I was able to get the horse I have now. Borthen was more of a father to me than my own. He did not wish to see me leave of course, but my happiness and freedom were more important to him than his."

Sarn went to the girl and hugged her as she cooked. Dagger, in the meantime, had been eating his meal trying to come up with another way into the castle. He had not considered the need to make another plan until now. He never had to make other plans in the past. No matter what the problem Dagger could always count on things working to his advantage. Things did not seem to be working that way this time. He was less sure how things would happen ever since Sala showed up at their camp that first night. He did know that she was meant to go with them and that she would always be part of the group. That was all he knew, at least all he knew for sure. Sarn kissed Sala before letting go of her and returning to the table.

Simon returned before they were finished eating. The short hunched over man following him through the door. Dagger thrust his hand in his cloak and grasped onto the crystal. The man behind Simon went immediately to Dagger, lowered his head and extended his hands.

"Ryn Mar," the man began as soon as he saw him, "I am at your service as always and forever."

"Thank you Kolas," Dagger returned, taking the old man's hands in his own, "It has been a long time."

"It has been too long between sightings my friend. Simon tells me that you have come for the tablet of spells that King Jares stole from the Keepers."

"If that is true," Dagger said letting go of his hand, "how do you think that you will be able to help me?"

"There is nothing I do not know about that castle or the palace," Kolas began. "Jares knows you are here. He has known that you were coming for some time now. How he found out or who told him you were coming I cannot say for certain. A few weeks ago Jares doubled the guards around himself and the castle. He paid soldiers from neighboring Kingdoms to keep watch for you and make sure that you did not get this far. How you got this far is your secret and I can only guess. I know that they were told to watch just for the two of you coming through the pass, that is you and Tig of course. They were not expecting three of you and you were only noticed when they finally saw your animal friend there. By then you were past all the traps that had been set for you. There is no way that you will be able to get in through any of the gates now, even if you had an invitation. As far as the tablet is concerned, I know where it is being kept. I am almost certain that I know how to get you into the palace without any of you being found by Jares' sentries at least until you get inside."

Dagger rose from his stool took Kolas by the shoulder and led him away from the others to the opposite side of the room. The two huddled together in the corner and continued their conversation in hushed tones.

"It has been a long time my Prince," Kolas began in a tongue that none else in the small hut had ever heard. "When was it, three years ago?"

"You must be careful what you call me," Dragger growled back in the same language. "If you do not I may just have to kill you."

"There is no one here that can understand what we speak, we can speak without worry."

"Then tell me what you have for me," Dagger growled again.

"This castle is a Valdore castle, is it not?"

"That is what I am led to believe," he returned, trying not to give away the fact that he knew exactly what castle it was.

"As you know a Valdore castle has many ways in and out of it especially if you know where to look," Kolas began, a smile forming on his face. "More than one of them is of course hidden from view, and at least one has never been discovered by its current occupier. And that my Prince is your way in. I have spent two weeks making ready one of those undiscovered entry ways on the chance that you might need my services."

"That may be the best way in, but getting there without any one seeing us is our next problem."

"There is going to be a festival at the castle in three days. We can use it to cover your movements."

"We cannot remain hidden here for that long," Dagger began. "The longer we are here the better the chance that we will be turned in."

"The reward is but five gold coins," Kolas returned hoping that he would not hear his lie.

"By day rise it will be three times that," Dagger moved even closer now as he spoke. "And at that cost I do not even trust you knowing where I am. No we must move under the cover of darkness later this night. Tell me more of this passage to the palace."

"As I said before, this castle was built for King Valdore, to be the fifth district of his Kingdom. Each of the Valdore castles were built with siege tunnels. They run under the castle walls out into the woods or meadows far from where any army would be likely to find them. They were built to store food and animals if attacked. It was hoped that they would be able to outlast even the longest of sieges. Each of the passages leads to a cluster of lower rooms. They also lead under the palace where the king and his family could be kept from harm and disease. There is a fire pit to cook on and the chimney is connected in with the palace chimney system. You could hide down there as long as you think is necessary, you could even wait for the festival if you want."

"Are you certain that the tunnels still exists and have not been discovered?" Dagger asked nodding his head. He knew of the tunnels that were said to lie beneath all the Valdore castles. Yet, in many places, some of the outer entrances had been discovered and destroyed over the years.

"Ryn I have been working in the castle for years. For the last week I have spent time making the room ready for your use, if you should need it."

Dagger sat thinking for a few minutes trying to decide if his old friend was telling him the truth.

"Come both of you," Sala interrupted Dagger's thoughts. "This food will be cold long before you solve your problem."

Dagger stood, still lost in thought and headed for the table. Taking two or three steps to the table he seemed to lose his way and bumped into a post in the middle of the room. Moving wide around the post he bounced off first one wall then another, finally reaching the table where he almost fell over his stool. Tig watched his master and then as if he could stand it no longer buried his head into little Simon, who was curled up next to him. Dagger laughed at his own folly. Kolas joined in his old friend's laughter while Sarn just shook his head.

"You never have figured how to see in this darkness have you?" Kolas shot at Dagger, still laughing.

Dagger found his seat and stared back at Kolas, making the man stop laughing and even cower a bit. Tera bade them all to give thanks and eat of the food, before going off on any plan.

"You will no doubt need all your energy," Tera added, as she and Sala finished placing the rest of the food in front of them.

They ate in silence, each of them thinking of what could happen next. Although Sarn was thinking further than that, his thoughts took him back to Penif, his friends, his home and his parents. He could not help from wondering if they were doing well and if Jhen was looking in on them as she had told him she would. Jhen was the tavern owner's daughter and had been his friend since the two were around four years old. They spent more and more time together the older they got. She was always telling Sarn how much she loved him and that they had been born to be together. She spent many weeks before he left trying to get him to stay. He spent as many weeks convincing her that he had to leave the village.

Dagger began to think of his life and the things he had seen and done. After having left his home there were many cases where to steal was to survive. Just weeks after leaving his home he was considered the finest little thief around. From then it was only a matter of time before he was sought out to use his skills on bigger and more dangerous jobs.

Sala kept looking at Sarn as he ate. She liked to watch him eat, and she watched him eat every night. She was always trying to imagine what the boy would be like in ten, or twenty years. How he would look holding their children as they grew up and holding her when the night came. Her life had meant nothing until she meet Sarn. She had resigned herself to live as a cook's helper and someday marrying the cook or tavern owners' son. She would have done anything to keep from having to sell her body to the men that would come through the tavern door. She had no intention of staying behind, whatever she needed to do or learn she was going to do it.

When he finished eating Kolas stood and walked to the fire pit. Leaning in he reached for a small piece of wood, pulled a short pipe from his coat and lit it with the flame from the wood.

"As soon as you are all ready I will take you to the lower siege rooms. You can hide there until it is safe to make your move," Kolas told them after lighting his pipe.

"Are we sure that King Jares does not know of this room?" asked Sarn.

"I am not sure that we have a choice in the matter," said Dagger. "We cannot stay here long. If we are here in the morning the sentries will no doubt find us. I am sure that they will search house to house looking for us soon enough. By then everyone in this house will be in as much danger, if not more than we are now."

"Then let us go into hiding," Sala spoke up. "I cannot bear the thought of anything happening to my grandparents because of me."

They looked at her as if she had never spoken before, and that none had ever expected her too.

"You will stay here," Kolas grumbled.

"I go where they go," she asserted, her voice trembling a little. "I am in as much danger here as Sarn and Dagger are. I have not been here in four years. How I appeared when all thought me dead will raise as much suspicion as the three of us hiding here."

"I do not want her to be in any danger," began Sarn, "but I do not see what harm she could do us if she came along."

"She could do us much harm with us as well as without us," Dagger said as if to end the debate.

"I will go with you or I will go to King Jares," Sala added. The threat was empty and she knew it but she hoped that it would work anyway.

Sarn laughed to himself knowing that if they did not take her along she would follow anyway. Dagger knew as well that it was an idle threat, but felt that he needed to put up a show of resistance in front of her grandparents and Kolas. Her grandparents would say nothing of their stay to no one other than Kolas, but they also would not want any harm to come to her.

"I would say then we have little choice but to let you come with us," Dagger chuckled.

"I knew you would not make me stay behind." Sala smiled as she began to dance about the room, hugging her grandparents in turn as she came to them.

An hour and many tears later the group was ready to leave the small home. With their horses' hooves wrapped in leather to help them make less noise and to help hide their steps, they slipped into the street. Tig made his way as fast as he could, keeping himself apart from the others so that he could watch for anyone that might see or follow them. They kept to the shadows as much as possible attempting to avoid being seen, walking their horses most of the way through the village, making certain at each turn that there was no one following them. Kolas led them out and away from the village and the castle as well. As the group passed the last building before the forest they mounted their horses again. Turning they made their way down a long gentle sloping hill. At the bottom of the hill the group found themselves in a grove of trees with low hanging branches. They began to follow the tree line under the cover of the branches until they came to a small stream. There they turned and followed it downstream. It was another ten minutes before they came to a small clearing in the grove. Moonlight filtered through the clouds and trees revealing a stone retaining wall. It was nearly as tall as their horses, and was overgrown with vines. The wall grew in height as it made its way along the edge of the narrow clearing. The stream weaving its way in and out from the wall several times before it came to a place where it touched the wall. Stopping there the group dismounted their horses and waited while Kolas began to feel his way along the wall. He pushed on some of the stones as he went, cursing himself when he did not get the reaction he was looking for. Here the wall was twice the height it had been when they first began to follow it. Tig pushed against his master and Dagger pulled his sword and turned to face the direction in which they had come. It was then that Kolas found the small opening in the wall he had been looking for. Reaching in up to his elbow Kolas grasped the handle that was hidden within it and pulled toward him. Water from the stream rushed to fill in the empty space as a section of the wall swung back to reveal the passage they were looking for. Dagger hurried the group into the passage, while Tig circled the area keeping low to the ground. He was above the group as they passed through the hidden door. As the last of the group stepped inside he caught sight of what he was looking for just a few yards behind them.

The two sentries had followed the group at a distance from the time they came out of the small stable. They were to have waited for Kolas to leave the house and then they were to enter and kill the thieves. At least that had been the plan that Kolas had set up with them before leaving the tavern. Although the plan he had given them had not included what to do if he had left with the thieves. So they decided to keep following them to see where they were going and then return for help or just report where they could be found.

As the last of the group disappeared into the darkness of the tunnel the two sentries moved into the small clearing. The two spoke for a second before one of them rode off.

Tig moved along the top of the wall making his way towards the departing sentry. When the man was deep enough in the grove Tig jumped behind him. His horse was the only one that noticed as it began to jump about almost knocking the sentry off. He quieted the animal as fast as he could before taking a few seconds to look around trying to see what spooked him before taking off again. Just as he kicked the animal forward Tig made his move, jumping toward the sentry and knocking his unaware prey to the ground. The sentry had little time to see Tig before he was tearing out his throat keeping him from screaming. Turning to the horse he tore at its hind leg crippling it, causing the horse to fall as it tried to run off. Knowing that the horse would return to its stable and raise suspicion Tig took the extra time to kill him as well. He then doubled back to where the other sentry had been. Having heard the horse of his friend call out in pain the remaining sentry dismounted pulling his sword free at the same time. He crouched ready to take on whatever was out there in the night. Dagger watched from the shadows as Tig moved through the trees behind the man. The sentry turned just in time to see Tig poised to pounce on him.

"If you think you can take me like you did him you are mistaken," he shouted, smiling as he swung his sword back and forth in front of him. "Come get me so that I can end your life."

Using the failure of the sentry to notice him, Dagger wrapped his hand around the crystal in his cloak and crept closer to him. Tig crept closer as well never once taking his eyes off the man. Dagger cocked his head then pointed toward the horse. Pulling one of his silver daggers he threw it toward the sentry, striking him in the back of the neck. The sentry fell forward, jerked once and never moved again. Tig turned his attention to the horse, but just as he was about to kill it Dagger whistled him away. Taking the still standing horse by its reins Dagger pulled a small pouch from his boot. Walking over to the dead sentry he shook a red powder over him. Moving to the other dead sentry and his horse he shook some of the powder over them as well before riding back to the stone wall. Once near the passageway he raised one hand, made a fist then brought it to his mouth. Lowering his hand again he opened it palm up revealing a red ball as he did so. The ball flew off the end of his hand and headed to where the dead sentries lay on the ground. As the ball struck the red powder it ignited, engulfing each one of them in the red light. When the light dissipated all signs of the horse and two sentries were gone. All that remained was the red powder floating just above the ground. A few seconds later it too was gone. The two slipped into the passageway and with the new horse in hand they rejoined the others. Kolas showed no sign of the fact that his plan had just been ruined. He could only hope that the now dead sentries' absence would cause some sort of concern or alarm to someone.

Kolas had pulled a torch from the wall and lit it as both Dagger and Tig rejoined the group. Holding the torch above his head Kolas led the way into the dark wet cavern. Water covered the floor of the tunnel and dripped from the ceiling and walls. Sarn and Sala kept the horses in tow while Dagger and Tig kept close behind Kolas. Sarn found another torch and lit it off the one Kolas was holding. The passage sloped down as it headed towards the castle. Before long the group found themselves walking in ever deepening water. It continued downward with the water reaching the group's knees before the floor finally began to rise. None spoke as they walked. The stench from the stagnant water made more than one of them wish they had taken their chances going through one of the many gates. Sarn guessed that they had been walking for about an hour before they finally reached a doorway. It was just large enough to get the horses through.

"We have reached the outer castle walls," Kolas told them after they passed through the doorway. "It will only be a short time more before we reach the center siege lodge."

The tunnel seemed to grow warmer and drier as they went. The floor, for the most part, leveled off once the group had passed through the door. The water that seeped in through the walls was collected and channeled in troths on each side of the walkway. Kolas told them that it was part of the lower castle's well system. All the troths from the many tunnels led to a well near the center siege lodge making it separate from the main well system. The water, he said was used to feed the animals and whoever else was in the lower castle during a siege.

A short time later the passageway opened to a large room that held several animal stalls and a few piles of hay. There were also four other doors with hallways leading away from the room they were standing in. One of the four doors was carved and adorned with silver hinges and handles. The three others were plain but taller than the passage they had just walked through. Kolas opened the ornate door to the lower lodge and led the group in. Sarn and Sala went to the fire pit near the center of the room. Sarn dropped his torch into the fire pit; the dry wood lit almost at once. Sala brought one of the torches from the wall to the fire pit and lit it, then lit the others about the room. Finding a chair Sarn kicked off his boots and sat next to the fire to dry off. The others joined him, although they seemed somewhat reluctant to do so.

"Are you sure that this added smoke will not be noticeable?" asked Dagger.

"Like I told you there is a fire going at all times in the main kitchen. This chimney is connected in with that system. The smoke from this fire will mix with the smoke from that fire and never be noticed," Kolas reassured them.

The room was furnished with several chairs, a long table and little else. The walls had once been covered with large wall hangings. But with years of neglect and the moisture in the room they were left as tattered rags. As they sat around the fire pit Kolas pointed to a wide stairwell tucked in the corner of one wall telling them it led up to the palace.

"It also goes to an anteroom on each floor of the palace," he told them. "When the time comes I will be happy to lead you up to the room where Jares is keeping the tablet."

The group rested and dried off while Dagger thought of the rest of his plan.

There were exactly six sitting rooms on the third floor of the palace. Yet only one looked toward the peasant village and the fields that surrounded it. It was in that sitting room that Jares stood looking out over the castle walls at the home that the thieves were hiding. The only problem was, he did not know in which of the ramshackle buildings they were. And yet he smiled with more than a little contentment just knowing that they were there. As far as he was concerned his only problem was what to do with the tablet while waiting for Lord Crel to arrive. He knew that his sentries would find the thieves before they could get into the palace. As poor as he kept his peasants, they would do anything for a handful for gold. They would even turn themselves in for something they did not do if it meant they could feed their family. Jares chuckled to himself as one of the many servants that made up the staff of the palace placed a plate in front of him. He despised eating in any of the dining rooms. Instead he took all his meals in his chambers or one of the many sitting rooms.

"Where is she?" he asked the female servant.

"I am sure that I do not know my lord," the servant said as she backed away from the small table.

"Then why did you not bring her dinner here with you as well?"

She did not answer him and knew that there was a chance

that she would end up paying for it. As luck would have it though, one of his close guards stepped through the open door. Close behind him was the dark haired girl he was looking for. She slipped in behind the guard carrying a tray filled with her dinner and wine.

"My lord," the guard interrupted his fist flying to his chest as he spoke, "we can no longer find any sign of the thieves."

"They are out there," Jares yelled back at the sentry. "You will find them or you will find yourself hanging by your thumbs in the court yard."

Jares threw his plate of food at the guard hitting him in the chest. He made no attempt to wipe it off until leaving the room. Not wanting to be the next to feel Jares' anger, the servant left close behind the guard.

"Fool," the sentry muttered as he walked away, grabbing his sword as he turned the corner at the end of the hall.

"Why must I be surrounded by imbeciles?" Jares grumbled as the sentry walked away. "How difficult can it be to find three strangers in a peasant village? If they do not stand out on their own then an orange and black animal must have been seen?"

The dark haired girl was now sitting beside him lowering her head as he spoke to keep him from taking his anger out on her, and from laughing. She was not sure why the three were so important to him nor did she care. She had her own reasons for being there. She laughed at Jares finally, unable to hold back any longer.

Jares turned and slapped her across the face.

"There is nothing to laugh about," he yelled pulling his hand back ready to strike again.

The dark haired girl slumped into the stool that she sat on lowering her head even further and looked away from him. She knew that it would only be a matter of time before she could enact her own revenge for the months that she had endured his abuse. Jares grabbed the girl by her hair. Pulling her off the stool, and knocking over the tray, he led her out of the room and down the hallway.

"Burn it," Jares yelled to anyone that could hear him. "If they do not turn the thieves over, burn the village to the ground."

Still pulling the girl along by her hair, Jares reached the first of his palace guards, where he repeated his demand. With his free hand he shoved the guard when he was finished. Jares continued to pull the girl along as he headed up a small set of stairs that led to his chambers. She did not struggle, not even when he had first grabbed her. She had learned early on that it was not in her best interest to struggle as it only made him stop long enough to hit her again. He threw her to the floor next to his bed before kicking her legs as she lay there.

"Where were you?" he screamed. "You are supposed to be near me at all times."

"I... I ... I am sorry my... my lord," she managed to stammer.

He sat on the edge of the bed and waited for her as she crawled toward him. She let her hands slide up his legs as she reached him. His lips formed a crooked smile as he hit her again. Taking a knife from his belt he slipped the blade between her breasts and began to cut her dress from her body.

Even though it was getting late activity inside the castle walls was still quite heavy. Most of the streets were full of people, many of the shops were open and the taverns were still doing a brisk business. Simon and his grandson wandered the streets of the city behind the castle walls, trying to find out what they could about the search for the group of thieves. They sat down outside one of the busiest taverns and waited. It was also the one most visited by Jares' guards. There were many things spoken of in the street, but as each group of two guards would pass another they would ask of the search for the thieves. The answer was always the same; none had seen them or had heard of anyone finding them. After a couple of hours of listening and begging for money they returned to their home. With each of them collecting more than a month's wages, and happy in the knowledge that the group had seemed to disappear.

"It is time," Dagger said as Sarn rolled away from Sala and began to wake.

Sarn grumbled, shaking his head as he came awake. He did not know how long he had been sleeping and was a bit angry with himself for having fallen asleep.

"I would not be too hard on yourself if I were you," Dagger told him. "It is a good thing that you have gotten some rest. I cannot say when we will get another chance to do so."

They gathered their now dry belongings and dressed. Dagger, Sarn, Kolas and Tig headed for the stairway leading up into the palace. Sala was to stay behind and have the horses ready to leave when they returned. Grabbing a torch and kissing Sala, Sarn led the way up the steps with Dagger and Tig close behind while Kolas followed. The stairs were steep and wound in a circular path as they went up. After several minutes they reached a landing with a stone door. It looked a lot like the rest of the wall except for a large pull ring. Stopping Dagger asked if it was the right door. Shaking his head Kolas pushed them on further up another set of stairs.

"This is the door that we need," Kolas told them in a low whisper.

Dagger pushed past Sarn, readying himself against the stone door.

"Do something with that torch," he whispered to Sarn.

Sarn tossed the torch down the flight of stairs hoping that it would stay lit to help them find their way back down to the siege lodge. They heard the torch sizzle as it hit the stairs and rolled down several more steps. A second later they were in the dark again. Dagger pushed against the door and as it opened the trio entered the semi dark room. Moonlight shone through the windows lighting the room.

Dagger asked Kolas what the room was used for. He told him that it once had been part of the Queen's chambers and as far as anyone could tell it had not been used for almost sixty years.

"Jares has no queen," Kolas continued. "He has a few women and..., but they have chambers elsewhere in the palace."

"So you are telling us that he has no idea of this door or the stairwell we just climbed?" Sarn half asked.

Dagger had noticed his friend's near slip of the tongue and wondered what he was going to say. He almost asked what it was, choosing instead not to let on that he had noticed it. He and Sarn found it hard to believe that no one had been in the room for sixty years that could not have found the doorway.

"I do not like this," Sarn added. "I have a bad feeling that there is...."

He abruptly stopped talking and began to push himself against the wall in the shadows. Tig was showing signs of his own nervousness as well as he began pacing the floor. Dagger and Sarn pulled their swords at the same time. Tig went to the far corner of the room and crouched as Dagger pulled the outer door of the chamber open. Light flooded in from the torches in the hallway and so did three guards that had been waiting just outside. Kolas stepped back into the darkness.

"I am sorry old friend but I ...." Kolas' voice trailed off as a silver dagger plunged into his chest, driving the old man back against the outer wall of the room.

The three guards pushed their way into the room as Kolas lifeless body dropped to the floor. A second silver dagger plunged into the first guard's throat, dropping him as well. Tig pounced on the second guard through the door, knocking him back into the hallway, as he tore at his throat. Sarn took on the third guard, driving him back toward the hall when Dagger slid his sword into the guard's side. The fight in the Queen's chamber was quick but bloody, leaving the three guards lying dead on the floor. Both Sarn and Dagger escaped the skirmish unharmed, but it was a long way from being over. They still needed to get the tablet and get back out.

There was little time for them to worry about much more than themselves as more of the palace guards made their way into the room. Tig was the first to react pouncing on the first of them taking him by surprise as he tore at his throat. Sarn and Dagger forced the others back into the hallway where they began dying one by one. Sarn took a hit to his hand and arm, while Dagger seemed to avoid the sword's strikes as well as all the advances of the guards. Tig appeared behind them with both silver daggers in his mouth and watched as the two would be thieves finished off the last of the guards.

"Are you injured?" Dagger asked as the last guard fell under his sword.

"Yes, but not badly," Sarn answered.

Dagger got Tig to drop his daggers from his blood covered face before giving him a short sword from one of the dead guards. Sending him back to the siege lodge he told him to take care of the girl. As Tig bounded back to their hiding place with the sword in his mouth, Sarn could not help but pray that Sala was still all right. Dagger also hoped that Tig was not too late.

"Let us see if we can still get the tablet out of here," Dagger said trying not to linger on his thoughts.

"I am sorry about your friend," Sarn returned.

"I never could trust him and I will miss him as much as I would miss a headache from too much drink." It would be all that Dagger would say about having killed Kolas before changing the subject. "Your wounds, are they bleeding much?"

"No, they should be fine until we get out of here." Sarn found himself chuckling over Dagger's statement and yet he was not sure why his friend's death did not seem to matter to him.

Dagger nodded in agreement as they headed down the

hallway towards the room that Kolas had told him that the tablet was in. They opened one door after another looking into each chamber in their search for the tablet. They did not find it, but they did find something else.

"Did you kill them?" Jares asked without turning his attention away from the naked dark-haired girl in his bed.

"No, I do not believe we killed all your guards, but I would say that it was enough that we are alone for the moment," Sarn said before ducking back into the hallway, keeping one eye behind them.

"Ryn Mar," Jares said more than just a little surprised to see Dagger. "I would have thought you would have learned by now that you cannot get away with anything in my Kingdom."

"If this were your Kingdom by law, then I might agree with you," Dagger snarled. "But, since it is not I think I will get away with as much as I would like, as always."

While the dark-haired girl did not know exactly what or who Ryn Mar was she knew that the time would not get any better to move on her plan. She reached under her torn dress pulling the knife that had cut it and held it to Jares' throat.

Sala heard the noise of the battle coming down the stairwell. She fought back the overwhelming feeling that she needed to join the others as long as she could. She was beginning to climb the steps when Tig appeared with the short sword in his mouth. Dropping the sword at her feet Tig leaned into her placing his head in her hand. Grabbing the sword she immediately turned from the stairs to finish her chore of seeing that the horses had been fed and watered. Making sure that everything was ready to leave as soon as the boys returned. She tied a packhorse to her horse and one to Pel as well. The remaining horse she tied to Daggers thinking it might come in handy, or perhaps they could always sell it.

Simon returned to his home just before the first of the guards entered the village with torches in hand. No one was questioned no homes were searched, and none of the villagers knew what was to happen next. When the sentries had surrounded the peasant's village, the leader raised his torch and tossed it onto the roof of the nearest hut. In seconds the entire village was ablaze and then they waited to kill all that ran from it. Those that were too afraid to run were burned alive in their homes.

"Chelseah," Jares pleaded, "what are you doing? You are my love, my life."

"I have waited a long time for this," Chelseah smiled.

"It seems that I am not the only one that would wish to kill you." Dagger said chuckling at Jares' situation.

"You have tried before Ryn Mar and failed, what brings you back?"

"You know what I am here for," Dagger told him stepping forward and pressing his sword to his chest.

"We have no time for this," Sarn interrupted. Knowing it was only a matter of time before the dead guards were found

"You heard the boy, tell us where the tablet is."

"The tablet," Jares scoffed. "What is it about that tablet that makes everyone want it so much?"

"Just tell me where it is," Dagger yelled pressing harder against his chest. Blood appeared from Jares' chest mixing with that of his guards on Dagger's sword.

Chelseah pressed the knife harder and pulled across his throat. Jares' eyes widened and his head fell back as the knife separated his skin. Jares' body went limp falling against Dagger's sword. Lowering his sword he let Jares fall to the floor.

"I hope you know where the tablet is," Sarn said as he crossed behind her.

"I will show you," she said smiling and stood naked from the bed.

She brushed against each of them, pausing against Dagger who immediately pushed her away.

"I have no time for your games," he told her

"I am sorry I did not mean to offend you sire I only meant...."

"I know exactly what it is that you meant," he said raising his sword up to her chest. "It would be a shame to waste such a body as yours, but I would not hesitate to do so."

"I happen to agree with you," Chelseah smiled at him and ran a hand down his chest before turning and walking out the door.

The two thieves followed the girl down the hall, as she led them past the dead guards. They went past several more doors before finally opening the door to one and leading them into the candlelit room.

The tablet lay on a table in the center of the room surrounded by candles.

"Is that it?" Sarn asked as Dagger ran his hands over it.

His hand touched each of the carved figures as if he were trying to recall each one of them from somewhere deep in his memory. It was smaller than Sarn thought it would be. Just about the size of one of his father's large books he thought.

"Yes, this is it," Dagger said as if he were coming out of some sort of trance.

Chelseah backed out of the room as they talked almost unnoticed by them.

"She is gone," Sarn said noticing first.

Dagger lifted the tablet from the table and slipped it into his cloak

"Then I guess we had better be on our way as well." Dagger added as he headed toward the door.

Once in the hallway the thieves headed back toward the stairway. Chelseah stood waiting for them just before the door to the Queen's chambers.

"They killed King Jares and have taken the tablet," she began yelling as the two headed towards her. "Do not let them get away."

Sala had just finished filling the water skins when Tig began to growl. Turning just in time she watched as Tig pounced on the first of three attackers. Grabbing at her own sword she stood facing her attackers. Having never swung her sword in anger she was more than a little unsure of herself. Yet, knowing it was her only hope she squared her shoulders, held the short sword ready and waited for them. Tig tore the throat out of the first attacker while the second slipped past him and swung his sword at Sala hitting her on the shoulder. The third while trying to keep out of Tig's way circled Sala and struck her across one leg, dropping her to one knee. She struggled to stand and faced the first guard again. Tig turned from the lifeless guard and caught up with the second one, taking him down by driving his head into his side, knocking him over. Sala kept pace with the two as the guard tumbled over the animal and plunged her sword into his chest as they stopped. The remaining guard lunged swinging his sword at Sala. Catching her on the left side and dropping her to the floor. Tig turned from the now dead guard and jumped to the remaining guard. He was too fast for the guard and was on him before he could pull his sword back from hitting Sala. His paws caught the man in his chest knocking him off his feet. Reaching in with his head he tore at the guard's throat and he was dead before the two hit the ground. When it was over he grabbed Sala by the back of her shirt and pulled her away from the dead bodies. Once she was far enough away he lay over the legs of the then unconscious girl and waited for his master to return.

Sarn ran to where the dark-haired girl stood, swung his sword taking her head. They were in the Queen's chamber before her head bounced on the floor. Running down the dark stairway Dagger held onto Sarn's shoulder as they went. Reaching the bottom of the stairs they found Tig still laying over Sala. She struggled to raise her head as they approached. Sarn ran to her side, took her in his arms and held her.

"We need to get out of here," he said trying to stop the flow of Sala's blood.

"I am sure you are right," Dagger returned, "but if we do nothing now she will not make it through the night. If that happens then I am afraid that you will be useless."

Dagger reached into his cloak and pulled out a pouch. Taking the girl from Sarn's arms, he opened the pouch and sprinkled a white powder over Sala's wounds. Sarn watched as her wounds stopped bleeding almost as fast as they had begun.

"Find us another way out," Dagger called to Sarn. "I do not think it a good idea to go back the way we came. We would have to cross the valley and I am sure that they are searching everywhere for us by now. Try and see if you can find two large doors."

Sarn went out to where the horses were and began to check the other passageways. With Tig running up one then another, finally behind a pile of hay the two found the high wide doorway with twin wooden doors half open. He led the horses beyond the hay and waited for Dagger and Sala. The two appeared shortly after with a couple of new attackers close behind. Sarn fought them while Dagger got Sala on her horse.

Grabbing two torches from the wall he returned to the others, the guards following close behind him. Dagger mounted his horse as Sarn tossed one of the torches in the pile of hay catching both guards as they crossed the pile. The dry hay was quick to catch fire cutting them off from the guards. Sarn mounted Pel and holding the torch high the three headed down the passageway. He thought that he could hear screams coming from behind them. They rode down the passageway as fast as the torch would allow. The pathway led down for some time before it finally began to rise just as it had when they had come in the tunnel on the other end. They finally reached the end of the tunnel and Sarn dismounted searching for the way to open the door. That is, he hoped that it was a door. After several minutes and plenty of cursing he found a hole in the wall. Pushing his arm in as far as it would go his hand found what he hoped was a handle. Pulling on it did nothing and he cursed his luck. He gave the handle a twist and it pulled away from his hand. The wall shook, creaked and began to open into the tunnel. Tossing the torch in a puddle of water and plunging them back into darkness he pulled on the door. Dagger jumped off his horse to help, while Tig ran a short distance back into the passageway. Looking out from the tunnel Sarn saw nothing but the light of the moon and an open field facing the mountains. Leading the horses out into the fields they found themselves over two miles from the castle at the base of a hill. Hearing more guards behind them they pulled the door closed again. Remounting their horses they circled wide to avoid any outposts as they began making their way back to the mountain pass. Sala, weak from her blood loss, was hunched over her on horse, but was hanging on with all the strength she had. Tig took off out ahead of the thieves keeping watch for anyone that might be in front of the group. It took the rest of the night for them to reach the bottom of the pass. As the sun's rays reached the top of the surrounding mountains they began their ascent out of the valley.

They would be near the top of the pass before they could get a clear look back into the valley. Looking over her shoulder Sala was the first to notice the red smoke coming from the palace chimney. She also saw the black smoke rising from where her grandparents' village once stood. Her heart fell at the sight, but she knew that there was little that she could do to help her grandparents now. Going to them would only mean death to them if they were alive, and if they were dead there was nothing she could do but say a few words over them. Either way she knew she was not meant to go back and that her destiny lay elsewhere.

"Sarn," she called out.

Turning around he saw what she was about to tell him.

"Dagger, why would there be red smoke coming from the castle?" Sarn asked when he saw it.

"It means that we are not yet out of danger," he replied, as he pushed his horse up the road. "One hope is that the pass guards are still asleep."

"I would hope that we have more than just one," Sarn called back as he noticed the smoke rising from the village.

Tig took over the lead of the group while Sarn and Sala followed close behind Dagger as the travelers pressed on.

High in the mountain above the pass someone did notice the smoke coming from the palace. The small encampment was just coming awake as each member of the group woke to the red smoke that continued to roll out of the palace chimney.

"It would seem that the thief has struck," the tallest of the guards said.

"From the looks of the smoke he was successful," another said.

The third said nothing as he stood and looked down into the pass. The sun had not yet reached it and it was still in the shadow of the mountains.

"Well there are only a few ways in or out of the valley," the third said finally. "I hope that they come this way again."

"You just wish to use your new sword," returned the first sentry.

"It has yet to taste blood," the third informed the others. "It needs to kill."

"Your desire to kill disturbs me," the tallest added.

"You would think that you would not be disturbed by anything," the third returned laughing at him.

"It also looks as if Jares is dead," the tallest said looking out over the valley.

Blue smoke began to rise from another chimney. While on the other side of the palace yellow smoke poured out of yet another. Each color mingling with the red smoke that continued to come from the palace.

"What do you think we should do now?" the third asked.

"We could return to the castle and join the others in the search," the tallest began. "We could try and stop the thieves ourselves, or we could just leave the valley and forget this place all together."

"It has been some time since we have been paid," the third chimed in, "and since Jares had no heir, I doubt we will be any time soon."

While the outpost sentries were trying to figure out what they were going to do, the travelers passed below. Stopping at the top of the pass they looked back to the valley, watching the smoke come from the castle and from where the village once stood.

"I am sorry my love," Sarn began. "I will understand if you want to go back to find your grandparents."

Dagger tilted his head in confusion before reaching in and

grabbing the small crystal in his cloak. Seeing the smoke from the village he told the girl that she should go back.

"No," Sala returned, tears forming in her eyes. "My heart is here. If they are dead there is little I can do. If they are alive, I might bring them death. I cannot go back; I am condemning myself to an eternity of heartache no matter what I do."

Neither Sarn nor Dagger said anything as they looked down into the valley. After several minutes of watching the two nodded knowing that what Sala had said was right. There was nothing she or they could ever do to help the villagers. Turning away they headed off down the other side of the pass putting more distance between them and the fifth castle of Valdore.

The small family of three stood in the relative safety of the tree line of the nearby forest. They watched as the smoke rose from their still smoldering home. They were not alone as others that had managed to somehow escape their homes stood with them or not far from them. Standing close by too were two others dressed in long dark blue hooded cloaks

"See, did I not tell you that they would not get caught," the taller of the two said.

"But they could have," the other chimed in. "I am growing more frustrated with you each day."

"I suppose then that I should be happy that you will still have anything to do with me."

The taller of the two turned away, shaking their head as they went.

Two weeks later the travelers arrived at Galdar's country estate. A few miles before the main house they came on an old tree. It had been dead for many years, twisted and crooked, ravaged by a fire that had come through the area some years earlier. Near the base of the tree just a foot or so from the ground was a wide crack in its trunk. Getting down, Dagger felt around in the crack. When he seemed satisfied he slid the tablet inside before remounting his horse and heading to the main house.

"You do not trust the man that hired you to get the tablet?" Sala asked. She had recovered from her wounds in no time and in just a few days she was herself again, showing no lasting effects of the fight at the castle.

"It is easier to trust no one than it is to trust everyone or to try and figure out who to trust," replied Dagger.

They rode to the main house and were greeted by Galdar.

"I see that you have returned. I trust that you were successful in your thievery." Galdar greeted them, opening his arms wide as if he wished to embrace them.

"If we were not, I would have not returned," Dagger shot back.

"Come, let me see the tablet I am paying for," Galdar insisted, before noticing Sala for the first time. "Where did you find the woman? I should know as she does look more than a little familiar."

"Where she comes from and how she came to be here is of no concern of yours," Sarn said trying to be as forceful as he could.

"I remember now," Galdar said immediately as if he had known all along. "The tavern, you were one of Calid's women. Yes, how unfortunate for me that you ran away before I could have you. Perhaps we can change that while you are here."

Sala turned her horse toward him, pulling her sword as she came around, readying to jump down to face Galdar. Dagger stopped her before she could do so, telling her that it was not the time to be offended.

"You would be wise not to bring that up again," Sarn told him as he stood in his saddle.

The travelers stayed motionless on their horses, waiting for Dagger to make the next move.

"Come my thieves, let us look at the tablet and have something to fill our insides with," Galdar insisted, throwing his arms open again in welcome, hoping that all could be well again.

"When I have the rest of our money perhaps we will join you and I will tell you where the tablet is and then you can send someone after it while we eat," Dagger told him still sitting on his horse.

"You do not trust me?"

"Could I ever?" answered Dagger. "I could not trust our old friend Kolas, and now he is dead so I do not think that I should trust you."

"Perhaps not," said Galdar shrugging his shoulders and tilting his head. "If that is the way it is to be then it must be so."

Five of Galdar's bodyguards began to appear on the side and behind them. Tig, who had been out by the burned out tree, came up behind them unnoticed. Sarn smiled to himself as he watched what was happening.

"Five ..., are they best that you have?" Dagger asked as a defiant smile formed on his lips. "Tig will be having their hearts for his midday meal before they are able to do us any harm."

"I doubt that," Galdar demanded. "The tablet, tell me where you hid it."

"My final payment and I will tell you."

"Very well," he conceded, after noticing Tig pacing behind his bodyguards.

He tossed the first bag to Sala followed by two more. She immediately opened them to make sure that they held gold coins and then tossed them to Sarn who began to count them.

"So little trust," he laughed. "I see you pass this lack of trust of yours to the boy as well."

Dagger ignored him as Sarn continued his count.

"They appear to all be here," Sarn told Dagger when he finished.

"Follow our trail and you will find the tablet in an old tree near the edge of your land," Dagger told him as he turned his horse and began to ride off.

Sarn and Sala followed close behind with the packhorses. Tig bounded after them, turning circles to ensure that they were not being followed by any of Galdar's men.

"Do you think that they will find the tablet?" Sarn asked when the group finally slowed down.

"Perhaps, if they hurry," said Dagger laughing. "But I am sure that the sisters or my cousins have already taken the tablet from the tree. They will see to it that it gets back to where it belongs and will do the most good."

Neither Sarn nor Sala knew who or what Dagger was speaking about, but both joined him in his laughter as they rode.

"I have a feeling that Galdar is not going to be a happy man,." Sala said after a while.

"I doubt he will complain," Dagger said still laughing. "I can always tell him that his men just looked in the wrong tree."

They had been on the move since leaving the castle city of Nefrendel. Avoiding as many villages and farms as they could as they went. They stopped only long enough to feed themselves and their animals, resting only a few hours at a time. Each stop would find them watching out for anyone that might have followed behind them. That is until late one afternoon when Dagger led them back onto the well-traveled road. A short time later they found themselves in a small village setting on the bank of a narrow river. It was quiet, but there were a few people in the street. The village often had strangers passing into or through it. So the small group's arrival did not cause any suspicion nor were they given a second thought. It wasn't until Tig bounded up behind the group that the villagers began to pay more than just passing attention to them. Word of their arrival spread fast through the village. It was not long before people were watching them from windows, around corners, or just stopping as they passed. Some of the older children began to reach out to pet Tig, while the smaller children could not keep their eyes off him. The animal tried his best to keep away from the children, not being sure what would happen if they were caught trying to pet him.

"Where is this place?" asked Sala as they passed through the central part of the village.

"What does it matter, a village is a village; the only ones that matter are the ones within a castle wall," Dagger replied.

"If it does not matter, then why enter it?" Sarn returned laughing a little, although he was not sure why.

"Perhaps he is in need of the pleasures of a good woman," Sala joined in with a joke of her own.

"I doubt he has ever been with a girl before let alone a woman," Sarn added playing along.

"That may or may not be true my friend. Then again I have often wondered if you had ever seen a girl before you met Sala," Dagger laughed. "I do believe you were afraid that you would never see another as well."

Sala shook her head, smiling at him holding back a laugh of her own.

"Tell me again why we are stopping here?" Sarn asked, changing the subject.

"We need to replenish our supplies," Dagger returned, not sure how much more he should tell him. "Your woman's cooking is not the best and I grow in need of a good meal."

"You never seem to mind my cooking as you eat it," Sala grumbled as she stared at the back of his head, wishing that she had something to throw at him.

"When it is all there is to eat, one does not complain, but when one has another choice, that is another story."

Dagger laughed telling her that he was not serious and that her cooking was far better than his own, but it did not help. Sala was still searching for something to toss at him. Sarn shook his head not sure what to say. Yet he had something to say for both sides, but he knew that no matter which side he picked he was going to be in trouble.

"Sarn," she returned, pleading with him to come to her rescue.

"I do believe that he was joking," he began trying his best to be diplomatic. "Especially since I do believe that he looks to have been gaining weight recently, but I beg you to not drag me any further into this. I think it is best if I leave it just between the two of you."

"Perhaps we can find someone here that you can learn cooking from." Dagger laughed as he spoke, no longer caring if he hurt her feelings or not. "We will rest here a few days just the same. Then we will work on your training and see what our next adventure will bring."

"Do you know what it is to be? Are you certain we will find it here? How long do you think we will have to stay here?" Sarn asked not sure if there was something that he was not telling him.

It was as if he was a child of five again asking his father questions. And yet he could not keep himself from being excited with the anticipation of another adventure. He did not know what had come over him but he felt his heart leap at the thought of a new adventure, or maybe it was just the thought of killing again. His hand trembled a little just the same at the thought of it all. He pushed Pel on ahead of the others trying to keep either of them from noticing. Dagger chuckled to himself as Sarn asked his questions. He knew that the boy was becoming excited about the possibility of both the killing and the danger. He had seen it all many times before. The problem was would the boy be able to control his excitement. He had trained others before him only to have them turned or killed. Would he be different than those that came before him? Did he know what he was supposed to know? Could he be taught everything that Dagger had to teach him, or would all the hours of training be a waste of time like the others?

On the banks of the river just a short distance from the center of the village the travelers found rooms in the village's only tavern. That night they sat at one of its tables drinking the local ale and listening to stories told by the villagers and other travelers. After a meal and more than their share of ales they disappeared into their rooms. Sarn and Sala shared a room, leaving Dagger to a room of his own. Tig seemed torn about which room he wanted to be in. Dagger won out, after of course he reminded the animal who had taken care of him longer.

Having taken little time for either for some time, they did little more than sleep and eat for the first few days. They saw no one but each other, even having their meals in their rooms. Tig had nothing to do with it as he spent most of his days wandering around the village, keeping on his guard for any kind of danger.

While the villagers seemed to welcome the travelers with open arms, they were a little cautious of Tig. They had never seen an animal exactly like him before, but they had heard about others like him. They also had heard that those like him were far from friendly. While they allowed him the freedom to roam about the village unharmed out of respect for the travelers they did keep a watchful eye on him. It would not be long before some the children became brave enough to begin to pet him. Being the type that loves attention he never once chased any of them away. It would not be long before all the children in the village were petting and playing with him. In return Tig began to be a bit protective of the children and would watch them as they played, keeping close by in case of any trouble. Being always the first by their side Tig would check them out if they had fallen, even helping them up if they needed it. When a toddler fell into the river, Tig was there in an instant pulling the young girl out by the scruff of her neck. The horror on the faces of those on the river bank as the girl fell in the water was nothing compared to when they saw her hanging from Tig's mouth. They realized at once that the girl was shaken by her trip into the water but unharmed from the jaws of Tig. His action made the animal somewhat of a hero in their eyes, and was no longer looked at with suspicion by anyone.

It was on the fourth day of their rest that Dagger, with the help of Tig, woke the two lovers early to tell them it was time to begin training again.

"If you had been better trained, you would not have been injured by Jares' guards," Dagger had told Sarn as he had looked after his wounds one day as they made their way to Galdar's estate. He reminded him again that day as he woke the sleeping couple.

Dagger had more on his mind that morning than just their continued training. He had been thinking of his family and wondering why they had not been trying to find him. They had not sent him a message for some months. It was unusual enough that they did not seem to be trying to find him, but they had always found a way to send him some kind of message. He had not thought of them as much as since that first night at Sarn's fire. Could that mean that there was a chance that the boy was who he had been told he was? He shook his head to get the thought out of his mind. It was best if he didn't even begin to think such thoughts like that; he knew how it would all end if he did. The travelers met again over a breakfast of chicken eggs and venison and cool cow's milk to wash it down with.

"Today we will return to your training," he told Sarn. "As for you girl, you might as well join us full time so that you will be better able to protect yourself as well. Since it would seem you are set on coming along and I cannot get you to leave no matter what I tell you, I had better teach you more than just how to protect yourself."

"I have not heard any complaints from you about my being around," Sala returned more than a little cross with him. "Besides I thought you wanted me to learn better cooking."

"I will just have to suffer your terrible cooking," Dagger returned. "You know it would have done me no good to have told you that you could not come along."

He knew that she would have followed them no matter what he had said that first night or since.

"At least I would have known you did not want me along," she grumbled, growing angrier.

Dagger had no answer but to take her hand and squeeze it.

"I think that means that he would not have it any other way," Sarn spoke up half laughing, trying to lighten the darkening mood.

Dagger smiled and nodded his head and pulled the ever-present hood of his cloak further down over his face. None in the party or any human that still lived had ever seen his full face without the hood of his cloak covering it. Going without the hood was left only for when he was alone or was sure that none else could see him. The only living thing that had seen his head fully uncovered since he left home, was Tig and he was telling no one what he saw. There were many times when Dagger had wanted to tell the couple his secret, but it was not the time. Perhaps someday he could tell them and live in the open without his ever present hood.

Their training took up the morning hours of each day. By the time the sun was high and hot enough the group would stop for the day and return to the tavern or sit in the shade by the river. They would often watch as the women of the village came to wash their clothes. There was always small children running naked in and out of the river, splashing water and chasing each other. The older children would swim farther upstream sometimes separate, and sometimes together. The travelers would always wait until dark to join any in the river. Dagger always begged off joining them claiming to "watch" over them just in case, ever on the lookout for trouble, or so he claimed. Each night Sala would help one of the servants set up a tub in Daggers room so that he could use it. Never wanting to let anyone think him grateful he would always complain of it. Depending on his mood would depend on what he would complain about. The water being cold or too hot or the tub in the wrong place, whatever it was he always found something wrong.

At night in the tavern Dagger was always turning down the advances of the tavern women. He was careful to keep to himself when the others were not with him. Sala was their acting servant and was the only one that Dagger would allow into his room, other than Sarn and Tig, when he was in it. She had been tempted to surprise him to learn of his secret. Although she always thought better of it every time she remembered the fate of Katryn, the blonde, back at Calid's tavern. She began to think that if he wanted her to learn of him, he would tell her himself.

It did not take long before news of the travelers reached neighboring villages. The curious would come and watch the strangers as they trained and often buy them ale or wine at the end of their day. Still others that came wanted to see those rumored to have killed King Jares and his mistress. Neither was well loved and would not be missed, nor would any come to arrest the travelers for killing them, at least not in that village.

No one was alarmed when a large group of men appeared in the small village the end of the second week of the travelers' stay. Unlike others that would come to watch, they sat on their horses as the three trained, staying back out of the way. It was not long before some in the village recognized one of the mounted men as King Gregor from a nearby Kingdom. As the word spread through the crowd the villagers turned and knelt, bowing their heads to the man in the light purple cloak. The trio continued their training even as the crowd about them grew. Dagger could tell that something was different, but since he did not have his hand on his crystal he could not see what was happening. He did not seem to care as he kept pressing the couple to continue.

Gregor dismounted his horse, and began to make his way through the crowd, taking their hands and lifting many of the villagers up as he came forward. Stopping each time as he did and speaking to them as if they were old friends that had not seen each other for some time. Once through the crowd he made his way to where Dagger stood and knelt before him.

"You have done a great service to this land," Gregor began, laying his sword on the ground at Dagger's feet. "I offer my sword for you to use as you wish."

Dagger seemed startled at first but was quick to recover, hoping no one noticed as he thrust his hand to his crystal. Smiling down at King Gregor he recognized him at once, the two having met several times before.

"We have little need of your sword my King," replied Dagger. "We offer our services and swords to you."

Dagger knelt before the still kneeling Gregor, Sala and Sarn following his lead. Gregor seemed upset at first, but soon saw that he meant no disrespect.

"We mean no disrespect your highness," said Sarn as he reached his knee. "Though your offer is high praise to us we cannot put ourselves above someone of your birth."

Gregor smiled as he rose up from his knee and looked close at the boy who had spoken to him. There was something familiar about him, not that he could place what it was right away. Perhaps, he thought later, there was a chance that he had met his parents before.

"I had heard that there were three travelers here training for battles," Gregor said as he reached his feet. "It is said that they are the ones that took the life of King Jares and his mistress Chelseah. I am not surprised to find that it is the great Dagger himself; and company of course. I am surprised though to find a young girl as part of that group, no matter the rumors. Even as I see this for myself it is hard for me to believe the truth of it," Gregor pointed to Sala.

She smiled and gave a quick curtsy in his direction.

"I have come for two reasons," he continued, thrusting the point of his sword into the ground, "that is other than to see if the rumors were true of course. First I come to pay my respects to those that ended Jares' reign as King and second, I am in need of your services."

Dagger stepped forward and placed his hand on the King's sword, followed by Sarn and then Sala.

"It would seem that our services are yours," Sarn told him smiling.

"I am sure that it will not come cheap, that is if I know you,"

King Gregor added grasping Dagger's shoulder.

"We can discuss the price when we know the full risk," Sala chimed in.

The King laughed loud and low, as Sala finished speaking.

"She has a tongue and a will," he said still laughing. "She will give you trouble one day."

Sala drew back from the group not knowing what to expect from Dagger. She stood behind them expecting one of them to reproach her.

"Perhaps," Dagger replied with a smile. "Until that day she is allowed her tongue."

Dagger was a little impressed that she spoke out, and to have been so accurate. Sarn laughed to himself thinking that Sala was getting through the cold facade that was Silver Dagger.

"You remind me of my own wife," King Gregor returned, still laughing while reaching out to her. "She too is outspoken and gives me much trouble most days, but I do not hold it against her, nor will I hold it against you."

She smiled back as she realized that Gregor had only been joking with her. Taking his outstretched hand she let him lead her away from the makeshift training field.

"Then I would say that we should be off to the tavern so that we may discuss your need over a meal and some ale," Dagger returned as he moved away from the group with Tig at his knees.

"No doubt from my pocket," added Gregor chuckling.

"But of course," Sala laughed as she reached Gregor's side and took his offered elbow.

The company was seated, the meal ordered and ales placed around before anyone spoke again.

"Your reputation for thievery and adventure are still well known in my Kingdom Ryn Mar. I take it that these two hold your trust," Gregor said, pointing to Sarn and Sala half huddled together at the end of the table. "The boy has a familiar look about him as if I know him. While the girl, I know for certain that I have never seen before."

"They have my trust as far as I trust anyone," Dagger returned. "They would not be here otherwise."

"Of what I know of you, that is not much."

"As you should well know Gregor, it is much easier to trust no one than it is to trust everyone."

Gregor chuckled in agreement, knowing exactly what Dagger had meant. The two talked of another time and of battles they had known before.

Their midday meal was placed before them and little else was discussed or thought of until it was consumed.

"Now let us get to your second reason for coming here?" Dagger asked Gregor as another round of ale was set before them.

"I only come to you as I no longer know who I can trust in my company," Gregor began, as he hefted his ale twice before taking a drink. "You must have been headed for Jares' Kingdom, when I was told that my son was taken from Lord Dermit's summer estate. We had gone there to visit for a few weeks and I had just left them to return to my Kingdom. I left half my men behind with them. I thought that with Lord Dermit's men there would be plenty to spell any trouble that would arise. Now it seems that it was his men that took my son for another. A lucky handful of my men were able to get my wife and daughters away without harm. Now Lord Dermit is feared dead and I have been told that for my son to be let go I must give up my throne and leave my Kingdom. If I refuse they will kill him, then hunt me and kill me taking my Kingdom by force."

"Just who is it that has him," Sarn interrupted.

"I am told that it is Lord Crel."

"We cannot help you," Dagger said slamming his mug to the table. "I am sorry that you wasted your time in coming here."

He reached inside of his cloak, stood and walked away from the table.

"I beg you," Gregor pleaded. "I was told that Crel has left Dermit's estate. He heads to Nefrendel to name a new puppet King. Those that hold him at the summer palace now are from the old eighth Kingdom of Valdore."

Dagger came back to the table and sat down across from Gregor. His hands seemed to make celebratory gestures as he surprised himself by sitting on the bench at his first attempt.

"King Foulas," Dagger laughed. "So the fool is still one of Crel's puppets. It will be a pleasure to take your gold to get at Foulas and his so called seer Solari. I owe them a great deal in the way of pain, and if I can get Crel to inflict it, so much the better."

Sarn and Sala sat huddled together in the corner drinking their ales and taking in all that was said. Neither knew anything of those that the two spoke of, but that did not stop them from being interested.

"Foulas was once said to be savior of the Valdore Kingdom. It was believed that he would be the one to reunite the fifty Kingdoms. Some believe that he was the chosen descendant of the king. Solari is supposed to be a seer, he appeared in Foulas' court three years ago; no one knows where he came from and he is not telling."

"I know where he comes from," laughed Dagger, "he is no more a seer than you are."

"Wherever he comes from he is more in charge of the Kingdom than Foulas. Nothing happens there unless he says or allows it to."

"And to release him they want you to step down?" asked Sarn before ordering another round of ale. Although he was not sure why, maybe it was the ale or maybe he just wanted to hear it again.

"I am to step down from my throne and turn it over to Foulas."

"Crel is attempting to gain control of the old Kingdoms," added Dagger.

"Yes and there is nothing he will not do to get what he wants," Gregor began again. "To be able to take the Kingdoms he wants by force, he needs more men and support. With six of the old Kingdoms he will have all the support and men that he needs to begin taking the rest. As each of the others fall his strength will grow. Although Jares was making a plan of his own when he stole the tablet. It is believed that he was attempting to break free from Crel. What he did not know was that Crel had sent Chelseah to keep an eye on him and keep him under control. With Jares dead Crel was to have stayed at Nefrendel and use it to support his growing army. But after the fire that swept through the valley, he will be lucky if anything grows there this year, giving him little help."

"Fire," Sala spoke up, almost as if it was the first time she had known of it.

"Yes, Jares' sentries set the village on fire when they could not find the three of you."

Sala had not thought of the smoke coming from the area of the village for some time. Not that she had forgotten, she just did not wish to remember. There were few days that she did not think of her grandparents or her little brother. She had not given any thought that they might be dead since that first day.

"What of the villagers?" she asked.

"Those that survived the fire and could have, left the valley, and those that could not are starving I am sure."

"Does anyone know who it is that survived the fire and which ones have left the valley?" she asked half pleading.

"I only know that there were some survivors, other than that I have no further knowledge of them."

Sala rose from the table wishing to hear no more, leaving the tavern she did not look back.

"Did I anger her?"

"No," Sarn replied, "she has, or rather had family in the village. They helped hide us, fed us and made sure that we got away to the caverns unnoticed."

"I am sorry," Gregor replied. "I will send someone as soon as I can to ask of the family."

"That would be kind of you," Dagger said knowing that there was little chance that there would be any word. "If just the village burned how are those left alive starving?"

"The village was just the beginning. It smoldered all day when the wind picked up just before dark sweeping remnants of it into the fields and trees. By morning it had spread into the fields and to the castle. The west wall was almost destroyed by the fire. If it had not begun to rain before it reached it, there would have been nothing left of it either. What was not burned before, Crel had it burned after he found out that you had stolen the tablet. He thought that you were still in hiding in the valley as you were not seen leaving it by any of the outposts. The entire valley is nothing but blackened ground now."

Dagger nodded his head as if he knew why they had not been seen leaving the valley but said nothing.

Leaving the tavern Sala walked to the river and sat on a large flat rock on its bank. She thought of nothing but her grandparents and little brother as she watched the women washing clothes at the river's edge. She hoped that they had made it out of the valley yet somewhere deep inside her, she knew that they had not. Some of the children noticed her there alone and rushed to her side.

The children in the village were quite taken by the travelers and would always be nearby as they trained and walked about. It would have been one thing if they had been giving the children treats and trinkets. It was something else that brought them around. In any village or castle there are always boys that will watch and follow along when there is any kind of training. And there were always young women watching the boys, picking which they wished to marry or would let kiss them. When the travelers would train it was not just the boys that followed along. None had ever heard of a woman that trained as Sala did. So whenever they would train it was not just the boys that would follow along. Sure there were the girls that still talked about the boys as they watched, but even the smallest of the girls were also trying to follow along. Tig watched from a distance much like he always did every day. Watching over just one of the travelers was not something that the animal seemed to enjoy. It took away from the attention that the children would give him. The attention that the travelers got in the village did make his job more enjoyable. There was always someone giving him attention and ready to feed or pet him, and to Tig attention was everything.

On the other side of the river two blue cloaked forms walked from the trees and knelt at its edge. Both knelt at the same time and placed a skin into the water, filling it before rising. The two waded across the river and into the crowd of women. Reaching out each of them touched as many as they could without disturbing them any more than they were by walking among them. The women did not seem to mind the interruption. They appeared to welcome the two and thank them for walking through their area of the river. Tig noticed them, watching every step they took as they crossed. It was not until they were standing on dry land did he move towards them.

Sala had seen them and was watching them as well. She was not sure what to do, deciding instead to take her lead from Tig, who at the time, was taking careful steps toward them with his head lowered as he did when around possible trouble. As he got closer he began to take longer strides toward the two strangers. When he reached them he wound his way around the legs of each of them then crouched at their feet. They mumbled something that Sala could not hear before the animal stood on his hind legs. Placing a front leg on either side of one of the figure's head he stuck his face up under the hood of their cloak. A hand reached out to pet his head before he moved onto the other one. Again a hand reached out to the animal scratching him behind his ears. Sala had never seen him act this way and did not take her eyes off of Tig from the second he crouched at their feet.

"Come child," the closest to her called. "Let us get a better look at the young woman that stands with the thieves."

"They are not criminals," the other spoke up. "Why must you

speak of them that way and not of what they are?"

"Oh, be quiet sister," the first said getting upset with the other. "You speak ahead of yourself, must I always correct you."

"I only want to keep you from making any more messes that I will have to clean up."

"They would not be messes if it were not for your meddling."

Sala, though puzzled by them, began laughing as she approached and heard them speak.

"Look at what you have done. She is laughing at us now."

"Forgive me I only laugh at your words, not at you," Sala replied reaching out to accept their outstretched hands. It did not help that their voices were so similar that she could not tell which was speaking without looking at them. It made their argument sound like it was being held by just one person.

"That is all right, my sister is always trying to be my mother."

"So you are the love of the youngest traveler," the other began, ignoring her sister. "Your heart is full of only him, yet you take care of them both and that is a good thing. You are worried about them and your family, are you not Sala?"

"Yes," she returned, shocked that the one knew her name though tried not to let it show. "Who are you that you know of me and I have yet to meet you?"

"Do not worry, we are friends," returned the first.

"And she is supposed to know," the second interrupted. "You are being foolish as always. Should we not tell her who we are before telling her that we know her name and that we are friends?"

"I wish you would quit doing that," the first said rolling her eyes and waving her hand around in the air.

Sala began laughing out loud again. She tried not to, but it was all just too much for her.

"Some call us the sisters, and some the sorceresses, or the witches, but we like the sisters better. Especially since we are sisters," the first said, finally letting go of Sala's hand. "We have come to thank Ryn and the other called Sarn for returning the tablet to its rightful keepers. But it appears that we also have you to thank, and that we did not know until now."

Sala bowed her head in acknowledgement.

"Now that we have introduced ourselves as it were, we want to hear about you and your heart," the second sister said, as they lead Sala and Tig to a tall shade tree so they could sit at its base.

The village children had been waiting and finally rushed to the sisters' side and began to play and dance about them as they walked. Tossing back the hoods of their cloaks the sisters took the children's hands and danced about with them. The older looking of the sisters had long flowing red hair while the younger of the two had shorter brown hair. They no longer seemed to be in any hurry to sit with Sala as they had been just a short time earlier.

She smiled as she watched the sisters dancing with the children. Everything around Sala and the sisters began to slow down. It seemed as if she were becoming one of the children playing at their feet. With each step they took, her mind wandered back to happier times. All the way back to when she was a little girl and she too used to dance in the late day sun of a summer's day. Her eyes fell closed as she lay back against the tree and watched her childhood pass in her mind.

Sala was still lost somewhere in her mind when the sisters dropped the hands of the children. They then placed their hands on her, pulling her memories into them. Kneeling down they hugged the girl and held her to them.

"You have had a hard life that gets no easier," the first sister whispered in Salas ear. "You have chosen a path that brings you in contact with great danger. You should not be worried as we will help you if ever we can."

"Take care of your charges," the second whispered. "They are important to us, keep them well."

The sisters kissed Sala on each cheek, rose, and walked away pulling their hoods back over their heads as they left. Wading back across the river and into the woods the sisters disappeared. Sala was left lying against the tree with her eyes closed and a smile on her face.

"Which was your Kingdom in Valdore's time?" asked Dagger tilting his head as he did the first night that Sarn met him.

"Mine was the tenth and five of Valdore," began Gregor. "As you may or may not know, according to lore and legend it is one of the key castles of Valdore's rein."

"Yes," Dagger added, "I know the history of Valdore. Yours was known as the center of Valdore, but not the most important to the Kingdom."

"That would be the lost castle and no one alive has any idea of where or which one that might be," Gregor added.

"The witches and the ancients know," Dagger began. "That

you can count on, they know of these things they know of all things."

"The witches?" Gregor asked.

"The sisters," he returned, "and there are those that believe that they were around before the Kingdom of Valdore. You know of course the first King was Tarin Valdore, son of a human and a fairy folk. The lost castle is where he is said to have ruled over the Kingdom. Just how he came to sit there is a matter of legend, truth or tale. I have not made up my mind one way or the other. They, from what I understand and have been told, are the only ones alive that would know of the lost castle."

Dagger stopped as if he had more to say about them, but stood and sniffed at the air instead.

"I had not thought about them." Gregor began before noticing that Dagger had stood.

Sarn, who had been sitting listening as intently as he could to the two speak, jumped up and grabbed at his sword.

"Dagger what is in the air that you smell, good or ill?" Gregor asked.

"Supper I believe," Dagger answered tilting his head laughing. "Innkeeper what is that you have cooking?"

"It is what you say," the Innkeeper said coming out from the back of the tavern. "I am roasting two deer over the pit, and that smell is a sauce that I was taught by another traveler. I felt that in honor of your visitor I would prepare a special meal, with your permission of course."

"Only if it tastes as good as it smells when it is finished roasting."

"Better," replied the innkeeper before disappearing into the back once again.

"We will discuss our fee later, after we have gorged ourselves on some of that fine smelling venison," Dagger told him. "I have to decide if it can even be done without the loss of your son and your Kingdom first.

"I am sure that if it can be done you are the only one that can do it," Gregor added. "That is why I have come to find you my friend."

Dagger staggered a bit as he walked away from the table, making his way across the room in his usual manner, bumping into everything between him and where he wanted to go. By now no one noticed or no longer paid any attention to him as he walked away. It was the same no matter if he had been drinking or just walking along sober. As long as he was without Tig by his side there was always something for him to stumble into whenever he was inside. Sarn watched his friend as he tried to sit down, or rather fall into a sitting position. After laughing with King Gregor he began trying to stand back up. After more than a few tries he finally made it to his feet and staggered out the door of the tavern.

Sala had no idea how long she had been sitting against the tree when she finally realized that she was sitting down. She shook her head trying to figure out just what had happened and how she ended up by the tree. Standing, she saw Tig out of the corner of her eye and it was the only time she wished that the animal could talk. Almost immediately he bounded over to her and begged for attention by rubbing his head against her hands. The large cat knew the sisters well. They had brought him from his native land when his mother and his siblings had been killed for having a farmer's sheep for a meal. Tig had been wounded when they found him, just having escaped being killed himself. The two took him away and nursed him back to health. Bringing him to Dagger's village they gave him to his grandparents to help protect the child from his parents. Tig became the child's only friend in no time. Dagger's parents had been banished just after his birth. The two grew up together learning to fend for themselves. He even learned how to fight alongside the striped animal. When Dagger ran off from his grandparents to keep hidden from his parents, Tig was right there with him. Now Tig was there to help Sala back to reality. The two walked along the water towards the tavern, the memory of the sister's visit disappearing with each step. By the time they reached the tavern it was as if the sisters had never been there. Her smile and those of the children were the only remaining signs that the two sisters had ever been in the small village.

Sarn watched as the two went up the outside steps to the second floor of the tavern. He wondered, though not for the first time, what his mother and father would think of the raven haired girl. One part of him wanted to take her back home and let them meet her. Yet there was still the feeling that he was supposed to continue his travels and adventures.

Sarn joined the girl upstairs who had felt tired and lay on the bed in their room. Tig left as soon as Sarn entered the room leaving the two alone he went to find Dagger.

"Are you feeling well?"

"I think so," she returned forcing a smile. "I just feel a little strange. Perhaps it was the ale so early in the day, and the heat of the outdoors."

The two lay together, drifting in and out of sleep.

Dagger wandered out to the creek where the women of the village were finishing their washing for the day. Each piled their still wet clothes together and carrying them on top of their heads as they walked away. The late afternoon sun was still warming the rocks at the edge of the creek. Dagger found the large rock where Sala had been sitting earlier, and sat down. With his hand still gripping the crystal in his cloak he watched as the last of the women walked away from the creek. Letting go of the crystal he began to feel a presence that he had felt a few times before. The warmth of the presence wrapped itself about him like an old comfortable blanket. Laying back on the rock he did something he had never allowed himself to do since the day he left home, he turned his face to the sun. Then closing his sightless eyes, he took in the loving warmth of it. Laying there he felt protected from his true self, protected from those that sought him out and protected from his secret.

Gregor was still dressing after spending some time in the cool waters of the river when Dagger called him. He waved the King over to the rock so that they could complete their plans.

"Once we have your son we will come straight to the castle," Dagger told him. "It will be up to you to see to it that we have enough to fight off any group that may have taken over your Kingdom in your absence."

"Do you think that the two are strong enough to take over while I am away?"

"I think that it may have already happened."

"Perhaps you are correct," Gregor added knowing that he was right. "I will send out word to those that can be trusted."

"It is already being spread," Dagger returned.

Gregor gave Dagger a puzzled look and was about to ask how he knew of such things, but before he could ask Dagger left him alone by the river.

It was a few hours later when the lovers woke from their dazed sleep. Sala lay on her lover's chest; looking up into his eyes she made a silent vow of her love to him. Sarn wiped the sleep from his eyes and looked down into her face as she stared into his.

"Why do you watch me so?" he asked her.

"I wish to remember this day for the rest of my life."

"I hope that you do not have to look into your memory to remember this day. Waking with you in my bed is something I wish to do until age takes my life."

Kissing him, she scrambled off the bed and began to dress. He grabbed at her in vain trying to pull her back into the bed before she got too many clothes about her. It was little use as she was too fast for him, so instead he joined her.

A short time later the group was sitting around the table where they had been for their midday meal. Dagger had his ever-present cloak hood pulled back just a little from his face, but yet still covering it. Sarn thought that he could almost make out his entire face, something that he was never able to do before. The hint of a smile was on all their faces but none more so than on Sala's. A round of mulled wine was placed before them as well as their first course. While the King had not shown himself, the three carried on without him. Tig in the meantime was comfortable where he was, curled up next to the cook. It was an easy life as he fed the animal strips of meat from the turning deer.

"There is one thing bothering me about this," Dagger said when Gregor finally joined the little group. "If you know where your son is being held and you know who it is that has him, why is it that you seek out my services to go after him?"

Sarn caught the puzzled look on the King's face as he took in Dagger's question.

The King sat back from his meal looked around the room and took a deep breath.

"I would hope that I would be better use to my Kingdom if I were still alive. I was told that if I sent my guards to return him, I would lose the guards as well as my son. The only way they will give him back to me is to step down from my throne. I thought that I told you that before."

"I guess I am having a hard time understanding it all."

"Do you think that he is not telling us the truth?" Sala asked, speaking up.

"A wench with the tongue," Gregor said as if he were scolding her. "She speaks. I do not like wenches that talk out of turn."

He seemed just the opposite man from the one that had sat with them earlier in the day. Sarn was getting ready to stand when Dagger put his hand on him to stop him. Surprising as it was to him, it was Dagger that stood to defend the girl. With a long odd shaped dagger he pushed the King back from the table. It was not one of his never ending silver daggers; this was of regular steel and one that the King no doubt had seen before.

"I do think that you will apologize to the lady for your last statement."

The King was too intent on looking at the knife to respond, his were eyes wide with recognition.

"I see that you recognize this knife." Dagger placed one hand over the King's eyes holding his head still. "You are correct in noticing this knife. It was given to me with some apprehension by the last man that owned it, and then of course I had to kill him with it."

"Dracor was not one to give anything to anyone."

"I did not say that he was all that giving of it," Dagger chuckled as he talked. "It was a bit more complicated than one of him giving it up free."

By now the group had the attention of everyone in the tavern. The Innkeeper was of course worried about his guests, and asked that they take the issue out into the night air. Of course Dagger was happy to do just that, as he pushed the King further back from the table. The two went out with Sarn, Sala and half the tavern close behind them. The rest, though interested in what may happen next seemed more concerned with Tig. The animal had left his spot of comfort and was now standing in the middle of the room pacing back and forth. It was just as well as Dagger had enough trouble going through the door as it was. He did not need any more people watching him.

They were followed out of the tavern by the crowd. Many grabbed at torches as they left, but the moon was near full and the front of the tavern was lit up almost as if it were daytime without them.

"Now tell me Zendar," Dagger said finally using the true name of the impostor. "What have you done with King Gregor?"

"I would refuse to tell you Ryn Mar even if your animal had its mouth about my neck."

"In that case I see no reason keep you alive." Dagger pushed the knife into his chest, drawing its first blood. "I shall give you one more opportunity to tell me what you have done with the King."

"I would see you rot in the ground first."

"As you wish," Dagger said, whistling twice before Tig came running from the tavern. Turning to the animal he spoke to him, "search for his friends, I am sure that you remember them."

Tig sniffed at Zendar, growled and then disappeared into the night. Sarn and Sala stood pulling their swords if only to have them at the ready, not that they yet knew if they needed them.

"I give you one last chance Zendar," Dagger said. "Tell me what have you done with King Gregor?"

"Kill me, and you will never know."

"I watched the King's men leave a few hours ago." The Innkeeper said walking up to Dagger. "It was not long after I saw another group ride in. I did not see if the King had been with them."

Sarn looked down at Zendar and for the first time saw him as the man he was and not the one he was pretending to be.

"It is no wonder I could not find him," Zendar began, "I thought that I had beaten him here at first. It was only luck that I found his cloak still hanging on the post in the tavern. Unfortunately it would seem it was your luck and not mine."

"So it will be," Dagger laughed.

Dagger thrust the knife deep into his chest, leaving his life blood pouring out of him and onto the ground. In just a few seconds the man that was Zendar lay dead in the dirt that was the village street. Dagger wiped the knife on the dead man's cloak before slipping it back into its hiding place.

The crowd made their way back inside to finish their respective meals. Some of them were talking amongst themselves. None of them seemed concerned that they had just watched someone being killed.

"I am Willie," the man slurred as he staggered back into the tavern. "I can beat any man here."

Taking two more steps further the man fell to the floor face first before he could return to his table. Those that had turned as he spoke did nothing but shake their heads before turning back to what they were doing beforehand. Those still making their way back in stepped over or just went around him as he lay on the floor.

To Sarn the air in the tavern felt somewhat different than it had before the killing of Zendar. Losing his seat in his mind Dagger fell to the floor twice before he was able to return to his meal. Each time he fell to the floor, he would stand, shrug his shoulders, shake his head and try again. Dagger saw the bench in his mind as always, well almost always. He would sometimes miss his seat or run into things to try and make his companions laugh. It was like his many attempts to tell jokes around their campfire though none of them were funny to anyone but him.

Sarn could not help but wonder why Dagger was not worried about his killing of Zendar and his lack of concern over the missing Gregor. As always though Sarn took his lead from his friend and tried hard not to show any concern either. Sala in the meantime was looking over their shoulders. She knew from being in Calid's tavern what happened when someone was killed in or out of it. She knew that it was only a matter of time before someone would show up and begin their questions. She asked Dagger about his lack of concern.

"There is nothing out there for them to find," Dagger replied. A smile crossed his face as he spoke, but it was almost impossible to see under the hood of his cloak.

Sarn and Sala both tilted their heads to the side, just like Tig would do when he did not understand what was going on. Dagger laughed to himself, as if he had seen the display and not just felt it.

"Do either of you not know that Zendar was a demon and that the ending of his physical life was the end of his physical being."

Again the two tilted their heads, this time trying hard not to laugh aloud. Demons were in tales told to young children to keep them from misbehaving.

"When a demon is killed the body they occupied returns to what or where it came from," Dagger began to explain to them. "If it comes from another human it returns where it was taken. If it came from the ashes of a dead human then it once again returns to ashes. The only difference is that the ashes catch the wind and are carried away."

While Dagger told them the theory of demon deaths the truth was unfolding outside. A shadowy figure swept back and forth across the body of Zendar. A low groan came from the shadow of a nearby tree, while laughter began rising from the ground. A moment later a short figure passed the front of the tavern, picking up the body as it passed. Tossing Zendar over his shoulder the figure and his burden vanished in a ball of flames. This all happened unseen by everyone, except for the two blue cloaked figures standing on the other side of the river.

About the same time that the body of Zendar was being taken away Tig came across the three men that traveled with him. They sat on their horses watching unnoticed as King Gregor and his guards crossed a stream. Tig sniffed at the air before turning away from the King. He worked his way behind the three men while keeping an eye on the King at the same time. Just as one of the three began his move Tig was on him tearing at his neck. The screams of the other two brought the attention of King Gregor and his guards. Two arrows came at them in answer, catching one in the heart and the other on his right side.

"How could you have missed him?" taunted one of the guards.

"Me! That was your arrow."

"Do not argue just make sure they are dead," the King chided them.

As one of them turned toward the trio on the small hill they watched as Tig tossed them by the neck one by one over and down the hill.

"I would say that the thief's animal has done that for us."

"Then make sure there are no others."

Two of the King's guards rode up the hill and watched as Tig tore again at each of the throats of his victims. They were hesitant to be near the animal and drew their bows pointing them at Tig. Tig looked up as if in a daze. His face was covered in the blood of the men, shaking his head he turned and bounded away from them.

"No, do not harm him, he was not sent for us," the King called out to his guards. "Had he been, we would be the ones on the ground missing our throats."

King Gregor smiled as his guards lowered their bows and returned to his side.

"I sure hope there are no others following us."

"If there were, Dagger's animal has already killed them," King Gregor said laughing as the two guards shivered at the thought of having the striped animal pounce on them.

"I would not wish to die that way," one of the guards said as they turned away from the creek.

Dagger's fellow traveler's tilted their heads to one side again, not quite understanding what he had just said. This time the two could hold back no longer and began laughing aloud. Dagger joined in their laughter causing many in the room to turn to look at the group.

"Tell me who this Dracor was?" Sarn asked of his friend.

"He was a demon and he is dead," Dagger began, "that is all that you need to know."

"So there is no reason for us to believe that any of his other friends or associates will be looking for you," Sala added.

"No," Dagger said after a long pause, as if he were disgusted by the conversation.

"So what do we do now?" Sarn asked Dagger.

"We do what needs to be done."

"You mean his son is in danger?" Sala asked.

"Danger," Dagger laughed, "danger is only a matter of the mind, and yes he is."

"I take it then that there is a fair amount of gold in this affair?" Sarn added.

"Not everything in life is about gold my friend," Dagger pointed out to them. "Some things are like this deer that gave its life for us to eat this wonderful meal. It lives its life for but a few purposes; one to eat the grass in the meadows and the forest floor so that it will grow big and strong. Its second purpose is to have offspring of its own so that there will be more of them. Finally it is meant be the meal of another. So you see, it grew by eating the grass and helped the forest. From what the innkeeper has told me it was of good size, so it is safe to say that it sired many offspring. Now it has become the meal of another being. This adventure my friend, much like the life of this deer, is about destiny."

"Ours or yours?" Sarn asked before downing his wine.

No further words were spoken between them for the rest of the meal. For that matter few words were spoken to each other for the rest of the evening. They ordered their ales and wine between stories coming from some of the other travelers and an occasional one from Dagger. Later Sala prepared a bath for her charges. Knowing that they would be leaving in the morning she knew it would be awhile before any of them would feel hot water again.

In the morning Sarn saw to the horses, and Sala took care of their needed provisions. It was up to Dagger who went around picking up and paying for the other items they would need. With swords, daggers and clothes in hand he returned to the tavern. When all was in order the travelers set out on their next adventure leaving the village behind them.

It would be about an hour before sunset before the travelers would stop and camp by a small stream that cut through a meadow. They decided it best to be safe and not attract anyone by lighting a fire that night. It was something that they had not worried about on their last adventure until after they had taken the tablet. That evening they ate a small cold meal in a moonlit campsite, while Tig, ever vigilant watched over them. The next morning Dagger and Tig led the group to a well-traveled road that pointed north and told Sarn that it was his turn to lead the way. Tig had begun following the trio from a distance crossing from side to side to help make sure that they were not being followed.

Over the next week the group avoided staying in any of the villages they came upon. Instead they camped along the road with any number of tradesmen and families they would find along the way. Some days they would even travel with a trade caravan or a few of the families that had grouped together. Dagger reasoned that they may as well hide in a group than to try to hide alone, being easier to spot by themselves. Not that he ever said who it was that might be looking for them, but neither Sala nor Sarn ventured any further with the discussion. After all, there always was the slight chance that Galdar might still have someone wanting to find them. The one thing that was beginning to bother the couple was the change in Dagger's mood. With each passing day it grew darker. When this happened, Tig would hide off in some field or group of trees. There had been many times that he had been like this before and the animal was quite used to it. One might have argued that it made his job of watching over them that much easier. That is until there would be children around and then the animal would act nervous. He would pace all night wanting to be in the camp for the attention they would give him.

After a week of going out of their way to avoid others, they camped at the edge of a dense strip of forest. There were many travelers camped there that were happy to share their food and stories with them. Many were families with small children, some moving to another village for a new start. Others were just headed into the next village to visit family or seek items they could not make on their farms. That next evening after having spent the day with a trade caravan they set up their camp at a crossroads. There was no village around, not even a farm or home could be seen. An area of lush grass surrounded the crossroads as far as the eye could see in two directions. Behind them were the farms and villages, and ahead of them was the edge of a dark and forbidding looking forest. The strip of grass seemed to act as a buffer between them.

"I never like it when we come this way," one of the tradesmen told the travelers as they sat eating an evening meal. "This place troubles me and yet I cannot say why."

Dagger chuckled as if he knew the reasons why. It was also the only sign of a light mood they had seen from him in weeks.

"Do any of these roads led to King Gregor's Kingdom?" Sarn asked of the tradesman.

"I cannot say for sure, I have only ever traveled in that direction and back," he said pointing to the left road.

"What of the forest road?" Sala asked almost in a whisper.

"I know of no one that ever goes or that has ever come from that direction."

Dagger grumbled, stood and stumbled away from the group and began whistling for Tig.

The following morning after a quick meal of leftovers, the travelers left the caravan and headed up the road and into the forest. With Dagger edging them ahead from the rear, his mood getting ever darker, they pushed on into the heavy forest. It did not seem as forbidding as it had the evening before. The sun poked its way through the forest canopy here and there, but still Sarn was starting to feel uneasy as they passed into it.

To Sarn the day seemed to take forever to pass or maybe it was just the fact that he could not follow the path of the sun as they went. He remarked on it but neither Dagger nor Sala agreed with him. At least he thought that Dagger did not agree. It was hard for him to make out any real words that he had used in return to the question. It was just past midday, or seemed to be anyway, when the group came to an opening in the forest canopy. On the other side of a large meadow sat a tavern, almost hidden from view at the edge of the trees. White smoke spiraled its way up from its chimney making the place look warm and inviting, yet cold and forbidding at the same time. There near the front of the tavern two roads met at another crossroad, each looked well-traveled and each empty but for the four of them. The tavern was not much to look at. It was a bit run down, two stories tall with a thick thatched roof that seemed a bit out of place so deep in the forest. There were a couple of out buildings on the side with a fenced in area in the back that stretched out and away from the tavern. An old man and a young boy were unloading split wood from a cart and stacking it against the outside wall of the tavern. As the travelers stopped the boy left the wood pile and ran to take their horses as they dismounted. Dagger leaned in and said something to the boy who took hold of the reins of all the horses and led them behind the tavern. Pel, however, made a stand and pulled away from the boy and looked back. Sarn nodded and the horse followed behind the others without having to be led. After speaking to the boy Dagger went inside and ordered a meal and a pitcher of ale for each of them. When they questioned his reasoning for the stopping, Dagger just told them that they needed to eat. With his darkening mood and short quick answers to questions over the last few days Sarn figured that ale was just what he needed. After all it just might help to lighten him up a little. It was quiet inside. They were the only ones there except for the three women that worked its board and scullery. The travelers spent the afternoon eating and drinking ale, while Tig lay asleep at their feet.

Dagger made arrangements for the group to stay over at the country tavern. After a lengthy conversation with the woman he paid her the price of their rooms for three nights. When his reason was questioned again he ignored them, leaving it unanswered and continued to drink.

"It looks as if we get to have a bed and a bath," Sarn told Sala, "for better or worse anyway."

"It is almost as if he is afraid to go on," Sala whispered in return. "We have not been traveling as fast as I had thought we would be."

"Of that I cannot say for sure, but I think that there may be something else that is keeping us here."

"With his mood I think it would not be wise to question his reasons, at least for now."

As Dagger ordered more ale his mood seemed to get even darker. The hood of his ever present cloak was pulled down over his face so that his companions could not even make out his mouth. It was not long before the effect of the ale was noticeable in Dagger. Tig raised his head for a second as Dagger rose and bounced his way to the outhouse. To Sarn Tig did not seem as protective as he had in the past. It was as if the animal was disconnected from its master. Any normal time Tig would jump when Dagger would so much as shift his weight. His indifference began to bother Sarn and it seemed almost as if the two had never known each other. The two lovers discussed the possible reasons why Dagger decided to stop and drink in the middle of the day. Neither of them knew any good reason, guessing would be all they could do. All the while Tig continued to nap under the table paying little if any attention to the passing of those around him. Sarn decided it might be best if he were to watch how much ale he was drinking, Sala did the same as well. They did not have to count for long as an hour later Dagger left them alone. Telling them to enjoy themselves he staggered and bumped his way up the flight of stairs and to his room.

Upstairs kneeling on the floor next to the bed Dagger bent his head. Looking at the floor, he began to talk aloud.

"I come again to this unholy land. Keep me still in the hands of those that would protect me and keep me from those that would find me if it were not for you."

Dagger stayed kneeling for an hour before reaching for his bed. Lying on top of it, still clothed, the boy fell asleep. As the sun began to set Tig appeared outside under his master's window; he paced back and forth for a bit before disappearing down the road.

After being shown to their room Sala and Sarn sat once again in the tavern sipping on wine and eating the evening meal. They kept to themselves as long as they could, with the youngest of the three women in the tavern serving them. It was not difficult for her to keep up with them as they were still the only ones in the place.

It was some time just before dark when a group of three weary travelers entered the small country tavern.

"I must say," the tallest of the travelers said when he saw the couple huddled together in a corner of the room, "I am glad to see that you have one woman out here in this god forsaken place."

Sarn wrapped his hand around his short sword as the tavern owner spoke up.

"That woman does not belong to me."

"Ah, then she is fair game," the tallest replied, as he walked closer to the two lovers.

Reaching out the tallest of the travelers took ahold of Sala by her hair. Just as the man was about to pull her from her seat he felt the piercing of Sarn's short sword under his chin and another piercing his chest. Letting go he began laughing when he saw where the second sword had come from. While Sarn had his short sword placed under his chin, Sala had hers all but planted in his chest.

"What do we have here?" the assailant grumbled. "All I am after is a kiss from this beauty."

Sarn stepped back while Sala continued to press her sword to his chest.

"It looks to me that the price of that kiss is going to be high," another of the three said.

"High indeed," the tallest replied. "But, not that high I think."

"It shall be the highest and last price you ever pay for anything," Sala added as she pushed harder into his chest.

Sarn showed concern but stood back to keep an eye on the

others. He still held his sword, but his empty hand was reaching for his broad sword. Tig seemed to come from nowhere as he appeared behind the other two men.

"You do not have the courage to finish," the tall man told her.

"I have the courage to," Sala returned stepping into the man. "The question should be, do you want to pay the price."

The tall man looked to his friends as they began to laugh. The tavern owner came around the boards with a large club in her hand.

"You three have worn out your welcome," she said holding the club over her head. "Leave now or never leave."

The owner watched as Sarn pulled his broad sword and pointed it at the other two strangers. At first the two laughed and pointed at him.

"Just what do you think you are going to do with that boy?" asked the taller of the two.

The other was quiet as he looked at Sarn, stepping back from his companion and right into Tig's path.

"I do not intend to leave this place without getting my kiss," the tallest responded.

Sarn gave a quick glance toward the man and noticed blood beginning to appear on the outside of his shirt.

"Innkeeper," Sarn quizzed, "just how long does it take for the local magistrate to arrive here?"

"If they refuse to leave any longer you may do with them what you will. I just ask that you take the bodies outside so that they can be burned."

"I have traveled from the Kingdom of Nefrendel," the tallest began expecting to get a rise from the two travelers. "I have been in search of the King's killers. While I have not found them yet, I do have the need of a woman, and now I have found the one that will meet my needs. Lord Crel is my master. That should be all you and anyone here need to know. My bidding will be done by anyone that I choose."

Grabbing her by the back of her head he leaned into Sala and puckered his lips.

With his eyes ever widening, he died by her sword as it pierced his heart. Sarn took two steps forward and planted his broad sword into the neck of the closest intruder as he cleared his sword from its sheath. The third one was trying to back out of the tavern as Tig took his ankle in his mouth and bit down, holding the man still as he yelled out in pain. Sarn laughed to himself as the man struggled with his sword. Tig just shook his large head, tearing at the man's flesh, his screams increasing as he tried to beg for his life, Sarn called to the animal and he let go. Almost falling to the floor from the pain he was now able to pull his sword and he swung back at the animal. Sarn did not wait to see the outcome of the swing as he spun around with his sword, catching the former guard on the neck removing his head.

With the innkeeper's help the two travelers pulled the bodies outside to a large pit. Then they proceeded to toss branches and anything else they could find in the near darkness over them. When they were finished, the cook came out of the tavern with a bucket of hot coals and tossed them onto the pile. It took several minutes, but the pile caught fire, burning hot and quick. The four went back into the tavern where the innkeeper's daughter was scrubbing the floor where the three had just been killed. The woman invited the travelers to sit back down while she brought them some wine. Accepting her offer they sat back down in their corner. While the two had been drinking for many hours, killing the men had a sobering effect on them, making the wine taste fresh and new. Tig found himself back under the table and seemed even less concerned about his master. The couple sat, keeping an eye on the fire in the pit outside through the open door. They were not alone for long. Soon two wagons pulled up out front and a family of four asked if they might camp for the night next to the burning fire pit. They explained that they had lost their way earlier in the day and thought that they would be home by night fall. The other wagon was filled with travelers going to a festival and they too wished to camp there in front of the inn. The innkeeper allowed them the privilege and offered them free hot food. She had no intention of allowing them to cook over the pit fire until she could get the remains of the strangers out of it. They accepted the food and accepted her return request of keeping the fire blazing. She explained that it was lit as a beacon when there was no moon, for travelers like themselves to find their way through the forest. By the way she talked Sarn got the idea that this was not the first time that the pit had been used for the same purpose it had just been used for.

It was near midnight before the couple staggered off to their room with Tig close at hand. As they passed Dagger's door Tig paused, sniffing at the air twice before he seemed satisfied. Then he followed the couple to their room where he made himself a spot on the end of the bed at the foot of the lovers.

About an hour later Dagger woke suddenly. Sitting upright in his bed he began turning his head back and forth and tilting it side to side. He grabbed at the places he kept his weapons to see if any had fallen out onto the bed as he slept. Sitting on the edge of the bed, he reached inside his cloak and grabbed at the crystal in his pocket. Searching the room he noticed that Tig was not there. He wandered out into the hall and down to his companion's room. Putting his ear to the door, he heard the couple breathing and then heard Tig jump off the bed and come toward the door. As he pressed against the door Tig sniffed at the air. Turning away the animal went back to the bed and laid down where he had been before the interruption. The animal lifted his head for a brief second as Dagger looked in. He took a quick look toward his master before turning his head away from him. Dagger backed out as the animal pushed his head between his paws as if he were disgusted with his old friend.

Making his way down the stairs and out the front door Dagger searched over the family and the festival goers. Searching but not finding what he was looking for, the happier thief took off down the road. Less than a mile away he turned off the road and started up a much neglected path. Being careful of low hanging branches and tree roots breaking the ground, he let go of the crystal and let his memory take him up the path. A half hour later Dagger stood in front of a cabin with its roof sagging and near collapse and its door having fallen off its hinges.

Dagger pulled his broad sword and slammed it point first into the ground. He knelt before the sword placing his left hand on it, while reaching into his shirt with his right. Out of a pocket on the inside of his shirt he pulled out a pendant made of hand hammered gold with a tiny green stone in the middle. Where there once had been readable words hammered in the gold the words were now worn and illegible. He ran his fingers over it before placing the pendant around his neck, then lowered his hand to the ground.

He began to speak low and in a language that only he seemed to know. He spoke the words he had learned as a child over and over from memory, lowering his head as he spoke them and then raising it before starting over again.

The stone on the pendant began to glow, and the ground began to shake. The green light from the pendant grew brighter and larger, before long the light engulfed Dagger and then the cabin. Soon the light moved to cover just the cabin. Dagger was still speaking the words as the roof lifted back into place and the door returned to its hinges. When it was done he continued to speak the words, the ground shaking harder, the light turning from green to white. Just as it began it stopped; rising he tucked the pendant into his shirt. Leaving his broad sword stuck into the ground in front of the cabin he flipped the hood of the cloak off his head. Looking over each shoulder, he walked to the door without his usual awkwardness and bumbling. He knocked twice at the center of the door and then twice more at the upper right hand corner. Taking a step back, he turned left and disappeared into thousands of tiny green points of light.

Sala woke a short time before daylight. Getting out of bed she ran her fingers over Tig's back causing him to lift his head and then follow his charge. In the twilight she walked down the steps of the tavern and out among the lost family and the festival goers' camp. She looked into each face as if she was expecting to find someone, or maybe she was just hoping and wishing. When she was done, she took off running up the road in the direction they had come the day before. Tig watched her run, tilted and then shook his head as he took off after her, following at a distance.

Running naked, her bare feet pounded at the dirt and stones of the road. Her breathing getting shorter more labored as she went, her feet bruising on the rocks but she seemed not to notice. When she was some distance away from the tavern she began to yell. Tig closed in on his charge trying hard not to knock her down but it was getting more difficult to hold back. Catching up to her he began slowing her down by running around her. Finally she stopped and fell to the ground. She screamed as she landed on her knees. Whether she screamed out of the pain from the rocks as they pushed into her knees or out of frustration, one could not tell and she would not remember.

Tig pushed at his charge to get her off the road, crying Sala crawled into the woods. He stood over the top of the girl alert to the sounds of the surrounding woods. Deep from within the forest a layer of fog rolled toward the pair. Somewhere in the middle, moving as if they were floating along with it, the two figures used the fog to hide their movements. The hoods of their cloaks were pulled tight about their heads as if they were trying to hide from the fog while using it at the same time. When they reached the pair, Tig stepped away from the girl and sniffed at their hands.

Tossing back her hood the oldest of the two looked down at the crying girl, while the other knelt beside her. The older red haired woman held her hands over the girl, her palms facing down. She began to move them in opposite circles against each other.

"I need to find the other," her sister told her.

"Wait until I take care of Sala," replied the red head.

"We need to find the other," her sister argued.

"Then you should help me take care of her first. It will be quicker if I go too."

Her sister agreed, though she was a bit reluctant, and took over from her. A white light came from the hooded sister's hands, bathing Sala in the warm light.

The red haired sister backed away from the two pulling her hood back over her head. She held her hands out to her side and began speaking in a low voice. She repeated the words over and over again as she had been taught.

As she spoke she was enveloped in white light and a second later she disappeared into thousands of points of light.

"I hate it when she does that," the remaining sister said aloud.

Reaching out she took Sala's hand and lifted her from her curled up position. She took the girl into her arms, picking her up as she continued crying. The fog closed in around them as she began to carry her back down the road. Tig seemed beside himself as he circled the two then ran down the road over and over again. After several times she told Tig to go to Sarn and watch over him.

"I will see that this member of your charge returns without further harm."

Tig bounded away stopping once to look over his shoulder, just long enough for the brown haired sister to nod her head and motion for him to keep going.

Hidden within the fog she carried Sala back through the woods towards the tavern. When the two were just out of site of the tavern, the sister set the girl down again. Placing a hand on either side of Sala's face, a low blue light began to come from them lighting up her face.

Sala's crying slowly stopped. Looking up for the first time she recognized the voice and the sister's face, but was not sure from where.

"My dear Sala, your mind is lost and your heart is tearing apart," the sister began. "Your thoughts are with your grandparents and your brother. Your heart is tearing apart because you want to search for them, but you cannot make yourself leave him. He too is in your thoughts and heart."

Sala's eyes were empty and cold as she looked up at the sister.

"To search for them is noble, but I can tell you now that there is no need. Finding them will not heal your heart. Staying here is what you are meant to do. You will fight alongside your love and Dagger and you will honor yourself and your family name by doing so." The sister let go of Sala's face, and sat down in front of her. "Your Destiny is here, running from it will not change it."

As the sister stood back up the fog began to dissipate. They were just a short way from the tavern as the sister took three steps back before turning away from Sala. She looked toward the tavern for a second before disappearing with the fog.

Outside of the little cabin, daylight had begun chasing away the night. Inside Dagger sat huddled next to the small fire he had lit in the fireplace. Not so much for the warmth of it as the security he found in the flames. He was not sure why he was summoned there, he only knew who summoned him. It was not the first time he had been there and he doubted it would be the last. He knew only that as much as he hated to come here there was no way that he could ignore their summoning of him.

"It is good to see you again," the voice called from across the room. "You have been away from me for too long this time."

"I stay away for good reason and you know it."

"Your father is not here, there is nothing to fear from him."

"If it were just him," Dagger began, "perhaps I would have come back before now and more often."

"And you hide from us every day. It is as if you do not trust us or want us around."

"Yet you continue to look for me," Dagger said almost spitting out the words. "You would think that by now you would trust that I would come when summoned, as I did this time."

"Yes, I did," Brunella, his mother began. "Your father and I miss you."

"You miss fighting with each other you mean."

"Your father and I only want what is best for you, and for you to accept your destiny and join your brothers and sisters. Your family needs you. Our time is near, and we cannot join the fight without you."

"I have renounced my destiny and family as well. I did so the day I left home to hide as I do," Dagger said as he began to move away from the fireplace.

"Renounced? You can no more renounce your destiny than you can renounce who it is that you are."

Dagger took another step from the fireplace. As much as he knew his mother was right he also knew that he could change his destiny. Each day he lived he was proof of that. As long as he had been away from his family, he had lived the other side of what he had always been told was his destiny.

"So, you summon me and think that I will run back here and take my place. All because you wish to join in a fight that even with me you cannot win?"

"We have no intention of winning, at least not until we find the one true adventurer."

"I think you are a little too old to still believe in the folktales and myths."

"You have been away too long my son. You seem to have forgotten where you come from and just who your ancestors are," Brunella said, beginning to laugh as she spoke. "You are those folktales and myths."

"So I have been told since my birth," Dagger began. "I am only who I am, nothing more, no matter where I came from."

Dagger stood tall before his mother. A band of fabric wrapped around his head, covering his forehead and ears while keeping his reddish brown shoulder length hair in place. Reaching out his mother removed the band and tossed it to the floor.

"Now that is more like the child I remember giving birth to."

Dagger reached up to cover the odd shaped ears. His mother pushed aside his hands and caressed the tiny almost unnoticeable points that poked up out of the top of his ear.

"I remember you used to love having your ears rubbed when you were a baby."

"When were you ever around when I was a baby?"

"That does not matter," Brunella responded quick and flippant. "You are who you are, you are half elf and half witch. There is little in the world of mortals that is worthy of your attention or your time."

"Perhaps, but it is where I wish to be and will continue to be."

A figure began to appear behind him, and then one on either side of him.

"Well, who do we have here? This cannot be our missing sibling," the figure behind him said and the others repeated as they too appeared.

Dagger lowered his head further and let out a long sigh knowing that he had messed up by not keeping his back against the stone fireplace.

They stepped closer as a group and reached for him. At the same time Dagger dropped to one knee. Reaching into his cloak he grabbed at his crystal with one hand and pulled out a small leather pouch with the other. As he stood back up he opened the pouch and began to toss its contents about as he spun around. As the powder made contact with the air it began to swirl about him, hiding him in a green cloud.

Hidden from the others he began to mumble the same words he had earlier. Letting go of his crystal, he pulled his short sword from its hiding place. Waving it over his head Dagger took one step forward, turned to the right and disappeared.

"I told you not to come so soon," his mother yelled as the green points of light vanished with her son.

"But they were the ones that said you were ready."

"What do you mean ready? She hadn't put him under yet."

"I almost had him but you three were too impatient. He must have had help from his father."

"Father, why do you think father would want to help him?"

He could hear them arguing with each other as he left them. He laughed knowing that he would be gone long before they were done. After flipping his hood back over his head, he pulled his broad sword from the ground where he had left it. Wrapping his hand back around the crystal in his pocket he began laughing, and took off on a run away from the cabin. He fled through the woods as another swirl of lights appeared in the cabin.

"Well what do we have here?" Brunella asked. "To what do I owe a visit from one of the sisters?"

As Sala lay beside the road in front of the tavern she kept trying to make sense of what had happened to her. She did not and could not remember leaving the tavern let alone her lover's side. Her mind was soon to forget the visit from the sister and what she had said and done for her. Sitting up on a fallen tree and with her eyes burning from tears that had just begun to stop, she felt lighter, almost happy. It was a bit like she had felt after her nap next to the river. She could not remember what day it had been now, or how long it had been since, but she did remember her nap and the happiness she felt afterward. Wiping her eyes for the fifth time in as many minutes she stood up and felt the pain from the bruises on her feet. Looking down she shook her head and wondered just what it was that made her leave a warm bed and go naked and bare foot into the woods. Testing each step as she went, she made her way across the road toward the tavern.

Up in their room Sarn woke disoriented with Tig pushing on his chest. It took him several seconds to realize that he was not in his room in his father's house. Sitting on the edge of the bed and shaking the dreams out of his head, he started to come awake. He was not surprised that Sala was not there. She would often wake before him and leave his side. Tig paced around the room as Sarn dressed. He was not quite sure what he should do about Sala at the moment, but he knew that waking him had been important. Once Sarn was dressed he went down the stairs and out into the morning. The fire pit lay smoldered and the overnight guests seemed to be still asleep. In the twilight it took him sometime to notice Sala limping out of the woods. Running to her side he lifted her into his arms and carried her back to their room. Once Sarn had her in bed and covered he went back downstairs and found the cook. Tig remained in the room, continuing to pace near the bed after Sarn left. He again took on his role of watcher and protector. Finding the tavern owner's daughter in the scullery, Sarn managed to get her to heat up enough water so that Sala could bathe.

Dagger made his way down the path and stood at the edge of the road, waiting as two carts and several horses passed him. Keeping his head lowered as they passed no one on the horses or carts paid any attention to him. It was a trick that he learned early in his life; if he did not look at them as they passed by they would pay little or no attention to him. After the group disappeared around a corner Dagger walked across the road. Thrusting his hand back into his cloak, he grabbed at his crystal and pushed his way into the forest. It took him almost an hour to reach the old path he was looking for. Turning up it he began to walk quicker, almost as if someone was following him. Sunlight filtered through the trees making Dagger move faster, almost running down the path. Tripping over a tree root and falling to the ground he began cursing as he brushed himself off and stood up. Soon he was running as he worked his way along the path, ducking as he went under the few low hanging branches. He laughed a little as one of them knocked the hood of his cloak back and off his head. The next low branch left him on his back, face up looking at the sky, cursing as he went down. He was unconscious as soon as he hit the ground.

When Sala finished her bath and a morning meal, she and Sarn settled back on the bed. After she drifted off to sleep, Sarn left her to go to Dagger's room. Tig jumped up and kept walking in front of him slowing him down before finally not letting him go any further.

"I get it Tig," Sarn said petting the animal, "you want to keep me from your master. Why, is your own reason I guess, but if there is something wrong, then perhaps we should look in on him."

Tig leaned into Sarn pushing him back away from his master's room. Taking the hint he turned and went down into the tavern. Finding the owner cleaning behind the planks he offered his help but she declined it. It even sounded to him as if she growled at him. Going out into the yard he found that the campers had left and he had not even heard them leave. The old man was in the fire pit going through the remaining hot coals and ashes. Again he offered his help, and again it was declined. He stood watching as the old man came across a piece of bone from one of the men that had been put in the pit the night before. The old man tossed the bone into a pile on a blanket that had others in it, and then went back to his search. When he was satisfied that he had found them all, he took up the blanket and carried it to the edge of the woods. Picking up a shovel Sarn followed him and helped him dig a hole just inside the edge of the trees. Once it was deep enough the old man shook out the blanket and buried what was left of the intruders.

"These men traveled a long way just to die here," he said once the bones were under the ground.

"I should have not killed them I suppose," Sarn returned.

"If you had not killed them, there is no doubt that they would have killed you and your girl. It would have taken them a few minutes, but they would have recognized the two of you from your killing of their King."

"That is impossible," Sarn replied. "We did not kill the King. We killed his mistress, she is the one that slit his throat."

"Whatever you think," the old man said smiling.

"It is the truth."

"You will find that no one wants to believe the truth when the lie is more believable."

"And you think that the lie is more believable?"

"In this case," the old man paused just long enough to toss the blanket over his shoulder. "The lie may not be more believable, but it makes a better truth than the truth ever would if the truth were ever known to be true."

Sarn shook his head not even pretending to understand what he had just said.

"Does it bother you?" he asked.

"Does what bother me?"

"That people want to believe that you and your hooded friend killed King Jares."

"I cannot say for sure, I have yet to give it thought."

"It does not bother you that being your age you have already killed more people than some kill their whole lives?"

"If you were my conscious I would know what to say."

"But since I am just an old man outside some tavern you know nothing?"

"I am beginning to think that you may know more than you are letting on."

"Perhaps I do, but of that I cannot tell you. I can tell you that I think you are too young to be here, let alone doing any killing."

"Then perhaps I should get my traveling companions and be on our way."

"There is just the two of you and that animal here now. I doubt you can leave without your blind friend, and by now he is nowhere near."

Sarn stood staring at the old man not quite sure what to say in return.

"I can tell you that this is not the first time your friend has been here. Although it has been a while since he has brought anyone with him. Then again I suspect that he will return in two or three days as he usually does."

"How many times has he been here?"

"At least once a year, sometimes twice a year and I have been here all my life."

"You have been here all your life? When did he start coming here and how can you be sure it is the same person?"

"The animal is how I remember him, and if I remember it right, he first came here just before the mister passed and that was about ten years or so now. I was born in a small cabin about a mile from here. I would come every day and do little things like cleaning, carrying wood, or whatever else I could do or they wanted me to do. I was 'bout six years old then, and now I am near on 'bout … . Well let us just say I have been here a long time."

"You never wanted to go anywhere or do anything else?"

"I could never think of anywhere I wanted to go but here; besides I have seen almost everything there is to see right here at this tavern."

Sarn could not see how there was any chance to see that much in this remote area. Shaking his head he began to walk away but was stopped short by the old man as he spoke again.

"You think that it is a bad thing that I have never wanted to go anywhere?"

"No," Sarn said turning back to him.

"Perhaps one day you will wish you had never left home."

"Perhaps," Sarn added agreeing with him. It was more to keep him from continuing the conversation, than to agree with him.

"Yes, I believe that one day you will regret leaving that home of yours next to that lake."

Sarn took a hard look at him, trying to figure out how he could know anything about his home.

"Well, there is one thing for certain young man," he said as he finished hiding the hole. "You and your friends no longer have to worry about these three."

"As true as that is, I am finding it hard to feel regret for having killed them. I know that it was them or us and I am not ready to let them kill me."

The old man shrugged his shoulders and began to walk back toward the fire pit.

"Oh, where is that boy?" he half yelled sounding disgusted. "I guess I never should have sent him out to do his job without me to look over him."

"Would you like me to look for him?"

"He will be along soon enough. It would not strike him that he could go anywhere from here."

Sarn almost wanted to toss him into the pit for his statement about the boy. It was only a matter of minutes before a barefoot boy appeared heading toward them on the road leading a horse and cart filled with dead tree limbs. He walked away as the old man saw the boy and began yelling at him, thinking it best to leave them alone. The verbal assault on the barefoot boy continued as Sarn went back to check in on his charge.

Inside of the tavern the two women that had been working the night before were sitting in the corner next to the fire place. They were in a heated debate over what they were going to do with a couple of intruders. When they saw Sarn coming they stopped, leaving him to believe that they were the intruders that they were talking about. He went up to his room to find Sala getting dressed as Tig paced about.

"How are your feet?"

"My feet?" Sala asked a bit confused. "They are sore for some reason, but since we will be riding I will be fine."

"Good, but Dagger is not in his room nor can I find him anywhere," he replied not realizing what she had just said. "So it looks as if we have to either wait for him or go back."

"No, we cannot go back and we cannot go forward without Dagger," she said as she began to get more than a little confused. "He is the only among us that knows where we are going, and what we are getting into."

"That may be true but I am not so sure that we are welcome here after last night."

"Last night, what happened last night?"

"You mean to tell me that you do not remember us having to kill three people last night?"

"No, did we?"

"How about being in the woods this morning?"

"I was in the woods?"

Sarn's concern was deepening. Reaching out he took her hand and sat on the edge of the bed with her.

"Tell me the last that you remember yesterday?"

"I remember going out to the creek, sitting on a rock and watching the village women washing clothes."

Sarn was having a hard time thinking of anything to say to her that she would believe without too much trouble.

"Look around my love; this is not the same room. Look outside, we are no longer in that village, we are in the middle of nowhere."

Sala limped to the window and looked out. She began shaking her head and turned around with a confused look on her face, her eyes wide as she tried to make sense of what was happening. Still shaking her head she went to Sarn and wrapped her arms around him, trying not to cry.

"I do not understand," she whispered in his ear.

"I am not sure I do either."

"Tell me," she began. "Please tell me what I cannot remember."

Sitting her back down Sarn told her what she, for some reason, could not remember. Neither had any idea of the reason that she no longer knew of the past week. When he finished she found it all hard to believe, but the one thing she knew for sure was that they were no longer in the village.

In the pantry the women from the night before were huddled together.

"We should just ask them," the tavern owner said to the two other women.

"We know less of them than we know of him. If the cousin was still here maybe we could, but he is gone again."

"They killed those three last night with no hesitation or remorse," Mara the owner's daughter said.

"I get the feeling that they are the ones those three were looking for. How do we know that they had not already fought before last night," Janua, the tavern owner, added.

"That just may be," said Marna, Janua's sister, "but you must remember where we are."

"I can never forget that we live in the middle of nowhere," Janua returned.

"No," Marna shot back, "you know what I meant."

"The edge," Mara said throwing her hands in the air. "The edge, the edge, I am tired of hearing that we live on the edge. The edge of what, is something that we never talk about...."

Janua reached over and put her hand on her daughter's mouth to keep her from continuing.

"Do not continue," Marna admonished. "You can never speak of that when there are guests here."

"You can never speak of it," Janua said removing her hand. "You can never tell who is about. We are here for a reason and do not forget that."

"How can I forget," Mara added a bit frustrated. "You tell us every day. I am young. I want to go out into the world. I want to see the places that I hear about."

"You know what will happen if you leave here."

"I know only what you tell me will happen if I leave here."

"What is your plan to get rid of that man and the boy?" Mara asked changing the subject.

"They only come when Dagger does, and then they leave

when they know he has gone."

"That may be sister," Marna returned, "but your cousin has gone and that man is still here."

Coming to as the sun reached its midday pinnacle Dagger found a tree with branches that lay just inches off the ground. Climbing under them he sought protection from the heat of the day and the prying eyes that were watching his every move.

"Why can you not just leave me alone!" he yelled as he reached the deep shade under the tree.

"Because I am your father," the voice returned.

"Father," he laughed, "that is the last thing in this world I would call you."

"Why not come back out into the sun where I may be able to look at you?"

"You have looked at me more than enough for one day. Now you can tell me why you have insisted that I come here?"

"You have come on your own as you always do."

"Never without your help and you know it," Dagger yelled back, but began to calm down some. "Tell me why I am here so that I can get back to my companions and we can continue our quest."

"More acts of thievery no doubt."

"That is funny coming from you."

"There are many other things that we could talk of if you came to visit more often."

"You sound as if you were my mother."

"Being your father means nothing to you?"

"Please, all the two of you ever do is fight over me. This is the only place in the world that I can come to that neither of you can touch me nor force me into your service."

"And that would be a bad thing?"

"No good would come of it that I can assure you. So tell me what it is that makes you summon me."

"Your time as thief and adventurer has come to an end."

"Have you been asleep for the past few years or so?"

"You know I can never sleep. It is time for us to join the battle."

"The battle," Dagger returned growing even angrier at his father. "Not the battle again; I am tired of you and mother telling me how important I am to the battle. This is the battle that you tell me has waged for hundreds, perhaps thousands of years without me. Now I am told that I am so important that it cannot carry on another day without me. If it were another time I would have more to say to about this. But I have other things that I must be doing than arguing with you."

"You must feel them call you."

"By them you mean my mother and my siblings? Yes I had a quick visit with them earlier. And now it is you that seems to want to keep me from my latest quest."

"That would be the rescue of the son of Gregor."

"How is it that you know of this?"

"My dear Ryn, you know that I can always find you."

"It was the healing potion that I used on the girl. You followed the trail of the residuals to the village. Then you listened into what we were told, and since you knew that I had to come this way you set this all up."

"You have learned well. It is just too bad that you no longer need that knowledge, besides you know just half of it."

Dagger pushed the hood of his cloak back for the second time that day. He scratched hard at his head with both hands as if he were trying to rid himself of some memory.

"I should have known that you are the one who sent Zendar to act as King Gregor." Dagger shook his head in disgust.

"Come from under those branches," he added paying no attention to him. "It has been a long time; please allow me to gaze upon you."

"You should have joined mother in the cabin earlier if you wished to gaze upon me."

"You know that it is not that easy."

"I am glad of that," Dagger laughed. "Then again I thought you were supposed to be an all-powerful being."

He was trying to figure out a way to slip out from under the tree and get away from his father. The only problem was that the only way he could get away from him at that point would be to use the magic that his father followed in the first place. There were only two places for him to go in the area to hide, and the tavern was not an option. The other, home, or where he called home anyway. If his father caught him before he got there his whole world would end and his father would win, and that too was not an option. He needed to wait for just the right time when his father would be less likely to follow him.

"I take it then that you still have not completed your given quest from the ancients."

"I do as I wish," he chuckled. "The ancients do not control me or tell me where to go. I am here to fill my pouch with gold and my mind with stories for my old age. If the ancients wish me to do anything for them, I will decide to accept it or not as I do everything. If it does not fill my pouch with gold, I doubt that I will accept it."

He knew that the best way to avoid his father's questions was to keep him asking the same ones and then not tell him everything.

"I see that you are still avoiding me," his father said sounding more than a little upset with him. "Just what is it going to take for you to tell me what I want to hear?"

"All you have to do is tell me what it is that you want me to say."

His answers did nothing but anger his father and that is exactly what he wanted to do. The ground shook under Dagger and the tree branches began to move. He felt the ground rise under him as he sat, roots from the tree pulled from under him. Rising as the tree did, Dagger pulled his hood back over his face. Reaching in his cloak and pulling out the pouch from earlier he tossed more of the contents in the air around him. As the contents hit the air the green cloud hid him further from his father. Then just as hours earlier, he disappeared. He could not return to the tavern; that was clear. There was only one place for him to go now and that was not as good an option as it had been when he left the old cabin earlier. It was only a slim chance that his father could not follow or find him there, but he felt it was his only way out and he had taken it.

"I just wanted to see you. Why do you always deny me?" his father screamed tossing the uprooted tree aside, knowing how hard it would be for him to follow his child in this land of his birth. There were too many other forces at work in the forest.

His voice carried across the top of the trees and hills of the forest just to the edge and no further.

Dagger laughed aloud and pushed his voice so that his father could hear him. He knew that it would only serve to make him more obsessed in finding him again, but it was a risk that he was going to have to take. There was one place that Dagger could be sure of not being found, and that is exactly where he reappeared.

The canopy of the trees kept the small clearing cool and shaded from the daily sun. A small cooking fire was smoldering to one side of the clearing as the points of green light filtered down from the canopy. They swirled around the clearing before coming to rest on a flat rock close to the fire.

"I have been expecting you Ryn," a voice called from the other side of the fire.

Dagger appeared sitting on the rock, looking tired and ready for sleep.

"Sleep my child. We will protect you as we always do. You are safe now with us."

Laying down he curled up with his back against another rock and drifted off to sleep.

Sarn looked up to the sun for what seemed the tenth time since the midday meal. Sitting out in front of the tavern he took in the warmth of the sun. With Pel and the other horses taken care of he had little else to do but take care of Sala and drink ale under the sun.

"Is the ale good?" asked Janua.

"It is fine, I have tasted none like it," Sarn lied but he wanted to keep on the good side of the woman.

"You lied, but that is fine. Tonight I will treat you to an ale that I keep in the cellar in the room where we put ice in the winter."

"You bring in ice to keep in a room?"

"Yes, it is something that my husband always wanted to try to keep our stores of food longer into the spring."

"I would like to see this room." Sarn spoke before he thought about it, almost wishing he could back out of it as soon as he said it.

"Perhaps when you are sure of just how safe you are here."

Sarn laughed, knowing that she felt his reservations.

"My name is Sarn, just in case you wanted to know."

It was her turn to laugh as she realized that they had not known each other's names. It took her a minute to return the introduction as she then found herself trying to think of where she heard his name before.

"I am called Janua and my sister is Marna and my daughter who you talked to this morning is Mara." She stopped for a second not sure if she should talk of the old man. "That old man you see around here is my husband's brother and his apprentice. They like to come by every now and then to see if we have walked away from the place. He just shows up and does things around here as if it is his. I think he likes to think that it is his and was not his brothers. He involves himself in things that, well that he has no reason to," Janua caught herself and stopped from saying more.

"Perhaps I should go and check on Sala," Sarn said, noticing her sudden hesitation.

"That would be your girl, yes?"

Sarn nodded as he stood and headed to their room.

"Perhaps you should bring her down to sit in the sun."

Sala was sitting on the floor petting Tig when he came in the room. He talked her into coming out into the sun, not that it was a hard sell but she did need his help. Her bruised feet where not capable of holding her own weight as well as she would have liked. At least it was a good enough excuse to get him to carry her. Well, she liked it when carried her in his arms anyway; she felt safe there. Tig went out ahead of them running across the grass to the edge of the forest and back several times. It was a behavior that neither of them had seen before. They reasoned that he was always watchful of Dagger and would not allow himself the pleasure if Dagger were there.

"The animal is always playful when his master is not around," Janua called from behind the planks.

"You mean Dagger has been here before?" Sala questioned.

"Dagger?" she asked. "Oh, you mean Ryn. Yes, Ryn has been here many times. He usually comes in the spring or winter, once in a while he will come in the summer like now. When he comes he always leaves his animal for us to look after. He is usually gone for just a few days. Then other times he will come for a month or so and never leaves him with us."

"Then how come you never... last night when...," Sarn said trying to put all his thoughts into one word.

"We are never certain if it is safe for us to know him," she chuckled. "So we rarely speak on his first night just in case someone comes to him as those three did for you last night."

"That would explain why you were so calm last night."

"It has happened before, yes," she giggled.

Marna came from behind the tavern carrying a small basket filled with pastries. She offered them to each of them before setting the basket on a table nearby.

Sarn kept looking up at the sky wondering how long this day was getting to be. It seemed to him that the day was turning out to last forever.

"Is it me or is it this place? The sun has been hanging just past that tree since I came out here with my first ale."

Janua and Marna both looked up and then to each other, but

neither said a word. Sala, having been upstairs was unable to attest to anything that had happened outside. He decided that he would wait and check again, and made a mental note of the position of the sun. Marna announced that she needed an ale. Janua said that some cold ale would be a perfect addition to their day. Marna laughed waving her hands in the air as she went to the cellar. She returned a few minutes later with ale for each of them from the tavern's special storage.

The five of them enjoyed the cool feeling of the ale as they sat in what was beginning to seem like an everlasting day. Tig rolled in the grass stretching out under the sun and playing with an unseen playmate. Sometime later Sarn looked up again noticing that the sun had moved, but just one point from its spot.

"I know you ladies must know the reason behind my mystery."

"You have a mystery?" Janua asked. "You should know that some mysteries do not have a reason. They just are. But if you tell us what your mystery is there might be a solution to yours."

Sarn told them what he had been noticing with the sun's movements, or rather the lack thereof. The two women glanced at each other for a second before Janua spoke up.

"We can only tell of the tales," she began.

"Then tell of this tale. Perhaps it is just what we need to help pass the afternoon."

"One that is told is about an elf and a witch that had a child together," Janua began again in a hushed tone. "Unlike their other children this child, the youngest, was said to have been born with or would inherit every power of both the witches and the elves. It is believed that the child is to have a hand in reuniting the kingdoms of the world. Whether they are to lead that fight or just participate in it is unclear. The child's parents believe that the child was to lead and that their family is meant to rule afterwards. Each parent believed they fought for the right side and yet each sought to take over the world and rule it as their own. After several attempts to take over, the ancients put an end to it. The mother and father were held and charged for their actions. After being found guilty they were banished from this world, the mother to the moon and the father to the sun. Their older children, who had each taken a part in their parent's attempts, were banished to the stars. The youngest child being too young at the time, had no part in it and was taken by the ancients and given to its grandparents. Whether it was the father's parents or the mothers has never been told, and makes little difference as I see it. Several years went by and the child grew and learned how to use the powers it had been born with. As the child grew stronger it became harder for the grandparents to protect it from the parents. Soon it was obvious that the parents would do anything to control the child or kill it to keep the other from having it. So now the grandparents hide the child to keep it safe."

Janua stopped long enough to take a drink of her ale and decide just how much more she should tell them. She did not want to give away more than needed. Besides she knew that there were parts of the tale that the two of them would not believe anyway.

"When the sun and moon are in the sky at the same time," she began again, "the child is said to be close by or that it has been found. It is the most dangerous time for the child because that is when the parents are the strongest. They are weakest when one of them blocks the other or when there is no moon at night. Still they search every day, the father during the day and the mother at night. If the child uses any of its powers or magic given by birthright it can be found them. That is when the child is at its weakest to hide from them. They can summon the child, but only the child can decide to meet with them. Of course the child is vulnerable if they meet with either of them. Now if the child meets with one of them the other parent can stay in sky to look for the child as long as they want or until the child is in a safe place. From what I understand there are few places the child can go where it will always be safe, one of those is with its grandparents. It does not matter which ones but it is said that one side wants nothing to do with the child."

"So you are trying to tell me that the father is searching for his child right now?" Sarn asked, more than a little skeptical. "Of all the tales I have heard and read this has to be the strangest of all by far."

"I did not tell this tale for entertainment. You asked why it seemed that the sun was not moving and I told of what I know," Janua said trying not to get upset with him. "This has happened here before. I believe that somewhere in this forest live those that know if the tale is truth or lie. I also think that the child comes to this forest when summoned. If that is so then this must be where the child was born, or where one of the grandparents lives. I know it is hard to believe, but many strange things happen in this forest. I can tell you that much is true because I have seen my fair share of them. I can also tell you that I believe this is a place that the gods have both forsaken and blessed. Which way you find it would depend, I suppose, on what you believe."

Dagger woke disoriented from his sleep to the sounds of clanging metal. Under the clanging he heard voices speaking the language of the ancients, helping him to remember where he was.

"How long have I slept?" Dagger asked of any that would answer.

"Four, maybe five hours, it is hard to say," said a familiar voice from behind the fire. "He knows that you are still in the forest and continues to search it. Hoping that he can track your magic, but it will do him no good I have hidden it from just past the tree. He is lost in his own madness. Nothing will stop him as long as you are in the forest. I will send you back to your companions; that will force him to move on again."

"No, I no longer wish this game. I want to end this hiding and running from them."

"Then they will win and nothing will be as it was or should be."

"You speak of them as if you are not part of them."

"I never have been a part of them, nor any that are here; we all hide from them just as you do. This safe spot only exists because of those here. If you do not think that we are on the same path, then perhaps you should go and be with the rest of your family. Perhaps there is room for you with your mother."

Dagger sat up, ran his fingers through his hair and pushed his hood back off his head.

"Just as I remember you," the voice said. "Now child, let us eat and you can share with me stories of your adventures. Perhaps some wine and a bath would be welcome as well."

Dagger nodded and crawled over to the small cooking fire. A stone to one side of the fire had been carved to make a chair. He sat down facing the fire, his feet tucked up under himself, hunching down he accepted a small bowl that was handed to him.

The figures of those around him started to become clear. Just the same he never seemed to be able to get used to being around his cousins. Perhaps it was because he never spent that much time with them. Then again he was never able to tell if they even liked him; he got the feeling that they resented him for who he was.

"Grandfather," Dagger began, "will I ever be able to walk the world as I am, and let the warm sun light my face?"

141

"Patience," his grandfather began, "you need just to follow your heart."

"It is my heart that troubles me."

"Torn again between your parents?"

"I do not believe so. Yet sometimes I wonder if I am doing the right thing; if I am even following the right path."

"There are many paths to take in one's lifetime; some we walk down and some that we do not. Sometimes it is the right one and others it is not. Who is to say which one is the correct one to take when we take it? Some think that it matters little which path one takes when young. They believe that it is where one ends that matters in life, and that is the only thing that has been written before we are born. No matter the path we take we end up at the same place that destiny has given us." His grandfather leaned forward and took his hand as he finished.

"As always you are not being much help" Dagger sighed.

"Will," said another voice from behind his grandfather, "you must not try to talk in riddles and circles. You know you are no good at it. Do not mind him Ryn; your grandfather has never been much help when it comes to advice. Sometimes I think that you know more about life than your grandfather and I will ever know. You have been away for so long, your visits are never long enough for us to learn of everything you have done and have learned of the world."

"Yes, but Bel, you need not remind me how long Ryn has been in hiding. If it were not for our help it would have lasted less than a week."

Bel reached out and placed a hand on either side of Ryn's head. As she touched him a red glow began to come from her hands. Looking up into her eyes for the first time in almost two years he saw the gray hues that sparkled in her eyes. Dagger began to cry, tears running down his face.

"Please grandmother," he pleaded. "It is too painful for me to sit here and see you all like this, then leave and never see again until I am once again in your hands."

"I took your sight to help keep you safe. You were given Tig to watch over you. I would have a hard time with you here knowing that you cannot look into my eyes and see me as I am."

"I am sorry grandmother, it is just that it is so hard for me to see and then not see again. We have had this argument so many times before."

"I know my child but you deserve to see us"

"Why did they send Dracor after me?" he asked trying to change the subject.

"So, you are the one that killed him," his grandfather added.

"I did."

"Just how were you able to kill him without using your magic?"

"How do you know I did not use magic?"

"I know the same way that your parents know when you use your magic."

"I killed him with a dagger."

"This dagger, what did it look like?"

"It looked like this," Dagger said. Pulling the knife he had used to kill Zendar from its hiding place he tossed it toward his grandfather.

The knife fell short of where he had intended, falling instead just out of his grandfather's reach.

"Could you not have gotten it a bit closer?" Will said as he reached out to grab it, almost falling off his seat.

"I might have if I could not see you," Dagger smiled. Something he rarely did, but it was his grandmother that came to his rescue.

"Father," Bel began, "you know as well as I do that Ryn was not serious."

Will grumbled as he sat back in his seat and looked over the dagger. He spent most of his time looking at the blade with Dagger staring at him trying to memorize his grandfather's face. It was something that he never seemed to been able to do no matter how many times he tried.

"Are you sure that you got this from Dracor?"

"Where else could I have gotten it?" Dagger asked getting a little upset that he did not believe him. "He pulled it out as we fought. I knocked if from his hand more than once before I could reach it. There was one more struggle for it before I was able to finally get it away from him. I grew frustrated that I could not get him with my sword so I threw the knife at him. He turned to run, but the knife followed him and it struck him in the heart. A second later he burst into flames and was gone. When it was all over the only thing that was left was the knife."

Will grumbled again, sure that his grandson was forgetting to tell him something. Just as he was sure that Dracor did not run for his life. If there had been anything about Dracor that could be said in the open, it was that he feared nothing. Nothing that is except maybe the knife that had killed him and that was the one the old man was now holding.

"I need three new daggers," Dagger said, almost whispering, trying to avoid any further questioning from his grandfather.

"You have not lost any, why is it that you need them?" his grandfather asked as he weighed the dagger he had been given.

"Just have them made Will. You know why they are needed. Why torture the child over it?"

"Whatever you say Mother; tell me, how do you want them made?"

"Special," he said, saying no more about them.

His grandfather nodded knowing just what it was that his grandchild wanted, and what it was that he needed to do. Dagger sat back and closed his eyes wanting to forget everything that had happened to him.

The sun finally moved from its peak, but not far before stopping again. After several minutes Dagger took his grandfather's outstretched hands and the two walked to the edge of the small village.

"Are you ready?" he asked his grandfather.

They looked briefly at each other before raising their hands to the sky and began turning around in circles in opposite directions.

Soon they began to speak in a soft slow almost melodic voice. It was something they had done many times since he had first taught it to his grandchild. They repeated it several times turning themselves in their circle and then they were done. Neither of them looked at each other as they turned and went back to where they had been sitting and waited for their meal to be ready.

No sooner had they sat down when the sun, that had just minutes before been close to its highest point of the day, began to set. Somewhere in the forest, if there had been anyone other than the animals that lived there, they would have heard the scream of the father.

The tavern began to get its daily customers just as the sun moved across the sky. While it was nothing for those in the area to watch Sarn found it all very interesting as the sun moved from a point that it had been at for several hours to setting in just a matter minutes. Shaking his head he took Sala's hand and as the couple continued to watch the sun. He wondered if any of what Janua had said were true or if maybe he had just fallen asleep and didn't know it. Of course had she told him the full truth, he still would not have believed it.

"So you see now for yourself," Marna called out to him, "just how fast the day can actually go by here."

Sarn shook his head again chuckling a bit, not quite sure what to say back to her. Going back inside Marna told him that it would be getting cooler fast and that perhaps he should at least bring Sala inside.

"Besides," she added over her shoulder, "I am making something special for you both for tonight's meal."

"Mara is more than willing to help you two if you should need it," Janua said quickly as she walked past the front door.

Sarn told her that he was sure that he could care for Sala. Sala however was determined not to be taken care of by Sarn. After all it was her job to take care of him; that was the way she had been raised. It was his job to provide and hers to take care of his needs. Tig seemed more than worn out from his day of running and rolling around in the field but was still reluctant to go inside. Instead he lay in the grass a short distance from the tavern and enjoyed the coming of night, his favorite time.

As the sun was about set Sarn picked up the girl and carried her inside. They took a table in the back of the tavern where the couple could sit nearly unseen and Tig could still be close to the fire where he liked nothing more than curling up next to it.

Later that night a fire was made in the middle of the clearing. It was not long before many of Dagger's cousins came out from the cover of the forest. Each greeted his grandparents as they passed them and began to dance to a drum beat around the flickering fire. Dagger recognized some of them as they went around the circle but none of them acknowledged his presence. As more of his cousins joined in some of the dancers seemed to rise off the ground as they went around the fire. Each step they took taking them higher into the air. As more entered the dance, the circle grew larger and went higher still. Soon the drums around the edge of the circle were joined by others from somewhere deep within the forest. Each addition kept the beat growing as yet even more drums were added from yet other parts of the forest.

The sound carried across the tops of the trees and into a large meadow far off in the distance, a figure stirred under a layer of grass.

"Why can he not do one thing for himself," the figure said aloud, though no one was there to hear him, yet knew that Dagger would. "I will return when I return. If you had not made it so difficult to find the tablet I would have been there by now. You cannot wait for me I know where you are headed and you can count on my help as always."

Dagger snapped his head back, looked straight up into the sky and screamed. Flames from the fire leapt higher, as more wood was added, sparks began to filter up above the trees and took to the wind.

"At what point do you take sides?" his grandfather asked.

Dagger ignored his question. Instead he sat and stared at him, his eyes trying to memorize each line in his face, each hair on his head. Someday, he thought, there would come a time when he would no longer be able to look upon his face. When that day came he hoped that there might be a chance that he would finally be able to see him in his mind. That was just one of the many things taking his eyesight did to him to help hide and protect him from his parents.

As the darkness of the night deepened the drums and dancers continued on in a never ending beat. As one row of dancers rose into the air another would take their place on the ground; soon the flames and the dancers were high above the trees. In groups of two the dancers would take each other's hands and together the two would come back to the ground only to rejoin the line again.

After watching them Dagger stood and made his way to join his cousins around the fire. In a short time he was laughing with them and smiling at each one as he passed them. They in turn reached out to touch him as he passed. It was as if they were touching him like he was their long lost friend. The truth of it though was as hard to believe as following it.

Pel reared up in the small stable behind the tavern. It was a matter of seconds that Tig was out at the stable looking at what it was that was disturbing his friend. Points of light began to swirl about the stable and the horses. Tig slipped under the gate and hid in the darkest corner of the stable, crouched and ready to pounce on whatever appeared. Seconds later the points of light began to settle behind the horses as figures began to appear. Tig watched and waited, sniffing at the air. One by one two figures appeared and stood behind Pel and the others. Tig crept closer and just as the two began to pull knives from their belts Tig jumped them from behind knocking each to the ground. Mara came running in from the dark swinging a sword from one of Dagger's packs he had left behind.

Tig tore into the first figure ripping out its throat, his head shaking as he pulled back. No screams escaped from his victims, his paws clawing, and tearing the throat of the second as his mouth ripped at the first. Mara stood over them with Dagger's sword raised above her head with the blade pointing down. As the animal finished she drove the blade through first one figure and then the other. Tig pulled back away from the lifeless bodies that were now under him.

Mara let go of the sword and ran screaming into the tavern. She told her mother what had happened out in the stable. The problem was that she was so excited that she had to retell what happened several times before Janua understood what her daughter was saying. Overhearing them, Sarn ran to his room and retrieved his broad sword and jumped out of his window. Rolling as he landed he was at the gate of the stable within seconds of hearing Mara, and in just a few seconds more was in with Pel and the others. It did not take him long to find Dagger's sword pushed into the ground. What he did not find were bodies. The only thing that he could see that Mara was telling the truth was the blood that had been left behind. Tig came from the darkness with his victims' blood still visible on his paws, and dripping from his face and whiskers. Sarn shook his head and pointed toward the stream that ran several yards behind the tavern. Tig lowered his head as he passed him, and then ran off dunking his head several times under the water until the blood was gone. Tig was in no hurry to go back to the tavern even though the fire was inviting. He found himself wanting to play in the water, running up and down the stream until he could find a deep enough spot to lie in with just his head breaking the surface. Lying in the water he let it run over his body several minutes before shaking himself off and running back to the tavern to dry next to the fire. Both Sala and Sarn laughed at him as he slipped through the back door as if he owned the place. Sarn had replaced Dagger's sword before returning to Sala and their table. He tossed a piece of fabric that had been on the end of Dagger's sword onto the fire. A white flame engulfed the fabric and in an instant it was gone.

"What do you think happened," Sala asked, after Sarn and Mara finished telling what had happened in the stable.

"The only thing I can think of, there was no time for," Sarn joked.

"What is that?" Mara asked.

"Tig ate them, but there was not enough time and no bones."

"Then he could not have," Sala added playing along.

"You have never been in this forest before, have you?" Mara asked shaking her head.

"No, this is the first that we have been here."

"It is true that Tig had no time to eat them. Although there was enough time for them to come and take the bodies," Mara began. Getting her mother's attention she ordered some wine for the three of them. "The two were of magic, no doubt of evil magic. They may have even been demons. You know of course when demons are killed their bodies are carried off. Normally though there is nothing left behind. Those pieces of their clothes, they must have been in a hurry to have left any trace of them behind; it is good that you burned them. I took the hay that was covered in their blood to the pit so that it can be burned later tonight."

When she finished she stood and left the couple alone and returned to her job. Sala and Sarn only looked at each other not wanting to comment on what she had just said. Thinking that while they found it hard to believe, she believed in what she was saying.

"Why does everyone around us spin stories of magic and fairies and then look upon us as if we know nothing when we do not react as they think we should?" Sala asked.

Sarn chuckled a little not quite knowing what she wanted to hear. Instead he leaned into her and kissed her cheek.

"Why is it that you wanted to come with me?" Sarn asked. It was something he had never thought to ask her. More because he was not sure he wanted to know than he was afraid to know.

"Love," she answered him laying her head on his shoulder. "Besides, someone needed to come along to look after you."

Sarn laughed at her and pulled her close to him.

"You two should retire to your room if you wish privacy," Marna called from her spot in front of the fire.

The couple smiled back, raised their mugs and drank to the woman, but stayed where they were. They were enjoying the other guests at the tavern as they told stories of their travels and of the things they had seen. Every now and again one of them would even break into song. About midnight a tall man made his way into the tavern. He was carrying a walking stick that was as tall as he was and his cloak was the color of an autumn leaf.

"Blessed be all that enter this door," he proclaimed as he closed the door behind him.

"May your feet be light as you travel your journeys," Janua

called back from behind the planks.

"Thank you mistress and I will have a tankard of your best ale if it pleases you."

"It has been a long time since you have graced us with your presence, Gramfor of Van Mourn. What great adventure has brought your feet once again to my humble inn?" Janua asked, taking the big man into her arms and hugging him close.

"I missed your special ale and Marna's cooking," he told her letting go and accepting Marna's hug.

"Oh, look Mother, my Prince has come to take me away at last," Mara added laughing from behind the new arrival.

"Now there is an offer I am almost tempted to take you up on."

"That would be the day," she said kissing him on the cheek as she took his cloak from his shoulders. "I am sure that the Princess would have more than just a little to say about that. What is her name again?"

"I think that she mourns me not," he laughed as he moved back near the couple and sat by the fire. "I think it would be wise of me to not tell you her name.

All eyes had been on him and everyone hung on his words as he spoke. Soon though, they were back talking amongst themselves ignoring him and not sharing any more stories. It was as if they had no longer any stories left to tell.

"Some of the stories were his that the others were telling earlier," Mara whispered to Sarn and Sala. "Now they are afraid that he will tell one of the same ones, making the other travelers here ask too many questions about them."

"Tell us a story," Sala called out to the newcomer.

The big man turned around to see who it was that had spoken, he looked right past Sarn to the raven haired girl on the other side of him.

"Janua," he said staring at Sala. "How did you get such a beautiful woman to come and work in this place so far from nowhere?"

"You know better than that," she told him shaking her finger at him. "You know I have never had that here. No sir, she belongs to that young man right there by her side."

"Well perhaps he is willing share," the man said standing and starting toward the couple. "What do you say to that?"

"I say that you had better sit back down over there so that you may stay alive," Sarn told him moving his hand toward his sword that was now leaning against the bench beside him.

"I think that you do not know who I am."

"I do not think he cares who you are," Marna said trying to stop him. "I watched him kill two men last night without thinking twice."

Tig picked his head up from his paws and watched the man walking toward the two. He crawled out from under the table and began to make his way around to the other side of the man.

"Why should that bother me?" he asked stepping closer. "He is just a boy."

Sarn stood, keeping one eye on Tig and the other on the man. Sala took his free hand and pulled him back down beside her. He sat back down with little resistance, although he was not sure why.

"I am no tavern girl," Sala began, "now if you would be so kind and go back to your place before I let go of him and slit your throat myself."

"A woman with a tongue," he said leaning over the table reaching across toward her. "How have you made it this far without being taken over a knee and taught a lesson?"

Before he could reach her Sarn had the point of his sword poking him under his chin and Tig had his mouth open and ready to tear at the man's ankle. The sword came so fast that he did not see where it came from.

"I think it is I that gets the lesson," the big man said backing away from the couple chuckling a bit at his situation. "Janua buy this loving couple an ale or two on me."

He made his way back to his table and only then did he notice the big animal that had worked his way behind him.

"I guess I should pay better attention. The four legged one there could have hurt me."

Janua and Mara laughed at him and the rest of the tavern guests joined in.

"It seems to me that you may have finally found your match big man." Mara told him patting him on his back. "I think you need more than just ale tonight."

"I suppose you are right child," he returned. "I only wish we were not so far out in the middle of nowhere, so that I may have at least one woman to pick from."

"What of me?" Mara asked.

"You are too much like my own daughter to think of that way," he almost laughed at her but thought better of it and stopped. "Besides, I am sure that you would be more than I could deal with."

Janua, who herself was far from being old or ugly, took hold of his hand and sat next to him for a minute.

"Don't worry my friend; I think that if you can hold out I am sure that I can take care of you as always."

"Now that is more like the treatment I am used to getting."

"Nothing is too great for my Prince," Janua said snuggling up to him.

He grumbled at her a bit, but kissed her on the cheek.

"I know, I know, you hate being called Prince," she said before standing back up. "But I just cannot help myself."

Sala begged Sarn to help her upstairs, and asked Mara to bring them a pitcher of ale. He carried the girl on his back, while she carried his sword. Tig waited for them to top the stairs before he too followed them. When the couple reached their room, he lay her down on the bed and listened as the three women chased out those that were not staying there. It was a little while later before Mara came to the door with the ale that they had wanted. She brought them two pitchers of ale, some meat that had been left over, and three mugs. Sarn looked to Sala who nodded her head as the girl poured ale in all the mugs.

"I asked Mara to get something ready for us," she said limping across the room. "I know that you are going to like it."

Pushing back a folding screen, Sala revealed a rather large tub filled with water.

"Now come here my love and let us take care of you."

Mara took his hand and led him over to the tub, and with Sala's help undressed him. He in turn helped them to undress and get into the tub before joining them.

Dagger and his cousins continued the dance. It was as if every elf in the forest was there or soon would be. The flames from the fire reached far above the trees and into the night sky. His cousins were treating him as if they would never see him again, touching his face, his hair and his hands. Pulling Dagger into the circle he was the only one that did not dance into the air, but the rest seemed not to notice or care. The drums slowed and voices took over the rhythm carrying the dancers even higher. Like the drums, the chanting seemed to carry in from places unseen within the forest. Dagger joined in the chant throwing his arms out and his head back. In that instant his feet left the ground and he rose into the air. Soon he was above the trees with the dancers surrounding him. When he reached the top of the tower of dancers, they lifted him on their shoulders and tossed him higher into the air. With his arms still outstretched and his head still back the starlit sky went black. The only light to be seen for miles was that of the fire. When the dancers completed a full rotation from ground to sky and back, the flames caught Dagger lifting him and pushing him higher. As each of the dancers floated back to the ground they sat around the fire in the open space between it and the forest. Soon there were only the flames and Dagger high above the trees. Those that were sitting around the fire continued to chant. They then lowered and cupped their hands together as if they were a bowl. After several beats of the drums they each began scooping at air from the ground as if they were digging into the soil. Then with every beat one of them would lift their hands above their heads and spread their arms wide as if in offering. Soon the hands began to look like a ripple in water.

Dagger began to turn in the air as the fire leapt one more time and began to swirl about him. The flames were spinning out around and down the length of his arms, extending out past his hands. They soon appeared to be shooting out of his mouth as they again went higher. Then just as it started the flames began to die down, lowering Dagger in a slow spin to the ground. When he reached the ground, the fire went out and it was as if there had been no fire at all. Dagger fell first to his knees and then on his back. As his head hit the ground several of his cousins came to him, lifted him up and carried him off into the forest.

"Do you think that Ryn will leave us again soon?" asked one of them as they passed his grandparents.

"Yes, but we will watch over and take care of our cousin until then," another returned.

As the sun began to filter its way into the room the three lay naked and entangled with each other. Mara woke first untangling herself from the other two, leaning in she kissed them both before reaching for her clothes. Sarn stirred in his sleep pulling Sala closer to him and she in turn grabbed at him trying to get even closer yet. Opening his eyes Sarn smiled at Mara as she slipped her shirt over her head.

"I am going for a morning meal for us," she said leaning in again, kissing him full on the lips and caressing Sala's arm where it crossed his chest.

"That sounds good," he returned after she kissed him,

"perhaps some fresh cow's milk?"

"Of course," she called back as she left the room.

A few minutes later Sala woke pulling him to her, kissing his face and body.

"You seem to be in a rather happy mind this morning," he whispered as her hands began to caress his chest.

"I am always in a happy mind when I wake next to you my love." She smiled looking about the room. "Where is Mara? I would like to thank her in private for last night."

"She is making us a morning meal and promises to return."

The two settled back into their bed, with Sala doing her best to keep him occupied. It was only a short time before Mara returned with a small meal for the three of them. She joined them back in bed as they sat huddled together feeding each other. When they were finished Sala set their platters and mugs aside and the three curled up together.

"I have all day," Mara giggled.

"Your mother will not be mad?" asked Sarn.

"Mother will be happy that I have found someone loving enough not to beat me, not that a good spanking would be a bad thing." She added laughing, crawling over Sarn's legs.

Sala joined her across her lover's legs slapping Mara on her bottom as she crawled over him. The three laughed and Sarn slapped them both.

Dagger woke naked on a bed of moss covered with deer and bear furs. It took him several seconds before realizing that he was in a safe place and did not need to hide. Still he dressed in a hurry before anyone noticed that he was awake. Just as he finished, one of his cousins brought him his morning meal.

"I am sorry that you are already dressed."

"Do you think I would let you see me naked in the daylight?" said Dagger, laughing a little.

"Well it would have been fun again."

"I do not remember anything after beginning to dance," he lied. But only just a little as he remembered floating above the trees wrapped in the flames keeping him safe and little more.

"Then perhaps I should remind you."

"No, I have ... I have other things to do than to sit here in this place."

"So I am aware of," his grandfather said entering the small hut. "As always you can see we have taken good care of your home.

Your grandmother and I wait for the day when you to return to us to stay forever. "

"You know that I must complete my tasks and quests. You talk as if I did not have to hide myself from those that should care for me and not want to use or kill me," he returned, his hands becoming fists. "Would you have me to ignore the ancients and what they have done and have given me? You know that I do as they ask of me when I can. It is my journey that I must complete before I can begin to think of coming home. I know you must realize that there is nothing here that will help me or anyone else. While you and grandmother have 'hidden' me from my parents they are the ones that saw to it that I have lived this long."

"Who gave these tasks to you? Not the ancients," his grandfather began to get angry at him, "and not your ancestors. They would not do such a thing. No it was just some dream that you think was an ancient. Your grandmother and I wait for you to take your place here and you play games while in hiding from your parents. You wander around the outside world stealing and killing. I do not begin to understand this fascination with it all."

"Grandfather," Dagger began. "I left here to get away from my parents I did not ask to be blinded. I did not ask them to spend their lives calling out to me and looking for me. It was the ancients that separated them and brought me here, not you, not grandmother. I know I was not supposed to be on this journey, but I also was not meant to be fighting some ancient battle either. My life would be so much simpler if you would all just leave me alone. You, grandmother, my parents, the ancients, our ancestors, the voices that tell me where to travel and what to do; I have had enough of it. I want to live my own life. I want to be able to let someone get close to me, someone I can trust, and someone I can ...."

Dagger was in tears by the time he finished. His grandfather tried to hug him but he pushed him away.

"Then stay here," his cousin added.

But Dagger could not look at the cousin, but the cousin understood and left the two alone.

"Your cousin is right, you could stay here."

"They would not let me stay here for long."

"Tell me of these voices. Do you know who they are, have you met them before?"

"I am not sure I think some of the voices belong to the sisters."

"The sisters would talk to their own family before talking to an elf."

"What makes you so sure?" Dagger asked looking his grandfather in the eyes. "Were they not the ones that brought Tig to you to give to me? Perhaps he has something to do with it, some connection with them. How am I to know for sure?"

"Why would they turn to an elf?" his grandfather asked tossing his hands in the air and looking away. "It makes no sense."

"As usual you ignore me, as if what I think does not matter. You still continue to treat me as a child."

"In many ways you still are."

"You never seem to let me forget," Dagger snapped back.

"Do you think that your grandmother and I sit here in this forest and come up with ways to lead you away from a task that you feel is more important?"

"As a matter of fact, yes, sometimes I do think that," Dagger added laughing just a little.

"Then you are mistaken my child."

"Then why are we arguing?" Dagger said and tossed his arms out wide in frustration. "You should be working on my daggers today."

"In that instance, let us get to the forge and have our way with some metal."

Dagger chuckled again taking his grandfather's hand and letting him lead the way to the forge.

"Tell me what you intend with these knives?"

"I intend for them to be used. I want you to make them and I will get part of their magic from another."

Will looked at his grandchild with more than a little concern. He knew that the only magic he could ever want that he did not have himself was that of his witch cousin Tobias.

"Tobias is coming here?"

"He should be here just after the midday meal."

"Is there a reason that you cannot go to him?"

"Grandfather, you know that the magic needs to be added before it is hammered out. It is the only way that it will work."

"I guess I just have a hard time trusting him."

"Is it him, or witches that you have a hard time trusting?"

"It is the witches that continue to try and turn you."

"And the elves are innocent? You know as well as I do that both sides of my family are trying to push me over to serve Lord Crel."

"As well as I am, I suppose."

"You have your moments." Dagger stared at his grandfather waiting for him to deny that he had never tried to get him to do evil with his magic.

The two spoke no further as they gathered the material to make the new daggers.

"We could always make a new sword if you want," Will told Ryn, measuring the material that was at hand.

"No, three daggers, that is what I want," Ryn replied tossing a large piece of oak onto the fire.

Will placed the materials into three separate pots and then set the pots deep into the fire.

"This reminds me of when we made your first daggers, do you remember?"

"Grandpa I was five, I barely remember last week like it was last week, let alone when I was five," Dagger lied. He remembered everything as if it was yesterday, and that too was part of his curse.

Will and Ryn spent time getting the rest of the forge ready to do the work needed to make the daggers. While his grandfather packed an area in sand to pour the molten metal once it was ready, he worked on their handles. Hearing the call for midday meal they left the forge and went to eat leaving two of the cousins to watch over it.

The family sat together over a meal of fresh rabbit and vegetables. They said little to each other of any importance. They talked about their garden and if Will's brother would be coming to an upcoming festival. It could have been a conversation in any home anywhere. Not that everything that his grandparents had to say was vital to him or the world. It just seemed strange to him to have someone he knew talking about things that were trivial in his mind. When they finished with the meal, Ryn grabbed a large pitcher of wine and headed back to the forge to wait for Tobias and for the metal to be ready. He checked the ore before sitting out under a tree and pouring himself a glass of the wine. He closed his eyes for what seemed a second and was awakened by Tobias' voice in his ear.

"Wake up, blind boy; it's time to earn your keep."

Dagger startled and in an instant had a knife to his cousin's belly before realizing that he was safe and the voice was that of his cousin.

"Perhaps next time I will not be so quick to stop myself," Ryn replied, lowering his head.

"Perhaps next time I will not give warning that I am here," Tobias told him, laughing at his cousin. "You would not be able to find me with your dark eyes, and where is that beast of yours? I usually trip over him several times before I can get close to you."

"He never comes this far with me," he responded, "besides he has a job to do elsewhere at the moment."

"He is guarding your new charge from the voices no doubt."

"What do you know of him?" asked Will.

"Nothing," Tobias answered, becoming a bit suspicious. "I was only guessing, I am surprised you do not know everything yourself by now."

It was unusual that Will would not know of his charge, if he had one or who he was training. It always seemed that he knew where Ryn was going and who he was traveling with.

"It has been a long time Will," Tobias said. "It is good to see you again."

"I have never looked forward to your visits so I cannot agree that it is good to see you."

"I did not know that you felt that way."

"I tell you every time you come through the forest and happen past my home. Just so there is no more confusion. I do not like you, I have never liked you, and I do not like what you do to my grandchild when the two of you get together."

"He helps, Grandfather. If it was not for his help the tablet would not have made it back to where it belongs."

"And how many times has he shown your parents where you were so that they could come and hurt you. You were lucky that your father was not strong enough to come here looking for you."

"Mother was strong enough to come after me."

"But she was not strong enough to catch you though and that is a good thing."

"She had help. I almost did not make it out of the cabin."

"Your siblings I would guess."

"Yes, and something more; something was throwing me off not letting me see what was going on. Something was keeping me from finding out her true intentions until it was almost too late."

"That was when the sister came in behind you," Tobias added.

"I saw no sister."

"She came just as you turned to leave, and kept your mother from following you."

Will went about checking the metal and making sure that everything was ready, leaving the two to talk.

"How is it that you know this?"

"I saw them last night," he lied. "They told me that I needed to come here and that you needed something of mine. I always thought that you possessed every magic, between your elf half and your witch half."

"I have all but a few. And I will come into those when the time is right," Ryn began, knowing that Tobias was lying to him, but refusing to acknowledge it. "Until then I need you to cast a beacon spell and a protection spell for three daggers."

"That explains why we are standing near a large pit of burning charcoal and those two are pumping air into the middle of the flames."

Dagger walked away from his cousin shaking his head. He did not wanting to continue their conversation, but he knew that he had little chance of him going away just yet.

"I take it you want it to work more than just one time. What is it that you are protecting them from?"

"It might need to be used more than one time; that is true. The protection spell is to keep it so that person and I are the only ones that can find it once it is used."

"I cannot keep the beacon from being seen by anyone other than you, if you know what I mean."

"Yes, you mean that my parents will see that magic is being used and that it calls to me."

"Exactly," his cousin added.

"Then let us hope that I am not too far away when it is used," Dagger laughed.

"I think they are ready," Will said as he scraped the impurities from the top of the molten metal.

Tobias pulled a small blue pouch from a pack that he carried on his back. Will lifted one of the small pots from the fire and held it on a block of wood using metal tongs. Tobias tossed a small handful of light blue powder into the molten metal. The powder flared as it caught fire from the heat of the pot and the flames that shot up from the wood under the pot. They repeated the process for the other two pots of metal, stirring each of them as they returned them to the fire. He began mumbling to himself as he took another pouch from his pack. Reaching into it he tossed some of the contents onto the fire itself and then into each of the three pots. The flames of the fire leapt every time air was pumped into the pit, but he did not move back from it. Moving his hands over the pots of metal, he continued to mumble the words he learned as a child.

When Tobias was finished, he left the forge without saying a word and went to Ryn's pitcher of wine and drank from it.

"We have things they call mugs for drinking from."

"I was too thirsty," Tobias laughed. "You need only to allow them to cool now and then get them into the shape you wish."

Will pulled the three pots one at a time from the fire and poured the molten metal into the three forms he had pounded into sand.

"Are you planning to stay the night?" asked Will as he finished.

"If it would be no trouble," Tobias replied.

"It may be trouble but I think it would be best."

"If you are worried that I will tell them where this one is," Tobias said pointing to Ryn. "You should not be, even if I did tell of where he is they cannot bother him here and you know that."

Will did not answer him and Dagger was too busy putting finishing touches on the handles of the knives to have heard what they were saying. As the other metal cooled, Dagger sat under a tree outside of the forge hammering and shaping some silver tips to put on the handles. It was not hard, and he kept the design simple, carrying it out through them all. As he shaped and hammered he mumbled to himself. It was a chant that he remembered, one that if he was asked he could not tell how he knew it. That was, as he learned throughout his young life, the way he knew of almost his entire 'gift' as some might say. There were a few things about his gift that were taught to him over the years. Some of them were taught to him by his grandmother, but not that many. Every once in a while though another would come along and teach him something new, or at least try to. Whatever they would try to teach him, he would be able to finish it even before they spoke it. It seemed to him that each day he would learn a little more of the magic that ran through his blood. Just before sunset he finished the handle pieces. He turned his attention to the now cooling metal bars, thrusting them one by one back into the fire. His evening meal was brought to him by one of his cousins that tended the forge's fire. Setting it near the fire to keep it warm they once again took on the duty of pumping air into the coals of the forge. Dagger ate his meal between hammering the bars of metal together. Then he folded them over and over making one new bar before cutting it into three pieces again. Once they were again three separate bars he closed his eyes as he worked and began to sing a low soft song. His words could not be heard by anyone but himself but the melodic sounds were soothing to anyone that was close enough to hear. Working into the night he kept hammering until the metal cooled too much to be worked. Then he would place it back into the fire and move onto the next blade. Near the middle of the night he set his hammer down, satisfied that they were exactly as he wanted them. Once he was finished he handed them to a cousin to add the handles and polish them. In turn that cousin gave them to yet another one who sharpened the points and the edges of the knives. Dagger watched over them as they worked admiring not only his work but that of his cousins as well. When the first one was finished, he lifted it feeling its weight before throwing it over his shoulder as if he were tossing it away. The knife flew from the experienced hand sinking half way up the blade into a large beam in the forge. He smiled as each blade found its way next to its brother, buried in the beam no more and no less than the one before it. Pulling each one from the beam he mumbled over each of them in turn. Standing over the fire pit he placed the knives one at a time into the fire handle first. Then he started waving his hands over the top of the points of the knives in a circular motion in opposite directions. A white light began to shine at the tips of his fingers before spreading across his hands and enveloping the knife blades. Soon the only lights seen in the forge were that from Ryn's hands and the soft orange glow from the fire.

Just before dawn Ryn took the knives back from the fire and put them in a small pack. Waking his grandmother he asked that she not blind him again.

"You will not be safe," Bel whispered.

"Please, at least wait until tomorrow, there is something I wish to see before I go on."

"Then I will get your aunt and we will send you back to the tavern and into your room."

"You better hurry, it is almost sunrise."

It took only a minute for Bel to leave and return with a tall light skinned woman, her black hair almost white from age. She hugged Ryn tight before giving him several small pouches and another smaller pack.

"These will replenish what you need," she told him as she handed them to him. "And in this pack you will find a couple of potions that you will need in the future. You will know when you need them."

"Auntie you know that I can make the potions and the powders that are in here."

"You know that you never have the chance or the time that you need to do that."

He said nothing in return just stepped back into his aunt's arms and hugged her.

She reached out behind him and took his grandmother's hands. As he let go the two began to turn around him. From his aunt's hands a light blue powder began to fall to the ground as they turned.

"In our hearts you will stay forever, but your journey is not yet over. We return you now to your friends, keeping yourself safe until you come again," the two chanted in unison.

It was not long before a light blue glow surrounded the three. Auntie and Bel, still chanting backed away, leaving him the only one in the light. Turning to the left and smiling at the two of them, he disappeared in thousands of tiny points of blue light.

Tig raised his head and went to the door sniffing the air, putting his nose to the crack at the bottom of it. Letting out a soft low growl and pushing against the door the animal began to dance back and forth on his paws. A blue light appeared for a second under the door. Backing up a bit Tig began lifting his paws several inches off the floor, making it look as if he were dancing from side to side. Soon the door opened and Dagger stepped into the room. Tig rose up and placed his front paws on his master's shoulders and nuzzled his neck. Smiling he took his friend's head in his hands and gave it a good rub and buried his face into the animal's fur.

"Wait for me here," he whispered to the animal. "I will join you in a moment."

Dropping to the floor Tig wound himself around Dagger's legs once before he left him alone.

Slipping to the side of the bed Dagger pulled back the covers from the lovers. Sarn rolled toward him and grabbed for the covers. Dagger stared at them trying to memorize each curve of his friends' faces. Raising his right hand, a white ball of light appeared in his palm. He lifted it to his face, and blew against the ball pushing it over the sleeping lovers. Lighting their faces, it made it easier for him to see them. He touched Sarn's face, running his fingers over it. Then he touched Sala's cheek before pulling the covers back over the lovers and leaving the room. Dagger stopped in the hall giving the sleepy looking, but walking

Mara a hug and a kiss on the cheek.

"Should I tell them you are back?" she asked whispering.

"No cousin," he whispered back. "I am tired and will need my sleep before I am ready to leave here."

She nodded and told him of Sala's bruised feet. He handed her a bit of powder and told her to put it into a bath.

"And make sure that she stays in the bath for at least an hour."

Mara nodded and hesitated, lowering her head. Reaching out and cupping her chin with a hand he lifted her face to look at him.

"You have been with them?" he asked.

She nodded and tried not to look ashamed.

"You like them, do you not?"

"Yes cousin," she returned, her face turning red.

"You have nothing to worry about and you have all day and another night to take care of them. Tell your mother that I am here, and have your aunt see to my meals. And to answer your question, it will not harm you if you and he join her in that bath. But she must not to leave it until after the hour, understand?"

Mara smiled nodding her head, leaning in she hugged him again and kissed him full on the lips. Turning away she smiled over her shoulder at her blind cousin.

"Just one more thing," Dagger said smiling. "You keep getting prettier each time I am here."

"You mean grandmother ... " she began, "you can see?"

"Just a few hours more," Dagger told her.

"Is it worth being discovered?"

Dagger thought for a second of his companions, looked her straight in the eye and turned away.

"Very much so," he told her, opening his door and disappearing inside.

Tig was lying beside the bed watching his master move about removing his clothes, before he fell into the soft folds of the bed. Pulling the covers up over his head, he was asleep before Tig climbed up and lay across his back.

Mara made her way down to the pantry where Marna was awake and working on the day's meals. She told her aunt of Dagger's return before grabbing some meat, eggs, platters and a pan.

"I see you intend on feeding them in their room again." Marna giggled.

"Of course, I must keep them from that boorish man that sleeps in my mother's bed."

"He leaves us today," she returned, "besides, I thought you liked him?"

"Not that much, he is a braggart, and an oaf."

"You just do not know him that well, he grows on you. It would be nice if you would give him the time to."

"Perhaps," she said pulling her robe tighter about her and arranging her loot on a large tray, "but not today. Today I have more interesting and fun things planned."

"Just as you spent your day yesterday I will bet."

"Are you jealous?"

"No," Marna began. "Just know that he will leave with her and not with you."

"I wish I could go with them both," Mara nodded knowing that she could not follow them. "I know, so I plan to spend this day with them just as yesterday and when they return I will be with them again until they leave."

Marna kissed her niece's cheek and gave the girl a quick hug before sending her off with her best wishes.

"I will look after our Ryn and you look after his companions."

Tobias woke in the home of his cousin, with a handwritten note on the side table. Rubbing his eyes he read the ink that had been scrawled on the paper. He shook his head, crumpled the paper and threw it at the wall.

"Bad news?" Bel asked entering the room.

"You have read it, you tell me."

"I guess it would all depend on how one looks at the words. What will you do now?"

"Go home I guess, if Ryn no longer wants me to follow."

"You will no more go home than you will quit following."

"I find it difficult to understand that I can no longer do what was asked of me ...."

"You were doing nothing more than keeping an eye on him for his parents," Bel interrupted. "Even I know that, but you could never get close enough to do any great harm. So now you need to go home and tell your father that where Ryn is headed you can no longer follow."

"I know where Ryn is now. I can go there today and make them to understand."

"If it were that easy, it would have been done already. You need to understand the path that Ryn is following comes from somewhere else. It has been his given path from birth, and that is

163

something that you or I cannot change. I have made it easier for that path to be followed in a way, but I have also made it more difficult. I sometimes wish I could go back and use a different spell than I did, but it is too late now. Someday perhaps I can remove it for good, but until then, this is the safest thing to do."

Bel turned to leave when she finished talking, a tear forming in the corner of her eye. She did all she could to keep from turning around and yelling at him. She knew that he had been the one that had told Ryn's parents where he was heading each time they had gotten close. He may have been responsible for the one time they had taken him. Stopping just before the front door she turned back to face Tobias.

"I suppose you're going to be leaving today."

"I do have things that need seeing to."

"Like visiting your aunt?" Bel asked.

"I am nearby. It would be a shame to have come this far and not."

"I think you need to spend a couple of days here before that time," Bel said, waving her arm toward him.

Tobias' eyes widened as he was lifted into the air and shoved back into a small pantry, the door slamming shut as he hit the wall behind him.

"You have no right," he screamed after hitting the floor.

"You will be safe here, and as soon as I arrange it you'll be let out of there so you can feed yourself and stretch."

"If you think you can hold me old woman, then you forget what I am."

"No sir, I have not forgotten, you are a witch, but until the day comes when elves no longer have magic you will always be weaker than I am."

"There is no way I am going to let you keep me here. I will be getting out, you can count on it hag!"

Bel laughed and swung her arm toward the pantry, and walked away.

"We will see how well you can travel blind," Bel whispered closing the front door of the house. "Not as easy as your cousin I am sure."

Dagger woke just after midday to find a small fire in his fire place, and a stew simmering to the side of it. He looked around smiling, letting his eyes take in as much of the sights around him as possible. He took in the colors of the blankets that were on his bed, the orange, the black and the white of his friend. It had been a long time since he had been able to talk his grandmother into leaving him his eyesight for any length of time after he left her. He went to the window and looked out at the stable. Looking at the horses he noticed Pel immediately, his white body stood out among the rest. He told himself that he would have to get Sarn to lose the horse somewhere along the way. It was too noticeable and someday might lead to a problem. He wanted to spend time with his companions, but knew that it would be impossible. At least without letting on that he could see, even if it was only just for a few more hours.

Dishing up some stew for the three of them, Mara let it slip that Dagger had returned. She kept them from going immediately to see him, but she knew it would not be long before one of them would go and wake him. They agreed to let him sleep more. But Sarn promised himself that he would go to his room before much longer and see if he would tell him where he had disappeared to.

Once Mara and Sala returned the leftovers of their meal to the scullery, he slipped out behind them and went to his friend's door. He entered the room without knocking; Tig tilted his head and looked at him from his master's bed. Looking about the room he found Dagger sitting with his back to him in front of the fire in a large chair, wrapped in a bulky robe, eating his stew.

"I need to remember to lock the door next time," Dagger said, not turning around to look at his friend.

"So, this is what you look like without the hood of your cloak pulled over your face."

Dagger waved his hand over his head feeling for the hood, pulling at the robe trying to pull it up around his head before finally giving up.

"It took you long enough," Dagger said between mouthfuls, trying not to show how upset he was with himself for not locking the door.

"Had you wanted to talk to me you could have seen me when you returned."

"I did look in on you and Sala, but you were both asleep and I could not interrupt you lying there all naked. What would you have thought of me? You might have thought I was just out to gaze upon her body."

"That is a good excuse," Sarn returned shaking his head, "but for the fact that you are blind. I doubt that whatever it is that makes you able to walk about without help lets you see that well."

"You can be sure of that my friend."

Dagger finished eating and turned to look at him. He looked into his companion's eyes for the first time without the help of the crystal in his pocket. He noticed right away that they were the same color of green as the crystal. He tried hard not to stare at him, but neither found themselves able to not stare at the other.

"Just do not get used to my face," Dagger said realizing what he was doing. "We leave again in the morning."

"Just like that," Sarn said, tossing his hands up. "You disappear for two full days, returning on the third as if nothing happened. You offer no explanation, just, I am back and we leave in the morning."

"I had to talk to someone. You would not understand."

"How can you tell that I would not understand if you do not tell me?" he began, trying not to look at his friend any longer. "We thought that something had happened to you. That is until Janua told us that you often disappear when you come here. Only to return after a day or two and on rare occasions three days. She told us that we should feel privileged as you have never brought anyone with you before. Forgive me if I do not feel so privileged. Sala and I were forced to kill three guards that came looking for us. Then the next morning I find her naked out at the edge of the forest with her feet and knees so bruised she could not walk."

"Things happen here," he returned, pulling the collar of his robe closer about his neck, "many that cannot be explained. You have to understand that. As for this I cannot tell you why or what happened, I can only say it happens here. There is something different about this forest and those that live among these trees. Legends tell of something of great importance that happened right outside of this tavern."

Sarn shook his head, but continued to tell Dagger everything that happened, making sure that he understood it. When he was done, Dagger nodded his head, shrugged his shoulders, sat back in the chair, closed his eyes and fell back asleep. Sarn took the bowl from his friend's hand and wrapped a blanket around him before leaving the room.

He slipped out to the stable to care for their animals and make sure that everything they needed was still in their packs. He was still checking them when Mara came out to look after the animals as well.

"Do you not trust us?" she asked him as she reached the gate.

"I needed to see for myself," he replied, "besides I needed to get away from the room for a minute. I could not face her or you after talking with him and getting the uncaring response that I did."

"Dagger cares what happens to the two of you, that I can promise," she told him as she brushed Dagger's horse. "It is just that when he comes back he is tired and unable to even protect himself. That is why he comes here. We make sure he is safe and taken care of until he is ready to leave again."

"Where does he go?"

"If he did not tell you then I cannot as well," she said trying not to hurt his feelings. "No, that he must tell you himself."

"Well," Sarn added chuckling, trying to change the mood of their conversation. "It would seem that you have all the answers. Is Sala in the room?"

"I left her in the tub, Ryn gave me something for...," Mara stopped before she said anything more than she should have.

"So you talked to him before he went to his room?"

Mara nodded her head almost afraid to answer him.

"He gave me something to help her bruises," she added lowering her head. "We are to keep her in the water for a least an hour."

"Then I would think that we had better hurry with our chores and get back to her."

Mara smiled as she turned back to her chores.

About an hour before dawn, hidden once again under the hood of his cloak, Dagger gathered the group together. They each said their goodbyes and left the remote tavern behind them. While he did talk to them it was only about what lie ahead of them and what they might expect to find. He continued to shy away from the questions the couple kept asking that concerned where he had been for two days. When the travelers broke free from the forest canopy sometime late in the afternoon, Dagger lost his eyesight. He wanted to scream out in frustration but held back to keep from alarming his companions. Instead he reached into his pocket, held onto his crystal and kept moving.

That night around the cooking fire for the first time Sala told stories of her childhood. Sarn and Dagger listened but where not paying attention. They seemed more intent on what the other was thinking. Dagger was worried that they would ask him about his disappearance again. At the same time Sarn was wondering if he was going to offer an explanation for his disappearance or if he had to ask.

Sala paid no attention to them or what they said or did not say. She just kept on telling her story of how she and an older sister would flirt with the young boys that were trying to become guards for the crown. Sarn did wonder if these were her stories, or if they belonged to one of the other girls in Calid's tavern. In a way it did not matter, it was better than a quiet night. Other nights their conversations had been about their evenings or days of training in the past. It was unusual that any of them would tell some story or other, even one they had heard in any of the places they had been. When she told the last story the three fell asleep with Tig keeping watch a few paces away as always.

In the morning the group left their campsite just before dawn. Dagger began telling them that they needed to move faster if they were to make it in time to save the child.

"Would we not have been further along had we not spent three days at Janua's tavern?" Sarn returned.

"Is that the best you can do?" Dagger said, sounding more than a little grumpy, pulling his cloak hood even further down over his face. "If you thought that it was such a bad thing to stay at the tavern, then why did you not begin without me?"

"You are the one that has said that we needed to hurry," Sarn shot back. "Tell us then why it was so important to you that we had to spend the time that we now need to make up. Besides you are the only one that knows the way to where we are going."

Sala motioned for him to stop and not to continue to question him. He nodded at her and waved one of his hands to tell her that he understood and would stop even though he did not want to. Throughout the morning the couple kept a bit behind their leader. They kept to themselves pointing out different birds or maybe a deer off in the distance at the edge of some meadow or grove. Dagger never turned or looked in the direction they were talking about and did not answer or speak again until just before midday.

"By this time tomorrow we should be in sight of the country home we need," Dagger said, stopping his horse and waiting for them to catch up. "I..., I had to visit... my family."

As he finished he kicked his horse and took off again. The couple was not sure what to say in return, so they left it alone for the moment. Shaking their heads they pushed their horses to catch up with him, pulling the two packhorses behind them.

True to his word the following day the group rode up over a small rise and looked out across a shallow valley at the summer house of Lord Dermit.

"What do we do now?" Sala asked hoping that one of them had thought about what they were going to do next.

"First we need to find a place to camp here on the ridge," Dagger began. "It will be cold meals tonight and perhaps until we can get the boy out of this place, so let us hope that it is soon."

"We have enough food for only three days of cold meals," Sala told them.

"I suppose we should have restored our provisions at the tavern," Dagger grumbled.

"There was not enough for us to take from Janua to restore all our provisions but she gave us what she could spare," Sala returned.

"It would seem I have been put in my place," Dagger said faking a bit of laughter. Though it fell more than a little short as his irritable mood showed through just the same.

They moved along the ridge until they could look into the front gate and at the front doors of the summer estate. Dagger gripped his crystal tighter looking through it to see the country house and its buildings. Jumping off his horse he called Tig to his side. Kneeling he placed a brown leather collar with a green crystal embedded in it around the animal's neck and then stood back up. Tig stood on his hind legs, placed a paw on either side of his master's head, nuzzled his face and then dropped back to all fours. Dagger leaned down, gave his old friend one last pet on his head then pointed his finger toward the house in the valley. Tig took off on a run while Dagger found himself a rock that he could sit on while taking the crystal from his pocket. Sitting down in the middle of the rock he put the crystal to his forehead.

"I guess this must be the place," Sala giggled getting off her horse.

She saw to their provisions while Sarn moved the horses to a grassy area nearby. It was a ritual that just worked itself out from the second night after she had joined the two. After setting the horses to a line at the edge of a small grove Sarn walked a circle around where they would be camped. It was not a normal thing that he would do, but he felt that if Tig were out ahead of them then he should get an idea what was around them.

"We will move closer again tomorrow," Dagger told him when he returned. "If anyone comes, we are hunters and we are safe here as this is not royal land; that begins at the river."

Sarn and Sala looked out across the valley to the river and up to the house.

"It is a large place," Sarn began. "How are we going to find a small boy in a place like that?"

"We need to find someone that knows where he is in that house or we are going to need someone to go inside and look around for him."

Sarn got a puzzled look on his face while Sala just got scared.

"Yes, that means that if we have to you will go there and get a job in the scullery so that you can look around." Dagger didn't even look up as he spoke, keeping the crystal to his forehead.

"That stone, does it see for you?" Sala asked trying not to sound as scared as she was beginning to feel.

Sarn looked to her and rolled his eyes. Even he knew that no one could see just by putting some stone to their forehead. He was certain of that, but how else could he explain that Dagger could lead them without being able to see? Well even he was not sure, but he knew it had to be something to do with Tig or his horse, and not some stone.

"This stone is a crystal," Dagger snarled back, "and if need be you will go to the house and do your part."

His attitude had been the subject of quiet conversation between the couple since his return from his family. Once again each day he seemed to get a bit more irritable than the last. If at all possible it was even worse than before they had arrived at the tavern. They were sure that it would only be a matter of time before he would lose himself in anger.

Sarn found a place from where he could keep an eye on Dagger and the approach to the campsite. It was here that he set up a place for himself for the night.

"So you would rather sit here apart from me and stare out into the night?" Sala said curling up next Sarn in his hiding place.

"With Tig off to Lord Dermit's summer palace and Dagger sitting on his rock, one of us needs to be looking out for the rest of us," he told her.

"My protector," she said looking up into his eyes. "What would I do without you?"

"Kill them yourself I suppose," Sarn said chuckling.

She hugged him and joined in on his laughter.

"I wish I had met you before leaving home," he said looking back at her.

"Why would you wish that?"

"Then I would never have had to leave my home."

"Something tells me that you would have," she added as if she knew exactly why he was there.

"Perhaps, but I would have had something to come back to."

"I was not going to let you go off without me when you found me," she added. "What makes you think that I would have let you leave your home without me?"

Sarn stared off into the coming darkness, and reached to touch her face.

"I think that you must have me mistaken with a weak stay behind kind of girl."

"Weak maybe," he chuckled, "never a stay behind kind of girl. I doubt that even if I had begged you to stay that you would have."

"True and you did tell me that you could not take me along with you."

"No, I said that I did not know what to do."

"Either way you meant that you could not, and look how much I have helped."

"You seem to know so much about my mind tell me then, what it is that I am thinking at this moment?"

"You are making a jest, I hope."

Sarn looked to her and smiled, and then without saying a word looked back to woods. He knew that his mother would be telling him that he was too young to know what his heart wanted. He was also sure that she would be more than happy to welcome the girl into her own heart as family.

"One thing is sure, without you I may well have starved by now," he told her trying not to laugh.

"Now there is something that I know to be true," she returned, looking up to him and stroking his cheek.

Her smile had captivated him from the first minute he had seen it, and then there was something about her eyes.

"How would you like to be a bride?"

His question came as no surprise to her, she had been hoping that he would ask but she was not ready for the question just at that moment. She stopped stroking his cheek and looked to him just as the last light of the day hit his face and she could no longer look away.

"I think that you are making fun of me and my feelings. That is what I think of this question of yours."

She tried hard to sound as if he were making a joke, knowing that at any time on any of their adventures that they could be killed. In her mind they were already married and she did not need anyone else to tell them that they were.

He shook his head and figured it better if he just left things as they were and not ask her again, at least for some time anyway. While it occurred to him that he should be upset, it also occurred to him that if she was unhappy there had been several chances for her to leave.

As the light of day faded to darkness Tig found himself close to the summer palace, laying under some brush at the edge of the lawn. As midnight approached, Tig moved closer to the palace. In just a few steps he was moving around the patrolling guards being as quiet as possible. As he made his way around the tiny crystal embedded in the collar around his neck began to glow almost unnoticeable. Sniffing at the ground as he went, Tig tried to find the scent he was looking for, the one that was different from the others. When it was safe and he was sure that he would not be seen he lifted himself up to look into the ground floor windows. The rooms may have been dark but Tig saw into them what he needed to see. He found his way back into hiding were he could keep a watchful eye on the palace throughout the night.

As the sun began to rise, Dagger remained sitting where he had been the night before, on his rock with the crystal pressed to his forehead. Sarn had kept up his vigilant watch over the campsite and his companions, while Sala slept at his side. Trying not to wake her he slipped away from his spot and went to Dagger's side.

"Did you find a way in?" he asked.

"What makes you think I can see anything?" Dagger asked him.

"Well I am not going to swallow this whole magic and legends thing," Sarn smiled as he spoke, "but I figure if you think it works for you then who am I to question it."

"If it works for me, huh?" Dagger huffed. "It works for this world my friend and some day you will see the truth."

"I guess there could be these things as you say, but I doubt if I will ever believe them," Sarn chuckled, unable to hold it back any longer.

"Laugh if you feel you must, but do not close your mind. You were privileged to witness something the other day that only a few people ever get to see. Yet you still do not believe what your eyes have shown you. I feel a bit of pity for you my friend."

Sarn shook his head before asking him if he was hungry and

walking away. Dagger turned his head toward his companion for a second before turning back and placing the crystal again to his forehead.

"You did not answer my question," Sarn called from the other side of the campsite.

"I may have, but we need to be closer to have another look."

"Then I guess we will be finding another campsite after the morning meal."

"Yes, we will."

Sarn shook his head and walked back to where Sala was still sleeping and woke her.

"We need to move the camp."

"I thought that we might," she returned, wiping the sleep from her eyes. "I hope it will be down near the creek, I would like to bathe."

"You just bathed a couple of days ago," he laughed at her. "You cannot be in need of a bath already."

"I do not need one, I want one, and perhaps you will join me as well."

"I should think that you would have had your fill of me for a few days yet."

"Never enough of you my love," she added.

He laughed again, not quite sure what to say to her.

"Then I will just have to plead to one that is higher," she said as she stood. She looked over her shoulder smiling at him as she went toward Dagger.

"Yes girl," he said just before she reached him, "we will be next to the creek this afternoon."

On an impulse she leaned in and kissed him on the cheek and immediately regretted it.

"Never do that again," Dagger screamed. "You must never do that, it... it... well, it just is not a good idea."

He began to regret his words the moment he said them. Sala backed away begging for forgiveness offering to do anything to make up for it.

"I should be the one who is sorry," he told her, softening to her pleading. "I was just surprised and was not ready for it. You and Sarn have grown close to me and I should not be so resistant to some things."

She looked at him raising an eyebrow and tried to figure out if in fact he was the same person. He had always seemed distant from the two of them. Quite often she could not tell if he was with them or if in fact his mind was somewhere else.

"I am sorry that I bothered you. I did not mean any harm. I only meant to thank you."

"Of that I realize, but the next time, try giving me some sort of warning or something just to be on the safe side."

"Perhaps next time I should touch you for a second or two before going in for the kiss."

"Or you could just forget the kiss," he said, still not moving from his spot. "One would think that you would have no kisses left after a night with Sarn."

She giggled and walked away from him, her face turning red.

"Your face turns a nice shade," he said to her as she walked away. "Perhaps we should find us someone to marry you two after this is over."

"I just might have to let you," her smile growing as she got farther away from him.

She returned to the rock and Dagger a short time later with some cheese and bread for him to eat. It would be a short ride down the hill and to the creek but she figured they might as well have something to eat before they left. Sarn gathered the horses together and joined the two at the rock.

"Are the two of you going to sit here all day and discuss my life, or are we going to move this camp and perhaps rescue a boy?"

"We cannot rescue him today, perhaps tomorrow," Dagger said, standing from his rock and grabbing at his horse. "For now how about we find us a deer or bear and have a good hearty meal."

Dagger mounted his horse as he finished and waited for the others to do the same.

"I thought you told us that we would have to have a cold camp until we rescued him," Sala said as she mounted her horse.

"Yes, but that was before," Dagger replied and spurred his horse away from the group.

Sarn shrugged his shoulders and shook his head before giving Pel a pat on the neck. Moving the horse forward he pulled the reins of the packhorses as they too began following behind.

"You would think that we would be used to the way he talked to us," Sala called after him.

"You would think that, but it seems we forget every day."

Sala only laughed knowing that he was trying to make her feel better about the way Dagger had always seemed to treat them.

She felt as if he was shutting them out from his life and the things that they would be doing together. She had always known that it was not going to be an easy life. She also knew that she would be risking her own life just to be with Sarn, but somehow being there made perfect sense to her.

Tig was waiting for the group next to the creek by the time they reached its bank. He was lying on a large rock on the bank of the creek just above the top of the water waiting for his master. The small crystal no longer glowed as he held the collar in his mouth. It looked as if he were playing with it in his mouth as he waited. Flipping the collar up over his nose then raising his head he would let it hang just off the front of his nose. He shook his head from side to side with each flip of the collar as if he were showing it off to the animals in the woods around him. When the travelers arrived at his rock, he dropped his head as if he were a child and had just been caught doing something he was told not to do. Sala and Sarn laughed at him while Dagger, not quite sure what it was they were laughing at, just shook his head. Tig jumped off the rock and began to run circles around Sala and her horse. Laughing, she got down and the animal jumped up and placed a paw on either side of her face and began licking it. Giggling, she kept pushing Tig's face away from her own trying to get away from him, but with no success. After a while she just gave in and let him have his way.

"That would be enough Tig," Dagger called out after what seemed several minutes.

"You would think that he had not seen you in months and not just a few hours ago," Sarn added.

"I have not seen him act this way with anyone else. Just what were the two of you doing to my animal while I was away?"

Tig let go of Sala and wound his way around Sarn's legs several times before joining his master on the rock. Dagger took the animal by the neck and scratched at his ears and under his chin before the two sat together.

"You might want to find us a deer," Dagger said pulling the crystal from his pocket. "I think that we would all like a nice hot meal and I know that Tig is getting hungry. We kept him from hunting last night."

"Deer hunting," Sarn started, "I hope no one is that hungry."

"Tig can go with you. You will find him quite helpful when stalking prey, and if you get my bow from my horse you will have an easier time."

"You have a bow? You mean to tell me that you have been having me hunt all this time with my knife and you have a bow?"

"Yes, how could you have missed it? It is right there next to my broad sword."

"I never noticed it I suppose."

"Then you should pay closer attention. I have been telling you for weeks now that you needed to be more observant. You cannot continue to act as if there is a place that you can bury your head."

"I understand," was all Sarn said as he reached for the bow.

Dagger walked to him and showed him how to bend the bow and attach the string.

"You will need to find something to use for arrow shafts as I do not carry them, but you will find some points in one of the packs."

Sala grabbed his packs and began looking though them, while Sarn set about finding some branches to use for the shafts. It did not take him long to find three small branches that he felt he would be able to strip and turn into an arrow. Sala found the points and the two sat side by side at the base of the rock where Dagger and Tig sat and worked. It did not take them long to come up with three good arrows that he could use.

"Make sure that you find us a good deer," Dagger told him when he was finished.

Leaning into Tig he whispered into his ear before telling him to go off with Sarn. Sala kissed them both goodbye and headed for the creek.

Tig took the lead as he bounced off into the woods, with Sarn following close behind.

When the two were far enough away Dagger rose and went over to the creek and slipped in near where Sala was beginning her bath. He began removing his clothes once in the water before tossing them back toward the bank. Sala was a bit surprised to see him in the water but made no attempt to get out.

"This is something new," she called out to him.

"I have taken baths before," Dagger returned a bit startled.

"I just have never seen you do it in front of anyone until now."

"Well I ...," he began trying to think of what to tell her. "I just needed a bath is all."

In truth Dagger had not been paying attention and he had thought that she had gone with Sarn and not to the creek.

"I will stay downstream and you can bathe where you are. That way everything will stay proper and your man will have nothing to fear from me," he added.

"I would think that he has nothing to fear from you just the same."

"Perhaps, but just you stay on your end any way. My cousin would be upset I think if I caused any harm to your arrangement with Sarn."

"Your cousin?" Sala asked.

"Mara," he said, "she seems to have taken a liking to the two of you."

"She is your cousin?" Sala asked again, turning a deep shade of red and turning away out of habit.

"That she is. I have known of her all her life, but I have never known her to take to anyone like she has to the two of you."

Sala turned a deeper shade of red and stumbled on a rock on the bottom of the creek.

"Well," she returned as soon as she caught her thoughts again. "She is an attentive girl and quite likable, I believe that we like her just as much."

"She will be happy to hear that the next time we pass through there," he said turning away from her and moving just a bit further downstream.

Sala smiled and moved a little farther away from him as well.

"Well Tig, where do you suppose we can find us a big buck for our dinner?" Sarn asked as if he believed that Tig knew just what it was that he was saying.

Tig pushed against him forcing him to turn to his left.

"Over there, is that where they are?" Sarn chuckled as he went the way that Tig wanted him to go. "Maybe I should listen to you after all; you do have the bigger nose."

Tig lowered and shook his head as they went along.

"If I thought about it long enough, I might have to start believing that you just might understand what it is that I am saying."

Tig pushed Sarn to a place just on the edge of a small meadow. He found a place to hide among some bushes and crouched behind some of its branches. Tig went around the meadow and began to work his way toward the center. Sarn watched him move across the meadow as if he were crawling, his nose stuck to the ground one second then in the air the next. He chuckled a little to himself as the action of the animal reminded him of the turtles he used to watch on the shores of the lake back home. He did watch him close though trying to see if he could find what it was that Tig was tracking. Testing the bow he waited hoping that it was a deer that he was sniffing for. Just as Tig reached half the distance across the meadow he saw it rising from the tall grass. Just the horns at first, then the top of its head; he cursed himself for not having found a higher place to hide. Tig stopped mid stride as the deer tossed its nose to the air. Sarn sat motionless as he watched the animal's nostrils flare as it sniffed at the air for a second before lowering its head again. Tig began to move again, his head low to the ground as he went. Only now he knew where the animal was. Testing the bow Sarn stood up in his hiding place and waited for the deer to rise again. Tig began circling to the outside of where the deer lay. Sarn stepped back breaking a twig causing the animal to jump from his hiding place. Not wanting to miss what might be his only chance he let the arrow fly towards the large animal. He cursed himself again as he knew that there was no way that the arrow would reach its intended target. He watched as the poorly timed arrow flew into the grass less than half the distance to where the deer had been hiding. He could do nothing but watch as the deer bolted away.

"Just as well I guess," he muttered. "I never could have carried that back to the campsite anyway."

Tig looked for a second to Sarn and shook his head before turning and going after the fleeing animal. Noticing what was happening Sarn jumped from the bushes and at the same time made another arrow ready in his bow. Catching up with the deer Tig jumped in front of it forcing it to turn back toward the hurried Sarn. It seemed to take the boy several seconds to aim and pull the arrow back in the bow, but when he felt sure it was all the way back he let the arrow fly. It was a lucky shot as he would tell himself later, but that would not be the story he would tell Sala and Dagger later as they ate it. The arrow struck the deer in the neck burying itself half way up its shaft and completely through it. He could have sworn he saw the arrow turn into the animal as it flew away from him. The animal carried on for several minutes into the forest before it finally dropped. It left behind a large blood trail that he and Tig followed with ease.

"Lucky for us that it turned towards our camp," Sarn said as he gutted the animal. "I think I just may have saved us a step or two."

Tig disappeared as the animal finally dropped and returned with the lost arrow.

"I am glad that you thought of getting this," he said as Tig dropped the arrow at his feet. "I do not think that your master would be happy with us if we had not returned with the same amount of arrows."

As he finished gutting the deer Sarn cut a piece from the stomach and tossed it to Tig. The animal made no pretense of waiting to be joined as he took the piece and made quick work of eating it. Once he had the animal gutted he hefted it testing its weight. It was a bit heavier than he had hoped, but then again he realized from the beginning that it was not going to be easy. He lifted the deer again, put it across his shoulders and began to make his way back to the campsite. While the way was not hard going or long, he did need to stop several times before he was able to make it back.

Sala saw him coming through the trees and went to help him, giving Dagger an opening to get out of the creek. Slipping behind a bush near the creek Dagger waited until Tig got closer so that he could get him to get his clothes.

"I think I may have gone too far with this deer," Sarn said setting it down as Sala reached him.

"Do you think it too small?"

"Funny," Sarn added wiping sweat from his forehead.

She took hold of the hind legs and allowed him the pleasure of the front, as she put it. The two carried the animal into the campsite. Sarn grabbed a rope from the packhorses and tossed an end over a large low hanging branch from one of the nearby trees. They lifted the dead animal off the ground by its hind legs and Sala began to strip it of its hide.

"Why not go to the creek and take a bath," she told him, as she pulled her cooking knives and sharpening stone from a small pack. "I have little intention in sleeping next to your blood stained body."

"And here I thought that you liked it when I got all bloody."

"From battle perhaps, not from dinner, but worry not you will be rewarded well for bringing in such a wonderful dinner." She smiled and waved him to the creek.

"In that case I think that I can arrange a proper bath," he chuckled before running toward the creek.

Running over the rock he jumped into the creek clothes and all. Dagger tossed him some soap as he came from the bush that he had used to dress behind.

"You might want to use some of this," he said as Sarn caught it.

"Do you think I need it?" Sarn asked as a joke

"Unless I am mistaken you carried your kill on your shoulders. Unless you did not clean it at the spot it fell then you should have a bloody neck and back, perhaps even some on the front of you."

"I got a deer, what more do you expect of me?"

"Perhaps, you should have dragged it instead or brought it back here before you cleaned it."

Once he was in the water Sarn took off his clothes washing the blood from each piece before tossing the cleaned item onto the creek bank. Tig took his place on the rock while looking back and forth between the three of them.

"It took him long enough to get back with it," Dagger said as he walked up to Sala and touched the animal. "At least it is of good size. I am surprised that he was able to carry it by himself."

Sala shook her head and rolled her eyes.

"I had hoped that you would have gone with him to help so that we could eat sooner."

"May I suggest then that you start a fire," she returned.

"I am not sure that I can do that."

"Well of course not, you can only complain that you are hungry," she snapped back. "I find it hard to believe that you can find your way down a road and into a tavern, but you cannot see to gather up a few sticks and start a fire. I am beginning to wonder how you survived on your own for so long."

"Hmm, it seems to me I have just been put in my place once again."

Smiling Dagger turned away from her and left her to her chore. Sala shook her head surprised at herself, and yet had no idea where what she had just said had come from. Dagger called to Tig and they headed towards the tree line grabbing a few downed branches as they went. It was not long before Sarn returned and wrapped his arms around her as she tried to work. Holding her from behind, he began kissing her neck.

"You had better be careful," she half joked. "We may never get this deer butchered in time for us to have a midnight meal, let alone an evening meal."

"Then perhaps I should give you a hand," he told her picking up one of her knives.

As the travelers worked in their camp, a fire was lit on the lawn at the summer estate of Lord Dermit. It was still daylight as the guards at the palace lay torches to a pile of tree limbs and broken furniture. The guards had spent all morning and part of the afternoon piling the branches near the house so they would not be noticed from a distance. When the time came they used it to make several piles on the lawn. Tig turned first, sniffing at the air and tilting his head from side to side. It was not long before Dagger noticed the change in the air as well. Turning toward the palace he dropped his armload of branches and reached into his cloak for the crystal. Gripping it tight he watched as the guards were lighting another fire. Cursing, he let go of the crystal and picked his load of branches back up. He wasted no time in bringing them out of the woods and setting them down a short way from the water's edge near the rock. Tig led his master, pulling a good sized limb behind him with his teeth.

Sala notice his efforts and when he dropped the tree limb she rewarded him by throwing a fist sized piece of meat at him. Tig jumped toward the meat and caught it in the air.

"Try not to swallow that whole," she called to him as he caught it.

"Now I know why he likes the two of you better, you feed him."

"Not that you do anymore," she returned.

"What do you guess that is all about?" She asked as she saw the fires that were now beginning to burn on the palace lawn.

Sarn turned from his work as a third fire was lit. The travelers watched as the guards worked around the fire. It was as if they were in a trance for a few seconds, not speaking, perhaps not seeing either.

"Do you think that they saw Tig last night?" Sarn asked finally.

"I do not think so or they would have come looking for him today."

"What do you think the reason for the fires?" he asked him. "You do not think that they have seen us?"

"They may have seen us," Dagger returned. "But I do not think that they believe us a threat or they would have come to us."

"Unless, perhaps, they do not have enough guards there and they wish us to believe that there are more of them," Sala chimed in.

"Perhaps," Sarn and Dagger said together nodding their heads.

"Then again," Dagger said, "there just might be more guards up in that small palace than the three of us could deal with in a week."

"In that case cousin," a voice from behind them called out, "I suppose that you will need our help."

Turning the three watched as a group walked out from the woods.

"If you think that deer is large enough to feed all of us you will be sadly mistaken."

"Canis," Dagger called out. "From what swamp is it that you crawled out of this day?"

"Cousin Ryn," Canis called back, "please do not tell of family dirt in front of my troops."

"What are you talking about? Half of them crawled out of the same swamp."

The two cousins embraced, each laughing at the other. Each member of his group carried an armload of branches. They dropped them one at time with the ones that Dagger had brought from the woods. Two of them stepped in and took over the job of butchering the deer, while the rest went off into the woods in different directions.

Dagger introduced the couple to his cousin.

"The rest of them," Canis said pointing in the directions that the others had gone. "Well, let us just say that you will have little time to learn their names, and they are not important anyway. Besides, if you did learn them you could face other problems just for knowing of them."

"What took you so long?" asked Dagger, pulling his cousin away from his companions.

The two talked as they walked to the rock. Each looked to the summer palace before sitting down and huddling together.

"I will only say that you made things a bit more difficult than we had talked about the last time we met," Canis began. "If you remember you had told me that you were going to meet me in the mountains after you took back the tablet."

"Is Tobias to join us?" Ryn asked, interrupting him and avoiding his statement.

"Tobias," Canis laughed, "when I saw him last he was locked in your home guarded by not less than eight of our brethren."

"Who locked him up?" Dagger asked, but was sure that he already knew the answer.

"Who is it that you think?"

"Grandmother never did like him, or grandfather for that matter."

"I cannot say as I blame them. As for myself I agree with their reasons. If it were not for him your parents would not have found you the time they locked you in that cage."

"That cage gave you a chance to show off for me," Dagger chuckled, "besides he has his uses."

"None that we can use on this occasion," Canis returned. "Not that showing off has ever done me any good, judging by your present company."

"The company that I keep today has nothing to do with whether you impressed me by your actions that day."

"I only ever asked to join you."

"It is not possible, you know that," Dagger turned away and looked to the palace as he spoke. "I must do this alone. You and I are destined to cross paths only as needed, nothing more."

"I would understand it better if I knew just what your path was."

"I am not even sure if I understand it all."

"Then why is it that you continue to follow it at all."

"I am not ready to quit. Besides, look at those two. Do you think they would have any chance of getting where they need to go without me?"

"It is where they are going that concerns me."

"Why should it concern you?" Dagger asked in return. "It does not seem to worry them and they do not know what their destiny is either."

"And I imagine that you do?"

"No, my destiny is not known," returned Dagger, trying to keep from having to say any more about his companions.

"Tell me then why it is that you accept it without looking where it will take you?"

Dagger chuckled under his breath and pointed to his face.

"That is not the way it was meant and you know it."

"I know cousin."

"It is just that everything you do seems to have no real purpose," Canis continued. You do not seem committed to protecting any of what our ancestors pledged to protect. You spent so much time training this boy that we almost lost the tablet."

"We got the tablet. Why are you concerned with how much time it took me to train him? He was worth the time and effort even if it had taken longer."

"Perhaps that is true, but we would have gotten it weeks earlier and perhaps this would not have happened."

"Cousin, the two are no more connected than I am to this rock and the air that surrounds it." Dagger tossed his hands in the air annoyed with the conversation. "You know nothing of my path, nothing of what I am meant to do."

"And according to you, you know only a little of it yourself."

"The difference is I am the one living it." Dagger leaned in closer to Canis and took hold of his hands. "We are here for a more important purpose. Do not let feelings get into the way of that."

"I know we are here to rescue a future King from certain harm and return him to his family." he said putting his hands on his hips and thrusting his chest out. "Now there is something that has never been done before."

Dagger nodded his head ignoring his cousin, knowing that there was more to it than just a rescue, much more. Instead he turned away and watched Sarn and Sala. The two worked in silence, building the fire getting it ready to cook over. One by one the men reappeared. Two carried a smaller deer between them on a pole, while others had some wild vegetables. The men made quick work of getting everything ready for the cooking fire. All while keeping an eye on the six fires that were now burning around the summer palace.

Dagger and Canis stayed together on the rock as those around them went about their chores. Dagger facing the palace holding the crystal to his forehead again, while Canis watched over the group. The camp became a flurry of activity. Some of them were cleaning and cutting up the two deer while the rest were busy sharpening their swords and fashioning arrows. None of the new arrivals spoke to the three travelers, not that Sala wanted to speak to them anyway. The larger of the two deer was placed over the fire, while the smaller one was cut to smaller pieces to be dried during the night. Sarn was busy watching over her while Dagger with the crystal to his head, was not paying attention to any of them. There was something about them that kept Sarn wary of the new arrivals. He could not understand why he felt the way he did, he just hoped that he was wrong. All the while from a point somewhere outside the camp, Tig lay content watching over them all.

"I should hope that one of you is planning to get some more wood for this fire or we will not eat this eve," Canis said, standing and stepping off the rock. "That will take until morning at this rate and I for one am hungry now."

Three of his troops shook their heads and went out into the woods. One of them handed Sala some of the strips of meat to add to the heat of the fire. She did not seem to mind, but Sarn was a bit put out that she was expected to cook for them as well. Then again, he doubted that they had ever been around a woman that was not in camp to do anything, but cook and see to their needs. Sala staked out the strips of meat and set them over the fire. Sarn grabbed his sword and walked to the edge of the creek and looked out over the meadows on the other side to the palace. His mind wandered to thoughts of home as he began thinking of his mother. He wondered who was helping them with their garden and the grass that would be needed for the livestock for the winter.

With their evening meal complete, the remaining strips of meat were placed over the fire to be smoked over what remained of the fire. The company then found themselves sitting around laughing and swapping stories. They still kept to themselves speaking in hushed tones, forcing Sarn and Sala out of their circle. It did not seem to bother them as the two shook their heads and left them to their stories. The couple found a comfortable spot next to a large tree and curled up with each other on the thick moss that grew there. A cheer went up as Canis joined his men around the fire. The company of men paid little attention to the palace or the guards, leaving all of that to Dagger.

"It is best that you do not get to know them that well anyway," Dagger told the two as he came over to where they were curled up. "Tig will be close by. These men need but one reason to slit our throats."

"You do not trust your own cousin?" Sarn asked.

"Him, yes, these other swamp bred elves, no."

"You and your folktales," Sarn said shaking his head not believing his friend. "I wish I knew where it was that you get your stories from."

"What is it that you find so hard to believe?" Dagger asked. "If I were to tell you that I was half elf, what would you say to that?"

"I would ask you what you did to your ears."

"My ears?" he asked.

"Yes, they are not pointed," Sarn chuckled.

"Pointed? You listen to wives tales and believe them. Yet when you are told the truth, you think it is all lies. I am half elf," he began. "Canis is more so than I, none of my family has pointed ears or the green skin that we are supposed to have."

"And what of the magic that you elves are said to have?"

"Magic, what do you know of magic?" Dagger asked walking

away from the two.

"You should not have attacked him so," Sala whispered into his ear as he left.

"He speaks as if fairy tales are real."

"How can you attack fairy tales?" Sala began. "Have you forgotten some of the things that you have seen; what of my wounds? How many hours did we sit in front of Janua's tavern without the sun moving across the sky? When it did move, do you remember how fast it set? One moment it was high in the sky and the next it was almost night. Say what you want my love, but I for one believe many of those fairy tales I was told as a child."

"My mother would tell me tales when I was younger, but I always found them hard to believe." Sarn began remembering the nights sitting at his mother's feet in front of the fireplace on some cold winter night. "My father would laugh at them and tell me how it was not possible for some of them to be true and how he doubted that any could be true. I guess I just believe him more than my mother or Dagger. I do not understand how you could believe in them."

"Perhaps it is because I have seen more of what happens in this world than you have. I cannot believe I ever fell in love with a person like you, someone who cannot see what is as plain as his face."

"It must have been the way I am with you under the covers," he said chuckling, pulling her close and kissing her.

"Yes, I am sure that is what I found so worthy in you to love."

The two chuckled and rolled to the ground in the other's arms. They pulled their blankets up over them and began to fall asleep on the soft bed of moss. Dagger was sitting once again on the rock with the crystal to his forehead. He looked over at the two for a second as they curled up under their blankets before looking back at the palace and its fires.

"Sleep well," he whispered, "everything is going to be fine."

Tig, who had been lying next to Dagger on his rock, stood, walked around his master twice before lying at the feet of the couple.

At the palace, the guards in fact had noticed the group on the other side of the creek as soon as they had arrived earlier in the day. One of them had gone to the edge of the creek and found Dagger and Sala bathing in it. He watched for a while and returned to the palace when Sarn had returned with the deer reporting what he had seen to his superior. It was then that he ordered the fires, as he put it, to keep the hunters away and aware of their presence.

"What if they are more than hunters?"

"If there are just the three we will kill them like the others. We keep the boy here and alive just like we have been ordered to do."

"And if more arrive?" asked a third guard.

"You will watch for more if it will rest your thoughts," the commanding guard told him. "I have little doubt that there will be more of them. These are good hunting grounds and we are not but three days from the nearest village."

"These are but children," the first said nodding his head in agreement. "I do not think we have anything to worry from them."

An hour after the sun went down in a room overlooking the fires on the palace grounds, the prisoner peered out the window. His eyes immediately went to the small fire on the other side of the creek. He had overheard some of his guards earlier talking about what was believed to be a small hunting party. They had said they were not worried about them being rescuers, but did order the boy to be kept on the upper floors.

"Do you think that they have come to rescue us?" the boy asked.

"If they catch you looking out they will throw you in the cellar again," she warned him. Even though she knew it would do no good to tell him.

"What do you know, you are just a girl?"

"I am older than you are," she returned.

"I am a prince you are not," he returned, with the spoiled attitude that he was noted for.

"Your mother told me to look out for you before we left the palace," she said taking his attitude all in stride. "I would like to think that she would want me to keep doing so."

The Prince shook his head and walked away from the window. He did not look up as he walked past the girl and went out of the room. The captors had allowed the two to roam about the old palace. They found it much easier to deal with their charge if he was not confined to just one room. The few hidden passages in the palace were known and had been blocked before they could be found by young Gregor. The Prince went up to the next floor and went into the room where his parents had stayed and sat on the window seat.

"Do you think they miss me?" the boy asked her as he looked

out into the night.

"I think that they want you safe."

"We have been here for months, why have they not come for me, us?"

"It is just a matter of time before some of your father's men come to take you to him."

"You mean like the day after we were taken?"

"You do remember what happened to those soldiers?"

He nodded his head as the vision of the mutilated bodies flashed through his mind.

"Then I would think that you would not wish that for any more of your father's men to come after you." She was trying not to talk anymore of what had happened that day. "If he would only pay them what they want, you could be home in just a few days."

"I do not think that these men are after a payment of gold for my return. I heard one saying that they wanted father to give up his Kingdom for my return."

The boy pushed aside the heavy fabric and stared out the window across the creek, watching the light from the small fire flicker in the darkness. He could not help himself from wondering if perhaps the fire was not that of his father's men. In a way he prayed that they were, but then again he hoped that they were not.

With the crystal in his hand Dagger watched the boy as he peered out from behind the heavy window covers.

"There you are your majesty," Dagger whispered. "Now let me just look a bit closer; keep looking at me just a little bit longer."

Placing the crystal back on his forehead, he counted the guards and worked his way into the summer palace. He saw each room through the eyes of the boy, each step counted, each door opened. He smiled to himself as he lowered the crystal and returned it to his pocket. The camp had finally become quiet, Canis and his men having fallen asleep sometime after the middle of the night. An hour later he called out to Tig in a near whisper, and then woke his two companions.

"Are you sure you have thought this through?" Sarn asked him after he told him his plan.

"That is the beauty of it," Dagger returned. "Come let us rescue ourselves a prince."

"If we are going to do this by ourselves, then pray tell me what are they doing here?" Sala asked.

"They are here to be here," Dagger laughed as he grabbed at

one of his packs and opened it checking its contents. Satisfied he tossed the pack to Sarn and sent the couple to get two more packs from the horses along with their weapons.

"I guess that means that we are going to cross the creek," Sarn joked as the two grabbed their weapons.

Sala shook her head unsure if they were doing the right thing, but where they went, she would go. Tig watched over the sleeping men as the travelers gathered everything they would need.

The rescuers waded into the creek several yards upstream of their camp, Sarn and Sala followed close behind by Dagger and Tig. The water was not as deep as in front of their campsite but it still reached their waists before reaching the other side. Once there they crawled behind a group of bushes making sure that each was all right before going any further. Taking the lead Sarn stepped around the bushes before bumping into the point of a spear.

"Stand," demanded the voice at the end of the spear.

Sarn finished coming out of hiding and stood, trying to make out in the dark just how far away the man was from him.

He felt the air move before he heard it and dropped to his knees as a knife passed over his head. Staying low he heard another pass over him even closer to his head. The guard let out a groan and fell to the ground.

"You missed," Sarn said as the guard went down.

"You had better look again," Sala answered. "I got him with both of them."

Dagger laughed and pushed Sarn aside. Tig rubbed against the two of them as he passed and went on ahead. Sala pulled the first knife from the guard's right shoulder and the second from his neck. She took time in wiping them on the dead man's clothes before they moved on.

"I think that perhaps you have trained her too well," Sarn whispered as Dagger moved past him.

"Are you afraid of her now?"

"I think that I do not want to ever make her angry at me from across the room."

Dagger chuckled and Sala joined him.

The path was dark, but well defined even in the near pitch black of the night. Keeping to the shadows the travelers crept over the short wall and to the edge of the lawn. Dagger pointed his finger toward the other side of the palace and the two nodded and followed Tig. The fires surrounded the palace. It was not exactly what he had hoped for, but with a little luck they would at least still be able to get inside. Finding what he felt was a spot that was not guarded as well the rest, Dagger held up his hand and waved the others closer.

Tig crouched just inside of the tree line and as a guard passed he circled around and shoved the guard into the trees. Sarn covered the guard's mouth and hit him over the head. Removing his uniform each of the three soon found that it was too large for any of them.

Shrugging his shoulders, Sarn's smile seemed to say, 'next'. They waited as the next guard passed and Tig did his part, again knocking him into the trees. The three went to work at his uniform, again finding that it was too large for any of them. They tied the two guards and gagged them before covering them with some dead branches. Wasting no more time they crept closer to the tree line before sprinting toward the palace and took cover behind the bushes that ran the length of the palace. The rescuers crept along the wall looking for the opening that Tig had found the night before. Dagger took a second and placed the crystal to his forehead and looked around ensuring himself that they could still not be seen. Satisfied, he pointed Sarn and Sala toward the small door at the foot of the wall.

There was a space in the bushes that hid them exposing the door and them. Sala went first, her sword drawn at the ready. The door was easy to open, and she slipped inside. Sarn followed as did Tig and Dagger. The four of them found themselves sliding down an incline and falling into a pile of wood. There was little they could do about the noise, but after waiting for a response from the guards the three let out a nervous chuckle. Tig was already searching for the door that would lead them out of the cellar. Joining Tig in his search Sarn felt along the walls looking for a door. It did not take them long before they found it. Turning, he called to his companions before pulling on the door. Dagger stood with his sword ready at the opening of the door and Sala with hers just to the side. They were relieved to find that there was no one on the other side and the crept into the scullery. The cooking fire lit the room just enough for them to see where they were headed. Crossing the room and heading out to the hallway the rescuers made their way deeper into the palace.

"Where are the guards?" Sala asked.

Dagger put his finger to his lips to quiet her, and then pointed ahead of them. The others caught on trying to walk as quiet as possible through the hall. Tig sniffed at the air and stopped in their path, causing Dagger to almost trip over him. Sarn heard the movement behind them before he saw it. Crouching with his sword pointed to the floor he waited as the guard turned the corner behind them.

Before the guard could react, Sarn swung his blade up and caught the man under his chin. He pushed just hard enough to get his attention.

"Do we need him?" he asked.

The guard swallowed hard, terror in his eyes as he closed them as if to pray.

"We may have use for him. Bring him forward."

Sarn pushed him forward as the guard breathed a sigh of relief.

"That does not mean that I will not kill you if you prove me wrong," Dagger told the man, pressing one of his silver daggers into the soft flesh below his ribs.

Sweat began to form on his forehead in the relative cool of the hallway.

"Take us to the Prince."

"No."

"Then we will just kill you here," Dagger said before calling Tig. "My friend here will make sure that it is a painful death."

If the guard had seen the animal before it clamped its large jaws around his leg, he had not let on. As Tig growled and bit down just a little more, an unmistakable odor began to fill the air.

"I think he is afraid now," Sala said chuckling a little.

Sarn smiled and shook his head trying not to laugh. He knew that if the roles were reversed, he might have done the same thing.

"Did you forget to relieve yourself before coming on duty?" Dagger asked trying to be serious about the matter. "Now will you take us to the Prince?"

With his eyes wide open and his body shaking in what could only be fear, the man nodded his head.

Sala took a strip of cloth and pushed it into his mouth, then pulled it tight around his head to keep him quiet, before tying his hands together.

"I will tell you this," Dagger added. "If you take us anywhere but to the Prince, my friend there will be more than happy to feed on your remains. That is, after of course, he tears out your throat."

He was still shaking in fear but he nodded his head in

agreement.

Tig followed close to the guard as he led the way down the hall to the stairs. He kept bumping against the guard as they walked, as if to remind him that he was still close by. The group looked around before disappearing up the stairs.

Canis snapped awake and looked over to the rock where Dagger had been sitting. He shook his head as he noticed that the three of them were gone. He didn't have to look around to know that Tig was with them. Getting up, he woke the closest man to him.

"You will need to cross the creek and stand watch."

"What of your cousin and his animal?"

"Unless I am mistaken they have begun their rescue."

"What is it with him? Why does he ask our help if he does not use it?"

"I promise you will bloody your sword many times before the sunrises this day."

"Why does he always seem to go alone?" he asked, half knowing the answer to his own question.

"Alone?" Canis replied. "He is with them and they are to help him in this part. We are here to see to it that they get a chance to return the boy to his home. If we were all to rush...."

"Then none of us would get any of the reward," the other interrupted. He stood and sliced off a large chunk of the venison being kept warm over the fire. "We should see to it that the rest of this is not wasted."

"I will have the others take care of that. You get over there and make sure we don't have any visitors," Canis called after the man.

Waking another of his men, Canis gave him orders to wake the others and to be ready to leave.

His troops woke mumbling profanities, but they rose and set about their chores.

Many asked about the girl and why she was not the one doing the work. Canis told them where she was and no more was said of the matter.

"You come across one woman, and you all grow soft. Maybe it will be a good thing if I no longer allow you close to another woman again."

They voiced their objections with a few brief well-chosen words before returning to the chore of breaking camp, storing things as best they could in the packs and seeing to the loading of the horses. The remaining meat was carved up and what was not ready was tossed into the fire. Some of the meat was portioned out to the men to carry while a majority of it was wrapped in salt and placed in the horses' packs.

A couple of the men began admiring the travelers' horses. They even began a small argument about which one would get Pel when the rescuers did not return. When the men turned back to continue their chores, Pel turned and backed away from the group, pushing Sala's and Dagger's horses away with him. Followed by their packhorses Pel led them away from the men. Sala's horse followed behind the others as they found their way across the creek.

Reaching the top of the stairs they made their way through the dim light of the upper hallway. Again Sarn felt that someone else was nearby before he could hear or see them. When he came to the first doorway he stopped and backed against the closed door as the others continued along the hallway. Pushing up against it he tried to become as small as possible. The low light of the lamps at either end of the hallway cast crossing shadows down the hall. He began to blend into his surroundings, completely hidden in the shadow of the doorway. Had anyone been watching, they would have claimed the boy had disappeared or had become part of the wall surrounding him. He counted each set of footsteps as they came behind them.

"Two," he said under his breath, "no three."

He listened as his companions reached the end of the hall and turned the corner. As the oncoming footsteps got closer he took a deep breath, holding it deep in his chest and waited. Watching as they passed in front of him, they were three steps beyond him when he stepped out behind them. Following them, Sarn echoed the steps of the guards as they walked.

'What am I doing?' he thought, 'I am behind three guards that would kill me if they saw me. If they see me, when they see me is more like it.'

He kept behind them as they reached the end of the hall. Turning, the guards began down the same hall as his companions. Halfway down he stopped and stepped into the next doorway pushing into the darkness again. He was not sure why he did it until the three turned suddenly and headed back in the direction they came. Sarn waited several seconds until he slipped out of the shadows again and went to rejoin the others.

"Where did you go?" Sala asked when he reached them.

"He was following us," Dagger said, stopping short of a true explanation."

Sarn was glad that Dagger answered her for him, he was sure that she would not have liked the truth. Somehow even he could not have told her everything and believed it. Dagger poked the guard again, pushing him to move. As they turned down the front hallway Sarn again slipped into the shadows of a doorway. Pressing into the shadows he held his breath and listened to the footsteps. He then began separating those of his companions and those of the guards by the rhythm of their walks. If he had been asked about it, he would not have been able to say how he was able to separate the footsteps of each person, it just seemed to happen. Dagger's footsteps were first, then Sala's and Tig's and then those of the bound guard. That left him with just his own heartbeat and the footsteps of two others. He waited as they turned and went into a room further down the hall. He was about to step out behind the two guards as they passed him, yet, something told him that there was at least one more. Counting off their beat as they walked, he singled them out and listened again to another rhythm of steps. They were trying to echo those steps of the guards to hide in their sounds as he had done before. Only this one was just a little off the beat of the others. He pushed himself even further into the wall as if he were trying to become part of it. Closing his eyes he felt his heart beating harder in his chest. As the footsteps stopped in front of him he felt their breath on his neck.

"With all the men in this Kingdom they send a boy retrieve their Prince."

Sarn swallowed hard squeezing his eyes shut tighter, as if he were playing a child's game.

"Closing your eyes will not help hide you from me."

"It could not hurt," Sarn said, opening his eyes.

The dark figure loomed over his head and he looked straight into the covered face.

"I know you," the voice said, "but ... where?"

"I do not believe that we have ever met. I am certain that I would remember an ugly face such as yours."

He was surprised at how calm he had become as he spoke. It was as if something deep inside him had told him that he had little to fear from the person behind the voice.

"If you could see it that is," he said turning away from Sarn.

"True," Sarn lied. His face was just as clear to him as if it they were outside in the daytime.

"Do not bother swinging that sword at me. It does not have the power to kill me."

Tilting his head as if he were trying to figure out how he knew what he was doing, Sarn lowered his sword.

"I would guess that your companions have already made their way into the Prince's room, and at this moment are waiting for you to join them before trying to get out of here."

"Perhaps," Sarn said. "Then again I could be here alone."

"I doubt that, Sarn of Penif," the figure laughed as if he had just figured out who he was talking to. "The great thief Ryn Mar would not allow you with in a thousand leagues of this place alone."

"If I agree with you, what happens then?"

"Nothing," the figure returned, surprised that he had not lied. "Neither of you have a chance of getting out of here alive."

"A bit of a fairy tale saying, but I will allow you to use it." He had no idea how he collected so much courage to think it, let alone say it.

"Fairy tales, ah yes, that is right you are not a believer; no doubt your father's idea."

"What do you know of my father?"

"I met him once, hiding as a stone cutter if I remember."

"My father hides from no man."

"True, he does not hide from a man, only from his heritage, just as he keeps it from you," the man said walking away from him. "Let us go and see if you are alone Sarn of Penif."

He was not sure why he seemed so obedient in following the man, but he did, keeping his sword ready to strike.

The man laughed as they reached the door that the others had entered. He pushed the door open without saying a word. Sala stood alone in the middle of the room with her back to them and her arms out to her side, not that she was surprised by their appearance. Dagger had warned her that she should expect the tall man in black.

"Ah, well, it would appear that you have come with someone. You must be the scullery wench, Sala. Where have Ryn and that animal gone to? Has he taken our Prince away and left the two of you behind to pay the price? It would not surprise me in the least if they are gone. I do believe that it would not be the first time that it has been done by them. I seem to remember another time. But that is a story that is better left for another time."

"He has not gone far and will not leave without us I am sure," Sarn replied.

"I would think a second time if I were you, as I said it is not the first time Ryn has slipped away leaving others to pay for his crimes. It is just as well, because you my boy will bring and even better prize than Prince Gregor could ever bring. As for your woman there I am sure that my men will be happy when I give her to them for their pleasures."

Turning around and facing the two, she watched wide eyed as Sarn swung his sword catching the tall man across the back of his head. Falling to his knees the man laughed as Sarn hit him again before plunging his sword into his back. Still laughing he leaned to one side and ended up on the floor. A few seconds later the man lay silent as his blood spilled from the wound made by Sarn's sword.

"Where did Dagger go to?" he asked Sala.

"Come on you two," Dagger called from the hall. "Take Prince Gregor and head to the front door and wait for me there."

"I will not leave without my friend," Gregor said.

"And with any luck you will not. Now leave with them, they will protect you."

Grabbing the boy by the arm Sarn led him out and down the hall. Dagger made a quick whistle and Tig bounded out the door behind the others. Kneeling next to the body on the floor he placed a hand on the man's shoulder and leaned closer.

"He may not be able to kill you right now and I am not sure if I can either," Dagger began. "What I can do, is make it difficult for you to follow us any time soon."

The man groaned as he rolled over. Sarn' s sword had entered his lung and he was having some trouble with his breathing. Yet as Dagger looked down, his bleeding stopped and the wound began to heal.

"Now that had to hurt. I can only guess how much your head still hurts," Dagger added once the man was looking up at him.

"I have no fear of you Ryn Mar, for I am above you," he said trying to laugh. "You are nothing but a breed, and breeds are worthless in this world."

"In that case, I have something for you." Dagger reached into his cloak, pulling out the dagger he had used to kill Zendar. "I am quite sure that you recognize it."

Dagger held the knife close his face to make sure that he saw the blade. He thought he heard him gasp but the man had just struggled to take a deeper breath.

"Ah, yes, you are correct. It is the blade of Dracor. Do you remember him or is his memory completely gone now?"

"Never gone thief; he is part of me, never gone."

"I know you still remember Zendar and Polav. Oh, and of course you could never forget my personal favorite, Genevieve."

The man screamed, taking a swing at Dagger but missing him.

"How dare you speak that name thief! You are not worthy enough to speak that name!"

"Then stand and face me Crel so that we can end this game, for now at least. I have many leagues to go before the sun rises."

Struggling, Crel rose to his feet.

"For someone who claims that he cannot be killed, you are having a hard time getting off the floor."

"When you have been on this plane as long as I have it will take some effort for you to pick yourself up off the floor as well."

Dagger laughed as he lifted his sword in one hand and the dagger in his other.

"You do know of course, that even that dagger you hold in your hand cannot kill me."

"That is the trouble with you Crel, you always think that I want to kill you." It was Dagger's turn to laugh now. "I know that I am not allowed to kill you and that is why I do not have that power. Yet I do so enjoy all the times that you have tried to kill me."

Crel raised his hands and flicked his fingers toward Dagger, lifting him up off the floor and throwing him across the room.

"You are no match for me Ryn Mar," Crel laughed as Dagger shook his head and stood up.

Charging again, Crel flicked his fingers and again Dagger flew across the room.

"I thought that you wished this over."

"And I thought you were all powerful," Dagger said standing and charging again.

"Will you never give up?" Crel lifted his hands above his head and threw them down and toward the charging Dagger.

As he was lifted off his feet Ryn threw the dagger as hard as he could toward Crel. The dagger sailed through the air and struck Crel in the chest driving him back several feet. Ryn slammed up against the wall on the other side of the room as the dagger found its mark. Seeming to bounce off the wall he landed on his feet and ran toward him again. This time there was little

Crel could do to stop him, swinging his sword as he neared him and catching him on his neck, lifting his head from his body. Crel's body fell lifeless as his head rolled across the floor and out into the hallway. Not wanting to waste more time Ryn pulled the knife from Crel's chest and wiped the blood off on the headless man's cloak before he returned it to his own.

"This ought to keep you in your own castle for several months," Dagger said as he turned to leave.

"You really are an ugly man. No wonder the parents locked you in your castle," he said lifting Crel's head by his hair. "I think I will hide this just to keep your men busy for a while. That is if I decide to let any of them live when we leave."

Crel's body began to shake as Dagger walked away carrying his head.

Sarn and Sala were waiting for Dagger at the top of the front stairway. Sitting on the top step the Prince again protested against his treatment, telling all within hearing distance that he would not leave without his friend.

"If you do not move now," Dagger yelled as he reached them, "I will see to it that you do not leave at all."

Prince Gregor turned and screamed when he saw the head of the girl in Dagger's hand. Tig came running from behind them, growling as he went past them and down the stairs.

"What are you doing? Get him out of here," Dagger told the two. "The guards are not just going to sit around and let us leave. You should have been gone long before now."

He took off his weapons pack and slipped the head of Crel inside. Prince Gregor still refused to move from his spot; struggling with Sarn as he tried to pull him to his feet. Frustrated, Sarn stepped closer and threw the boy over his shoulder. The three ran down the steps to catch up with Tig who had already reached the front door. The sound of guards running toward them from deep inside the palace echoed through the halls.

"Here they come," Dagger said, sounding as calm as possible.

Tig bounded back to the stairs and crouched at the bottom of them waiting for the guards to arrive. The guards reached them three at a time; Dagger and Sala took on the first two as Tig took hold of the last one by his ankle. The battle was short lived as the first two were quick to fall to their swords. Tig, having tripped up the last guard, was making a quick end to his life as well ripping out a large chunk of his throat.

Outside the battle had begun just as they had reached the top of the stairs. Canis and his men rounded the first fire and then another, killing everything in their path as they went.

Arrows flew through the air, most of them hitting their intended targets. Any that were missed were taken down by the next man to pass.

"Cousin," Canis called out, "get out of there!"

He knew that the words would go unheard as he pushed onto the front door of the palace. Running to the next guard that was still standing, Canis plunged his sword through the man. Lifting the man up and continuing he used his lifeless body as a battering ram to open the doors. Breaking through, the two fell to the floor in a heap. Tig had just finished tearing out the throat of the last guard as Canis tumbled through the door.

"I am sorry; had I known that it would take all four of you to kill three guards I would have come sooner." Canis stood and pulled his sword from the body of the guard.

"Then what took you so long," Sarn answered.

"If you had not just snuck off, I would no doubt have been much earlier."

"Now is not the time Canis," Dagger said pushing Sarn out into the night.

Carrying Prince Gregor proved to be easier than Sarn had first imagined. The boy was light; except for the occasional struggling, he may have forgotten he was there at all.

Once out from the palace it was a quick but bloody retreat for the rescuers and their charge. While Canis and his men had taken all the guards that had been on watch, the rest were pouring out of the temporary barracks next to the stable. By the time they reached the low wall surrounding the palace, the ground was littered with dead and dying guards as well as some of Canis' men. The guards did not chase them past the green lawn of the palace. For whatever reason, they seemed to have no heart for a chase. Dagger, Sarn and Prince Gregor were the only ones that escaped without an injury. Sala, having received a minor hit to her left arm, was the only one of the three to be injured.

The rescuers made their way to the banks of the creek with Canis and what few of his men that remained close behind them.

"I would have brought your horses," Canis told them, "but they took off from the campsite heading in the opposite direction."

Setting Prince Gregor on the ground, Sarn stepped away from the group and slipped into the shadows.

"Where do you think you are going?" Canis asked as he

disappeared.

"You need only to worry about why we have no horses," Dagger told him.

"I told you that they ran off."

"That horse of his would never run off, unless someone was going to harm him."

Dagger knelt, pulled out one of his silver daggers and began to dig in the soft ground next to the creek.

"Canis, take the boy and your men and follow the path toward the next village," Dagger said once he had his hole dug. "Sala, find the guard we tied earlier and bring him here."

"What of you and the others?" Canis asked, sounding a little concerned.

"We will be behind you," Dagger said knowing that his cousin was far from concerned about him. "I can promise you that."

Sala headed off in the direction of the guard as Canis took the young Prince by the hand and led him away. Dagger finished the hole he was working on as the others left him. Looking about he opened his weapons pack and pulled out Crel's head. He placed it on the ground next to the hole and pulled a small pouch from the same pack. Tossing its contents into the hole Dagger spread it around mumbling as he did so.

"What are you doing?" Crel's eyes opened wide in surprise. "What is that you are saying?"

"I am preparing a burial ground for your head," Dagger answered trying not to look at it.

"Why are you doing that? There is no need for that, just leave me in the brush where I can be found by my followers."

"I cannot make it so easy for you to be found. We are not far from the summer palace. It should only take you a day or two to find your head."

"Prince Gregor needs me. He will call for me and I will find you and kill all of you."

"By sunrise tomorrow the boy will have forgotten the girl that helped take him prisoner, and your hold over him will be gone."

"That will be an impossible task without your magic."

"Just as finding us by tomorrow morning will be for you without your head," he said tossing the head into the hole.

"I will find you again Ryn Mar."

"And I will have to kill you again. At least do something like this again."

"You can never kill me. You know you do not have the power."

"Perhaps I do not, but I believe that I know who will, and until that time we will continue as we have been. Now I will bury your head to make it harder for you to follow us."

"I will find you, I will always find you. And next time I will kill you."

"You do not have the knowledge to begin to know how to kill me. You can only throw me against walls or down stairs. If in fact you could kill me, you would have done so long ago."

"You are not that powerful Ryn Mar," Crel began. "I will kill you one day, you will see. You will not always be protected by the ancestors."

"I wait the day with great pleasure for you to end my hiding and pain," Dagger said as he began pulling the dirt back into the hole. "If you believe that it is the ancestors' protection that keeps you from killing me, then I am afraid you have been speaking to the wrong spirits. Then again perhaps they are the right ones to speak to after all. Now I am tired of talking to you."

He heard Sala returning from the woods and Tig finally came down the path behind them, his fur covered in blood. Walking past his master the animal went into the creek and plunged himself into the water. Standing up Dagger stomped several times on the overturned ground compacting it. Sala pushed at the guard with her sword forcing him through the woods and onto the path.

"Go to your man," Dagger told her.

"What of you?"

"I will be along," he added. "You need to see to it that Canis does not harm Gregor."

Sala went off with no further protest running in the direction of Sarn had gone.

"Your master will need you now," Dagger said, cutting the guard's hands free and pushing him away with his own sword. "I want you to go to the summer palace and see to him. I have buried his head somewhere near here and he will need your help in finding it."

He tossed a handful of earth at the guard and mumbled a few words under his breath.

"I was beginning to think you had decided to stay behind us," he said, turning toward the creek. "Are you are done playing in the water? We need to go help our friends."

Tig dipped below the water one more time before getting out. Reaching his master the animal shook his wet body before rubbing against his legs.

"Now that is one thing that you do that always makes me want to have you around," he laughed a little. As he spoke he reached down to give his wet friend a quick scratch between his ears. "Go to them."

As Tig bounded off toward Sarn and the others, Dagger thrust his fist into his pocket and wrapped his hand around the crystal. With a smile on his face he stepped one more time on Crel's head before turning and going into the woods.

"Good bye for now Lord Crel," he laughed as he walked away.

Dagger was still laughing when he caught up with Sala.

"I have never heard you laugh quite like this. Is there something you wish to share?"

"If only I could … if only I could, just know that we are all safe for some time, but not forever."

"Are you saying that we will not be traveling for a time?" she asked, stopping just a short distance from where he had buried Lord Crel's head.

"Once we return him to his home we will need to protect him until …," Dagger stopped, unsure what words he should use or even if he should say more. "Well, until his family can return."

"Good," Sala said knowing that even if she questioned him about it he would not tell her any more.

"Yes, you will be able to give birth to your son there once the King returns."

"But I am not with child," she returned.

"Yes you are. It will come near spring if I am right. Do not worry, I will leave the telling to you."

"If I do not know and have told no one, how is it that you know?"

"You should be catching on by now," Dagger said smiling from under his ever present hood. "Even if your man does not wish to believe, you are aware of what I am."

"I have seen more than he has in this life and I understand that not everything that happens can be explained away. My grandmother used to tell me tales of her ancestors and of magic and other beings. I never believed her until I began to see some things for myself. I have seen more since I have been with the two of you than I have ever seen before and yes, it all begins to make sense to me."

"You have been chosen."

"Am I of magic?" she asked, knowing he might not tell her anyway. "You know it would have been just as easy for me to have fallen for you."

"True, but it has happened the way it is supposed to, besides not all is as you see it."

"I know you have not hidden all from me." She took Dagger's free hand and started along the path again. "You are safe with me."

"If I was not, you would not be here."

Nothing more was said and a minute later they found Sarn waiting with Pel and the other horses. Canis and his men were nowhere to be found.

"Has Canis found you?"

"No, but I heard them passing." Sarn answered looking around. "Is the Prince with you?"

"No," Sala said. "He is still with Canis and his men."

"Can you find him?" Dagger asked.

"I think so," Sarn said dropping Pel's reins and turning into the shadows of the coming dawn.

Sala jumped on Pel and Dagger got on his horse. They led the others away from the creek and followed after Sarn.

"You had better go with him," Dagger said to Tig. "I am sure he will no doubt get lost before he finds them, and you will be useless until you catch up with him."

Tig took off after Sarn but kept some distance behind him as if he did not want the boy to know he was following him.

The sun, while still low, was beginning to filter through the trees by the time Sarn caught up with Canis and his men. Prince Gregor was tied to a pole and was being carried between two men as if he were an animal that had been killed in a hunt. He watched as one punched the crying Prince, telling him to be quiet. Crouched behind a tree an idea came to him.

"How long do you think it will be before your cousin and his apprentice catch up to us?" one of the men asked.

"I think we will have a few hours. They will need to find their horses first," Canis replied. "I only wish that we could have found them and brought them with us. I would feel much more comfortable knowing that they would not be able to follow so quickly once they do find them."

"We have covered our path well I think just the same," another of the men replied.

"Yes, I do believe you are right," Canis said reaching back into his pack and pulling out a large pouch. Opening it he began to spill some of the contents onto the ground. "Before you know it

Craden you will be drunk with your share of the ransom that we will get for this boy."

"To the highest bidder!" a bunch of them yelled in unison.

"The highest bidder," Canis began to chuckle. "It is just too bad that Ryn will not pay us more for our help. I have to admit, Galdar sure was happy to see that tablet. What should we care of his need or use of it."

Sarn kept his eyes on Canis and his men. Watching every step they took, he measured the distance between them. He then figured out how long it would take him to reach them from where he stood. He paid little if any attention to the green powder that seemed to float to the ground as it poured out. If he had, he would have seen that as it covered the ground a rolling cloud of dust gathered inches above it brushing away the tracks of the men. As the dust settled to the ground patches of grass began to grow further covering the path. In minutes the path that had existed looked more like the forest around it than a long traveled well-worn path.

Sarn slipped from tree to tree until he was almost beside them. Pulling his knife and short sword he readied himself to take on the men one at a time. Just as he began to stand, Tig pushed against him knocking him back to his knees. Smiling at the animal he scratched him behind the ears. Tig left him and began to sneak up the line of men. Sarn followed him taking his lead and waited until the cat made his move jumping straight for Canis. Sarn was right behind him, taking the last man in line before working forward through the line of men. First one then the next fell to Tig and Sarn. He began to use the men that fell as stepping stones to the next man. His sword was like an extension of his hand as it sliced and thrust its way into and out of the men as he reached them. Catching an axe to his legs he fell to the ground but shoved his sword deep into the chest of the man that hit him before he landed on his back. In an instant he was back to his feet. Grabbing for his knife he tossed it, catching another of the men in the back as he tried to flee the area. Taking the axe from the dead man's hand he threw it sideways making the axe spin parallel to the ground. It connected with and took the head of the first man that carried the Prince on the pole. Removing his sword he turned to face the next man. Yelling, he dove toward him sticking the man in the neck with his knife as he pushed his sword into the chest of the next man behind him. Tig had watched Sarn once he had taken Canis, as if he were either unsure of which to kill next or if he was even needed. As another of the men began to run away Tig jumped from his spot taking him down. He caught a sword to his back dropping the big animal, but not for long as he turned and tore out the throat of his attacker. The last man holding the Prince dropped his end and began to run, although he did not get far away as a knife caught him square in the back dropping him to his knees screaming in pain. Tig not to be outdone by Sarn, worked his way through the remaining four men to the front of the line tearing and biting as he went. The animal was hit several times before he could finally go no further, falling near where the Prince was lying on the ground, still tied to the pole.

Tig lie bleeding but not moving when Sarn reached him. His breathing was heavy but at least he was still breathing. Taking his shirt off, he pressed it into the wounds of his friend.

"You just lie still," he told him before turning to check on the Prince.

He cut him loose from the pole but did not free his hands or feet. He hesitated to remove the gag that had been placed over his mouth, but after looking into the frightened boy's eyes he thought it the better idea.

"Please, spare me," the boy begged. "I can get you all the gold you can carry."

"I did not save you to kill you; as for the gold, well we will talk of that after we return you to your father."

Sarn began to turn his head from side to side, his eyes searching the trees. Removing his cloak he folded it and placed it over more of Tig's wounds.

"Put your hand here and do not let go," he told the boy, moving him to where Tig was lying.

Tig opened his eyes and tried to move but Sarn again told him to be still.

"It is my turn to protect you my friend," he said before jumping into the cover of the trees.

He was sure that there was still one more of them out there somewhere. He had seen him slipping away from the rest as Tig had jumped Canis.

Prince Gregor did not move. As much as he wanted to run, he could not seem to make himself move. The vision of Sarn coming out from the bushes and attacking the men that were holding him kept running through his mind. He had immediately seen Tig charging out from trees and jumping toward Canis, but to him Sarn seemed to appear from nowhere as he struck the first man and then another. With the speed that Sarn had moved, the boy was surprised to see that he had been wounded at all. He was a blur of activity to Gregor. As he had seen it there was only a brief minute from the time he appeared until he took off his shirt to place it on the animal. Thinking it best, he decided that it might not be wise for him to move. Instead he held the cloak to the bleeding animal as best as his shaking hands would let him.

Sarn lay under the cover of a large tree, waiting and listening to the air around him. With his wound still bleeding heavily, he became weaker by the minute. He tilted his head before looking down and found a cut across his stomach and wondered when and which of the men had hit him there. He moved to another tree, listening again before closing his eyes as the pain from his wounds seemed to finally hit him.

"Listen to me," a voice seemed to call him. "You must stay awake. Think of me son, think of me."

He shook his head and tried to move again as his mind began to fog from the pain and loss of blood. 'Think of me' the words echoed in his head as he tried to focus on where they were coming from. Crawling to his next hiding spot he attempted to push out the pain to listen for the voice that had slipped away. He knew that the escaping man was near so he lifted himself to his feet and waited for him. Turning towards the sound of a breaking branch he tripped over a rock at his feet, landing face down at the base of a bush. From somewhere deep within him he forced himself to his knees just as the escaping man came into a small open area between the trees. The sword flew from his hand blade first as the man cleared the trees. The fleeing man saw him just as the sword was released. He tried to duck but noticed that the sword seemed to lower as he did so. He twisted to one side and then the other, but still the sword seemed to follow him. Giving up he stared in disbelief as it found his throat. It looked as if it slid into him in slow motion. The man's eyes followed every inch until all he could see was the hilt, if in fact he could see anything at the time. Where Sarn had gotten the strength to lift his sword, let alone throw it, is impossible to say. At least that is what he would say some time later as he told the story.

Listening to the wind, Sarn found a tree with low hanging branches and crawled under it, fearing that there may yet be someone else nearby. He was still on his knees as he lowered his head to the ground and waited, for the next man or death, whichever it was to be. His mind was a jumble of images as he clutched at his stomach. His blood poured from his wounds, yet it was the image of his father that stood out most in his mind. Sala was there in his mind as well, but he found himself thinking of his father the most as he began to gather his energy.

Sala saw the bodies of Canis and his men first before spotting Tig. She pushed Pel to him and found Prince Gregor hiding behind the large animal. Gregor looked scared but still held Sarn's shirt to Tig's wound. Dagger was just a few seconds behind; jumping from his horse he grabbed one of the packs that his aunt had given him. It was only a few steps before he was at friend's side. Moving the boy's hands and lifting the shirt from the wound he felt his way along Tig's body. Opening the pack he pulled out two pouches. From one he took out a handful of the white powder and sprinkled it in all the wounds he could see. He pulled several leaves from the second pouch, breaking them one at a time at the base a thick liquid began to run from the stem of each of the leaves. He let the liquid drip into the wound across his friend's back until he was sure that each leaf held no more.

Sala laid a hand on Tig's head while pulling the still crying Prince to her. Cutting his hands and feet free from the ropes she asked him if he knew where Sarn had gone.

"He went into the trees," he said pointing in the direction that Sarn had gone in. "He was wounded, bad I think."

She looked at Dagger who just pointed her in the right direction in which to go. Telling the boy that he was going to be fine she left him with Dagger and took off into the trees. Seconds later Gregor ran to follow her, not wanting to be alone. He was beginning to think that Sala had been the girl that was with him in the palace. He even called out the name of the girl Crel had disguised himself as so that he could befriend the boy.

Once they were gone Dagger placed his hands over Tig's wounds. Moving his hands in small circles a white light appeared surrounding them, growing brighter with each second. Tig lifted his head for a second and looked over his shoulder before falling unconscious again. The wounds under Dagger's hands stopped bleeding and began to heal over. After several minutes the light began to fade and when Dagger removed his hands there was no sign of the wounds. Standing Dagger moved his hands back and forth over the length of Tig. He began to mumble again as a red light began to consume the animal. Once the light covered Tig completely he raised his arms and the animal began to lift up from the ground. With Tig suspended in the air Dagger lifted him up and over to his horse and lowered him down atop it.

Sala stopped next to a tree and waited for Gregor to catch up to her. Looking back, she watched amazed as Dagger lifted Tig to his horse. She had a feeling about Dagger the minute they had met. Her grandmother had always told her that she would have a strange warm feeling the moment she met someone with magic. She had never believed her, but now that she had seen it, she knew exactly what she had meant by it. Gregor brought her attention back to her search by pointing out a small pool of blood. Following the trail of blood he left behind they traced Sarn's path through the trees. It was not long before they found him face down half in the bushes and half under the tree. She ran to his side, turned him over and called out to Dagger. Reaching down and tossing his arm over her shoulders, she lifted him from the ground and with the help of Gregor they went back to Dagger and the horses. Dagger tossed some of the white powder into his wounds, placing a hand over each one, stopping the bleeding. He hesitated to heal the wounds entirely as he had with Tig, not wanting to use the magic that it took to do it. It was not that he was worried about being traced, he had already used more than enough for that. Instead he thought it better not to show more of himself in front of Sala and the boy. After covering his wounds they placed the still unconscious Sarn on Pel. Sala mounted behind him to help keep him from falling off the horse. While Dagger put Gregor on his horse with Tig, leaving him with Sala's horse.

"Take them up the path," he told Sala, "I need to see to something here first."

Sala, not wanting to know what it was that he needed to do nodded and led the small troop up the path. He waited until they were out of sight until he climbed back down off the horse. Bending down to Canis he reached into his dead cousin's cloak and pulled out a long pouch.

"I am sorry cousin, but you should not have crossed me this way. I cannot be sure what your plan was, but it was not what we agreed upon," Dagger said as he opened the pouch and began pouring its contents over the dead men. "If it makes you feel any better, I would have killed you for this as well. I have always told you that what I do can only go one way."

Dagger walked back and forth between Canis and the others. Each time he came back to Canis' corpse he spoke to it.

"I guess I should have told you that I had beheaded Crel and your payment would not have been waiting for you."

When the pouch was half empty, he went to where Sarn had killed the last of the men. He pulled Sarn's sword from the neck of the man before covering him with the powder as well. Taking his time returning to the main body of men, he was sure to cover the trail of blood that Sarn had left behind.

"Although, I do regret that I was unable to find out why you turned against me and the ancients this way," Dagger continued when he reached Canis again. "I guess I cannot understand why you did not kill us when you first arrived. With this being your plan all along, you should have killed us at the creek. Then again, I suppose that you did not think that you could get into the palace and retrieve the boy. Even if you had killed us then, my regret would be that it still would have ended with you dead. Even if you killed me first I know that Tig would have torn out your throat long before you could have killed him. I am being honest when I say that I take no pleasure in seeing you this way, but you did make your choice. "

He climbed back on the horse and headed up the path behind the others. When he reached a point where the path turned, he stopped the horse and turned in his saddle to face the bodies. He raised one hand, made a fist then brought it to his mouth for a second. Lowering his arm he opened the fist, palm up revealing a glowing red ball.

"Good bye cousin," he said throwing the ball back toward the bodies. Turning back in his saddle he pushed the horse forward.

When the ball reached its intended targets it slammed into a pile of the red powder. Bursting into flames the red powder began burning away every sign that anyone had been there, let alone been killed there. As the fire diminished a cloud of dust formed just inches above the ground, just as the powder Canis had used earlier had done. The dust hung just off the ground for several seconds before settling on it, turning the blackened area into a lush forest floor.

Catching up to the others he pointed out a safe place for them to stop. It was next to the creek with a rock ledge and base forming the creek's bank. Dagger lowered Tig and put him next to the rock wall, before helping Sala place Sarn next to him. Telling her they would be safe there he sat next to Tig with his back to the ledge. Pushing his hood back just a bit he put the green crystal to his forehead.

Sala enlisted the help of Gregor in gathering wood and lighting a fire. The two worked at setting up a small camp. She checked on Tig and Sarn often as they worked.

"You need not worry of them," Dagger told her. "You need only worry of the campsite and the boy."

"It would be easier if you helped."

"It may not seem it, but that is exactly what I am doing."

"But, I...," Sala started, but she could not finish her thought, knowing that he was right and was doing just what needed to be done.

Sarn woke several hours later looking up at the late day sun.

"You had me worried," she said looking down into his eyes. "I think you even had Dagger concerned."

"Tig," was all he managed to say.

"He still has not moved, but he will," Dagger told him.

"And the Prince?" he asked.

"He is taking a nap. Your woman is warming some meat for a meal," Dagger added. "We will be safe here until morning. By then Tig will be well enough to move."

"You mean he is going to be alright?" Sarn asked trying to sit up, but the pain stopped him.

"We reached him in time, and you," Dagger said reaching out and touching Sarn's shoulder. "You will be just fine as well."

"Well, I am glad to see that you took the time to help me," Sarn returned, trying to smile.

"Anything for a friend," he told him patting his shoulder.

Sarn shook his head and lay back down. Falling asleep he dreamed of home and of his parents. He was sitting next to the fireplace while his father was in his favorite chair reading a book. His mother was seated next to his father working on a piece of lace.

"You have done a brave thing," his mother said, "and this girl that is with you, she is brave as well; take good care of her."

"He knows to take care of her," his father said. "You have taught him of that."

"You are right of course, Father," his mother returned looking up for a second from her lace work. "I should not have brought it up."

"Your mother is always worried that she did not teach you well enough. I keep reminding her that if she had not, I would not have let you go until she had. Be well my son...."

His dream ended with an image of Crel laughing as it faded

away.

Once Sala had made sure the group was fed she left them and waded into the water. She took her time cleaning her clothes and herself of blood. Before she knew it Dagger and Prince Gregor had fallen asleep next to Tig and Sarn. Climbing out of the creek she shed most of her clothes and laid them on the rocks near the fire in the sun. Sitting across from Sarn and the others she leaned against a tree and closed her eyes.

The sisters moved across the creek without making a sound.

"See," one said to the other, "I told you that they would be safe."

"I still say that we should have done what we were told to do."

"How many times must we go through this? There is no way we can do that."

"Enough, let us just make sure that everything is well so that we can watch over them while they rest."

"Good day to you," Sala said opening her eyes.

"And good day to you Sala," the sisters said together.

"It is good to see you again," one of them said. "Close your eyes and go to sleep. We will watch over the five of you for the rest of this day and through the night. No harm will come to you here."

Sala smiled, closed her eyes and drifted back to sleep. With the rescuers and the rescued asleep the sisters crossed to where Dagger and Sarn lay sleeping.

"He looks well sister."

"They all do considering what has happened. Do you think we should tell them what will happen next?"

"We are not allowed to tell of what is to come next."

"And you think that we will be in any less trouble if we do?"

"If we tell him of his heritage, he will die. You saw it, just as did I."

"Then I guess if we keep that from him, we should keep everything."

The two crossed the creek again. Standing on the other side, they turned to watch the travelers.

"Do you think we should tell Sala of her child?"

"She will find out soon enough. Besides Dagger has told her already, yet she does not believe."

"Just keep the fire going when it gets dark, it will be cold tonight."

"I wish I could have been there when Dagger took his head."

"We could have made it permanent had we done what were told."

"Will you stop?"

"I cannot. I just have the feeling that one day it will be yet another mess that I will have to clean up for you."

The two continued arguing over what they should have done and what they should do and not do. They even argued over which spell to use to keep the rescuers' fire going. They were so busy arguing that neither of them noticed the figure coming up the path behind them.

"To what do I owe the pleasure of a visit from the sisters to my forest?"

Startled, the two quit arguing and turned to the figure.

"Did I interrupt anything?"

"No, not at all," Caitlin said pushing back the hood of her cloak.

"That is too bad. I had hoped that I would have surprised you."

"You surprised us," Meglyn said. "You just did not interrupt us."

"When did this become your forest?" Caitlin asked

"It always has been mine."

"It has never been yours," said Caitlin.

"Whichever you believe, it does not explain why you are here."

"We are helping our niece," Meglyn said pointing to Sala. "She is on a quest to find her true love."

"What are you doing in this part of the forest?" Caitlin asked.

"I am looking for something that was stolen from me."

"I was of the belief Foulas, that you had nothing worthy of being stolen."

Keeping to the sunlit ground Foulas crossed the gap between him and the sisters.

"Are you afraid?" Caitlin asked him.

"I am Foulas. I fear no one that exists on this plane."

"Yet you do not allow your feet to touch the shadows," Meglyn pointed out.

"I serve a higher master than either of you."

"Your higher master has lost his head," Caitlin told him. "He is near powerless now, and his hold over you gets weaker. Can you not feel the powers that he has given you slipping away?"

"That may be," Foulas said, "but soon he will be resurrected and my powers will be restored."

"Whichever you believe," Meglyn said. "Just know that what

you have lost is not here. As you can see there is none but our niece in this place."

"So you tell me, but I feel magic. I may not be able to see it, but it is here." Foulas began to get angry, his face changing colors as he spoke.

"Are you forgetting that we are magic?"

"I forget nothing," Foulas returned. Looking around he began to get confused. "Where is my master, have you seen my master?"

"Have you been to the tower on the lake? Perhaps he is there waiting for you."

"He told me that he would be here in my forest." Foulas' voice began to turn childlike and more confused as he talked.

"The forest is large and you are in but a small part of it. Could he be in another part?"

"That could be," Foulas looked around again. "Do you know where I should look?"

The sisters shook their heads trying not to say anymore to him.

"Why do we not just discharge him?" Caitlin asked

"In other words kill him," Meglyn began. "You know we are not allowed to do that. The ancients definitely would not approve."

"It would solve many problems later on. Then again with Crel using his powers to find his head and then to heal himself. It will take many weeks before he finds his way out of the forest."

"He does grow more childlike. How old was he when Crel made him a follower?"

"He was about Prince Gregor's age I think, perhaps much younger."

"Good day pretty ladies. My name is Foulas. My daddy says that I was named for ...," Foulas stopped not remembering what he was saying. "I lost something can you help me?"

"Sure thing sweetie," Meglyn said. "You go over on the other side of the creek and look downstream from here. My sister and I will look over here and then upstream. If we find your master we will tell him how to find you."

"Alright," Foulas said heading toward the creek bank. "Is the water deep? I have not yet learned to swim."

"If you promise not to tell anyone that we have helped you, we will get you across the creek," Caitlin told him. "We are not allowed to use our magic for just whatever purpose suits us or anyone else for that matter."

"I would not know who to tell that you have helped me with magic," Foulas returned. "Neither would I know who you are that would help me."

Meglyn smiled to her sister then turned to where Foulas was standing. Closing her eyes she lifted one hand, causing him to rise just off the ground. Then with one smooth motion she pushed out at the air and away from her body. Foulas floated through the air over the creek and onto the opposite bank.

He turned around in a circle, waved to the sisters and ran off into the trees singing a children's song of faries.

"The only problem as I see it sister," Caitlin said as he ran off, "is that in few weeks he will be back to his evil doing self."

"Why must you always spoil my good deeds," Meglyn replied. "I will say one thing for you, I may not like what you have to say but you do have a way with words."

Just before nightfall the sisters slipped out of the make shift camp and moved to where they could watch them without being seen.

In the morning as the sun began to filter its way to the forest floor, the rescuers woke huddled together at the bottom of the rock ledge. Tig was the first to move, tentative steps at first, but soon he found himself in the cool water of the creek. Standing mid-stream he let the water wash away the dried blood from his face and body while dunking in the water over and over. Sarn was still a bit weak, but the pain was gone and his wounds had healed over. From their hiding spot the sisters watched as the rescuers woke to face the day. Meglyn recanted the spell that she and Caitlin had cast to keep them safe. Having used so much of his magic he made it possible for his parents to find and trace his path. Having used the rock ledge as their camp nothing needed to be done to keep them safe during the day. It was the night time that it had proven necessary for the spell. After arguing over which spell was best to use, Meglyn made a choice. Her choice though, was not without the disapproval of Caitlin.

"I find that the best time of day to watch people is at night. There is less chance of them seeing you."

The sisters turned to face the voice, standing beside them.

"I would think that you of all creatures would find that hard to accomplish Garrick," Caitlin said, turning to the new visitor.

"There was a time Caitlin, that you did not think me a creature."

"I would like to say how happy we are to see you. After all you are family, sort of," Meglyn said interrupting the exchange of words that was about to erupt between the two. "But I get the feeling this is not a friendly visit."

"I am surprised that you think it anything else."

"It is not what I think," Meglyn returned, "it is what I know."

"I come to see that my child is safe."

"Since when did you ever care if Ryn was safe?" Caitlin added. "Your only concern has been to bend him to your ways, just as his mother always tries."

"And here I thought the two of you were so all knowing," Garrick returned. "Listening to you only proves to me how little you know. There is but one way for this all to end."

"Yet you continue to try and change the end," Meglyn said.

"I try to change nothing more than you and your ever meddling sister do."

"I think that it is time for you go back to where you came from," Caitlin returned. Trying not to sound angry with him and for what she knew was meant to enrage her, and allow him to see through their magic. "You need to worry less about what we do and say. Perhaps you should be worrying about what your punishment will be for leaving your home."

"Punish me?" he said laughing at Caitlin. "Who is powerful enough to punish me any more than I already have been by the parents? Living my life forever looking down on a world that I should be ruling."

"You will never learn, will you?"

Raising their hands, a blue light sprung from their palms engulfing the man.

"Before we finish your punishment will begin," the sisters spoke almost in unison. "From the sun's warmth to the moon's cold, they share the skies together. Though they sometimes pass they never meet. The sun is where you are supposed to be. Somewhere between them is where you will be now and until the moon blocks the sun once again."

"No you cannot, I need more time I... no!"

The light swirled around the man before he disappeared within it, circling around him and rolling itself into a ball before shooting straight into the morning sky.

Turning back as if nothing had happened, the sisters watched the group before slipping away into trees.

After a morning meal and washing the blood from their clothes the rescuers broke camp and moved up the path.

"I am sorry about your cousin," Sarn said as the group started out.

"It was not your fault that he turned from his path."

"How can I be so sure that he had? I cannot help but think that I may have acted too quick."

"Do you think that you were too quick to kill the guards at the summer palace?"

"They were holding Gregor, and it is not as if they were just going to hand him over because we wanted them to."

"Do you think that Canis was just going to turn him over to you?"

"I never asked," Sarn said stopping Pel.

"You must learn to trust your instincts. It is the only thing that you can rely on all the time," Dagger replied.

He made no further attempt to help Sarn understand or explain how he knew that he had made the right decision. Without another word between them on the subject, the travelers continued on their way to Gregor's Kingdom.

Far upstream near the buried head of Lord Crel, the sisters stood once again in heavy debate.

"Are you sure this will work?"

"Of course it will. If we overflow the banks of the creek we will make it harder for them to find it."

"What if you are wrong? What if it just uncovers it, making it easier for them to find?"

"Why must you be this way? Why must you always second guess everything that we do? You are always trying to stop me from doing something."

"If only to keep me from having to fix it later on; I still think that I will have to fix everything before we face our brother again."

"Then perhaps it will be best if we stay away from him for a while."

"I am beginning to think that you should do this by yourself," Meglyn told her, sounding a bit more resolute than in the past. "I cannot continue to go against what we are supposed to do any longer. All this running around to cover up something or make something more difficult is not what we are supposed to do. This should not even need doing if we had only done what we were supposed to in the first place."

"You do realize of course," Caitlin began trying not to sound too smug. "That since we did not tell him we need to stay close and make sure that nothing happens to him."

"Then I am going to tell him so that we can get back to our duties."

"These are our duties. This is what we are supposed to do."

"I still cannot believe that I let you talk me into this."

"Come on, help me swell the creek so that they cannot find Crel's head for a few weeks."

Meglyn turned away from her sister and folded her arms. Shaking her head Caitlin lifted her arms, pointed to the sky and began her spell.

"Rumble, roar, shake and rattle, clouds roll in...."

"If you are going to do it," Meglyn began. "Then you need to do it right."

Pushing her sister aside, she lifted her arms to the sky and began mumbling the words she had learned as a child

The cloudless sky began to fill with dark rain clouds. Lightning struck a tree a few hundred feet from the sisters as a light rain began to fall around them. It was not long before the rain began to fall heavier the water filling the stream as inch after inch of rain began to fall.

"How long do you think it will take for the creek to overflow its banks?"

"About three or four hours of rain like this," she said.

"Good, but it needs more I think," Caitlin returned.

Lifting her face to the rain she began to speak in a language that had not been heard in the forest for a long time.

"What did you just do?" Meglyn asked when she finished

"I have made it so that it will rain for a week and a half, keeping the creek overflowing for as long as possible."

"I know what you have done. I just want to know why."

"For the same reason that we wanted to overflow the creek in the first place," Meglyn said turning and moving away from the creek. "Besides, if a little is good, more is better."

Caitlin shook her head and followed her sister, arguing as they went. The rain seemed to fall around them, almost as if they were being shielded from it in some way.

Once they had gotten far enough from the summer palace, Gregor had indeed forgotten the girl that had befriended him. He had begun remembering only that he had been held alone in the palace. Every morning he would tell them how much better they were treating him than the guards at the palace.

"They would not let me go when my father asked them to. I heard him outside asking them to let me come home with him, but they refused."

Every morning the boy would say the same thing and nothing more for the rest of the day. Both Sarn and Tig grew stronger each day. Yet while Tig was eating twice what he normally ate, Sarn was eating less. The only one that was concerned with it was Sala.

It was late in the sixth day after the rescue when they reached the edge of the forest. There across a wheat field, beyond some barns and few houses laid Tenisfie, the tenth and five castle of the Kingdom of Valdore. Built on what seemed like an out of place hill, the large castle city stood out among the fields and forests that surrounded it. Its stark white walls rose from the lush green hill seeming to stand like a beacon in the land. The castle had not been the largest in the time of the old Kingdom, yet there had been several additions to it since then. The older part of the castle held the King's palace and was there in the time of Valdore. The gray wall that surrounded the original village stood out against the newer sections its high ramparts standing guard in silence over the village that spread out in front of it.

"Legends tell that the palace was built over a burial mound from the time of the ancients. The mound is believed to hold the remains of two lovers whose families had forbidden them to be together." Dagger spoke easy as the travelers looked out from the forest. "Turning their backs on their families the two were said to have ran away from home and ended up here. They carved a home and farm out of the forest and managed to have five children before their families found them."

"When they found them, the lovers were killed," Dagger's voice seemed to turn bitter as he spoke. "One can only guess why they did not kill the children as well. Perhaps they did not have the heart for it. Whatever their reasoning may have been, the youngest children were sent to live in separate parts of the world. They were all said to be of magical birth and that the ancients worried that they would tear the world around them apart if left together. Of what magic they were born is lost to time, forgotten or just never known. Although one cannot say for sure if it is true, as it is only believed that they were of magic. While four of the children were sent in opposite directions, the fifth and oldest was left here, for what reason one could not say. Who knows what goes through the minds of those that may be feeling guilty for killing someone that is of the same blood?"

Dagger paused for a minute but did not move. Sarn of course could not, or would not believe the tale that Dagger was telling, yet he did not interrupt. Instead he jumped off Pel and lifted Prince Gregor from in front of Sala.

"The two families stripped him of any powers that he may have had or would ever have then erased the memories of his siblings. All he remembered is that his parents had died in the night of a fever and not that they had been killed by their own family," Dagger began again. His voice changed back and forth as he talked, from sounding bitter to sad. "Condemned to live within just a few miles of his parents' grave he spent his life building the hill the Palace now stands on to honor them. Over the years some claimed that many strange things happened on that hill. Lovers found, things given that were asked for, lives returned from dead, even the sick healed. Many of the things that happen on the hill and around the fields are attributed to the lovers. What is true or just tales is anyone's guess, but one thing for sure; some type of energy comes from that hill. This is the reason that Valdore ordered a castle to be built here. Some believe that the hill and the lovers gave Valdore the ability to conquer his enemies and unite the Kingdoms of the world. Others think ... well, that there is nothing special about this place. They say it is just a tale made up to help children go to sleep."

When he finished, Dagger jumped down from his horse and picked up a handful of dead leaves off the forest floor. Running his fingers over them he seemed to get a little lost about where and what he was doing. Several minutes passed without anything being said as if each of the travelers were lost in their own thoughts. Sala could not help but think of her grandparents while Sarn as always, thought of his home. Dagger could not help but think of how this adventure was to end and what would come next.

The young Prince began to run around the travelers and their horses as if he had just realized that he was being taken home. It was the sudden outburst of excitement that would bring the travelers back from their thoughts and to the present.

"How are we supposed to get in?" Sarn asked.

"Can you not see the gate?" Dagger asked back.

"Do you think it wise to just ride into the castle with the Prince out in the open," he returned ignoring his friend.

"It may not be the best thing we have done on this trip, but it would not go well were we to hide him only to have him discovered at the gate."

"Then we should change him," Sala said.

"I always knew you would be helpful if you came along," Dagger returned.

"Is that why you did not speak to me for almost a week?"

"I did not speak to you because I had nothing to say to you."

"Do you have many friends there?" Sala asked laughing.

"Friends... where... what?"

"In the world that you live in. Do you have many friends there?"

Dagger huffed and moved away from the others. He just lowered his head and gave no response to their laughter.

Sala took charge of changing the Prince. When she was finished he looked more like a girl than the nine year old boy that he was. It was an easy ride across the fields to the castle walls, with the group keeping close to each other. Just before they reached the gate Sala jumped down from her horse leaving the Prince alone on it for the first time since they rescued him. Tying a short rope around the neck of Tig to keep the locals from chasing him off or killing him on sight, they walked through the open gate. The guards paid close attention to the rescuers as they rode past their posts. Prince Gregor wanted to holler out to the guards and tell them who he was, but something stopped him, instead he lowered his head as they passed them. Reaching the first tavern the group stopped and went inside.

"Do you smell the villages that have taverns?" Sala asked. "There are times you cannot find your horse, yet you always seem to go right to a tavern."

Sarn and Dagger laughed, saying nothing in return.

The tavern was quite crowded, which surprised Dagger some considering it was still early in the day. He tripped more than once as they worked their way toward an empty table. He made his apologies to more than one table and post along the way. Keeping to themselves they sat near the back of the room and ordered a meal.

"Well, we made it this far, what is our next move?" asked Sarn once the serving girl had left them.

"I am not sure, do you have any ideas?" Dagger asked back.

"You two cannot be serious. I cannot believe that neither of you have thought about what would happen next," Sala added. "I thought that the two of you were some kind of one mind where you each knew what the other was thinking."

Both Sarn and Dagger laughed at what she had said. It was unusual for them to laugh together. It was even more unusual that Dagger would laugh at all. His mood seemed to become lighter with each day that passed since the night of the rescue of the young Prince Gregor.

When their meal arrived the server looked hard at the Prince. They could not tell if the girl had recognized him or not. Chances were that she had never seen the Prince before. It might have only been a slim chance, but Dagger pushed the Prince further into the dark corner just the same.

"There is little need to hide the child," the girl said returning with some goat's milk. "That is if you are hiding one that belongs here."

"Who is to say where one belongs," Dagger returned. "There are many places that one can belong to, not everyone can belong everywhere. Some may choose to hide and others may not, no matter where they are from. The need to hide is only as equal to the need for them to be found."

"Perhaps," the girl added, "but it would be best to hide the one that is missing for now."

"Would you know of a place to hide? That is if indeed there was someone that was in need of hiding?" Sala asked.

"When you are ready, meet me down the street behind the brewery," she said going back to her work.

The four looked at each other as she left them, not quite sure if she could be trusted.

"Do you know her?" Sarn asked the Prince.

He watched the girls every move as they ate, then admitted that there was a chance that he had seen her in the palace before but could not be sure.

Sarn picked some meat off of his plate and tossed it under the table for Tig. Giving a quick glance at Dagger before getting up he leaned over and kissed Sala on the forehead before making his way out of the Inn.

Dagger watched him go and a smile formed on his lips, as he nodded his head.

"You know where he's going?" Sala asked, though it was more of a statement than a question.

"I cannot say, but he will be safe."

"I know he will be safe. That is not what I want to know."

Dagger reached across the table and touched her hand reassuring her that her man would be fine.

Once outside Sarn slid the hood of his cloak over his head and made his way to the brewery. He kept close to the buildings and tried not to trip over any of the beggars. He was almost run over by a few carts of wheat and hay as they rolled past him. He stepped back against one of the many shops that lined the street after the third one just about knocked him down. He stood watching the line of people and carts as they made their way to wherever they were going. He had never seen so many people in one place at one time before. As he look around him taking in the sights of the street he spent a few seconds on each person as if he were trying to memorize each face. Then the second time that his eyes swept those on the street he began to hear what each one was saying. It was just as if he were standing next to them and carrying on a conversation. He shook his head trying to make sense of what was happening. There was no way that he could have heard them; he began to feel confused. In his confusion he stepped away from the shops and into the street. It was only a second before he saw the cart coming at him. Over the noise of the street he heard the dull thud of empty barrels sliding back and forth against each other on the cart. He even heard the hooves of the ox beating the cobblestone street that pulled it. Jumping out of the way, he tripped over a boy playing near the street and tumbled to the ground. After almost being run over again he picked himself up and jumped in behind the cart. He was still not sure how he had heard the cart before it had run into him. He wasted no time trying to figure it out. Instead he pushed everything that had happened out of his thoughts.

When the cart reached the brewery, he listened as two men argued over the price of the barrels. When they came to an agreement, the men walked off as the barrels were unloaded. He watched and waited even though he was not sure what it was he was waiting for. Before anyone wondered what he was doing he began to look for some doorway or ledge that he could use to hide in or under. Spotting what he was looking for he snuck around the front of the cart and slid into a deep recess in a nearby wall. Pushing himself against the wall and into the shadow he waited to see what would happen next.

A tall man wearing an apron came running around the corner and down the alley toward him. He was met at the front of the cart by one of the men that were unloading the barrels.

"What is it now Garis?" the tall man asked.

"He is here."

"Are you certain?" he returned, sounding a little suspicious. "You have said this before and I was not happy when it was not."

"The girl recognized him."

"Is there anyone else that knows?"

"No one that I can be certain of."

"Is he by himself?"

Garis told him of the others with the Prince and described them to him.

"The animal with them, is he a large cat, orange, black and white in color?"

"Yes, do you know this animal?"

"I might," he replied. "Go back and see that no one else finds the Prince."

"You mean you want me to...."

"I want you to watch them and that is all I want you to do."

"Herina told them to meet her here after their meal."

"That will not be necessary," the tall man said. "I will come to them when I am through here."

Sarn did not get any kind of bad feeling about the tall man but he did not get a good one either. Keeping himself pressed into the shadow of the doorway he waited. When the men finished unloading the barrels, the tall man took two of them by the shoulder, leading them away from the brewery and closer to the place where Sarn was hiding.

"We have to make sure that no one outside of the circle finds out, you both understand that right?"

They both nodded their agreement.

"Good," the tall man said. "Then what I tell you goes only to those in the circle, no matter what happens to you."

Both men again nodded their understanding.

"The Prince is back," the tall man began again. "Those that have brought him have little idea about what they have brought him back to. I know of one of them. Tell the circle that he is here and that it is the seer that brings him. Go now and remember that no one outside of the circle finds out no matter what the cost."

The two men walked to the end of the alley and turned in opposite directions. The tall man followed them after several minutes, turning toward the inn. Sarn waited for the man to leave his sight before following, making sure that he was not seen. The tall man made his way to the inn and went inside with Sarn close behind him. Once inside he caught the eye of Herina, who motioned him to the table where the group was sitting.

Dagger was the first to notice the man coming toward them. He made no movement to acknowledge the tall man's presence, but he did make a move toward his daggers. A few moments later Dagger noticed Sarn slipping his way in through the door behind another patron. The Prince, sitting between Sala and Dagger noticed the man next and buried his head under her arm.

"This is not your concern traveler," said Garis, as he stuck out his arm to stop Sarn.

"And who are you to say it is not?" Sarn replied, keeping watch over the group and the man at the same time.

"I am the man that will kill you if you interfere," Garis began until he felt the pressure from one of Sarn's daggers, "or not."

"I thought that you might change your mind. Who is that man and what is his place?"

"His name is Harindes," Garis told him. "He was a Captain of King Gregor's royal guard."

"If he means no harm then there is little to worry about," Sarn whispered. "But know this; I will kill you first before moving to him."

The man nodded his head and lowered his arm. Harindes placed his hands on the table as he sat down with the rescuers.

"If you are who I think you are, then we have business to discuss," Harindes began.

"And if I am not?" returned Dagger.

"Then I have been misinformed and I will bid you good day and then be on my way."

"I think then I will let you talk before I decide," he said laying two of his silver daggers on the table in front of him.

Garis turned to the door and stood just to the side, opening it a little, looking out through the small opening. Sarn kept a close eye on Harindes and a dagger pushed to the side of Garis.

"Speak your mind," Sala told him.

"There is nothing worse than a wench with a tongue," Harindes said looking hard at Sala.

"I will decide who speaks at my table," Dagger said lifting one of the daggers and pointing it at him.

"Very well," he said turning back towards Dagger. "Your name, unless I am mistaken, is Ryn Mar. You are here to either return my Prince or you are here to extract money from Foulas to return a fake."

"And what would the difference be as far as you would concern yourself with?"

"If you are a fake I will leave you to the whim of Foulas. But if you are Ryn Mar, that would make that little girl over there my King's son. In which case I will take you into our circle and protect you and your group until the time is right for his return."

"I was of the belief that your Prince was being held by Foulas at Lord Dermit's summer palace."

"Up until a few days ago, yes, but my sources tell me that the thief Ryn Mar and a band of elves took him from there."

"A band of elves you say?" Dagger chuckled. "And of what concern should this be of mine?"

"None, unless you are Ryn Mar," Harindes added again, sounding annoyed.

Dagger lowered his head and placed his hands on either side of his daggers before speaking.

"If your Prince is free of Crel at the moment then why would he have to go into hiding until, as you say, the time is right?" Dagger spoke soft and deliberate almost as if he were trying to anger Harindes. "Is it not always the proper time to return one that has been stolen away?"

Harindes looked to the still hiding Prince before standing and leaving the inn.

"I would caution you to keep your companions in check," Harindes said to Sarn as he walked past him.

Sarn turned to watch him leave the inn, not quite sure what to think of him. After rejoining the others he tried to put it all together before telling Dagger what had happened behind the brewery.

"Do you think he is telling the truth?"

"Gregor could tell us better than I."

They looked to Gregor, who was still huddled close to Sala, for the answer.

"Do you think that what he says is the truth?" Sala asked the boy.

"Yes, but I cannot be sure that he is not one of those that helped to steal me away from here."

"In that case," Dagger said rising from the table, "let Tig free from his rope and let us find our way out of this tavern. Trust none but each other until we can be sure who is on the side of the Prince."

"Wait," the Prince said, "there might be another way to know for sure. My father used to walk from one end of this street to the other. He used to greet the shop owners and they would say something back to him. If I could remember what it was, then maybe we can tell who we can trust."

"That is all well," Sarn added, "I would still wonder how we can be sure that they are trusting and not just knowledgeable."

"There was also a greeting that only Balmore and those close to him used."

"And if you cannot remember it, then it does us little good," said Dagger.

"I think that we need to remove ourselves from this place before more of the patrons are replaced," Sala added looking around the room.

The travelers watched, as men entered the inn and began to make some of the others leave. It was a subtle move, and unless anyone was paying close attention they would not have noticed it happening. Sarn found himself looking for the shadows of the room, but Dagger placed a hand on his shoulder stopping him from getting up. Tig however, was already hunting his first victim, crawling from table to table. Pulling their swords, the travelers prepared themselves for what they felt was inevitable. Sala pushed the Prince behind her with the two making their way to the nearest wall.

"I do not wish to state the obvious," Sala began.

"Then I would suggest that you do not," Sarn returned.

Dagger giggled and joined his companions near the wall and readied themselves for what they felt was yet to come.

"How many do you think that there are in this room?" asked Dagger.

"More than I wish to take the time and count," Sarn replied.

"That is heartening to know," Dagger returned almost laughing.

"You did ask me."

"You have no reason to fight those here. Their only concern is for the boy," Herina said stepping in front of the group.

"It is why they are concerned for him that bothers me," Dagger said.

"I know that you are Ryn Mar. I know that you are the thief of Macenis, and that you are the one that King Gregor set out to find and get to return his son. There are those in this castle that do not wish the return of the Prince, and there are those that would do anything to affect his return."

"God bless and protect all here," Balmore said walking into the inn.

"With the shields of Gregor so he shall," answered every man in unison that was now sitting or standing in the room.

"I think we just might be onto something here," Sarn whispered in Daggers direction.

"Yes," Dagger returned. "It would seem so. Whether it is for good or ill we shall soon find out."

"With my sword and yours we shall return the rightful heir," Balmore finished and went over to the travelers. "I am sorry your majesty. I was to have met with the rescuers before they reached the summer palace, but was delayed."

Sala, Dagger and Sarn each raised their sword and pointed it in the direction of Balmore.

"Or you were never coming and are now going to take him from those of us that did risk their lives," said Dagger taking a step forward.

Prince Gregor stepped behind Dagger and hid, while Sala and Sarn stepped to Dagger's side.

"If we are to wait until the time is right," Dagger began, reaching for his crystal, "we will need to find a safe place somewhere in the castle walls to stay hidden until then."

"We will take him and will hide him," Balmore added. "You can be sure that he will be safe with us until his father returns and we can take our Kingdom back."

"I think it best if you let us leave this place so we can hide on our own," Dagger returned looking into Balmore's eyes as he spoke.

"There is no place that you will be safe to hide. We are the only hope for you and for our Prince," returned Balmore.

"There may be something to what you say. But since your Prince cowers and hides form you," Sarn interrupted, "I think that you have little choice in the matter."

"Is this something that you know or is it just something that you suspect?" Dagger whispered to him.

"I do not know for sure," Sarn returned in a whisper. "But I think there might be something to what Balmore says about needing to keep the Prince hidden."

"Then we will see what comes our way over the next day or two," added Dagger

The group lowered their swords and moved back to the table.

"We will hang onto the Prince until we can be sure of what is going to happen next," added Sala after sitting down.

"I would prefer that he come with me."

"Then we all come with you," said Sarn stepping back from the table again.

"I will not go anywhere without them," the boy interrupted, taking Sala's hand.

Balmore studied the boy closer before agreeing to his demand.

"If you feel that strong about it, I can make the necessary changes within the circle."

"No," Dagger returned. "We need only a place to hide, nothing more."

"As you wish, but you must leave this inn. It will not be safe here much longer. I am afraid that the movement of the circle will be noticed."

"Then perhaps you should not all meet in one place at the same time."

"This is but a handful of the circle," Balmore said looking about the inn. "We are near five hundred."

"Then I would think that it would be rather easy to overthrow Foulas and his men."

"It would not have been wise to do so with the Prince locked away in Lord Dermit's summer palace. He would have been dead before we took the last man."

"Now he is here," Sarn said moving to the side of Sala and the Prince. "And soon he will be where he belongs. Let us not waste this man's time any longer."

"I am in no hurry to die. I think we can protect the Prince and still be in the company of these men. If you are having second thoughts, we can discuss them as soon as we are in a good hiding place," Dagger told Sarn, knowing that they would need Balmore to keep them safe, at least for now.

It mattered little to Dagger if Balmore meant to harm the Prince or not. He only knew that until King Gregor returned and there were enough men to rid them of Foulas and his men they were his only hope. Dagger whistled twice for Tig, and the travelers made their way through the crowd of bowing men. Each offered their sword to the Prince; who took the time to touch each of the men on the head as he passed. Once near the door Garis led the way out of the inn and down the street. People seemed to part before them as they went and Sarn thought that he even caught one or two of them bowing as they went. It was an almost unnoticeable motion in most of them, but for some it was not so subtle and he was certain that they had bowed.

Garis led the travelers down several streets and more than one alley before they stopped. It was near an outside wall of the castle and not a place that Dagger would have chosen for them.

"This belongs to the best baker in the village," Garis told them as he opened the door of the stable. "You can stay here in the loft. We will bring you everything you need to be comfortable and the baker will get you whatever else you might need."

Dagger thanked Garis as the travelers saw to their horses. When they were finished they were shown the hayloft and introduced to the baker, his wife, and their five children. Three of the children were around the same age as Prince Gregor making them perfect to help keep him from being bored. Making themselves at home with the help of several blankets they made themselves beds in the hay. All the baker's children helped by clearing part of the loft, making room for some chairs and a table that were brought up to them by two of Balmore's men. Following close behind were more of his men with two small barrels of wine and two of ale.

"All the comforts of home," Dagger said once the men had gone.

"So it would seem," Sarn returned. "I get the feeling that they intend on keeping us here and keeping the Prince elsewhere."

"I will not go with them without you," Prince Gregor added grabbing Sala's hand.

"I am afraid that you have no choice," interrupted Balmore. "You are needed elsewhere."

"You told me that I would be allowed to stay with Sala. You told me that I did not have to leave them, you said...."

"I know what I said and I know what needs to be done."

"Then if in fact you are taking him from us, you can pay us what is owed and we will be on our way," Dagger added.

"You have no agreement with me, so if you wish your blood money then you must stick around and get it from the King himself."

Dagger said nothing to Balmore, instead he turned away getting his own suspicions about the man.

"I will not leave them," Gregor said, taking more than two steps away from Sala for the first time since the day after he was rescued. "I do have a choice and I choose to stay here or they go with me. You are sworn to protect me, and to obey my orders. And now I order you to leave me here with my friends."

"As you wish Your Majesty," Balmore said. His face showed his distain and disapproval of Prince Gregor's choice.

"Besides I do not follow people that lie to me," Gregor added.

Balmore knelt before the Prince and asked his forgiveness in the matter. He shook his head and left the hayloft and then the stable. The travelers settled into what they hoped would be a short stay in the hayloft. Tig, ever vigilant, made his home at the top of the stairs while Dagger and Sarn placed several alarms around the loft itself. It did not take them long to settle into their new home. Dagger poured the first mug of ale and sat back on a pile of hay and sipped the dark amber colored liquid.

"If we need to hide I could think of worse places to have to hide in," he said wiping his mouth.

"And I could think of better places to be in," returned Sala.

"It is a good thing I never said you would get to live in luxury," Sarn laughed.

"I would say that it was a good thing too." She hugged Sarn and kissed his cheek. "I am going to go get some bread and a couple of cakes for later and find out more about this family."

The Prince clung to Sala's side as she headed down the stairs. Stopping halfway down she told him that he needed to stay up in the hay loft. It was a hard sell but he went back and sat with Tig at the top of the stairs to wait for her to return. He looked as if he had just lost his best friend in the whole world and did not move for the entire hour that Sala was gone.

Returning with some cakes and breads, Sala set them on the table only to find Gregor once again attached to her side. Dagger took the boy by the hand and led him from her. Placing him on his knees he told him that it was time he let go of the shirt tale of women and time that he learned a bit about protecting himself. He got Sarn to help him clear back more of the hay. When it was finished, he enlisted his help in the training of the young Prince. The three worked away the afternoon stopping only for water or to make sure that neither of them had hurt the boy. Sala watched from on top a pile of hay, applauding when the boy would manage to get the upper hand. More to the point, that is when the teachers would allow him the upper hand. That evening after their meal, Balmore tried again to remove the boy. Again Gregor admonished the guard for even trying. The Prince instead showed off his earlier lessons to Balmore before telling him to leave. As the sun left the sky and the hayloft grew dark the group settled in to their respective beds. While it was hard for them to convince the Prince to sleep in a bed of his own, after a while they managed it. Although, not without more than a little pouting coming from him.

A low rumble came from deep within the fortress that stood alone in the middle of the lake. Dark clouds closed in around it, cutting off the streaks of light that tried to make its way through them. The rumbling began to shake the lone tower that stood above the fortress. The water moved away from its outer walls in ripples, then waves. Soon the rumbling was followed by a low growling sound. A red glow became visible from the windows in the fortress. Loose stones rattled down the walls and landed in the courtyard and into the surrounding water.

Standing in the tower on its highest level a lone dark figure stood with his arms outstretched and his head tossed back. He was speaking in a language that had been lost. The words rang through the fortress, across the lake and into the forest.

A scream came from deep within the walls, the painful sound rising up to meet the dark figure. The scream ended and the rumbling stopped as quick as it had started.

"Welcome home," the dark figure whispered. When he finished he turned and descended deep into the tower.

The red glow faded. At its source stood Lord Crel, stretching out his arms and rolling his head as if he were testing his body.

"That gets more painful every time he does that."

"I still think that we should have waited longer. It would have been easier and perhaps less painful."

"I must move fast. If we wait too long we will lose and you know how I hate to lose."

"But you were not meant to fail. It is just a matter of time; it will happen soon enough."

"I am the one that is supposed to speak of patience."

"Then rejoin with me and we will be as we were meant."

"Yes, for now," the figure from the tower said stepping closer to the other.

"Live as one, be as one," the two said embracing each other.

The red glow reappeared as the two joined as one.

"We will wait and then I will go out again, leaving you behind. Soon our destiny will be reached."

Crel climbed the steps up to the top of the tower and looked out.

"I will return Ryn Mar. You have not seen the last of me, but of course you know that. And as for you Sarn of Penif," Crel laughed, "we have just begun our struggle. In the end I will kill you and everyone close to you."

Lightning struck the fortress as he finished speaking as if to seal his words.

"When I am ready, we will meet again Ryn Mar. You can be sure of that. Until then, I am sure that your parents will keep you busy, as I intend to show them everywhere you should be." Crel looked out over the lake, trying to see beyond it.

Standing at the edge of the lake the two sisters watched as the lightning bolt struck the tower.

"How long do you think it will take him to get out this time?"

"With any luck never," Meglyn said.

"Then you had better not interfere by casting a spell."

"What are you trying to say?"

"Nothing, it is just that, you know how you get," Caitlin said backing away from her sister.

"No, tell me how I get."

"It is just that I do not want to have to clean up after you again."

"Please, you never have to clean up after me."

"If I never cleaned up after you, we would still be chasing after Krenoras. You remember who he is?"

"Oh, sure, bring him into this argument. I forgot to say one thing and you have never let me forget. It has been over two hundred years. You would think that you would have at least forgiven me, if not forgotten it."

"You have no idea, do you?"

"I know exactly what I do every day."

"That, sister, is exactly what scares me."

Meglyn laughed and knelt down, placing a hand into the water.

"It feels worse than I remember."

Caitlin shook her head and tried to pull her sister away from the water.

"It should not be painful," a voice said behind them. "It should be free from pain."

"Great," Meglyn said "this is not turning out to be a good day."

"Hello brother," Caitlin said giving the man a hug. "It is good to see you again."

"It is always good to see you both," he told them. "You did do what you were supposed to?"

"Well ...," Caitlin began.

"Of course we did, why would you think that we did not?" Meglyn finished.

"It could be because Crel is in his fortress and not where he was supposed to be after the encounter."

"That half breed, Ryn Mar beat him to it," Meglyn said.

"I see, then he just allowed Ryn to bury his head so that it could be found and he could reincarnate?"

"Something like that," Caitlin answered.

"That is not his destiny. That is not what is supposed to have happened. This was to be over so that the next heir can rule the Kingdom."

"We have heard it all before. If you are trying to tell us something new then you are wasting your time," Meglyn said pointing her finger at him.

"Meglyn," Caitlin said grabbing at her sisters hand. "You know why he is asking these questions. There is nothing that we have done for him to think that we did as we were told. Crel has reincarnated in the tower, just as he has every time before."

"And the two of you were to have done something about that," he said looking at his sisters before walking into the lake. "But still, he grows stronger."

He went into the water to his waist, pulled a small book from his shirt pocket and began to read from it.

"Within the water keep, within these waters deep, release the pain, release those that are imprisoned here. Release the spirits from here that keep him strong."

"No, what are you doing?" Crel screamed from the tower window. "It is not the way it is to be! You cannot interfere!"

As he finished, the water began to glow a light blue and swirl around him. He held out his hands as the glow rose from the lake, running through his fingers, and then up into the sky. As the spirits of Lord Crel's victims rose up from the lake the brother laughed.

"Now, you must do as you have been told," he told them as he came out of the water. "I will not do this again. I should not have had to do this at all. If you two will just get it over with, we will all be able to rest."

The brother did not wait around for them to say anything more in their defense. Turning his back to them he walked away, never once looking back.

"If he thinks it is so important, why does he not tell him?" asked Meglyn. "Better still, why does he not finish Crel?"

"You know why he cannot do that."

"I do, but why does he have to be that way," Meglyn asked as they watched him walk off.

"Because he is right," Caitlin answered. "We have done nothing of what we were supposed to have done."

"It is not like you have gone out of your way to do it," Meglyn defended herself in her usual way of not taking any blame.

"And another mess I am sure that I will be blamed for." Caitlin looked at her sister then shook her head and walked away.

"If he is so powerful and we have messed it up so bad, then he should be the one to tell him," Meglyn called after her sister.

Caitlin stopped for a second, began to turn around before catching herself and continued walking.

"Where are you going?"

Caitlin did not answer her sister, knowing that anything she said would just prolong their argument. Making the easiest thing for her to do at that time was to just keep walking.

"You cannot interfere with this," Crel yelled again. "It is not supposed to be this way. You cannot interfere!"

Caitlin could barely hear it and stopped to listen to him.

"I will get out again. It is just a matter of time. It is just a matter of time before I see to it that your line is finished and never remembered," he said over and over.

She could hear him laughing as she started walking again. She wanted to laugh too, but she knew that he would get out of the tower and off the lake. It was just a matter of time and if Meglyn kept her from talking to their nephew, there was a good chance that he could win out after all. It was not as if they could do anything to keep him in the fortress forever and neither could the brothers. As it was the parents could only cast him into the tower. They were the ones that sent him there in the first place. Crel was the one that figured how to get off the lake by filling it with the spirits of his victims. The ancients were the ones who figured out who would be able to kill him once and for all.

Caitlin raised her hand over her head as she walked. Laughing, she pointed her finger toward the fortress. A white light shot from her finger and struck the fortress. For a brief moment the black looking tower turned bright white. Laughing louder, hoping that Crel would hear her, she raised her hand one more time. Again white light shot from her finger into the tower window, landing at Crel's feet. Stepping back from the bolt of light he shook his head, a little in disgust and a little in helplessness.

"You missed," He yelled, "Not that it is going to do you any good anyway. You are going to have to do little better than that."

"I know I cannot kill you," she yelled back to him before laughing again. "I just want to have some fun with you while I am here."

Over the next few weeks the travelers did little else but work on their training. Balmore came by everyday trying to remove the boy from the loft. Everyday young Gregor would reject him and send him off with nothing more than what he came with. After the first week Sala began to help in the bakery while the others took over the care of the animals. Gregor often felt that it was beneath him to help in the stable but after a while he began to look forward to the chore. After falling several times from the loft, Dagger, for the most part stayed there. Every few days though he would leave and would not tell of where he was going, or had been when he returned. Sarn had attempted several times to follow him when he left, but he would always lose him. At night Dagger would tell tales of his thievery, and each tale he told would become more unbelievable.

After some time Tig began moving away from the stairs. He was becoming bored in the confines of the loft and began to watch over the others by walking the beams over their heads. He had a pattern to his movements, twice over his master, three times over the Prince, and once over Sarn and Sala. Then he would lie for several minutes over the heads of Pel and the other horses watching the goats and the cows. He seemed restless and sleeping less, spending most of his time looking out the door that was used to bring in hay from the alley below.

The baker's oldest daughter would take the animals out of the castle every day to a field where they could spend the day grazing and exercising. Pel being himself would not let her get too close to him but did allow her to hold the rope that Sarn put around his neck. Pel also saw to it that none of the others ran off during their trips outside the walls.

"We will not be training tomorrow," Dagger announced one night after several hours of drinking.

While Sarn was curious he did not ask why. He accepted the break from the tedious days of training and thought that perhaps he would use it to exercise Pel himself. However, Sala saw it as a good reason to be able to spend the day doing some shopping.

The following morning after they had fed and milked the animals Sarn led Pel and the others out of the castle with the baker's daughter. Once through the gate he mounted Pel and rode off, with the other horses close behind. Even though it was raining a little he felt free being out from the loft and liked the feeling of the rain falling against his face. He could not help but begin to wonder what lie ahead for him. When he left home he had just wanted to travel and have a little adventure. He never gave it much thought about what he might do if in fact he got what he was looking for. Sala was a benefit that he had never thought of whenever he had thought of leaving home. Although, now that she was in his life he could not think of it without her. Dagger had even become more than a mentor. He had taught him more in a few short months than he could have ever thought he would learn in a lifetime. With only another month of good weather before the leaves would start to turn, he hoped that they would be able to take Foulas soon. He did not want to think of having to spend the winter in the hayloft. He rode Pel to the woods and began to turn to ride the edge around the fields back to the gate. As he turned, out of the corner of his eye he saw a movement in the wheat. Circling around, he moved closer to the movement. He could have kicked himself for not remembering to bring his sword along with him. Working his way closer to where he saw the movement he hoped he could cut in front of whatever it was that he had seen.

"Why are you hiding?" Sarn asked when he found the source of the movement.

"I am looking for my friend," answered Solari. "He is supposed to be around here somewhere."

"What is your friend's name, perhaps I know them."

"I doubt it, he was taken from his house over there and was supposed to have been somewhere else, but he was not there either. Maybe I need to go back home and try to find him there."

"Where is home?"

"It is... it... I ... I," Solari stuttered. "Maybe my other friend knows where my friend is. He is in the forest over there. He is waiting for another friend of ours."

"What is the name of your friend?" Sarn asked, but was pretty sure that he knew the answer. "Who is your other friend?"

"My friend is named Foulas," he said. "Oh... I do not know what his friend's name is."

Sarn searched the edge of forest hoping that he was wrong. Yet he knew he that was right, Prince Gregor was the friend that the two were both looking for.

"Tell me your friend's name. The one that you are looking for and I will ask around for you in the castle. If he is there I will tell him that you are looking for him and that he should come out to see you."

"You would do that for me? You are a good person, and you have such a beautiful horse too." Solari waved to Sarn before turning and running off back toward the forest.

Sarn rode in the same direction and manner as he had before seeing Solari in the hopes that he would not raise any suspicion. With the other horses close at hand again he took off toward the baker's daughter. He told her to take the animals back to the stable and to send word to Balmore that he needed to see him. Sarn was careful not to do anything to change the daily happenings in the fields. Just in case Foulas had been in the forest longer than that morning.

He passed through the gate just as easy as he had on the way out, leading Pel past the guards and up the streets to the stable next to the bakery. Once back in the stable Sarn found Dagger sitting cross legged in the middle of the loft floor. The Prince and Sala were nowhere to be found, while Tig was sound asleep on Dagger's blankets. With his head in his chest Dagger sat motionless. Sarn tried to talk to him, but he did not move or answer him. Going down into the bakery he found Gregor helping with pastries. When Gregor saw him he dropped what he was doing and ran to him and gave him a hug.

"I missed you while you were gone," the Prince began, "I came down here to help with the pastries while Sala went to the markets."

Sarn nodded and ran his hand through the boy's hair. He told the baker that he need to talk to Balmore and that he should keep the Prince with him until he returned. He agreed to try and keep him busy until then, but offered no guarantee that he would be able to. Smiling, he returned to the hayloft and tried not to get in the way of Dagger and whatever it was that he was doing. It was not long before the baker's daughter returned with the other animals. After returning them to their proper places she waved to Sarn and ran out the door.

She returned a short time later, but it would be an hour before Balmore arrived. Meeting him in the stable, he again argued the point of taking the Prince with him.

"Are you aware that Foulas is waiting in the forest for the Prince?" Sarn asked after allowing him to speak.

Balmore nodded his answer.

"When were we going to be told this?"

"Never," he answered almost defiant. "How did you find out?"

"I wanted to give Pel more exercise than he had been getting and I saw Solari searching the wheat fields for Gregor."

"The circle is aware of everything that Foulas does."

"Then why is he in the forest? Just what is he looking for and how long has he been there?"

"He looks for the Prince," Balmore began. "They both do. He thinks that your group has been delayed in the forest. He left with most of his army just days before you arrived here. He has been looking for you and the Prince since that time. He camps now in the forest to keep the Prince from getting to the gates."

"What good is the Prince to him alive if he believes the King is already dead?"

"That would be a question for Foulas. Although, I would think that you would not want to talk to him alone, considering that he thinks that you and your little group are supposed to be dead as well. If not dead, at the very least you are lost in the forest chasing after one of Ryn Mar's cousins."

"If you have known all this, why have you not told us before?" Sarn asked, not showing any emotion to what Balmore was telling him.

"It was not important that you knew," Balmore said growing impatient. "If we thought that you needed to know you would have been told."

"I see, and if Foulas is outside of the castle why are you and the circle not taking over the ramparts and parapets? Why is it that we are not making our way to the palace as we speak? What is it that you are waiting for?"

"He is waiting for Crel to come," Dagger said standing at the top of the stairs.

The two looked up at him. Sarn was not sure what to say to him and Balmore was too shocked that he knew the true reason for the wait.

"The head that I buried belonged to Crel," Dagger smiled from under the hood of his cloak. "He was the girl at the summer palace. They are no doubt still looking for his head. I am sure they have already found his body. I can only guess that the guard we freed has been unable to find the head that I buried or something else happened to him. Then again something could have happened to the head."

"The head?" Balmore said shivering, "Why would something

happen to his head?"

"It was not attached to his body when I buried it."

"I have heard stories of you. Until this moment I had always thought that they we just tall tales. Now I am beginning to think that more than one of them could be true."

"I am sure that more than one of them are true," Dagger said. "I happen to agree with my friend. Just what is your reason for not taking over the castle while Foulas is away?"

"It is just that I ...," Balmore stuttered, taking a few steps back from Sarn. "We were waiting for the right time."

"I would think that the timing would not be better," Sarn said. It was his turn to become impatient. "Unless of course there is something you continue to hide from us."

"I have told you everything," Balmore said turning and storming out of the stable.

"I think that there is more," Dagger said. "What do you think?"

Sarn nodded and went to get Gregor.

Dagger in turn whistled for Tig, who stretched as he stood before making his way to his master's side. He bent over and whispered in his friend's ear. When he was finished, Tig turned and went back up to the hayloft and curled up on his master's blankets.

Sarn found Gregor helping to mix a batter with the baker's youngest son who was just a year younger than the Prince himself. He sat on a stool near the door and watched the boy. It was good that he spent time with the child. It was almost an hour later before Sala and the baker's wife returned with their baskets full of fruits vegetables and meats. The baker's oldest son followed behind them carrying more packages.

"I do not that think they missed a shop," the boy said setting his burden down on the closest available table.

"I missed more than one shop my love," Sala said kissing Sarn on the cheek. "Besides I have more things to buy if we will be spending more time here. My birthday is coming soon and it is an old family tradition that a gift is given to the person born in that month. I see no reason that I should miss out just because I am no longer with any that have the same tradition, so I plan on making my own gift."

Sarn laughed and gave her a quick hug.

"Perhaps we should make you a gown that you can wear at the King's grand banquet that ends the annual battle of Tenisfie celebration. There will be jugglers, plays, shows of strength, and minstrels. If it entertains it will be here in the castle," the baker's wife said, holding up some of the fabric they had bought earlier.

It was not long before Sala found Gregor attached to her side once again. He moved as she moved; each step he followed with his own. The others looked, but said nothing; he just seemed to belong next to her. It was almost as if they were mother and son. It was a makeshift family at best but it was one that Sala did not shy away from. It was not as easy for Sarn knowing that when the King returned it would only make it harder for them to part, but he did his best not to interfere. As they were heading back to the stable Gregor took his hand as they followed Sala.

With Tig on his blankets sleeping again, Dagger waited until the others returned for him to leave the loft. He slipped out just as the family made their way up the steps. Sarn caught sight of him and waited just a few moments to follow him.

Dagger made his way down the streets with his hand thrust in his pocket holding tight to the crystal as he went. Sarn followed him as he went from shop to shop. He looked in on him through the windows to see what he was doing. Dagger talked for a moment with each of the shop owners before leaving and moving onto the next shop. He lost track of him after being distracted by a scuffle between a beggar and a guard. It would be several minutes before he was able to find him again. Looking into the shop he caught a glimpse of his friend going into the back room. Shaking his head as if he were ashamed of himself, he turned and went back to the hayloft. He could not tell why he even felt the need to follow his friend in the first place.

Sala stood at the top of the stairs looking out over the animals, running her hand over her stomach while Gregor sat at the table. She smiled to herself and began to hum a song that her grandmother used to sing to her when she was a little girl. She never could remember what the words were or where the song had come from. Over the years she had asked several musicians that she had met at Calid's tavern and none could say for certain what the words had been. She had not thought to ask her grandmother when she had seen her last. Her smile disappeared as she realized that she may never get the opportunity to ask her again. At the same time she could not help but wonder just how much longer they would have to stay there. It was not the best place to hide, and she knew it. It was only a matter of time before trouble would find them. It did not help that they had all done something that they should not have. Sarn having gone out to exercise the horses, she going to the shops, and now Dagger out and about the castle in the daylight. They should have all stayed where they were and spent the day resting. Dagger had said that there was a chance that they may have to spend the rest of the summer and into the fall there. She hoped that it was not true. She wanted to go somewhere where the winter would not be as harsh as the baker and his wife were saying that it usually was there. There were many other things for her to worry about other than what the weather might be during the winter. Deciding instead to worry only about what Sarn would say about her day of shopping. Laughing to herself she began going through the baskets that the baker's son brought up. Finding what she was looking for, she went to the corner of the loft. She stepped behind the blankets they had put up so that she and Sarn could have more privacy at night. By the time that Sarn returned she had changed into the dress that she had bought. She knew that she might not be able to bring it with them when they finally left Tenisfie, but until then she planned on wearing it often. If she were the type, she would want him to swear his everlasting love for her and get married as soon as the mood struck her. But that was far from what she wanted from him. She had his love, she had his body each night, and there was nothing more that she could get from him or give to him that she could ever want.

"Do you love me?" she asked after he complimented her on the dress.

"Love; what is this sudden interest in love?"

"I am a girl," she replied. "Half of my life is about love."

He took her in his arms and began kissing her on the neck, face and lips, ignoring her question.

"You two sure kiss a lot," Gregor chimed in.

The two laughed and turned toward the boy as if they had forgotten him.

"That is what you do when you feel as we do toward each other," Sala told him trying not to embarrass Sarn.

"My mother and father never kissed in front of me. I think I like seeing it," he said running up to them and hugging them both around the waist. "When I am King I will make everyone in the Kingdom kiss as often as the two of you do every day."

They laughed at his idea, not that it was bad idea it was just that it sounded silly when he said it. Sala turned them loose and started work on their evening meal.

Dagger returned a couple of hours later, handing Sala a small bundle tied with string. Sitting with the others at the table, they discussed their day as they ate. Each had their own theory about Foulas and the actual reason he had taken to the forest.

"Do you believe Balmore?" Sarn asked as Dagger sat down.

"No," Dagger answered trying not to give away too much in front of Gregor. "I think that perhaps Foulas did leave some time before we arrived, and I think he waits for Crel. There is another reason why they did not stop us from reaching the village."

"I cannot believe that he just now found out," Sala said sure that they were all thinking the same thing. "How can he have just found out? We have been here for weeks."

"We cannot be sure how long he has been there, can we?" Sarn asked.

"I guess the first thing we need to do is to find out how long he has been out there. Then perhaps we can know why he is there, unless ...," Dagger stood and walked to where Tig had been sleeping earlier. He crawled up onto the rafters of the loft, one hand in his pocket and the other balancing himself against the roof. "Unless, he has been there all along and is waiting for Lord Crel. He may have watched us come into the castle; he may be waiting for the circle to show with the Prince. Then again, I could be speaking out of turn and he has no idea what is going on around him."

"Solari said he was looking for their friend," Sarn began. "I thought that he meant Prince Gregor; it could be Crel I guess. Then again any of your ideas could be right. I have a feeling that he does not know the Prince is here. He is waiting for him; that I am almost sure. To kill him, perhaps; to steal him back is more likely. No, he thinks that we are still in the forest waiting for the right time to bring him in. Is the circle hoping that when Gregor returns Foulas will lay down his arms and let the young Prince have the throne? There is little chance of that happening. No, we need to let everyone know that he is alive; if not for the sake of this Kingdom, then for the sake of our own lives. I am quite certain that Balmore has no intention of letting him take over his father's throne. I am beginning to believe that he has his own plan and it does not include Gregor or us."

"Then what do you suggest?" Dagger asked sitting on the highest beam. With the crystal to his forehead he faced the now open door that Tig often looked out.

"We take the castle and place Gregor in power for as long as it takes," Sarn returned.

"For as long as it takes?" Sala asked beginning to get worried.

Laughter came from both Gregor and Dagger, but they waited for Sarn to explain.

Sarn stood and began to walk from one end of the loft to the other, then began to think out loud.

"If I were Crel what would the one thing be that I worried most about? Would it be the return of Gregor or his father? Would I be worried about the circle, or the man? Would I be worried about three thieves and their animal, or would I be worried about the peasants of the Kingdom? Should I have my puppet stay in the palace, or should I have him outside where he cannot be harmed by three thieves or the peasants?" He kept walking back and forth across the loft not stopping for some time.

Sala thought that they were quite the pair with Dagger in the rafters and Sarn walking the floor. She chuckled at them and smiled toward Gregor who joined her, before following Sarn step for step. Sala only laughed harder as she watched the three of them, Tig crept up behind his master and sat placing his head on his shoulder.

Look at my men she thought as she laughed. I will always think of this day when I think of us.

If Dagger knew any of the answers to the questions, he was not telling. He just sat in silence and continued to look out the open door.

That night behind the makeshift wall Sarn and Sala lay holding each other's hand with Gregor lying beside them.

"Do you think I will see my parents again?" he asked the two.

"I cannot be sure of that," Sarn answered.

"You will see them again," she told the boy, "sooner or later."

"You mean, here or in the after, right?"

Sala took her free hand and caressed the boy's face pushing a tuft of hair around on his head.

Sarn rolled his eyes at her, but it went unseen in the darkness of the hayloft.

Later that evening Dagger went to the open door in the rafters of the hayloft and crawled out, with Tig close behind him. The two made their way across the peak of the roof and stepped over to the baker's house. They moved in silence across the rooftops to the castle wall. It was a long leap from the last roof top to the parapets and Tig made it with ease.

"Show off," Dagger whispered as Tig landed on the walkway.

Reaching into his cloak he pulled out a short stick, set it on the edge of the roof and knelt down.

Holding his hands just above it he began to mumble a few unheard words. Soon a blue glow enveloped his hands and the stick. Soon it began to grow until it reached from the roof to the parapet.

He took a tentative step onto the temporary bridge.

"Well what do you know, it works," he whispered as he walked across it. "Maybe I should have given him more gold for it."

Reaching the other side, he knelt, held his hands over the bridge and spoke the words again. When the stick shrunk to its original size he picked it up and stuck it back into his cloak. Tig looked over the wall and with one leap dropped to the ground on the outside of the castle. Dagger shook his head as he made his way to the steps picking his way down the wall. He walked through the gate as if he did it every night. His cloak in its ever present position, pulled as far down over his head as he could get it. Using the crystal gripped in his hand he glanced behind him as he walked. He met up again with his friend a short ways from the castle wall. The two made their way as quick as the moonlight would let them, going across the fields and into the trees. Using the shadows to hide themselves the two worked their way to Foulas' camp. They seemed to have no concerns about their safety as they had not set a watch, making it much easier for the pair to get in close. Dagger pointed to the other side of the camp and Tig turned and went through the shadows across from him. Dagger held the crystal to his forehead and searched the encampment. He was not exactly sure what he was looking for, but he kept looking just the same. He began to get angry with himself for not having brought Sarn along. It may have made it easier to find what he was looking for. He began thinking of how he could have used this as more training for Sarn. He kept telling himself that weapons training would not be all he would need to survive. Dagger caught himself from thinking more. Shaking his head he brought his mind back to the task at hand.

Just as he caught himself, there was a movement to his right and he turned to face it.

"What are we looking for?" Tobias whispered.

"I could have killed you."

"As long as you did not, that is all that matters," he reached out and took hold of his cousin's arm. "Who is this that you watch, and where is the one that you are supposed to be training? Why are you here by yourself? Is Tig around? Has your charge been captured? Have you seen Canis? What of the boy you were to have rescued?"

"Do you have any other questions that you wish to ask?" he added before turning away from his cousin. Instead Dagger looked across to Tig through the crystal, who lowered his head as if he knew what his master was thinking.

"I am sure that I have more, but they can wait until I find out what is going on now," Tobias added.

"Then you must be quiet and say nothing until I say you can."

The two crouched in the brush at the edge of the encampment and waited in silence as the night wore on. It took longer than Dagger had hoped, but Foulas finally came out from his tent and moved among his men. Solari was close behind him dancing around and through the guards as if he were at a festival. Dagger watched each one close marking each of their actions to his memory. There was something about the two and the way they moved about that bothered him. He was not sure what it was that bothered him about their movements.

"They look as if they do not move on their own," Tobias pointed out.

"Just how would they be moving, together as one?" Dagger whispered.

"No, it is as if they are being told what to do. Watch that tall one there, the one watching the dancing fool. Tell me that a leader of men would stand by as this fool did those things to his men and not be laughing. If not laughing, what leader would not be telling him to stop."

Dagger shook his head before pointing out that the leader would be doing neither if they had enough of the other's antics. But there was also something to what Tobias had said. It was something that he could not overlook or pass off as his cousin talking too much as usual.

None of the men seemed to have a purpose. They were sitting in the woods as if they had just come to the forest to fish or hunt. They did not seem to be looking for anyone either, nor did they seem to be protecting anything. They were just sitting around their campfires talking to each other of the forest, their wives, the food, some tavern women, but nothing of why they might be there. One would expect that an army would be talking among themselves about what they were doing or where they were going. Dagger had set outside many encampments to listen to what was going on. He decided that they were far from being typical soldiers in an encampment and that bothered him a little. Lowering the crystal and turning away from the encampment he motioned for Tig. When they reached the edge of the forest Tobias stopped his cousin.

"What do we do now cousin?"

"We are going to do nothing. I want you to circle back around to the river and wait for me. I will be there in about a day or two," Dagger told him. "You must not search the other side of the castle for me. I need you to keep our escape open. Do you understand that?"

"Cousin," Tobias began, "I know what to do and I have done it before. You can count on me to do as you wish, as always."

Dagger shook his cousin's hand, before motioning Tig back toward the castle. Tobias ran toward the road and turned, following it into the forest.

"That is exactly why I told you not to look for me on the other side of the castle. I know that is exactly what you are going to do. You will no doubt also tell my parents that I am in the forest on the other side of the castle, keeping any harm coming to us from there." Dagger laughed to himself as he watched his cousin disappear into the trees. "Sometimes I think that I should be nicer to him, but only sometimes."

Turning, he slipped his hand into his cloak, wrapped it around the crystal and ran off toward the castle. He swung wide on the off chance that Tobias had found himself a hiding place where he could see the direction he was taking. Tig was waiting for his friend on the other side of the castle. Taking their time the pair made their way toward the far gate only to find it closed and guarded by three of Balmore's men.

"What should we do now old friend?" Dagger whispered.

Tig lowered his head and went behind his friend, sticking his head between Dagger's legs.

"You always know just the right thing," he told him, taking the animal's head between his hands.

As Dagger finished talking a white glow came from his hands. Tig twisted his head free and slid further under his master, as the glow began to engulf him. In the few seconds Tig began to change. His legs grew longer and thinner, his neck grew longer, and his fur changed from its orange and black stripes to a light brown. When it was over he had turned into a small pony. Dagger sat astride his friend with his feet just off the ground. They had traveled this way many times. Most of those times were after they had worn out their welcome in some Kingdom or another. It worked well after finishing a job of thievery and they needed a disguise to get away.

"I thought you hated this," Dagger chuckled as Tig began to move toward the gate. "I should ride you more often. Hmm, I think I will call you my trusty charger from now on."

Tig bucked a bit in answer before turning toward the gate, causing only laughter in return from Dagger.

"All this time I thought you liked the animal you are. Now I find you like this one better."

The guards did not question him as he approached. They just opened the gate and allowed him to pass.

Dagger was still laughing as they went under the arch that formed the gateway. The guards watched as the rider and small horse passed by them and pointed at the pair, joining Dagger's laughter. Once inside the two turned into a dark alley, Tig changing back to his normal self as they went.

As the sun began to filter through the cracks of the hayloft, Tig lifted his head and looked out over his charges. When he was satisfied that they were all where he had left them, he lowered his head back between his large paws and closed his eyes. Prince Gregor was the first of the group awake. It was as if Tig's movements had woken him up. Rubbing his eyes the boy slid from under Sala's arms taking great care not to disturb her. The young Prince sat at the table and waited for the others to join him. Tig raised his head again before jumping down from his post. Gregor smiled and pet the animal once before raising the pitcher of wine from the table and striking him over the head with it.

Tig blinked and went to his front knees. Shaking his head he looked up at the boy. Gregor pulled back and raised his arm to protect himself from what he was sure was going to happen. Instead Tig growled waking Sarn and Dagger. Sarn was first to the boy pulling him back and away from the animal. Dagger reached down and touched Tig's head, calming him.

"Why did you do that?" Dagger asked.

"I did nothing! He jumped down from his spot and began to growl at me and I was scared."

"Did you not hit him over the head?"

"No, I could not have, I love him. I would never hurt him."

Dagger took the boys hand and placed it on Tig's head, the

wine already making his coat sticky.

Gregor saw himself grabbing the pitcher and smashing it over Tig's head.

"So I did it. What can you do about it?"

"I should run you through with my sword!"

"Then you would have something to explain to Balmore and the circle," the boy said laughing a little.

"Tell me, what makes you so important that we sit here like trapped animals. Just waiting for the hunters to move in for the kill?" Dagger asked growing angrier.

"I am Gregor, Prince of this Kingdom and all that it holds," the boy began. "I am heir to the throne, mine to do with as I wish."

Dagger turned and placed his hand on the boy's head. Sarn thought that he saw a blue glow come from his friend's hand as it gripped the boy.

"Tell me again what makes you so important boy," Dagger demanded.

"I am Prince Gregor, I am the heir to this Kingdom..." he began again, "I am..."

Sala and Sarn watched as the boy's face changed before them. Dagger was quick to let go of the boy's head and jump back away from him.

Each of them looked at the boy and then each other as if to ask if they had seen what the other had. None of them spoke about it, but they all seemed to agree that something happened.

"What is it?" Gregor asked, looking to each of them in turn.

"It was nothing," Sala told him, taking his hand and leading him away.

"What was that?" Sarn asked when the two were far enough away.

"That, my friend, is why he is so valuable to Lord Crel," Dagger began. "I can tell you one thing; he is not the same Prince Gregor that left this castle some months ago. Lord Crel has corrupted his mind and has a hold on him. I had hoped that by beheading Crel we would have broken the bond between them."

"Then who is he," Sarn asked, still not exactly sure of what was going on around him.

"In body he is Prince Gregor, heir to this Kingdom; but in mind, who is to say at this moment," a voice said from behind them.

Both turned with their swords at the ready. Dagger slipped his free hand into his pocket, grabbing at the crystal as he turned.

"Will!" Dagger cried out, as he figured out who had snuck up

248

on them.

Putting his sword away he rushed to the old man that had shared Sarn's fire some months earlier.

"It has been too long old man," Dagger said after releasing the man from his arms.

"I see you found him. Have you taught him all he will need?" Will asked walking over to Sarn and stretching out his hand.

The old man walked around the boy before taking his returned hand.

"I am close," Dagger returned.

"Good," the old man said still holding Sarn's hand. "I see he has already shown his worth in battle, good. Preformed quite well too I see. A bit slow yet though, that will hurt. Well I guess he cannot be perfect immediately. Hmm, now there is something I did not expect, but she is pretty and quite a warrior herself. Where is she? I must meet her. Now that on the other hand is troubling, I must see to that soon." The old man let go of Sarn's hand and walked around the makeshift living area in the loft.

"She took Gregor to the bakery for some cakes," Dagger returned. "While she was gone I thought I would tell him of what is going on with the Prince."

"Perfect," the old man began again as he sat at the small table. "Perhaps you will allow me the honor of the telling."

Dagger nodded his head and waved his arm in Will's direction. Will chuckled looking at Sarn, who shifted his weight looking somewhat uncomfortable.

"That is if I can remember it all. No I guess I don't need to tell of the whole story, just what matters. There was a time when Lord Crel was in line to be a king. In most Kingdoms, royal marriages are arranged with the best interest of the Kingdom in mind. His marriage was no exception. The only difference is that just days before the wedding her family announced that the girl had died. Crel is said to have been devastated, some say he had grown fond of the girl. That is until he found out that she was still alive."

The old man stopped, poured himself a glass of wine and took a drink.

"Mmm, this wine is quite good." Wiping his mouth with the back of his hand he began again. "Where was I? Oh yes. When Crel learned of the deceit he led an army across the girl's Kingdom killing or enslaving everyone he found there. They burned the fields and villages on their march to the castle, turning the countryside black. Crel is said to be of the ancients and well versed in the secrets of the world. Collecting the souls of the dead and entrapping them he began to make himself more powerful. When he was strong enough he tore the rest of the Kingdom apart destroying the castle and all in it. Afterward, he learned that the Royal family had gotten away from him. By the time he found them again, the daughter had married. Some believe that the man she married was an heir to the Valdore throne. When they had their first child Crel kidnapped it, and after turning the boy's mind he returned him. As the child grew he began to have more control over him. When the boy was old enough Crel tried to get the child to kill his parents so that he could control that Kingdom through the child. Needless to say it failed. When it came to light what he had tried to do the ancients imprisoned him in a tower on a tiny island in the middle of a lake. The ancients tried to undo what Crel had done to the boy, but it was not possible. They say that the child wanders the world to this day looking for Crel."

Sarn looked at the old man as if he had just told him that the sky was the ground and the ground was the sky. As he struggled to believe the old man he paced the floor, stopping every other step to look back before shaking his head and turning away again.

"It would seem that your apprentice does not believe in the ancients and the history of the land in which he fights."

"I do not think he believes in much past his sword and his woman," Dagger answered. "Unless of course you count his mother and father as well."

"Ah, then it is not our place to teach him of these things," the old man said, letting a smile slip across his face. "I take it then you train him only to suit your own needs."

"I train him as I please, no more, no less." Dagger grew angry and turned toward the old man. "What should it matter to you, your place is not here anyway. You are supposed to be miles away from here. You were not to interfere with any of this. You were to go to the twins and stay there. You were not to be wandering around making trouble."

"I do as I please," he returned. "You of all people have no right to tell me of what I am to be doing. You were to be miles from here after returning the young Gregor. Yet here you are holed up in this ... this place."

"I am in my own time and I do as I please," Dagger said dropping to one knee. "You tell a good story, but why do I get the feeling that you are not who you show yourself to be."

With his hand on the crystal he looked deep into the old man's eyes. The old man tried to turn away, but it was too late, a glimmer of recognition was already there. Realizing that he had been discovered he began to rise wide eyed. But it was too late as Dagger was also standing back up. With a motion almost unseen he lifted the head of the old man from his body. Replacing his sword he looked to Sarn who stood wide eyed and mouth agape at what he had just seen.

"Why did you do that?" he asked.

"This was not the old man that you met beside the road," Dagger began. Taking Sarn by the shoulder and turning him away from the headless body. "I know that you do not remember him now, but some day you will. You will remember this day as well, and it will be clear to you then what has happened here. Now cover your eyes my friend, it will take but a moment."

A flash of light filled the area for a brief moment. As the light subsided the body and head of the old man were gone.

"You can uncover your eyes now," Dagger added turning his friend back around.

"Where did it go?"

"They took him," Dagger said as if it was something that happened every day and he was supposed to know who they were.

"They, who are they?"

"What does it matter, you would not believe me if I told you," Dagger said, lowering his head somewhat frustrated. Lifting his head he began again. "Why must you always do this to me? For once can you not send me a believer, just once; a believer. How can that be too much to ask for?"

Puzzled at his friend's words Sarn shrugged his shoulders and wondered who he was talking to, but decided not to ask.

"If these so called Ancients were unable to remove Crel's influence, and we have seen what ... that ...," he said, struggling to find the words and grasping what he was saying. "Are you saying that whatever happened with Gregor to make him break the pitcher of wine over Tig's head .... You mean to say that all that rescuing him from that place was all for nothing?"

"It was not up to them to remove his influence," Dagger said after a few minutes. "That was to have been your ... well it was hoped that he would not have been able to create such a strong bond with him."

A short time later, with Gregor in the relative safety of the baker and his family, the travelers made their way to the tavern.

Herina showed the travelers a table in the back of the tavern and took it upon herself to see to their needs.

Sala ordered a half ale, saying that she only felt like half drinking. While it gave them a good laugh, Sarn was beginning to think that there was something wrong with her.

"It was a good thought you had of coming here," Sala said as their first ales were placed in front of them.

"Are you feeling well?" Sarn asked.

"Of course my love," she answered him smiling and taking his hand. She was glad that she always rose before him each morning so that he would not see or hear her being sick. She just was not ready to tell him about the child she was now sure she was carrying.

Dagger had heard her over the past few mornings, and knowing the symptoms, knew that before spring another would be joining them. Since it was not his place to tell of such things he would continue keeping her secret as if it were his own.

"She is feeling better than you look my friend," Dagger said coming to her defense. "Drink your ale and let us enjoy the evening and stories."

As the evening wore on they were approached by several of the tavern women each trying to win the attention of Sarn and Dagger. Sala would laugh as the women were turned away. A couple of the women were more determined than the others. They would sit on their laps, pushing Sala aside and often knocking her off the bench they were sitting on. Sala laughed at them as both Dagger and Sarn would brush the women off by standing and dropping the women to the floor as they did so. It caused more than one argument among the women that were in the tavern looking for men. One argument even went as far as fighting between two of the girls.

"You call that a fight?" asked a man as he stood after it had ended. "I am Willie and I will take on all in this place. Now that will be a fight!"

The man that called himself Willie lifted his mug and tripped over his bench as he tried to take a drink. The three travelers glanced at each other, then shrugged their shoulders and continued drinking.

Near the end of the night Dagger slipped out of the tavern, unnoticed at first by his fellow travelers. Keeping to the shadows of the torchlight, he made his way along the narrow streets. Slipping from shadow to shadow he was unseen by those that roamed the late night. Turning down an alleyway he found himself in near total darkness. There were few people in the alley and most were too intent on their own survival to care anything of him or what he might be up to. Some women of the street did notice and approached him. Each girl he passed asked if he were looking for them. He answered them in turn with a stern no and laughing a bit to himself. Finally a young girl of about fourteen took his hand and looked up at him.

"It has been a long time traveler," she said as she took his hand.

Dagger stopped and smiled at the girl from under the hood of his cloak. The girl was dirty faced and dressed in clothes that were ripped and torn. The poorest of those that lived within the castle walls lived in and around the alley, and her looks made her fit in with them.

"Almost five years if I remember."

"Yet you look just as you did then," she told him.

She looked up at him, her eyes sparkling and a smile as big as she was. Dagger laughed and squeezed her hand tight as they began to walk.

"I have come to show you the way."

"I think it is too dangerous for you to come this far to show me the way."

"I am not afraid," she said squeezing his hand tighter. "No one noticed me from any of the others that live here."

"Lead the way then my young lover."

"Mother thinks I am too young yet, my love. Soon you will find me ready and as always waiting your tenderness and love." The young girl giggled as she spoke, yet she had been in love with the thief for as many years as she had known him. "I will be fifteen soon and then I will travel with you and care for you as the one that travels with you now."

"Ah, but she is not mine to care for," Dagger returned.

"I hear she looks after the nephew," the girl began. "That is a shame, for I hear he is quite handsome as well. I have heard that he is perhaps even more handsome than you, my love. I might have a hard time deciding between you and him, but for now you have nothing to worry about. I am sure that I would have you and you would have me."

They turned, hand in hand, around a corner in the alley into a narrow walkway. It was so narrow that they could no longer walk side by side. She moved ahead of him, never letting go of his hand.

"Why is it that your sister did not come this time?"

"She was almost noticed last time," she said, as the narrow walkway dead ended. "Father felt it too dangerous and was going to come himself, but mother forbid it. I begged them to let me come for you."

Turning to him she kissed his cheek and reached for the wall near him. Smiling up at him she pushed her hand into a barely noticeable opening in the near complete darkness of the walkway. A small click sounded loud in the quiet of the night, causing Dagger to reach for his sword.

"Do not worry my darling, we are safe here, the sound travels no further than the end of the walkway."

Slipping his hand around the crystal he turned back to look over his shoulder. She pushed against the wall in front of her. The wall slid open revealing a hidden walkway. She pulled him in quick as he continued to look behind them. He pushed the wall back into place behind them hoping that it had gone unnoticed. Pulling a short knife from the folds of her dress she struck the wall several times, causing a spark and lighting a torch that was waiting for them.

"This way," she whispered. "I doubt anyone was paying attention to us as we walked. They no doubt think you are having your way with me in the walkway; perhaps I will let you on our return."

Dagger laughed as he followed behind her. She would no doubt make the offer even if she sounded now as if she were only making a joke. She took his hand again and led the way as the floor beneath them lead down and began to spiral around.

"When you are old enough my young lover, I will be the first to take you up on your offer."

"Of course, and not until," she giggled as she answered him. "You are no fun my darling, no fun at all. Many girls my age are married and have at least one child. You would have me an old maid of about twenty before you believe me old enough."

"You will know your heart for sure by then."

They walked in silence for a while. He lost in his thoughts of the coming days and she dreaming of what it would be like to be close in his arms and kissing him.

"You always were a bit of a romantic," he said finally as if he had been reading her thoughts.

"It is all for you," she said half giggling.

Dagger smiled, not wanting to laugh aloud.

Reaching the bottom of the spiral walkway he pushed open a wooden door. The two stepped away from the walkway and into a large arched hallway that could fit eight men across on horseback. They walked for a short time more before coming to a set of double doors that spanned the width of the hallway. Two smaller hallways led away from the larger one in different directions. Built into one side of the double doors was a normal sized door. It opened into the royal family room, much like the room the travelers had been in before with the large fire pit to one side. The biggest difference was that this room, unlike the last, was occupied and held much more furniture.

"It is good to see you again," called a voice from the other side of the fire pit. "I hope that you have good news."

"It is good to see you again as well King Gregor," Dagger began. "News I have. Is it good is yet to be found, but it is time for us to find out."

King Gregor smiled and took his outstretched hand.

"I told you I would be able to bring him Father."

"Yes," Gregor said, smiling at his daughter. "I had every faith in you Phoebe."

Gregor led Dagger away from the others, talking among themselves as they went.

A soft white light began to glow from the shadows in the loft and drifted toward the sleeping travelers and their charge. It swirled around Tig and his master before lighting on the lovers, finally making its way to the young Prince.

The light engulfed the boy making him glow. Turning faster around him, the light began to change from white to blue before rising up and disappearing.

"Do you think that will be good enough?" the shadowy figure asked, before turning away.

"If it is not, then we will have one more thing to answer for."

Stepping out of the shadows the figure lowered the hood of their cloak revealing the long red hair of one of the sisters.

"What are you doing?" the other asked, turning and reaching out for her sister. "What if you are seen, what then?"

"Then I am seen, what can anyone do to me, to us?"

"We can be exposed and imprisoned. Then how could we protect the nephew from a dungeon?"

"Then maybe it is time I go down there and finally speak to

him. Then we can fulfill our destiny and help him in the open."

"Then shortly thereafter we will have to live our lives in that thing they call a village."

"It has been good enough for our brother for all these years, why would it not be good enough of us."

"He has a wife and the nephew and something to occupy himself. What do we have?"

"We have each other."

"No harm meant sister, but I think that if I had to spend two minutes in that place with just your company I would have to drown myself in that lake."

The redhead turned from her sister shaking her head. Reaching into her cloak she pulled out a short bent stick, waving it around in the air as she walked toward the ledge of the castle wall. Pointing it toward the ground, she took a step off the wall. As the stick reached the bottom of her stroke a blue light engulfed her and she disappeared.

"Show off," her sister said before she too did the same.

As the two sisters disappeared a tall man in a green half cloak stepped from inside the turret. Standing where the sisters had, he looked toward the baker's house.

"Why would the sisters be interested in the goings on of a baker?" he whispered as if anyone were there to hear him. "They are up to no good. I think I can be sure of that."

Turning back toward the turret, he raised his hand as if he were trying to reach something in the air. Waving his hand about before finally deciding on what it was that he wanted from the moonlit night sky. Pulling it back to him he opened his hand, revealing a tiny point of white light.

He lifted the point from his hand and placed it on the stone walkway. Stepping back he pulled a small pouch from around his waist. Opening it he took a pinch of its content and sprinkled it on the tiny light. As the contents hit the light it grew larger and began to dull. As the light finally faded a woman stood before him.

"Did you find him?" she asked as she appeared.

"Not yet, but he is here somewhere. I can feel him."

"I told you not to disturb me until you found him," she scolded raising her hand.

"But Mother, I know he is still here."

"But Mother, but Mother," she began, letting her hand fall across his face. "I grow tired of your halfhearted searches and your excuses. If you were not my son I would have killed you years ago. As it is I am thinking it just the same, except I am not sure how I would explain it to your father. Yet some days I think it would not be so hard after all."

She turned quick and lifted her nose to the night air. She sniffed at it as if she were a dog catching a scent.

"It would seem that you are right," she said, lifting her hand back to her son's face.

He pulled his head away, but she caught it and began caressing his chin.

"I owe you an apology," she said as she ran her hand over his face. "I can smell the magic that can only be a Mar magic."

"I told you that he was here."

"So it would seem, but remember he is not the only one with Mar magic that could be here."

"But, we have not heard from any of them in months and they could not be anywhere near here."

"You forget how close we are to their homes my son," the woman turned again to sniff at the air.

"We are not that close Mother; it has to be a good three weeks walk from here and through forest."

"Sisters," she said, sniffing around the walkway. "You said nothing of the sisters. The sisters were here on this wall as well this night. Why have you not told me of the sisters being here?"

"I thought nothing of it as we are not involved in their business and they are not in ours. I did think it a bit strange for them to have been here though."

"Idiot!" she screamed raising her hand once again, but stopped before striking him. "Those two are in everyone's business no matter the business. Tell me what they were doing."

"Bickering as always, only this time it is about some nephew or something, and they seemed rather interested in the baker's hayloft."

She grabbed her son by the throat and lifted the sizable man off the ground and tossed him against the high wall of the walkway.

"You idiot, that is where we will find Ryn," she said as if she were disgusted. "When you are finished picking yourself up off the ground you will need to get your brothers and sisters. And be quick about it."

"Yes Mother," he said getting up from the walkway and straightening his clothes.

When he was ready, he raised his hand back into the air and

waved it around again before settling on what he wanted. As with his mother he picked the four points from the air and set them on the walkway.

"You there, what are doing on the wall at this hour?" commanded a voice from below them.

"Why must these inferior things keep bothering me?" the mother said sounding disgusted. "Do something about him."

"I can only do one thing at a time Mother. I can either get my brothers and sisters or I can do something about that 'inferior thing'."

"Just hurry up and be done with it."

"Come down from there," called the guard from below.

As he had done before he sprinkled a pinch of powder over the tiny points of light, before turning his attention toward the guard.

Walking to the edge of the wall he poured a handful of powder from another pouch, lifted it and blew across his hand scattering it on the wind. The powder sparkled as if it were dust in the sunlight as it cascaded down over the edge of the wall and onto the guard below. As the sparkles reached the guard they seemed to begin to swirl about him. Soon the only thing that could be seen was the tiny flecks of powder. When all the powder had finally reached the ground the guard was gone.

"It took you long enough."

"I told you I could not do both at the same time."

"You are a Mar," replied one of his sisters. "The only thing that is not possible is what you do not try."

"Excelcia," began one of his brothers, "you must remember he is not exactly like the rest us. He is only Mar by proxy."

"Your brother is full Mar just as you all are," Brunella, their mother said. "We are here only for Ryn."

"What makes you think he will want to be with us?" Excelcia asked.

"I would think that Ryn would want to be with us, after all he is family. There is no reason that he should be here and we are not allowed."

"I keep telling you the reason that Ryn has been allowed to stay here," Creve, one of Dagger's brothers began. "Ryn was not old enough to have participated in our last attempt to 'take our rightful place in this world'. For that Ryn was not banished to the skies as we were. Besides, it is our grandparents that help to hide Ryn."

W. M. Stahl

Each time the brother said the name Ryn it was as if he was spitting it out, instead of saying it.

"Creve, you always think someone is getting more than you," Genna, Ryn's oldest sister said. "What makes you think that Ryn is better off than you are?"

"Ryn can walk the earth, we have to hide in the night sky and wish that we were here."

"If you were here, you would think that we were better off where we were, so just stop your complaining and live with it."

"Stop your complaining!" their mother yelled. "We have much bigger things to deal with."

The two stuck their tongues out at each other like two small children.

"Magic," the sister whispered.

"You don't think, that Brunella is..." the other started.

"She couldn't be, we sent her back. She cannot come back to ground for another... well however long it is, it is not time now."

"Do you think that she has had help?"

"Perhaps we missed one of the children."

"I was certain that we took care of all four of them."

"All four them," the sister groaned "there are six including Ryn."

"I guess you missed one of them."

"Me, you were supposed to make sure that we had sent them all back."

"If you had not distracted me by asking me if we had them all I would not have miscounted."

"How is it that we have gone so long without me strangling you?"

"You would not survive without me."

"If it were not for you, I would be done with all of this and finally be able to rest and perhaps marry."

"Who would marry someone like you?" the sister laughed aloud.

"I have been proposed to and you know it," the sister said, glaring out from under the hood of her cloak, her blue eyes turning blood red.

"I would guess that you are going to tell me it was some king."

"He was a prince."

"A prince," the sister laughed. "When have you ever met a prince?"

259

"This is getting us nowhere," the sister said finally changing the subject. "We need to get back to the castle and protect the nephew and his company."

Sarn woke with a start, as if he had fallen out of the makeshift bed. Looking around he struggled to see in the darkness of the hayloft, his eyes searching for whatever it was that woke him. Tig noticed the movement underneath him and lifted his head. The animal rose and in complete silence stepped across the beam that he had called home.

"Easy Tig," Sarn whispered.

Feeling around Sarn found the lamp on the small table.

"Not going to do us much good if we don't have something to light it with, is it," he whispered again setting the lamp back down.

In two more steps Tig was beside his master's friend moving around him in tight circles.

"Just you and me Tig," he added, reaching down and rubbing Tig's back. "Well I guess we can handle whatever it is, I hope."

Tig stopped and leaned into Sarn for a second in answer.

A red bolt of light shot out in the darkness striking Sarn in the chest. It lifted him off the floor and drove him backwards over the table and against a large beam. Sarn let out a groan as he hit the beam and fell to the floor. Tig leapt out in the direction of where the bolt of light came from. Another bolt struck Tig on the side of his head, tossing him to one side as if he were nothing but a rag. He landed in a pile of hay near where Ryn had been sleeping.

Dagger appeared at the top of the stairs and raised one hand shoulder high in front of him. A ball of red light formed in the palm of his hand. He pulled it back and let the ball fly across the dark room, hitting its intended target.

"How many times have I told you not to bother me?" he said as the intruder was thrown over the edge of the loft to the animal stalls below.

"It was not my idea, but you know how Mother is."

"I also do not like the way you treated my friend and my companion." Dagger said ignoring his sibling's remark.

"They are not necessary to what I am here for. They will be fine, and as I have no need of them they will continue to be as long as they stay out of my way."

"Which one are you?"

"I am Telman, your oldest brother." The intruder said jumping back up to the hayloft as if the ten feet were but one.

Dagger reached around on the table for the lamp before finding it. Flicking his fingers toward the wick, the lamp came to life lighting up the small area. Telman stood at one end of the table while Dagger at the other.

"What makes you think that I want anything to do with whatever it is that you or Mother is up to?"

"You are a Mar and every Mar must follow their destiny," Telman began. "None have turned away and none ever will. We are the chosen, and the chosen must take their place among the world, ours is to rule."

"I have no idea where it is written or said that you or any Mar is supposed to rule in this world or any other."

"We have been chosen. That is all I know."

"Who is it that tells you that we have been chosen?" he asked, "no one that I have ever heard."

"Do you not remember when you were small?" Ryn's brother began. "When we would sit by our grandparents' fire and Mother would tell us that one day a Mar would rule the Kingdom that was once Valdore? We are the chosen to lead the next coming."

"I may agree that we have been chosen," Ryn returned. "Except that we are not leaders; that is for another. No brother, Mother has turned your mind. She wishes to rule that is true, except only as Lord Crel wishes."

"Lord Crel would be no match to us if only you would join in."

"I did not know that you had a sense of humor Brother."

Behind the two family members Sarn finally came to. He watched the two as they spoke but he was unable to hear them. It was as if they were just mouthing the words or they were too far from him to hear. He grabbed his short sword and stood ready, waiting to see what would happen next.

Three large balls of red light came across the floor as if they were floating surrounding the pair, then another two did the same.

"Hello Mother," Ryn said as the five balls of light dissipated and the rest of his family appeared.

"Why must you be so stubborn?" she asked reaching out for Dagger.

"I am not stubborn Mother," Ryn began. "I am just better at knowing my reality and my destiny than you."

"Your destiny is with your family and your destiny is our destiny. You were meant to rule. The book tells that the young Mar will grow up and lead the Kingdoms of the world."

"Perhaps, but that is not me," Ryn chuckled. "If you had not insisted in going against King Valdore you would not have been sent to where you now live. You and father would still be walking the world together. There might even been another Mar born or you just might have had a grandchild by now."

Brunella looked at her youngest child as if she were confused. She turned to look at each of her children and then finally back to Ryn.

"I don't understand," she began finally. "You have become bolder and seem less afraid, why is that?"

"You do not hold the power here that you do in the forest of the Ancients. You cannot take me from here like you could have from there."

"I can take you from anywhere that is controlled by Lord Crel."

Dagger pulled his sword, put the point to the floor and leaned against it as if it were a walking stick.

"That may or may not be true," Dagger continued, "but I do not think that you will try it just now."

"What makes you say that?"

"You would have done it by now," Dagger added. "After all, you are arranged around me, Genna, Excelcia, Telman, Creve, Nefter, and yourself. You have all added your magic and tossed the proper powder on the floor. Yet here I stand waiting for you to spirit me away."

"Perhaps you are right, perhaps our combined magic is not enough to take you from this place," Genna began. "We can hold you here and we will hold you here. It will be daylight soon enough and then your father can join us. With him we can take you from here. Then we can take our rightful place on this world."

"You have no idea where you are," Ryn laughed as he watched Sarn over her shoulder lifting his sword.

Sala was awake now as well and was making her way to Sarn's side. Her sword too was pulled and ready for what may come their way. Tig jumped from his landing place and began walking around the circle of family members.

"Can you hear what they are saying?" Sala whispered as she reached his side.

"No," he began. "I do not know who they are either, but I am not going to take any chances. One of them tossed Tig and I around like we were but a rag using some sort of red ball."

"Magic," Sala whispered back.

"There is no such thing as magic. You have listened to too many fairy tales."

"How else would you explain that red ball" she asked him. "Have we not both been on the same journey? Have you not seen some of the things that have happened to us since leaving Calid's tavern?"

Sarn shook his head not believing or thinking of it as magic while taking a step closer to the group. Sala followed close behind him. With their swords raised they waited for Dagger to make the first move.

Standing on the window ledge the sisters watched and waited for the time that they would be needed.

"Not just yet. Wait to see if he can handle himself."

"We know he can handle himself against a sword. That is not why I dragged you back here."

"Their magic is no good against our nephew."

"If you would have let me talk to him and do everything we were supposed to have done sure, but now who is to say for certain."

"That is exactly my point."

The sister let out a sigh of pure exhaustion over the argument as she raised her hands.

"Wait," the other said stopping her sister then turning around. "There is only one of them in the circle, the rest are somewhere else."

"Where ...," the other said lowering her hands. "On the wall, the far parapet; you watch our nephew while I distract them."

The sister had no chance to answer as the other moved toward the group on the wall.

"I hope she does what needs to be done," the sister whispered after she left. "I am getting tired of cleaning up her messes, and this could be the biggest yet."

"How many times must we talk of this?" Dagger began again. "There is nothing that you can say that can make me leave with you. I am sure you must all tire of chasing after me. There must be something that you would rather be doing. Genna, what happened to your husband? How could you leave him alone for so long? I was told that you were in love with him and that you wanted to have a child. Creve, what of the maiden that you had asked to marry you, do you think that she will be waiting for you forever? There was another that had been after her, but she chose you. I do not think that she will live alone until you are again able to return to earth without having to hide in the shadows."

Sarn found his way around the circle and waited for Dagger to signal them.

"If that is true then you should help end their suffering and allow us to complete our destiny," his mother returned.

"There is nothing that you can say that will make me come with you."

"Nothing can stop us," Genna added. "If we want to we can take you with us anytime we wish."

Dagger took a step back and lifted his sword. Sarn and Sala stepped forward at the same time swinging at the heads of those in the circle. As each of their swords connected with the head of one of the figures it disappeared. The two continued around the circle until they were all gone but Telman. Dagger had turned to him and was pushing the point of his sword into his chest. He stopped just short of pushing it through the fabric of Telman's cloak. Sarn and Sala stood looking at each other with puzzled looks about their faces. Then she began to nod her head and mouthed the word 'magic' to him; he just shook his head and rolled his eyes in total disbelief.

"It would seem Brother, that we can stop you," Dagger said, his sword still pressed against the bother's chest.

"I had thought the two of you would have better things to do than to interrupt something that is none of your business," Brunella said when the sister had found them.

"Hello Brunella," the sister returned. "I would think that you would be too busy running from your husband to worry about the interests of those on this world."

"Since when have you worried about the happenings of my family?"

"Your family?" the sister questioned.

"My family; my sons and daughters they all need to be with me."

"Ah yes, the one they call Dagger is your only permanent connection to this world," the sister said moving closer as she talked. "It must be hard to take."

"At least I have a family," Brunella said is if she were trying to hurt the sister with her words. "I think that you are envious of me and my family. As it is my child, a Mar, that will rule the new Kingdom. You and your sister are powerless to stop destiny. Perhaps you think that you were to have the children to rule the new Kingdom. There is little chance of that. No, the ones that will rule are here in front of you now."

The sister counted the small group assuring herself that they were all there but one, excluding Dagger.

"Should I do away with her Mother," Nefter asked.

"Only if you wish to perish my son," Brunella warned.

"I see you are one short."

"You are one short as well Sister. I wonder which you are, the mess maker or the cleaner?"

"I will not be one short for long, but I fear that you are about to be one less for much longer."

At that moment above the animals, in the loft, behind the baker's home, Dagger leaned in close to his brother.

"Come after me no more," Dagger whispered.

The two stood face to face whispering. Reaching out the brother took hold of the sword that was pressed to his chest then grasped the handle over Dagger's hand.

"It is best this way Ryn," Telman began. "There have been too many things that have happened between us and our parents. You are the future of the family, not me. It is far better that I end here. I will look after you from the place of our ancestors. I will always watch over you and help you in your path. I believe our grandmother now. I believe that the path our mother wishes us to follow is not the path of our destiny."

"Then go back to our mother and make her see that hers is not the path to our destiny. Plead your case with the Ancients so that they will let you return."

"No Ryn, it is no longer for me," he said keeping his hand over Dagger's on the handle of the sword. "When you see my heart, tell her that I no longer pine for her. Tell her that my last words were of my love for her."

Telman grabbed the sword with both hands and pulled toward him. The sword pushed through his clothes, then deep into his rib cage before passing through his chest.

The sound of the crushing bone and slicing flesh seemed deafening to Sarn. Dagger struggled to pull the sword back but Telman was too strong and the sword was too deep for it to be pulled out in time to save the brother. Dagger knelt next to the dying Telman shaking his head and whispering in his ear.

"I did not want it to end this way Brother," Dagger whispered, looking deep into his eyes.

"I can no longer hide. This is a much better place to be, even in death." Telman smiled as he took his last breath. "I am yours now..."

"I will tell her that, and more dear bother," he whispered, reaching up he closed his brother's eyes

Dagger jumped to the rafters of the hayloft in one smooth motion. Running across the beam to the open window he leapt over the alley reaching the outer wall of the castle with ease. Sarn took two steps toward the ladder that led to the rafter, but Tig ran in front of him and leaned into him to stop him. The animal walked circles around the two keeping them both from following his master. Sarn and Sala could do nothing but look at each other as their friend ran out the window. Neither of them knew what to say to him or to each other, as a soft blue glow filled the hayloft and the body of Telman disappeared.

"I have seen it once before," Sala said after a few moments. "I was about eight, I think. My family was camped along a narrow river and an old man came and sat next to it. He did not move for a long time. So my father went to ask him if he was all right, and asked him to join us for our meal. After the meal he told us stories of magic and faeries. When we went to bed, he returned to the river and sat again on its bank. I was too excited over his stories and could not sleep so I laid there and watched him. He pulled out a small pouch and tossed it into the river. He was saying something, but his voice was low and he was too far away for me to hear what he was saying. I crawled out of my bed and got closer to see if I could hear his words, but no matter how close I got his words still sounded too far away. Finally, after a long silence he opened his arms, his body went slack and he fell over. I ran over to him and touched him. His body was cold, like death. At first I was scared, then as I watched as he disappeared. I was no longer scared. Then a warm breeze picked up for a second and then it was gone just as quick as the old man had gone. I told my mother what had happened in the morning. She told me that the man was of magic and that as he died his body went back to the earth, where all magic comes from."

"Magic," Sarn whispered half laughing. "I cannot be so sure of this magic. I think that you were told too many fairy tales when you were younger."

"Then you explain the way that body disappeared."

"Well, I ...."

"You cannot," she returned, "admit it."

"You are correct my love I cannot, but I do not believe in magic. There are explanations for everything in this world, including this."

"Yes, and magic is the explanation for this my sweet innocent lover." She reached out and pulled him to her kissing him and holding him to her.

"I think that in the morning we should take a walk the four of us," Sarn began changing the subject. "I think that it is time that I made you my wife."

She closed her eyes and kissed him harder.

"Oh my love," she whispered, "but you should know, I would take you without any ceremony or words read over a book."

Seconds later, each of the siblings that stood on the wall turned back into the points of light that they had been earlier floating up into the night sky.

"Why did Ryn have to kill Telman?" Brunella asked.

"I did not kill him Mother," Ryn said, walking up to her. "He pulled my sword into his chest in his own time. He told me he could no longer live in the world that you have been keeping him in."

"It would have been ended by now if you had just joined us from the start. You know how much I want for this family. I cannot believe that you have refused for so long and now I have lost a son, to your sword."

"Touch it," Dagger held out the sword that Telman had pulled into his chest. "See the truth for yourself mother."

Brunella reached out to touch the sword. Her fingers touched it for just a second before she too was returned to the point of light she had been not more than an hour earlier.

"I am sorry Ryn of Mar, but it was not the punishment of the parents that placed your mother where she is." The sister told him as the two stood alone on the wall.

"I am called Dagger, Sister," Ryn returned. "I do not know this Ryn of Mar that you speak. I am Dagger the thief, trained in the art of thievery and fighting. I am Dagger, cursed to hide and walk on this world blind. I am Dagger, sought after by the Ancients to train those that would be kings. I am Dagger the great thief, Dagger the great hunter, Dagger the great fighter, Dagger the trainer, Dagger the great, master of all that I am. That Sister is who I am. I am not this Ryn Mar that she or you think that I am."

Dagger turned and ran along the wall one hand deep in his

pocket.

"I know," the sister called after him. "You are Dagger the hidden, the keeper of the true path."

"You are the protector of the innocent and the unprotected, the keeper of the true king." The other sister whispered as she watched him jump from the wall to the roof of the bakery. "Keep yourself well Dagger, because soon you will need all your talents again."

Dagger stood at the peak of the bakery roof shaking his fist at the night sky, screaming out unheard by anyone that was near.

"I am Dagger the hunted, Dagger the hidden, Dagger the thief, Dagger the fighter, the protector of Kings and those that will be. I am not Ryn Mar. I am not. I am who I am. I am who the Ancients made me. They are the reason I am Dagger."

Sala turned her attention to the still sleeping Prince. While Sarn swept away the powder and cleared any sign of what had happened, what there was of it anyway.

The sisters stood in silence on either side of Dagger unseen. They stood watch over him as his sentinels through the rest of the night. Each stood not arguing or even speaking. Just as the light began to break in the distance, the sisters each touched the head of Dagger before disappearing into the morning mist.

"Why did we just spend all night there on that roof top?"

"Sister you cannot be serious in asking me that question."

"Well?"

"We kept watch for Ryn and the nephew to keep them safe."

"What of the battle that comes?"

"We have sent them everything and everyone they will need."

As the sun rose over the forest Dagger was still sitting on the peak of the roof. His head was still between his knees. Waking, his mind was a bit foggy at first, but then it began to clear. He remembered the sisters and smiled knowing that they had stood over him in his sleep.

"Yes," he whispered into the rising sun. "I am that Dagger."

Standing on the roof Dagger shook his fist at the rising sun.

"As for you," Dagger screamed, yet the only one that heard him was the object of his anger. "You are as responsible as Mother. You are to blame as well. I suppose that you will hunt me this day too."

"You are my child," was his answer. "I want that you are safe and that we are a family. How can you blame me for wanting my family together?"

"My path and destiny is here, not with you or with Mother."

"As you continue to say," his father said. "You do realize that I can see you where you are standing. It would be easy for me to just lift you from that place and bring you to me once and for all."

"You cannot, not without help," Dagger began. "There is no way that you could keep me there even if you did. Tell me again how you can take me from where I stand?"

"That is what I thought you were going to say," Dagger said when he received no answer.

Jumping down off the roof Dagger climbed through the window of the hayloft.

Dagger reached out and touched Sarn on his cheek, ran his fingers over Sala's face, turned to the young Prince and sat next to his bed.

"You are what this is all about," Dagger whispered. "You are the reason that we are here, the reason that we will risk our lives once again. We three that may not survive are here for you. The battle comes for your survival. It is about your parents' Kingdom and your Kingdom. Yet you are too young to realize the cost, and too young to fight for your own survival."

With the sun just rising on the castle, the morning dew was still heavy on the fields. Small groups of men began to cross the landscape and head toward the castle village. Coming in small parties of about twenty or less they arrived for the better part of the next four hours. Each group entered at the western and northern gates of the castle until more than three hundred had entered. It was only the latest group of men to have arrived at the castle in the last month. Over all the groups had been arriving for two weeks. That morning's group of men brought the total number to about three thousand.

The travelers went about their morning as they had every morning since coming to the castle, preparing breakfast and planning out the day's training and exercises for the horses. Although today was a little different, today began a week of celebration for the people and village of Tenisfie.

Dagger stood in front of the shop for several minutes before walking in. Sarn stood watching several shops away, trying to hide among the passing crowd of shoppers. It was easier this day than it had been the previous weeks. It was a day when everyone would come out to celebrate and to shop, with entertainment on every street. When the day was over there would be a large banquet. There would be one every night of the coming week, each one more elaborate than the night before. Sarn slipped through the crowds and looked in the shop window.

Ryn stood in front of the counter and was greeted by a woman that bowed before him. He accepted her extended hand as she led him behind the counter. Sarn watched from the front window as the two disappeared through a small curtained doorway. As he stood outside he could not help but hear his father's voice telling him that some secrets were his to keep and to tell of in their own time. He waited for a short time more before he began to feel guilty for having followed him and returned to the bakery.

"And just where have you been?" Sala asked laughing when he returned. "Where did you lose him this morning?"

She knew he had been out trying to follow him again. It was the same thing every time Dagger would leave by himself. Sarn would wait then leave behind him trying to find out where he would go.

"I followed him," Sarn began, shaking his head. "I followed and watched him go into a dressmaker's shop."

"Into what?" she asked still laughing. "What do you suppose he was doing in there?"

"I could not keep myself around long enough to figure it out," he told her as he headed down into the stable.

In the dressmaker's shop, Dagger paid for a package and left tucking it under his arm. Wrapping his hand around the crystal he made his way back to the bakery and their hiding spot.

Sala took Dagger by the arm as soon as he returned and led him behind the hanging blankets.

"You know I did not want you to come with us," Dagger began as soon as they were alone. "But you have proven yourself useful more than once."

"I know how you felt about me from the beginning. I want you to understand why I came along."

"You came because you felt a love for Sarn," Dagger began. "I know that you did not wish to never see him again."

"That is true, yes. But I did not come just because of feeling a love for Sarn," she began. Looking hard at Dagger's face she tried to see if there was anything she could read in his expression. "Something told me that this is what I was meant to be doing. That this is where I am supposed to be we three, together, here today in this castle and in this hayloft. This is my ... well my destiny is here together with you and him."

"I cannot say about your destiny," Dagger lied. "Whether you were meant to be here or not, but you are here just the same. It is true that we are here in this place at this time together. It is here that everything has led the three of us. Travelers we are and travelers we will be, in the light or in the dark, destiny or not."

She looked at Dagger and began to get a little confused, not so much from his words but more by the way he was beginning to move his head.

"Do not worry child I have not lost my mind," he laughed back at her and reached out and placed a hand on her stomach. "I do know what is happening around me. Your son has been waited for and will be well received by all, including your love."

It was not the first time he had talked about her having a child, but it was the first time since she knew for sure that she would have a child.

"I ... I ...," she stuttered not quite sure how to react to him. "I cannot be sure how you know these things, but I have my suspicions. He has asked me to marry him today, yet I have not said a word of his child."

"Then we must marry you," Dagger said as he held the package he had purchased at the dressmaker's shop. "You can tell him of the son later. Now we must get ready for your wedding."

Sala pushed him out from behind the wall of blankets before opening the package. Tearing it open she found the two dresses that were inside; one blue and one red. As she held the red one it seemed to make her eyes sparkle just a little more than they usually did.

"What of this blue one?" She called out.

"Blue one, what blue one?" Dagger answered his voice breaking just a bit.

"It is too small for me," she said, coming back around the blankets. Taking his hand she began to pull him behind the makeshift wall. "I would think that it would match your eyes better."

"S ... silly ... shop girl ... she ... uh must have made a mistake," Dagger stuttered as he tried to find the right words. "I ordered the red one for you and the blue was to be... for someone else. Yes, she must have put it in the wrong package... I meant it for the baker's daughter... yes that's it, it was meant for her. I bought it for her to show our thanks for all that she has done with the horses."

"If that is what you wish to tell me Dagger then it is the story I will believe," Sala said smiling at him. "Only I think it is not her color either; I would think a light green would be for her."

"Then there are two mistakes that they made," Dagger returned. He nodded his head as if to make his point stronger, or perhaps only to convince himself of the mistake.

"Where is your man?" Dagger asked.

"I am feeding your horse," Sarn's voice called from below.

"Then it is time you were dressed yourself. Come brother and let us prepare ourselves for your wedding."

"I thought we would ...," Sarn's voice trailed off as if he were trying to change the subject.

"Wait until tomorrow? No, come now brother this is the day," Dagger said standing at the top of the stairs that led to the stalls below. "Do you know what this day is?"

"No," the two lovers answered in near unison.

"Today is the anniversary of Tenisfie. It is the day when...." Dagger stopped in the middle of his words as if he did not know them, but in truth he did not say because Sarn at least would not believe him. "After the fall of Valdore, Tenisfie and the castle villages that had made up the Kingdom were given to the families that had watched over them. Many of the new rulers set out to regain the Kingdom that was Valdore. Some were successful in conquering others and some were not. Tenisfie being an important Castle village was fought over many times throughout the years. For almost a hundred years after the Valdore Kingdom was broken up there would be wars fought over the smaller lands trying to regain the old Kingdom."

"It has been the talk of the castle for about a week," Sarn interrupted. "What does that have to do with us and our wedding?"

"It is just the day," Dagger said smiling. "It is the day that you will be married and the day that life for the two of you begins. It is also when they celebrate the end of those wars and today begins that celebration."

Her red hair shone under the late morning sunlight; her fingers shook with nerves as she worked over the meal.

"Keep it together," she whispered. "You have done this every day for four years, there is nothing that makes today any different."

"Except you have never gone this far," she rolled her eyes as she answered her own dilemma.

She picked up the platter hiding the dagger under it. The knife made it difficult to balance and she almost dropped it. She gasped at the near loss but was quick to steady the platter with her free hand.

As she walked toward her master's tent she began to think about how long she had been with Foulas. It had been long enough that she could not remember where she came from. She only knew that she did not belong there. And that was the one thing she knew for sure. She had come from somewhere else and from a family that was so far in the past that she no longer had dreams of them.

"Now that you are the one Foulas trusts to cook and bring him his meal," they had started, "you will be in a position to do us a great favor one day."

She had heard of the sisters, her friend that now shared Foulas' bed used to tell her stories about them. The tales were told of how the two were magical and would grant wishes if you asked them kind enough or on a good day. Lorra just wanted to go home, to be with her parents and to live the life she was meant to, not that of some slave girl or servant and cook. Over the years she had done many favors for the sisters and they in turn kept promising that they would return her to her home and her parents. They had never asked much of her, but they would always come when they were least wanted.

Lorra had been taken from her parents when she was just a little girl, so long ago that she could no longer remember what her parents looked like. She could only guess how long it had been that she was taken from her home. When she was first taken she had told herself that she would never forget them and would always remember where she had come from. Now there was not one memory left of them no matter how much she had tried to bring them to mind. Through the years those memories of them had disappeared. At first she had remembered everything, right down to what she was planning that year for her birthday. But as the punishments and hunger had taken hold, her memories grew distant with each passing year. The sisters knew when Lorra had been taken. They also knew where she belonged.

With the knife hidden under the tray, she headed toward Foulas' tent each step becoming easier than the first and the one before. As she reached the tent she found that Foulas was not alone.

"It is about time you fed me," Foulas grumbled as she set the tray down.

She slipped the knife up the sleeve of her shirt and stepped away from the tray

"I had thought you were the leader of the circle?" Foulas asked Balmore.

"I am," he replied.

"You told me the circle counted one hundred of the King's most loyal and close men."

"They do my lord."

"Then tell me Balmore, why it is that you bring me less than those one hundred."

"It was not possible to get them all at once my lord. Many are still needed to keep up the appearance of our loyalty to King Gregor," Balmore explained, but was not sure if he was believed. "There are at least twenty that are with the coward King that hides rather than fight. Soon you need only to walk into the castle and take it over."

"As you have told me before, yet you do not tell me when this will be."

"After the celebration of this week, the castle and Kingdom will be yours for the taking. You have waited too long to take the castle and now it is filled with those that come to celebrate and to replay the battle for Tenisfie. It is a weeklong celebration, people have been coming for the festival for just about two weeks now, and it will end with the mock battle and a large feast. After that we will be able to do as we wish to this place."

Foulas only grunted and nodded his head as he turned to his food shoving Lorra away almost making her drop the knife.

"As long as you do not forget your promise," Balmore added, "we will get along just fine."

Foulas ignored him again having no intention of honoring his promise of giving him Tenisfie to watch over for his master. Tenisfie was to be for his master only, and from there the rest of the Valdore Kingdom would follow one by one, or so that was the belief.

With the bride and groom dressed, they gathered the baker and his family along with Prince Gregor. With Tig in the lead they began to walk through the crowded streets. The early revelers were spilling out from their homes, shops, and taverns. All had begun making their way through the markets that lined almost every street. Tables were set up in front of the taverns and bakeries in the hopes they might entice someone walking by into buying one of their ales or tasty cakes. As the travelers would pass a tavern those there would cheer the bride and groom and offer toasts to them. Wedding songs were sung as they passed the stands selling their food or wares. There were so many things it was impossible to name them all. Children that had once shied or had run from Tig were now reaching out to pet him or scratch him between his ears. If any in the crowd had noticed the young Prince none showed their recognition.

"I love it when the festival arrives," the baker's wife said as they went. "So many people that come from so far away with so many stories, and oh, the new recipes that I will get and trade for."

"She just likes to gossip and learn of other Kingdoms," the baker added. "If it were not for that, the days that we have spent getting ready for the festival would be too brutal for me to think about."

"There will also be friends that have moved away and those that we have met through the years," she returned, giving her husband a playful back hand to his shoulder.

"Well this will not be long," Dagger told them, "then you can return to your storefront; I do not think you will miss much."

"We would not have missed this for anything," they both seemed to say in unison.

"Papa," the baker's oldest daughter interrupted. "I think there are more here this year than last."

"Perhaps you are just not remembering last year that well," he returned, not showing any sign of worry.

Dagger became a bit uncomfortable and laughed, knowing that she was more right than even he wanted to let on.

Once they reached the large church they made their way inside. They were greeted by over a hundred sitting or standing around. As the group walked toward the altar everyone seemed to go silent and began to remove their hats and bowed as the travelers passed them. From behind them more entered the church, filling it until there was nowhere to move except down the center aisle.

"So many people," Sarn whispered. "To what do we owe so many people coming here this day?"

"I am sure it is just the festival," Dagger whispered back. "But, does not everyone like to see a wedding?"

"Perhaps," Sarn continued, "but they cannot know us."

"They know of you," the baker said. "They know of the travelers and of your saving of the Prince and bringing him home to them. They have come to see you and in their own way pay their respect for your deed."

"You see," Dagger added, "everyone knows of you and of your bride to be."

Tig walked ahead of the group and found himself a place away from his master and the others where he could watch them. Somewhere he could watch them all and yet was not too far from the travelers that he could not come to their aide if needed.

Meeting the priest at the altar they introduced themselves. The priest shook their hands and thanked them for returning the Prince and their continued protection of him. After asking them if they were sure they wished to be married he proceeded with the short ceremony. It seemed to go by fast and they were married almost before they realized it. Applause filled the church as they turned to face those that had come to see them wed.

"Guard the door," a voice called from within the crowd.

Confused, Sarn turned to Dagger, but before anything could be said King Gregor stepped from behind a tapestry on the other side of the altar. Queen Janelle and their two daughters the Princesses Kay and Phoebe were close behind him. Prince Gregor ran from where he was sitting with the baker and his family to his father's side. King Gregor lifted his son into his arms and held him close as he walked to where the travelers stood.

"Welcome Sarn," he greeted the new groom as he reached him.

All in attendance in the church bowed to the King and his presence.

"I am happy to see you again, and your new bride Sala," the King continued. "I want to thank you first for returning my son to us. I hope Sala; that he will still allow you your tongue to speak as you will."

The two laughed and Dagger joined in, with King Gregor adding his laughter to the crowd.

"I wish it were a day that we could have a feast to celebrate your marriage," the King began. "But today we will confront Foulas and Solari to take back my Kingdom. He waits in forest to confront me outside, before I can reach the protection of these walls. What he does not know is that I am already here as you can see. With your help, and those here and throughout the castle, waiting only for our signal, we will take on this false King and end his reign in

Tenisfie. We will feast to your wedding tomorrow and we will feast to our win as well. Now who is it that leads this group that has come to help us?"

"Jher Bratham," called a voice from the crowd again.

"Then where is this man?"

"I am here my Lord," answered a tall man standing to the side of the church. "I offer my sword and those that have followed me for you to use as you need."

"You have come as your own mind?"

"If not, the sisters would never let us sleep again," came the answer from somewhere in the crowd.

"Nor would the Ancients," answered another in the crowd.

The crowd laughed in unison, knowing full well that while it may have been said as a joke it was far from being untrue. Many believed that the sisters would indeed haunt them and that the Ancients would not allow them their rightful final resting place.

"We fight this day for Tenisfie and for the ancestors of the Kingdom of Valdore."

Sarn looked around and noticed that as King Gregor mentioned the old Kingdom of Valdore everyone in the church stood at once. Jher pulled his sword and began to tap it against the stone floor of the church. The noise of his sword began to fill the church. Soon the noise grew louder as more of the men joined him.

"It must be done this day?" Sarn asked turning to Dagger.

Dagger did not have the heart to tell the couple that it had all been planned months earlier. With the final preparations made just the day before, when the couple had decided to be married.

"Yes," he returned, "it must be done this day or it will be too late for Tenisfie. I am sorry that we could not have waited, but it will not be such a long battle and will be over for good or bad by the end of this day. Then we will spend the next six days drinking, toasting your wedding and your new life."

"Then we will fight side by side and we will make it a battle that will be celebrated through the years as the last one is now," Sarn added, getting caught in the moment of it all.

"No, you and Sala will go with Queen Janelle and protect her and the family."

"I will fight with you my friend."

"I will never forgive myself if anything were to happen to you or your bride on your wedding day. Let alone the fact that by spring you will be a father, and I will not allow your son to come into this world without his father."

Sarn turned to Sala who only lowered her head before smiling and answering him.

"So you see you will be safer if you are to protect the family. Besides, we are not sure but we think that the circle is no longer loyal to King Gregor. You will be with six of his closest guards and with luck, his most loyal. They have been with him for as long as he has been in hiding and have shown no sign of betrayal."

Sarn did not seem to hear him, he was too busy holding Sala close and kissing her.

The sound of the metal on stone became deafening in the church and soon it was carrying outside. It was not long before it was being repeated by the rest of the three thousand that had come to castle to join in the fight for Tenisfie. The noise was soon carried on throughout Tenisfie. It carried on over the walls, into the fields and the forest beyond for all to hear.

"Lorra," the sister began. "You must do this one last thing."

"I have tried but he is never alone," Lorra replied. "Besides you have promised this to me before. That I would only need to do this one last thing and you would return me to my family. Meglyn I grow tired of your promises. I want only to be with my family, to be back where I belong, wherever it is and in whatever position I belong."

The two stood to the side of the fire as Lorra worked on her master's midday meal. The sounds of metal on stone echoed from the castle, reaching them as they spoke.

"I know you have tried many times," Caitlin continued without correcting her on her identity. "Only now it has to be done again and this time you must not give up."

"Please take me home," Lorra seemed to beg. "Get me away from this. If you know where I come from, please take me there now. I am beginning to be afraid that I will never return to my family."

"We have told you many times that it is your destiny to return to your family." Caitlin said, trying to ease her mind and of course to get her to do what she wanted. "We have even told you that you will marry and have children in your husband's Kingdom."

"So you tell me, as if he will be some prince," Lorra shook her head as she finished talking.

The sisters had told her many times that she would marry and have children in her husband's Kingdom. It was almost impossible

278

to her that she would know a true prince let alone marry one.

"I only ask that you finally honor your promises for once and return me to my home," Lorra sighed. "I have done all that you have ever asked of me over the years and now I grow tired of this. I want to go home."

Lorra turned to where Caitlin had been only to find that she had gone and that she had been talking to herself.

The noise coming from the castle had kept her from hearing the sister leave and from hearing Solari as he approached her.

"It is good that you finally earn your stay," Solari grumbled as he walked by sniffing at the air, something he did everywhere he would go.

"I smell a sister," Solari said as he stopped and turned to her, sniffing the air around her and finally her. "Are you a sister slave?"

Lorra managed a cracked no, but nothing more.

"Hmmpff," Solari said as he stuck a crooked finger under her chin and lifted her from the ground. "You had better hope that you are not one of them!"

He began to let her down when he finally began to hear the sounds echoing from the castle, causing him to sniff the air around her.

"No," he said, "you are not a sister but somewhere close."

His anger deepened as he held her in the air. He lifted her higher until she was suspended from his outstretched arm at the point of his finger; his long fingernail cutting deep into her skin. He began to emit a grumbling noise from somewhere deep within him. She knew that nothing good was about to happen as he released the noise from his throat and removed his finger. Blood appeared from her chin as she stayed suspended in the air. His left hand rose up from under his long black cloak and pushed away from his body. He never once touched her with it, but as it came closer to her, a dark blue almost black light shot from his palm and she was shoved away from him. She flew over the cooking fire and past the circle of her work area. She continued out over the stumps of cut trees and young saplings, flying over the forest floor backwards. Screaming, she bounced off several tall trees and continued on deep into the forest. She finally slammed against a long out cropping of rocks, where she slumped and fell like a rag to the forest floor. Just out of sight Caitlin had seen it all happen, yet had done nothing to stop Solari, nor had she done anything to keep Lorra from hitting the rocks.

"These are for you," Dagger said handing Sarn the two silver daggers he had made for him.

Sarn began to speak, but Dagger stopped him, placing a hand on the back of his neck.

"And this," he said handing Sala the third dagger he had made, "is for you."

Sala hugged him close to her expecting him to back away, but he opened his arms and drew her even closer. She was surprised that he did not fight it or even try to back away from her.

"How unlike you," she said smiling as she let him go.

"Use them well," he began again, ignoring her comment. "If ever you are in need of me, push its blade into the crook of the nearest tree and I will come to you, if I am still alive. You must remember everything I have taught the two of you. I must tell you that you have more talent than any I have ever seen before now. As for you dear Sala, you have learned a great deal, and much faster than I thought you would."

"We will have plenty of time for this talk when the day is out and we are sitting around a fire drinking some of Tenisfie's finest ales eating its food, telling and listening to stories about the day," Sarn added, as if he were already back home walking to the local tavern for a night of storytelling.

"He does have something there," Sala began. "Besides we have a wedding feast to worry about later and there will be plenty of time for us to speak as if we are parting."

"Aye," Sarn finished. "With more than just a few adventures left before we do."

Dagger nodded his head in agreement and let out a nervous laugh, not that the others noticed. He lowered his head as if he knew more than he was telling, and he did. Of course he could not tell them everything that he knew. With that said between them, he left them to their charges. At the door of the church he turned and watched as they went to the altar to be with the Queen, her two daughters and of course Prince Gregor. Tig waited just outside of the church for his master.

"Sorry, not this time my old friend," Dagger began as he knelt next to him. "I want you to go with them. You will know what to do when it is time. For now I want you to help them protect the Queen and her children."

Tig rubbed his face against Dagger's. Giving him one last rub Tig followed after the couple.

"Until we meet again," he whispered and left the church.

It wasn't that Dagger knew exactly what would happen that day, but he knew for certain that they would not have time to speak of more favorable things. With the clinking of metal on stone still filling the church he found his horse and headed to the King's side.

"You will find your horses below," one of the guards told them as they reached the Queen, "They call me Yolo, but you can call me what you wish."

"I think Yolo will be fine for now," Sarn said turning to take the guard's outstretched hand.

"We have heard of you Master Sarn, and I must say I never thought I would have a chance to ever meet you let alone perhaps fight alongside of you."

Sarn looked at him a bit puzzled but figured that the he must have thought that he had been with Dagger on more of his adventures than he had been. Queen Janelle shook her head behind Sarn as if to tell Yolo not to say anything further.

"There are ten of us," Yolo began. "If you will allow me I will set three of them at the top stairwell under the church."

"I am sure that will be fine," Sarn told him as they began down the hidden stairway in the floor behind the altar.

The stairs were steep at first then lessened as they began to wrap around in a circular motion. Some sections of the stairs were slippery from water that seeped between the rocks of the wall. Sarn wondered just how many years it had taken for it to have been built and how many years it had stood. Yolo posted the guards three at a time as they went, with the last three at the bottom. When they reached the bottom of the stairs Sarn went to the stable area to look after their horses. Sala went with Gregor's sisters to an area surrounded by hanging tapestries and blankets from a few ropes, while the Queen sat with Gregor on her lap in a large chair near the fire pit.

After seeing that the horses were well cared for he returned to the great room. Taking some meat and scraps from the cooking area he tossed them to Tig, who had been pacing back and forth near the cooks as if he were stalking prey.

"Just make sure you come see me for any more food my friend," Sarn began. "We cannot have you scaring off the cooks and servants."

Tig looked at Sarn and tilted his head as if in answer before turning his attention back to the meat.

The Queen smiled at Sarn and whispered in Gregor's ear then

waved one of the servants closer. The Prince jumped down from his mother's lap and ran to his sisters and Sala. The Queen and the servant whispered together for a minute before they left and went out one of the many corridors that led away from the room. Smiling, the Queen got up from her large chair and went to where Sarn was laying his weapons out on a table.

"Checking to see if you are missing anything?" she asked as she got closer.

"No," he said. "I just cannot think of anything else to do."

The Queen smiled and placed her hand on his shoulder and sat down on the edge of the table next to him.

"I want to give you something," she began. "Dagger has said that you are not a believer in legends, destiny or magic. I know that you know nothing of the Kingdom of Valdore except what Dagger has told you and knowing Dagger, it was little if anything. There is so much that you need to know and much more that you will never believe until you find it out for yourself. You are a special person and there have been many that have waited for you, hoping that one day you would come.

"I have no idea what is it you are trying say," Sarn returned.

"You have no knowledge do you?" she said, turning Sarn's face to hers and looking into his eyes.

"I came here to return your son," Sarn interrupted, smiling at her. "Dagger taught me to protect myself and how use these to kill. He has taught me everything I know of them. If it were not for him I would know nothing, and for that I owe him everything."

"Yes," she said smiling back at him. "You owe him everything for that, but there is more that you will learn, so much more.

The servant returned and handed her a long bundle wrapped in cloth. Dismissing the servant she put the bundle on the table and began to unwrap it. Inside were three items; a longbow, a cloak, and medium sized box, each one light purple in color. She laid each of the three items as they were unwrapped next to Sarn's weapons.

"These are for you," the Queen said once she had all three items laid out before him. "They have been held here waiting for you ... to come for.... I am sorry I forget you are not a believer. In that case we will just say that these are just one payment for returning our son to us."

Sarn shook his head and rolled his eyes as she spoke but he accepted each item as she handed it to him and examined them.

"This cloak has many hiding places for your knives and other weapons. You will find it useful, as well as this longbow," the Queen continued. "In this box are the tools and some feathers you will need for your arrows. If you look closer, you will find some shafts for arrows hidden in the cloak. I would tell you of the wood and where it comes from but I am sure you will not believe me nor pay attention if I were to tell you. You will know where it comes from when you see it and then you can make more. "

He searched the cloak and opened the box and found everything there.

"I suppose I could always change the color of the cloak," he said finally.

"I would not, its color is a royal color," she said. "It is one that has not been seen here for a long time. It was once the color worn by the personal guards of the Valdore family. It will tell all that see you about who you are and your stand here in Tenisfie."

The Queen stopped telling of the cloak and the importance of it and of its color, still she knew that he was not paying attention to her nor would he even begin to believe her if she told him more. In truth it was left in Tenisfie long before he was born. The story behind the cloak was much more a tale of destiny than a tale of duty and honor or that of faith and service. It was kept in Tenisfie until the time would come that it could be given to the right person; him.

"This will become useful to you," she said. Placing it on his shoulder she tried hard not to tell him anymore about the cloak than he would believe. "Why not try it on? I think it will be a perfect fit."

The noise of metal on stone was deafening as the King, Jher, and Dagger led the group through the streets toward the main gate. Men that had spilled out to the streets at the first sounding of the call fell in behind the trio. By the time they reached the gate all were there, ready for what would be the battle for Tenisfie. As Dagger, King Gregor and Jher climbed the steps of the wall near the gate, they were joined by the man called Gramfor. Each had fought alongside the other at least once before, not that they all remembered it or each other. Jher had great faith in Gramfor and his ability to fight and lead men. While King Gregor knew little of Gramfor he had fought many battles with Dagger and had full faith in him as well. Once on the battlement they stood looking out to the forest where Foulas was waiting with his army. After a few minutes Jher took King Gregor and Dagger away from the front of the wall and finalized the plan for the battle ahead. While Gramfor, feeling a bit left out, stood near the wall with his arms folded and looked inward to the city. Dagger walked back and forth along the battlement for several minutes, while King Gregor stood just inside the nearest parapet not wanting to show himself to the enemy just yet. Jher stood just outside of the parapet close to where the King was standing looking over the fields toward the forest that did little to hide Foulas and his army.

"Now all we need to do is wait for them to fight," King Gregor laughed knowing that it was not an option that any would accept.

"We need to attack them while they are still weak and in the forest," Jher said opening the discussion. "Perhaps we should call them out into the open and split his army so that they cannot lay a siege against the castle."

"What I have been trying to figure is why they left the protection of the castle and went out to the forest in the first place," Gramfor added.

"If you think that all his army is in the forest, you would be mistaken. Then again it would not be the first time you have been mistaken," Dagger said ending any discussion of Foulas and his men.

The three men turned toward Dagger before looking past him to the old walls of the castle that lay around the palace. They were meant to be a final defense against any army and were once the original walls of the castle. They were built along with the palace; as its walls went up, so did the wall around it. The stones to build it were brought up from the tunnels that lay under it as well as from several quarries not so nearby.

"I can only hope that they are not behind us," Jher said finally after several minutes.

"You can hope all you want Jher, but they are behind us as well as in front of us in the forest. Perhaps even among us," Dagger said trying not to smile. "We will be at a disadvantage as well, because this plan will also split our army into two sections if not more."

As the four spoke atop the wall they were being watched by no fewer than one hundred of Foulas' men placed inside the castle walls. Many that were inside the walls were only waiting for the right moment to show themselves as traitors.

"If I were the one making the plan, I would be sure to send some men out in search for those of Foulas' men hiding out within the city and on the walls," Dagger said thrusting his hand in the pocket of his cloak and running down the stairs off the wall.

"What do you think you are doing?" Jher called after Dagger

"If you do not know then I cannot tell you," Dagger yelled back, taking the steps three at a time.

"That boy always amazes me," King Gregor smiled shaking his head as he watched Dagger bounce off the last step.

Dagger found his horse ready at the bottom, and stopped only long enough to speak to three men, pointing each to a different direction and yet to the same task. Mounting his horse Dagger turned and headed out the opening gate. As the main gate rattled open, Foulas' men made their presence known by signaling each other and those in the forest. Flashes of light blinked on and off around the city and then from the forest itself. As each glint of light showed from behind them a handful of men from the gathered army went on the hunt for its maker.

Leaving the castle walls behind him Dagger followed the road that cut between the fields. He kept on until he was almost to the forest before turning away into the fields. He rode toward the section of the forest that held Foulas and his army. Turning again just before the tree line he went along it until he was in line with the main gate of Tenisfie. From there he began riding his horse in an ever widening circle. On his third time around the first wave of the King's gathered army began pouring from the main gate. With their spears rising and falling with each step and the sun glinting off their shields they ran up the road toward the field. Stopping next to the area Dagger was they regrouped and waited. On his next circle Dagger reached behind him and pulled two small pouches from a pack on his horse. Standing on the back of his horse he stretched his arms out and began to pour the blue and green powder on the ground as he continued circling in the field. When he finished one circle he reached for two more pouches and went around again.

Foulas stood with Balmore and watched as Dagger made his circles and poured out his powders.

"What does he think he is doing?" Foulas asked Balmore.

"I would say that he thinks he is protecting himself from us," Balmore laughed.

"Perhaps, but I cannot just let him come and take us as we sit in the forest," Foulas said as he noticed the men coming out from the castle gate.

"Then I would say that we should not disappoint him," Balmore said as he gathered up his weapons and the men that came with him.

When the powder was gone he continued in his circle within the blue and green lines of powder on the ground. Dark clouds began to roll in across the sky turning the sunny day gray and dark. After his fourth time around he rode to the center of his circle. Jumping from his horse he pulled one sword then another pushing the point of the first into the ground and then took three steps away.

The two armies stood across from each other at the edge of the field. Foulas and his men were on the forest side and the army of King Gregor on the other, with Dagger between them.

As Dagger stood waiting for the first to venture out from the army the cloud cover began to slide away overhead. Except that is for those over the circle that Dagger created on the open field. It remained the clouded, shadow less gray of overcast skies. The rest of the field and castle were again bathed in the late summer sunlight.

"I am Dagger, I am the protector of this castle," Dagger yelled. "If you wish to claim it for yourself you must see me first."

He stood near the middle of the circle smiling and waiting.

"Could it be that you do not know me," he yelled out to any that might hear him. "Then pray let me tell you who I am. I am Dagger the thief, Dagger the protector, Dagger the warrior, Dagger killer of evil men. Come, you men of evil, come and have a taste of my blood. That is … if you can get close enough to me."

Dagger knelt down and ran his fingers over the cut ends of grass, and smiled.

The first of Balmore's men headed out to where Dagger stood

"You do not own Tenisfie we still hold it," Balmore yelled back. "You think that just because you brought the Prince home that it is yours. Just being within the walls of Tenisfie does not make him King. His father was the King and he is no longer alive."

"Perhaps you should take another look to the walls and make that statement again," Dagger returned laughing. "If you look close enough you will find King Gregor atop it and you will also find that his flag now flies high over the palace keep."

As he spoke the King's personal flag was unfurled in its place atop the palace.

Three of Foulas' men rode out from the edge of the field as Dagger and Balmore traded words.

"I believe that in a short moment or two you will no longer

matter in this fight," Balmore called out, trying not to show his surprise.

Dagger laughed again and stood up. He waited as the three got closer, bringing his hands together as they came and smiling. Pulling his hands apart the three fell off their horses one at a time, each impaled with a silver dagger. The horses kept running only to be stopped on the opposite side of the field by those of the King's gathered army.

"Are you sure that those were your best men Balmore?" Dagger taunted as he pulled the daggers from their necks. "Perhaps you need to check with Foulas to be certain that he is not planning on leaving you here to face his justice."

"I am sure my lord is quite capable and ready to overpower you and your ragged group of misfits," Balmore yelled back. "Your wit makes me weary; it is time that you died. Let us just see how you are at facing five men on your own."

Balmore raised his hand and five men left the line and headed toward Dagger. When they were on their way, he raised his hand again and ten more followed the first five. Dagger stood motionless in the center of the circle with his hands crossed on his chest and waited. Behind him the group of one hundred seemed to rush forward all at once. He raised his hand to stop them, but five kept coming to his side. As they reached him they spread out to either side of him and readied themselves. Dagger shook his head and smiled as he again pulled his hands apart and the first five dropped one at a time from their horses. Each one had a dagger sticking out of each of their chests. The following ten attackers were luckier as arrows fired from behind Dagger and company fell almost harmlessly into them. It succeeded only in slowing them down but not stopping them completely. Dagger soon ended the lives of the ten just as he had the others before them.

"Enough of this game," Balmore yelled. "I never was one to play this stupidity."

He turned to the men at his side and ordered them each out onto the field with their men. He knew that he could keep some of them back until the numbers of Dagger's men were lessened. Just how long the King would hesitate to commit more men he could not say. He knew that while King Gregor was well loved by his people, he also knew that he was not eager to order his men into a fight to the death. What Balmore did not know was that Jher was not the least bit hesitant, and ordered the next wave of men to the fields, with his old friend Gramfor to lead them. The man was a battle hardened warrior that had seen more battles in more Kingdoms than any man he had ever known. Although, had Jher known that a young girl and a mere boy had gotten the better of him some weeks earlier, he would have been sure to remind him of it as he gave him his orders.

Raising his battle axe to his chest, Gramfor mounted his horse and rode out the main gate ahead of his men. He knew only three of the men that he commanded but he had complete trust in them, knowing their loyalty to him and any cause they fought for.

Dagger knelt as ten riders rode past him as if they did not see him. Turing around, he separated his hands again. This time a red light came from his fingertips hitting the men in their backs and lifting them off their respective horses. They each landed hard on their backs before being swallowed up by Dagger's now charging men. Gramfor's men were not far behind them as the two armies began the battle. Dagger took time to round up his weapons once again. Then he stood near the center of his cloud covered shadow less circle, his sword surrounded by a dark blue light waiting for them to reach him. It would not be long before he would be fighting and killing all that dared to come near him.

Foulas watched the battle begin standing in the relative safety of the trees, waiting for his time to either escape or join the fight. Foulas was happy in the safety of the forest and nothing could make him leave it, for now anyway. Lord Crel was the only one that could force him into the battle.

"What is that smell?" the dark figure of Solari asked as he emerged from Foulas' tent. He stood a few steps away sniffing the air and then began to smile. "Magic ... mmmm yes it is, but not just any magic. I would know that magic anywhere. Yes, yes that is Mar magic. The blind one has shown himself once again. King Gregor puts his Kingdom's fate in Mar magic. It will be a sad day for him and his Kingdom."

As the battle for Tenisfie began many of the inhabitants of the city turned their attentions away from the party that had started the day. The anniversary celebration would wait as it was not every day that they were treated to a battle of armies in their own fields. Many carried their wine and ale barrels and food to a small rise not too far from the gate on a small rise outside of the castle. There they could drink and eat while they watched what they thought to be an impromptu act of the original battle for Tenisfie. Many had no idea of the reality of the battle; that is not until they heard the royal trumpets sound and saw the flag of their King flying over the castle. Cheers came from the revelers as the flags caught in the wind, and increased as they caught sight of King Gregor himself. He gave them all a quick wave but nothing more as the battle was the only thing that concerned him at the time.

With the battle having begun outside the walls of the castle, Sarn was busy learning the secrets of his new cloak. While Sala huddled with the Princesses and some of the youngest servant girls behind the tapestries, Tig was more than content lying next to the warmth of the fire pit.

It was not long before the sounds of fighting began to filter down the stairway. As the sounds reached them, the group in the lower room began to gather their charges and packs, getting everything ready to escape. Sarn grabbed his swords and ran to the sounds of fighting, leaving Sala and the royal family the task of preparing the horses.

Yolo was the first of the guards that Sarn caught up with.

"I think it is safe to say that we have been found," Sarn said when he reached him.

"It would seem that way," Yolo returned. "I have been worried about this happening. I am afraid that some of the guards are no longer loyal."

"You got started without us," Sarn said as he and Yolo joined the other guards.

"We had little choice in the matter and wish that we did not have to begin at all," One of the closer guards said as he backed away from the oncoming group.

Sarn slid back against the wall of the stairway and worked his way into the attackers. The noise rose in the stairway and no one seemed to notice Sarn as they fought. Once behind them Sarn began to swing his swords in swift circular motions dropping the disloyal guards one at a time. With Yolo and five of the loyal guards in front of them and Sarn behind, the nine assassins were soon dealt with. In total there were ten more bodies on the stairs that had not been there a few minutes earlier. It would have been easy to say that Yolo and his group had taken the most of the nine but it would not have been true. Sarn would have said that there was no chance that he had taken six of the nine lives in that stairway, but that was the truth. Yolo had fallen back from the fight after being relieved of his sword and he watched Sarn as he fought. As a boy he would listen to the royal guards talk while he was supposed to be cleaning their armor and swords or other chores that he was to be doing. He had heard them tell of the folktales and legend about the one that would come from Penif to do battle for Tenisfie, although he never had imagined that he would witness it for himself.

"Do you think you could have saved some of them for us," Yolo joked.

"I did not take so many as to leave you with none," Sarn began "Besides there were more of you than of me; I am sure you killed more of them than I could have."

"I guess you are right," one of the other guards said. "We were only six and you were, well you were like fifteen men."

All the guards nodded their heads in agreement, although none could say what exactly Sarn had done and how he had done it, considering that they were a bit busy at the time. It was Yolo that had seen it all but even he could not figure out how it he had done it. First, there was the puzzle of how Sarn had gotten behind the attackers. Second, there was the way his swords seemed to move in ways that he never could have imagined or believed if he had not seen it himself.

"Me, like fifteen men?" Sarn laughed and shook his head not believing them.

"I saw you take nine of them on your own," Yolo told him.

"How many of your company are left?" Sarn asked, changing the subject, again not believing him.

"Five, including me," Yolo returned.

"Then perhaps we better be ready to leave here if more come."

Stepping over the dead, Sarn ignored the three guards that were that were busy searching the bodies of any needed items. To some it may have seemed robbery, but if they had lost or needed repairs to their own weapons the use of those of the dead was a matter of survival. Taking their time they made sure that none of the dead had anything left that could be of use to anyone that may come behind them. Had they been outside or near the winter they would have also taken the boots of the dead along with any warm clothing that they may have worn. They did separate their dead friends from the pile of those of the traitors that had died on the stairway. They would take those below where they could be kept away from any that followed, and then burned at sunrise. Once the dead had been searched to their satisfaction, they were piled in the middle of the stairway where they had died.

They would serve in death as a way to slow anyone coming behind them.

As the traitors made themselves known, and the groups of men went after them, they began making their way to the tunnels and rooms below the castle. They would not have to wait long for the next round of attackers to find their way into the lower rooms. They spilled in from a stairway that led from one of the rooms of the palace itself, followed close behind by members of the gathered army.

Sarn did notice that their attackers were being followed by and fought by those of the defending army.

"It would seem that those were not the last of our troubles," Yolo stated, turning to the sounds of the oncoming fight.

"I had thought that many within the circle had turned with Balmore," returned one of Yolo's guards. "I only hope that there are enough of us left that have not done so."

"The circle was near five hundred at my last count," another of the guards added.

"I can say that they have not all turned," Yolo announced.

"We are not with them," the remaining five guards said almost in unison before laughing.

Sarn shook his head at what seemed to be a waste of time and went to the Queen and Sala and made sure that everyone was ready to leave. Finding everyone ready he returned to Yolo in time for the next group of attackers to reach the large chamber. They seemed more in retreat than in attack as some of the gathered men that had hunted them were pushing them from the other side. Sarn ordered Yolo and his company to send the Queen down the tunnel, telling them to be ready to close the doors and to set fire to the hay. He went to the oncoming group and joined the fight, Tig close at his side. With a sword in each hand Sarn made quick work of killing the first line of attackers. Any that happened to have escaped him were taken care of almost as fast by Tig. Those that would witness the killing done in that chamber would never be able to tell the tale and believe what they had seen. What they would tell is that the boy's swords never stopped moving until all the attackers were dead, and that as he fought a soft blue light encircled him and seemed to make him glow. They would add that it seemed that even before his sword was out of the last attacker it was already beginning to kill the next. Some told of witnessing him using each dead man as a stepping stone to advance within the attackers, and that it was only a matter of seconds before there were none left.

"Where is Sarn?" asked the Queen and Sala when Yolo had reached them.

He told the two what was happening and Sala went immediately to his side ignoring the objections of Queen Janella.

She found Sarn in the middle of the dead men as some of the men from the gathered army were greeting him and others were stripping the dead. He shook his head as she called to him and went to his side.

"More are coming," called one of two men as they came running down the steps.

It was not long before the next group of attackers appeared behind them.

"I want you with the others. They need you to protect them as well as Yolo and his men," he told her when she was near enough.

He expected her to protest his order and was full ready to have one of the guards drag her back to Yolo, but she did not.

"Be careful my husband," Sala whispered as Sarn pulled her to him. "I will only breathe again when we will be together."

"You will breathe my love, of that I am sure."

"Perhaps, but it will not be deep as when you are safe and again in my arms."

"Is that any way for a proper thief to speak?"

"Perhaps not," Sala sighed, "but it is the way that a wife speaks to her husband."

Sarn smiled as he turned back to the new group of attackers.

"You think you can do this without me?" Sala asked.

"No, but I am worried that you would take all the joy in the fight," Sarn returned, turning his back to the attackers.

"Maybe you are worried I am much better than you are at killing."

He laughed as he told Tig to follow and to stay with her. Turning back he met the new attackers. The attacking group was getting smaller and so was the group that was fighting them. The sounds of fighting in the chamber were soon added to by a new group of attackers fighting their way down another stairway. This one led from the royal stables, the same stairway that had brought Pel and the other horses down into the tunnels. The attackers once again began to outnumber Sarn and those left protecting the Queen. As the attackers pushed their way into them he pulled back.

Yolo and his men threw themselves at the attackers slowing them even further, hopping to give Sarn enough time to move the family and servants out from the tunnels.

"I think it is best if we move from here," Sarn told the Queen. "There is no telling how many more will make their way to the tunnels and keep us from our meal."

"I think that it is more than our meal that they wish to keep us from," the Queen returned, smiling toward her daughters and Sala.

"Then it would be best if we found a safer place for everyone," Sala added. "I only wish we had more choices than just this one tunnel."

"Unfortunately there is nothing from here to the end of the tunnel," replied the Queen, knowing that their only other choice would be another chamber or tunnel to hide in on the other side of the main chamber or below it. "When Gregor and I were children we used to play in these tunnels and chambers. There is nothing on this side until the forest. There is, of course, the door that blocks the way, but there are no chambers or other tunnels that lead into or out of this one. They used this tunnel to lead the livestock into and out of here. I guess they did not want them wandering off anywhere."

"Then if you and the others are ready," Sarn returned, "Yolo and I will find a way to slow them down."

Yolo instructed those guards that had been with him to remain with the Queen and to protect them and the others. They began to protest but he reminded them of their duty and oath to the royal family. With a nod of their heads they turned and stood ready to move or fight, whichever they were ordered.

Leaving Sarn and Yolo behind they fled down the tunnel that led away from the stable area of the hiding place. The Queen led the way followed by Sala, her sword drawn and at the ready. Tig was uneasy in the tunnel running ahead and then returning again. Each time he returned Sala could have sworn that he was covered in more blood, but she could not be sure.

Sarn fought with the others at ending the new attack, but they knew that it would not be long before more of them found their way to the tunnels. The number of the gathered rose and fell with those that were wounded or killed and by the next group of traitors being pursued. When the attack ended the remaining men wasted no time in pushing the large doors of the stables and the chamber closed behind them. Finding the heavy poles, made just for that purpose, they put them across the doors locking it.

The darkness of the tunnel along with its turns and uphill slant did not make for a quick escape. Sarn made his way to the front as he and the men caught up with the others. The three torches that were held by servants somewhere in the group offered little if no help to Sarn at the front. Queen Janella was already off her horse searching for the latch that held the door closed. He was quick to join her and take over, but she kept trying to help him just the same. She was not much help to him, but at least she was trying.

"There is a latch somewhere," the Queen told him. "Only I have never found it nor do I know how it works."

"Great," Sarn replied, "I am sure we will find it."

As Sarn began to feel along the wall the tips of his fingers seemed to begin to glow, but he did not seem to take any notice of it, if in fact he even noticed it at all. As his fingers found the latch the light seemed to be at its brightest. As the latch gave way his fingers stopped glowing. A low thud sounded in the tunnel as the stone door of the secret passage popped away from the wall. Sarn leaned into the door and pulled. It did not seem to move as he put his foot against the wall and pulled harder.

"Did you lose your strength?" Phoebe asked giggling.

"Perhaps you should come forward and pull on it for yourself Princess," Sarn returned not having the patience for her laughter. "Or have you just decided to chastise my work?"

Queen Janella scolded her daughter for her words. A few seconds later Yolo and a few others reached him and pulled at the door with Sarn. Soon the door inched back and away from the opening letting in the daylight.

Once outside Sarn made sure that the Queen and her children were together on their horses.

"Look," Prince Gregor said, pointing to the redheaded servant girl lying against the rock wall.

Sarn and Yolo ran over to the unconscious girl.

"Do you know her," Sarn asked.

He shook his head no even though he had seen her before.

"I do not think we should leave her here just the same," Yolo added as he began looking over the girl.

After giving her a quick check they placed her on Pel. Sarn gave the animal a pat on his chest before whispering in his ear. He gave the young Prince the responsibility of riding with her to make sure that she did not fall.

"I will take good care of her," he told him as he climbed onto Pel's back.

"Tig," Sarn began, "I know you wish to find and fight by Dagger, but I need you to see that the others make it to safety first."

Tig lowered his head as if he had been told to do something that he did not wish to do, but he would do it just the same. Raising his head again he turned in a circle, put his nose to the air and began to search for the safest way back to the castle.

"There on the hill beside the castle. Where everyone is gathering with the flags of the King," The Queen said; pointing to hill that was now filled with villagers.

"I think that you will be safe there as well," Sarn told her, "but keep close to Pel and Tig in case the need to flee arises."

She told him that they would do that, and for him and Sala to survive so that she may give them a proper wedding feast.

They smiled as the family rode off with Tig leading the way. Princess Kay joined her brother on Pel making sure that Lorra did not fall from the horse. Yolo, two of his guards, along with a handful of men that fought their way out of the tunnels were running behind them.

It was not long before three of the traitors found their way out of the long shaft and into daylight only to find Sala and Sarn waiting for them. Sala drew the first one out further into the woods. While Sarn waited and stepped out from behind a tree and toppled the man by slicing open the back of his neck. The second wanted nothing to do with them and began to run back to the fighting in the open field. Just the same it was too late, Sarn was before him within seconds, driving his sword up and into his chest. Sala took care of the third, almost taking his head with her sword.

"Well now that was not so difficult was it?" Sala asked

"No, but please my love remind me to never walk away from you if ever you are mad at me," Sarn chuckled and kissed her on the cheek.

"We need only to find Dagger now and tell him of our problem."

"I think he knows my love, look," she pointed past her husband out to the battle field where she saw Dagger running towards them.

"I think you might be right," he smiled and waited for his friend to reach him.

"The circle is no longer loyal to the King," Sarn said as soon as Dagger reached him.

"Yes, but it would seem that some still remain loyal," he returned pointing to Yolo and the two as they ran behind the Queen swords at the ready. "However, as much good that does us now we have many other problems."

"Would you care to tell us what some of those problems are?" Sala asked.

"We have little time to talk of the problems."

"I am sure of that," Sarn said taking Sala's hand. "Perhaps we should work our way to the King's side and fight beside him."

"He was not to leave the safety of the wall," he returned, sounding angry as he saw the King at the edge of the field of battle. "Go to him, he will need us there, but Sala must remain with the Queen. I will go with her to see that she makes it."

Dagger took Sala's hand from him and began to lead her away. He had wanted to protest but he knew that Dagger was right. She needed to be safe and she would be if she were with the Queen. He hated himself for being selfish and not making her go with them in the first place.

He called the other men that had made it out of the tunnels to join him. Together they watched the battle, looking for the best way to reach the King. It was only a second or so before he found it. Pulling both his swords from their hiding place he began to run into the battle. They began their charge with Sarn swinging his swords, stopping only long enough to drop the enemy nearest him.

Dagger pulled his hood further down over his face and began move faster. To Sala he seemed to be a little nervous and unsure of what he was doing, something she had never seen in him before. Even when he was bumping and bumbling his way through a tavern or down a road he always seemed sure of himself and what he was doing.

"Are you all right?" she asked him.

"I am... I am fine. Why do you ask?"

"You do not seem yourself, something is different."

Dagger laughed and let go of her hand and told her that it must be the excitement of the battle that made him seem this way. She knew that he had just lied to her. She could feel there was something troubling him. The two took three steps more when a figure in a long silver colored cloak appeared in front them.

"You cannot escape me now," the figure laughed and pushed

her aside as if she were nothing but air.

Sala fell to the ground as Dagger began swinging his sword. Lifting his hands the figure pushed out toward him as a black light came from his hands. His sword glanced up and away from the figure as the light struck it.

"Why do you think you can beat me with your sword?"

"I knew you would be the one that would come for me," he said ignoring the question, pulling his hood back and off his head.

"You should have known better than to have come out of your circle then."

It was Dagger's turn to laugh now.

"And now you show yourself. This is getting easier by the second."

"I cannot allow you to interfere here," Dagger returned. "You can take me away from here if you want, but you still will not make me fight with you."

Swinging his sword toward him again Dagger jumped to the right missing the bolt of black light that was directed at him. Just before the sword hit the figure a red light engulfed them both and they were gone. As Dagger and the figure disappeared the clouds that covered the circle that he had made on the field of battle began to dissipate.

Tig stood next the royal family and watched it unsure of what he should do. He bounced back and forth on his paws and even began to run several times, but each time he stopped. As Dagger disappeared he began to turn in circles torn between his master and the duty that he was told to do. Turning away he could no longer look on.

Sarn was just advancing when he heard her scream out his name. Jumping up from the men around him he stepped one foot then the other on the shoulders of one the men fighting with him. He saw her off in the distance just at the edge of the battle. She was lying on the ground. He looked around for Dagger, but he could not find him. Sarn leapt from one shoulder to the next until he ran out of places to step. His swords moved in circles, killing as he ran towards her, jumping over the fallen men at his feet. He watched helpless as a dark figure with a long knife moved toward her. He tried reaching for his own knife as he juggled the two swords but it fell from his hands. Since he was unable to use his knife he threw one of his swords striking the figure in the head. The figure went limp and the black cloak it wore fell to the ground in a pile along with Sarn's sword. His sword having hit the figure with the flat side of the blade against its head he could not have killed it. He shook his head as the cloak fell, cursing for having missed the one he thought had harmed his bride.

Sarn knelt at his new bride's side pushing at her bleeding wounds as if he could will the bleeding to stop. She looked up to him her eyes sparkling as they always did and she tried to smile.

"I missed you my love," She whispered.

"I tried to make it to you in time," he tried to explain to her, his eyes filling with tears.

"I saw you," she coughed, "my brave, brave husband, jumping over things and killing as you came. You even lost your favorite knife getting to me."

He could not help but smile at her words even as much as he knew she would be lost to him soon.

"Did the family make it to the hill and back to the castle? Did Tig and Pel get them through?"

"I need to find Dagger. He can fix you, I know he can," he said frustrated by his inability to do anything.

"He is gone my love," She whispered, trying to breathe. "They took him … right from there. Just as he was about kill the one that did this to me."

He looked over his shoulder as if there were a chance that if he knew where he had been taken from he could make them return him, but all he could see was Balmore smiling and pointing at him.

"Who took him?" he pleaded, his growing anger beginning to have a focus.

"A man … from there, gone he …," Sala answered, her words short between her labored breathing.

She never finished her answer as she took her last breath. Leaning over her he bent down to kiss her one last time, his lips tasting the blood that ran from her mouth as he held her close. Ignoring all that was going on around him he lay down next to her and pulled her to him. A light blue glow seemed to wrap around the couple as he lay next to her kissing her cheek and whispering in her ear. None went near them as they lay on the ground. It is hard to say why, perhaps they were not sure what had happened or would happen if they had. Later when they would speak of it around their fires or in the taverns at night none could say for sure why they had not gone to their aide.

Just how long Sarn lay on the ground with Sala he could not say, but to him it was not long enough. His anger rose with each kiss that she did not return and soon he was standing over her screaming Dagger's name. If anyone had been watching Sarn, and a few were, they would have found it hard to tell exactly what happened next, even though many tried. Picking up his thrown sword he drove it point first into the ground next to his love, as if to mark the spot where she lay. The blue glow around him seemed to pulse as if it were a heartbeat. If he noticed it, which was doubtful, and he would not have believed it if he did, Sarn paid no attention to the light as it encircled him.

Reaching into his cloak he pulled out one of the daggers he had just been given by Ryn. Some said he seemed to float up from the ground as he did so. Placing the dagger in his mouth he reached for Sala's sword and then one of his own. With a sword in each hand and the dagger in his mouth he ran toward King Gregor. Each of his swords found its mark and wounding if not killing its target as he ran. He used the falling dead and those already on the ground to step his way across the field, yet he seemed to float about waist high above those that littered the battle ground. However they saw it happen, Foulas' men still fell one by one as he made his way toward the King. His rage never faltered as he again saw the man that he thought had killed his love.

Balmore turned just in time for Sarn to pull the dagger from his mouth and throw it towards him. Balmore laughed again as he began to move out of the way, but the dagger seemed to follow his every move. Sarn followed the dagger's path, killing as he went. Balmore took two more steps before looking behind him again. It would be the last thing he saw as the dagger struck the man in the corner of one eye and buried itself into his skull.

Sarn reached down as he caught up with the now lifeless body, pulled the dagger from the dead man's eye and thrust Sala's sword into his chest cavity. His rage may have found its reason to end, yet he was far from ending his assault. Looking up Sarn caught sight of the King once again and ran towards him. Once at the King's side he began to tear at Foulas' men as they approached the now wounded King. Swing after swing of Sarn's swords took one man after another. His eyes seemed to have turned a bright red with his arms moving back and forth slashing at and tearing the flesh of any that came near him. His own body was not escaping the wrath of those that he was killing as swords cut across his arms and torso. None of their strikes seemed to register or harm him even though his blood was being spilled.

Sarn turned toward the King in time to see Jher lifting the wounded man to his feet.

"There," he shouted to Jher, "on the hill. His family is there, they are safe. They have the few remaining loyal guards with them."

"Then come along," Jher yelled back, "the castle is still ours, we can stand them off."

"Why stand them off when they can all be dead," Sarn yelled and turned back to the attackers.

Searching the field he spotted Foulas at the edge of the trees. Lifting his swords he pointed one to where Foulas stood and started to run towards him. The light blue glow encircled him again as he ran. Jumping over the bodies that littered the field he used many that were standing as if they were stepping stones to use to cross a stream. Foulas watched the boy running towards him but for a brief second before he himself turned to run. Sarn kept one sword pointed at the now running leader while using the second to fend off any that would confront him and try stopping his run. Foulas turned from the forest and began to run towards the hill that held the Queen and the rest of the royal family. It was as if Foulas were a magnet for Sarn's sword as it kept track of each step that the man made as he ran from him. Sarn did not stop even as Foulas knocked one of his men from a horse and jumped up on its back. The horse took two steps before being taken down by an arrow from an archer that had been standing near the King.

"It just were not fair of him getting on the horse eh?" Jher asked.

"Well …, I were not aiming for the horse, I were aiming for him. First time I caught sight of him since he give me this," the archer said pointing to the scare on his face that ran from the corner of his eye to his ear and then to the corner of his mouth. "I will take the reason to slow him down for the boy as just as good as killing him."

Foulas fell to the ground as the horse dropped from under him. He was unable to get away, as one leg was trapped under the horse. Sarn stepped onto the body of the dead horse and lifted both of his swords over his head. The blue glow that had wrapped around him was now a deep red matching that of his eyes.

"Who are you that you think you can kill me?" Foulas asked.

"I am Sarn of Penif," he answered as he shoved the first sword into him.

"That will not kill me," Foulas laughed as the sword entered his chest.

He said nothing more to the fallen Foulas as he shoved the second sword through his heart. Stepping on his chest Sarn pulled the first sword out before placing it next to the other. Twisting them both he smiled as Foulas lay wide eyed under the horse as he died. Pulling his swords, he picked up a battle axe that lay nearby. Lifting the axe over his head he smiled again as he let it fall, severing the head from its body.

"I guess I could kill you," Sarn yelled as he tossed the severed head toward the battle.

Dropping to one knee he felt himself growing weak. His strength was draining from him with each drop of blood that seeped from his wounds. It would not be long he thought and he would be able to join his love in the afterlife his father and mother had spoken of when he was younger. His father's face began to come at him as if he were in a cloud.

"Leave me alone father," he yelled. "I have no will or time, let me alone."

"Think of me my son I am here for you."

Sarn pushed his father from his mind as the red glow that some said surrounded him turned back to blue.

"This is where I belong. Leave me, I do not wish your strength." Sarn fought his way back to where Sala lay.

It was not a hard fight, as many stepped back to let him pass. The resistance of those that did fight against him fell as each could not reason as how the boy was still standing. That and a close look into his burning eyes and the men that were left near him ran from him in total fear of the crazed boy. When he reached Sala again he collapsed next her and pulled her to him. Holding her lifeless body he closed his eyes and waited.

"Get up!" the image of his father yelled as he floated above him in his mind.

"I am done Father, please let me alone now," Sarn whispered. "I have done all that I want to do. Without her there is nothing more that I wish to see or do. I have learned and fought and died for a cause. Let me die now on this field with my one and our child."

"Do you think that you were given to us for this one fight?" his father whispered. "Your destiny is far away from this place and much more important."

"I do not care I just want to be with my family, please Father let me go."

"You are not done," his father whispered. "Not done at all."

The image of his father drifted away and was replaced with that of Sala carrying him off the field and away from those that would harm him more. Even though Foulas was dead there was still some semblance of his army left on the field. They stayed away from the crazed boy that seemed to float over his enemies as he killed and wounded them. It seemed as if there were a ring of soldiers that continued to battle surrounding the couple. A few even claimed they could see that same soft blue light surrounding and covering the two lovers.

Sarn's actions had turned the battle for Tenisfie back to the forces of King Gregor. It was not long after Sarn had closed his eyes that King Gregor sent Jher and Gramfor to retrieve the couple from the field. No one approached them as Jher and Gramfor took the bodies of Sarn and Sala and carried the newlyweds off the field of the ongoing battle. The battle weary men and women stopped and looked up to watch the lifeless bodies of the newlyweds being carried off the field as they passed them. It was as if that sight alone was all that was needed to lift them from pits of despair and fill them with needed energy. Once they were off the field, the King turned and gave a cry to his men as they began a final charge against the onslaught. The King's cry was repeated over and over across the field, until all that could answer the cry were on their feet to the rally of the King. Those that were not wounded were first to move but it was not long before all that could walk and raise a weapon were moving in one direction. They began to drive at the attacking men and surrounded them for one final stand. With Foulas dead and Solari nowhere to be found it was not long before the leaderless and disoriented army met their final end.

"He is still alive my lord," Jher told King Gregor as he passed him with Sarn in his arms.

"Take him to my personal surgeon and have him cared for at once."

Jher nodded his head and continued with Sarn. Gramfor followed behind with Sala's lifeless body in his arms.

"Take her to the Queen. She will take care of her," King Gregor told Gramfor as he passed.

With the battle finally won and king Gregor claiming victory over Foulas' men there would now be time for the field to be searched for any other wounded soldiers of either side that would be in need of help. As the work of separating those wounded and those killed began the sun was beginning to set. They would continue as long as needed and torches would be brought out to light the field and trees would be cut to build the funeral pyres.

That night as they celebrated their victory over Solari and Foulas, a hush would come over them whenever Sarn and Sala were mentioned. They spoke too of Dagger and how he rode out in front of them all showing no fear, and how he just seemed to disappear from the battlefield. The large figure in the silver colored cloak wrapped their arms around the thief and in four or maybe five steps was gone from view. At any given moment the men would raise their ale and toast the missing thief. But it seemed the stories they were telling and listening to most were that of Sarn and his deeds on the field of battle.

"I do not believe that Foulas knew what was happening to him as Sarn swung that axe. He took his head as if it were a mere grape from a vine," Gramfor said, raising his ale and taking a long drink before slamming down the mug.

"I would not have believed it if I had not seen it with me own eyes," Jher began, taking up where Gramfor seemed to leave it. "I was heading toward the King when I heard this yell coming from behind me. There off a way were that boy. He seemed like he were running on the air. His feet were above the ground, there about to my waist, running toward King Gregor. I was sure he were going to kill him. His sword slicing at the air like a mill sail in the wind, cutting and tearing at those men that dared to stand against him. All the time he were missing each of those that were there to protect the King and myself as well. It were something to see there are no doubt about that. He spit that silver dagger out from his mouth and it flew to Balmore burying in him's eye and taking him's life."

"He could not have spit that knife into his eye, he had to have thrown it," someone in the crowd of men and women said.

"That may be the truth, but I never did see either of him's hands leave from them swords that he were swinging," Jher began again. "He were yelling out that wife of him's name and that of the thief as well as something about how could they have taken him. And who were they to take him when he were a needing him. I would not have thought a single person could go in so many directions all in the time of one and do so much damage to human life."

"I have seen him that way before," Prince Gregor chimed in and recounted the story of how Sarn and Tig had rescued him from Canis and his men.

They all nodded when the boy finished as if they all agreed to something, but none knew what they were agreeing on. King Gregor lifted his ale above his head and held it waiting for the silence to return.

"Let those that are present bare witness," the King began. "To Sarn of Penif, to him I pledge my sword and those of my men whenever and wherever he may have their need."

Tankards of ale flew up over the heads of those in the crowd, as those of the gathered army and others made the same pledge followed by cheers in support of Sarn. At the end of it there was a silence that seemed to last an hour, but it was just a brief moment. Somewhere in the crowd the noise began again as it had in the church so many hours earlier. The metal on stone chimed throughout the castle walls. Again the noise carried out across the battlefield, where the dead were being sorted out. The sound of the metal on stone carried on and into the dense forest beyond.

Although it was nearing the middle of the night, torches lit up the field as the work continued. The bodies and personal belongings that were not asked for would be burned. The King's men would build their own funeral pyre and light it at the rising of the sun, so that their souls would be able to go to wherever it was that soldiers' souls went. Some say they went to sit with their God, others said it was a place of honor in paradise that awaited them. Others say soldiers never die. They are reborn the instant of their death so that there will always be brave souls that would fight and die for a righteous cause. Foulas' men would not have such a ceremony. They would be tossed in a shallow grave, worthy not even that of a peasant.

Still the metal on stone sound chimed out across the fields carrying deep into the forest. It would be just a few days before everyone that had seen the battle began to call Sarn the savior of Tenisfie. Even the men that had been in battle gave the boy more credit for winning it than they gave themselves. Of course in later years they would all have claimed to be the one that fought next to him and inspired him to fight on.

Long past midnight as the workers were finishing on the battlefield and readying the funeral pyres a light mist began to fall.

"The ancients begin to weep," said one of the men. "They

weep for the dead and the injured."

"They weep for the bride," said another shaking his head as he worked.

"Aye" the rest replied nodding their heads in agreement.

Off in the distance on the other side of the castle the sisters moved along the road that led into the village. In the darkness of the night no one saw them as they entered the far gate. There were a few still wandering the streets after the night of festivities but no one paid attention to them or anything else. Most were either too drunk or too busy with each other to care what may have been happening around them.

"I told you this would happen," Meglyn whispered.

"How was I supposed to know?"

"How many times did I tell you that this would happen?"

"You never once told me that this would happen," Caitlin returned.

"I knew this was going to be another mess that I would have to fix."

"You ...," Caitlin laughed. "Since when have you ever fixed any mess? I am the one that has to fix your messes. I never make the mess, it is always you."

"Where did you say we needed to go," Meglyn asked changing the subject.

Caitlin did not answer her. Instead she pointed the way and moved ahead of her sister. Shaking her head Meglyn followed behind, but only because someone needed to fix what had gone wrong. The two made their way through the streets to and into the palace, searching from room to room until they found what they had come for.

"Well, what do we do now?" Caitlin asked.

"I cannot believe that after all these years you still surprise me."

Meglyn knelt next to the bed and Caitlin followed, each taking one hand as they knelt and lowered their heads. Soon the room began to fill with tiny blue points of light that began swirling around the sisters and the body of Sala. The lights moved faster around them until finally they became one and rolled into a large ball. Lifting up off the bed the light shot out through the door down the hall and out into the night sky. When it was gone, the sisters and Sala were gone as well. In the following days no one would ask of Sala's body and what had happened to it. All agreed or believed that her body had been given the highest place atop the pyres at sunrise.

It would not be until the next day that Lorra would finally come to, her whole body sore from hitting the stone wall.

"How do you feel?" Princess Kay asked her.

"I will tell you as soon as I figure out if I am alive or dead," Lorra returned.

The Princess laughed and told her that she was still alive.

"How did I get here then," Lorra asked.

Princess Kay told her the story of how they had found her the day before unconscious against the rock ledge.

The days passed and Sarn was moved from the tents on the field to the castle and finally into the palace. Each day the Queen, the Princesses, Lorra and even Prince Gregor would take turns sitting with him holding his hand or wiping his face; one of them was at his side at all times.

Each day the King would call his surgeon to ask of him, each day the surgeon could give no good report.

"There must be something that we can do," the King replied. "It has been almost fifteen days since the battle and still you cannot tell me any more than you could the first day."

"I think that he has given up the will to live," the surgeon returned. He guessed he had known it from the third day but had not allowed himself to believe that it could be possible. "All we can hope now is for a miracle, or magic."

King Gregor lowered his head and thought for a moment. Then as if he had been hit in the stomach he let out a hard breath of air, rose from his seat and ran toward the window. Looking out over the fields he seemed to be looking for something that only he could see.

"The sisters!" he cried out. "They must be found. They will be able to cure him."

Gregor ordered that the castle and surrounding lands be searched for signs of the sisters.

"The first to find them and tell them of our need will receive a thousand gold pieces and land title," Gregor ordered.

All Tenisfie was in on the search for the sisters, from the highest of the royal court to the lowest peasant. The reward of a thousand pieces of gold was more than enough enticement for them to search. The chance for title to land though was worth more to some of them than the gold.

Queen Janella and the Princesses took turns sitting by Sarn's bed and holding his hand. Lorra would come as well for a time each day. There was something about him that kept her coming back to his side. She had no idea why she was drawn to him. Yet every day from the day she woke after the battle, she made her way to him to look after him, even if only just a short time. It seemed that almost everyone in the village waited every day for even the smallest bit of information about how he was. Those that wished him well would come to palace and wait until they were told that there had been no change or until the sun would set. Powders and every other kind of healing remedy arrived to be used to try and heal the savior of Tenisfie.

It was Tig that they would find almost every hour of the day lying next to Sarn on the bed. The animal would only leave several times throughout the day, but never more than a few minutes at a time. Then late one night, Tig went into the palace stables and brought Pel and the rest of the travelers' horses out. He led them around the palace to the window of the room that held Sarn. It was quiet as Tig made his way back in and began to pull Sarn from his bed. He was as quiet as he could be, but Princess Phoebe had been sleeping nearby.

"Tig," she whispered, when he woke her. "What are you doing?"

Tig ignored her and kept pulling on Sarn. She stepped over Sarn and called out for help. It would be her mother that would be the first to reach the room.

Grabbing for Tig he growled at her to keep her from him. Queen Janella backed away from him, cursing the animal for having growled at her. It would be Prince Gregor that would stop her and anyone else that tried to stop the animal.

"No Mother," the young Prince said as he appeared behind her. "Let him go, I think he knows what to do."

His father agreed and arranged for a cart to be brought and hooked to the packhorses before stopping Tig.

"You can take him Tig," he said as he approached the animal. "Let us get him ready and help you."

Tig let go of Sarn and went to the King. Placing a paw on each of his shoulders the animal rubbed his face against the King's. When everything was ready they placed Sarn on the hay in the cart. King Gregor ordered several of his guards to go along and make sure that they arrived wherever it was that Tig wanted to take them. Tig however, had a different idea as he growled at the guards as they stepped forward to volunteer for the duty. Instead he went up to Gramfor and pulled him by his hand from where he was watching behind the guards. By the time the first rays of the sun began to fill the sky the small group led by Tig was making its way out of the castle gate.

"They are back," Marna yelled as she saw Pel and Tig coming down the road through the forest. "Sarn and Sala they are back!"

Janua, Marna, and Mara gathered out in front of the tavern paying little attention to those that were inside and waited for them.

Tig was in the lead as he had been every day since they had left the castle. The cart, pulled by the packhorses, rumbled behind him. Sarn was still cradled as best he could be by the hay. It had seemed to Gramfor that the animal had not only set the pace that the group traveled, he also made sure that nothing stopped them for long. From the time that King Gregor had hooked the cart to the packhorses and had laid Sarn in the back, Tig knew where he was going to go. Gramfor rode the whole way a short distance behind the cart and other horses, his head falling from side to side as he slept.

He could not remember how long they had been on the move. It seemed to him that they had been moving since, well they never stopped but for a few hours here and there since they left Tenisfie.

As they reached the tavern Mara went straight to Pel who only pushed her toward the cart and its occupant. He then turned to Gramfor and began pushing up against his thigh to wake him. Tig had kept the group traveling day and night for weeks. Now that they had made it to the tavern Pel went straight to the stables where Janua opened a pen and let him in. He collapsed to the ground laying his head on some hay in the clean stall. Gramfor tried to speak several times but Marna stopped him every time and told him that there would be enough time to talk later. Tig was the only one that seemed to have any energy left as he ran around the women as they helped first Gramfor and then Sarn into the tavern and up the stairs. There were many questions that needed to be answered but it all would have to wait.

www.ingramcontent.com/pod-product-compliance
Lightning Source LLC
Chambersburg PA
CBHW051407170626
46809CB00006B/2063